CHICKS
KICK
BUTT

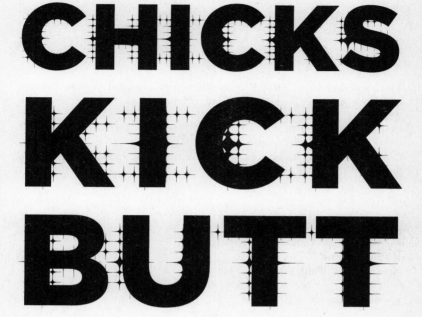

CHICKS KICK BUTT

EDITED BY

Rachel Caine

AND

Kerrie L. Hughes

TOR®

A Tom Doherty Associates Book
New York

CHICKS KICK BUTT

Copyright © 2011 by Roxanne Longstreet Conrad, Kerrie L. Hughes, and Tekno Books

A Tor Book
Published by Tom Doherty Associates, LLC
175 Fifth Avenue
New York, NY 10010

www.tor-forge.com

Tor® is a registered trademark of Tom Doherty Associates, LLC.

Library of Congress Cataloging-in-Publication Data

Chicks kick butt / edited by Rachel Caine and Kerrie L. Hughes. — 1st ed.
    p. cm.
  ISBN 978-0-7653-2577-8
  1. Fantasy fiction, American.   2. Occult fiction, American.   3. American
fiction—Women authors.   4. Vampires—Fiction.   5. Werewolves—
Fiction.   6. Demonology—Fiction.   I. Caine, Rachel.   II. Hughes, Kerrie.

  PS648.F3C49 2011
  813'.08766083522—dc22

                                                          2011011543

First Edition: June 2011

Printed in the United States of America

0   9   8   7   6   5   4   3   2   1

COPYRIGHT ACKNOWLEDGMENTS

CONTENTS

Introduction by Rachel Caine   11

Shiny by Rachel Caine   13

In Vino Veritas by Karen Chance   35

Hunt by Rachel Vincent   59

Monsters by Lilith Saintcrow   85

Vampires Prefer Blondes by P. N. Elrod   112

Nine-Tenths of the Law by Jenna Black   136

Double Dead by Cheyenne McCray   167

A Rose by Any Other Name Would Still Be Red
by Elizabeth A. Vaughan   194

Superman by Jeanne C. Stein   208

Monster Mash by Carole Nelson Douglas   230

Wanted: Dead or Alive by L. A. Banks   263

Mist by Susan Krinard   281

Beyond the Pale by Nancy Holder   309

INTRODUCTION

Rachel Caine

When I was growing up, I used to wonder why girls never got the cool stories. You know what I mean—the tales with knights fighting for right, with detectives prowling the mean streets to solve crimes, and the gritty stories about growing up on the wrong side of the tracks.

Instead, the books people thought *I* should read were about ballerinas. About good girls who did what they were told. About women who rarely had adventures, and when they did, rarely saved themselves, or anybody else.

I decided I didn't want to be the princess languishing in the tower—I wanted to be the knight battling to save her. So I grabbed all the adventure stories I could, and never looked back.

I'm particularly proud to be included in this collection of stories featuring powerful women, women who aren't afraid to kick a little butt—or a lot of it—when the situation calls for it. I'm also honored to be in the company of these fantastic storytellers, who kick some stereotyping butt of their own.

I'm proud to be a chick—never more than now.

Because chicks are awesome.

SHINY

A WEATHER WARDEN STORY

Rachel Caine

We were enjoying a rare day that did *not* include doom and apocalypse, and wonder of wonders, it was one of those balmy, beautiful early-summer days that reminded me why I lived in Florida.

It had been David's idea to do a beach picnic, which, given the lovely, mild weather, was a fantastic idea, but it had been mine to take a drive. A nice long one, on winding roads, for the sheer pleasure of putting tires to asphalt and seeing the world. So we had compromised on a long drive followed by a beach picnic, which was a perfect thing to do on such a lovely day.

Me, I loved to get behind the wheel even more than the prospect of the beach itself. I especially loved to drive really good cars, and this one, a Viper, was right up there in my ranking of awesome rides. Not as sweet as my long-lost Mustang Mona, who'd been a casualty of life in the Weather Warden ranks, but still: nice, and powerful.

David had never said one way or another whether he liked cars, but I suspected he did. Although not much impresses a Djinn. This is an unalterable fact of the world: Djinn—or genies—have been around since the dawn of time, although some are certainly newer than others, and one thing they all share is a sense of historical perspective. By the time you get to your first few hundred years, much less few thousand, I suspect, the "been there, done that" feeling is overwhelming.

Which is why it seemed so unusual to hear my Djinn lover David let out a low whistle as I powered through a turn, and say, "That's something you don't see every day."

I peeled my attention back from the curve and looked where he was looking. Just off the road, with the backdrop of the wetlands, was a mob of vehicles and people, and massive industrial video cameras—high-definition ones, I assumed. Everyone looked ridiculously casual in dress, and highly professional in what he or she was doing.

"Commercial shoot," I said. It wasn't that astonishing, in this part of the world. Everybody loved the colors and lifestyle here, and there were probably more still and video cameras clicking away here than anywhere else in the country, except Hollywood. And maybe New York City. "What's so special . . ."

And then I saw it.

It was a silvery vision of a car, elegant as something designed by a classical sculptor. Michelangelo, maybe, if he'd worked in metal and sheer engine power. I instinctively took my foot off the gas, staring, because in all my extensive years of car fetishizing, I'd never actually seen *anything* that cool with my own eyes.

I pulled the Viper over to the side of the road, barely noticing the crunch of tires on gravel, and stared. My mouth was probably hanging open, too. Honestly, David was right—you just did *not* see that every day. Or, in fact, any day, unless you worked at an Italian car manufacturer, or had $1.7 million to throw around on a set of wheels. "That," I said, "is a freaking Bugatti Veyron. In the Everglades." It wasn't the fastest car in the world—maybe number two?—but it was, to my mind, the most elegantly designed. And, not coincidentally, the most expensive.

David let out a little snort of laughter. "I wasn't talking about the car," he said. Well, of course he wasn't, but I was still adjusting to the fact that there was a *Bugatti Veyron* sitting there, not twenty feet away from me. A couple of staffers for the shoot were polishing it with soft cloths, not that it needed the help to look its best. I blinked and tried to see what *else* was in the picture.

Ah. He was talking about the girl. The one in the bikini.

The one in the *diamond* bikini. Not a bikini with diamonds, not a blinged-out piece of spandex . . . an actual bikini, made of diamonds. Now that I'd noticed her, it was hard to see how I'd missed her in the first place—the glitter of all those facets was blinding. The girl wearing the thing was getting herself powdered—last-minute primping, just like the car—and she looked almost as sleek and expensive as what she was wearing, and what her backdrop would be. I presumed she was a world-class model, or she wouldn't be here acting as the prop for all that loot. You didn't go cheap on the talent in a thing like this.

I blinked as a cloud blotted out the sun. No, not a cloud . . . a shadow, and then a body, big enough to present a solid flesh barrier to me catching any more glimpses of car, girl, or diamonds. He was, unmistakably, security. I could cleverly discern this by reading the giant letters in white on his black T-shirt, which read SECURITY, but even had he been unlabeled, there would really have been no mistaking him for anything else. He was professional muscle; whether he took it to bodyguarding a star, bouncing a club, or donning an overdone belt as a pro wrestler, he'd made a career out of intimidation.

"Hi," I said brightly. He scowled down at me from way, way up high. Tall, not only broadly built. "Just wanted to see what was going on."

"Nothing, ma'am," he said. "Move on, please."

"I'm not in the way." I had no real reason not to immediately put the Viper in gear and drive on, but I didn't like being scowled at. Or ordered around. "That's a Bugatti Veyron, right?"

"No idea. Move on."

"Look—what's your name?"

"Steve."

"Steve, I promise, I'm just looking. Give me a second and I'll go."

Instead, Steve took a step back and waved a hand, and from somewhere behind me, two uniformed Florida state troopers sauntered over, one on my side of the car, one on David's. The saunter was deceptive, because I didn't for a moment believe they were being relaxed about it. "Miss," said the one who bent over on my side of the window. He had a thick Southern accent, a little too Southern for Florida. I was guessing he was a Georgia transplant. "You need to move along now, unless you've got a pass."

David reached into the glove box and brought out something in an envelope, which he handed over without a word to the officer on his side of the car. The trooper unfolded the paper, read it, and said to his partner, "They've got a pass, Joe."

"They do? Let me see that!"

The two passed the paper back and forth for a while, then huddled with the security guard, who came back and leaned in David's window this time. David was noticeably not bothered or intimidated; he even looked amused, from the light glittering in his brown-bronze eyes. (He was trying to keep his Djinn side from showing, at least. Thankfully.)

"Where'd you get this?" Mr. Security demanded, flourishing the paper.

David jerked his chin at the model. "From her," he said. "She's my sister."

"Your *what*?" As if no supermodel in the world had siblings, or parents, or any kind of family. Well, they did often look lab-grown, that was a true fact.

"Ask her," David said, raising his eyebrows. The security dude stalked off, as much as someone so muscle-bound could effectively stalk, and arrived next to the diamond model. He bent over and spoke to her. She leaned past him, looking at David, and then smiled.

"David?" I asked, in a voice that was probably way too confused. "Who is that?"

He smiled, but didn't answer. Annoying.

Security Steve was trudging his way back, and he looked . . .

apologetic. Not that he had a very mobile sort of face, but I got the subtlety from the hangdog set of his slumped shoulders. He leaned in and said, in a much different kind of voice, "Sorry, sir. Didn't know who you were. Miss, why don't you park right over there, next to the director's car? Miss Whitney wants to say hello."

"Miss Whitney," I repeated, and followed parking instructions as David continued with that Cheshire cat grin. "Do I even want to know how you've picked up a sudden sister named Miss Whitney?"

"The usual way," he said. "At least, for me."

"She's Djinn," I guessed. "New Djinn."

"Not just new. She's only a few years old. Generationally, she's no older than you."

Okay, that was bad news. Whitney was a Djinn—okay, fine, I'd stopped trying to figure out why David liked me better than hot immortal chicks that could move mountains *and* look any way he wanted them. But the fact was, she was actually my own age, and looked about ten years younger, and at least a dozen points hotter, which already sucked. She was also wearing a couple of million dollars of high-carat diamonds in a skimpy little outfit that left nothing at all to the imagination, not even how expert her bikini wax was.

And she had a cute, infectious smile. The *bitch*. Honestly, that was just taking it too far.

And she *winked* at me as we walked toward her; then she swigged some bottled water, and shooed away the two walking-shorts-wearing prettifiers who were hovering around her touching her up. "Well," she said, with a distinct, low-pitched Southern drawl that made the trooper's sound like he came from Nebraska. "If it isn't Mr. Boss himself. Excuse me if I don't kneel. I think this bikini might leave scars."

David snorted, but he looked amused. "Whitney, what the *hell* is this?"

"Fun." She shrugged a little, which woke a blinding flash of diamonds that must have been a menace to low-flying aircraft. "I get bored just being all-powerful. Can't a girl have a little fun sometimes?" She must have learned the accent, I decided, from *Gone with the Wind*. "You're just jealous 'cause you know this little thing wouldn't fit you."

She was saying it to David, but her eyes changed focus, shifting over to me on the last word. *Ooooh.* I felt the burn, and the shock of getting a Djinn stare at full strength. Whitney's eyes were brilliant lavender blue, Liz Taylor's eyes on crack, and there was a lazy mischief in them that reminded me of cats and mice and unfortunate endings for the rodent in the equation.

I put on my best *shove-it* smile and held out my hand. "Joanne Baldwin," I said. "I don't think we've met."

"Only by rumor," Whitney agreed languidly, without accepting my handshake. She held up her own and blew on the long, beautifully shaped nails. "Sorry. Polish is still wet."

That was *so* lame an excuse that even David lost his smile. "Whit," he said. "Play nice."

"Or what, big daddy? You'll spank me? Mmmmm." Her tongue glided over her lower lip. Pure suggestion.

His eyes kindled in a hot bronze glow, trapping hers. *"Whitney."*

She looked away, and for the first time, I saw a flicker of fear. "Sorry," she said. "Didn't mean to be rude."

"Let's try this again. What are you doing here?"

She trailed a fingertip over the diamond-set strap of her bikini top, and tapped one of the stones as she lifted her eyebrow. David let out an impatient breath and said, "You can *make* one. Don't be stupid!"

"I can't make one like *this* one. *This* one is perfect. You know how I feel about having something that's perfect." She licked her lips and glanced over at the car. *"That's* perfect, too."

David growled, low in his throat, in total frustration. "You will *not* steal anything, Whitney. I've told you before. You're attracting attention with all this, and I won't have it. Have your fun. Do your photos, and go quietly. I'm warning you."

Whitney's purple eyes narrowed, and she tossed her liquidly dark hair back over her shoulders. Its shine and bounce were perfection itself. *She* didn't have to battle frizzy hair and uncontrollable curling. "You may be the big dog, David, but don't you bite too hard. We both know I can give you a street fight if you want it."

I had *never* heard anybody—except maybe Ashan, the leader of the other, older half of the Djinn, a right cold bastard—speak to David that way. When he talked, the New Djinn generally listened, and certainly obeyed when push came to shove.

But not this one.

David, though, wasn't having any nonsense. He smiled. It wasn't a pretty smile, and it reminded me that as much as I adored him, as much as he was all the good things that a Djinn could be, he had a dark streak. They all did. And his wasn't small, just deeply buried and tightly leashed. "Don't push me," he said. "Or I'll break you. For good."

Whitney *flipped him off,* drained the rest of her bottled water, and tossed the empty to a distantly hovering staffer, who fielded it with long practice. "I'm bored," she announced. "Let's get this show on the road, folks!"

She was the talent, which would normally make her pretty low on the order-giving totem pole—but it seemed like Whitney had already established a brand-new paradigm here in the middle of nowhere. The director—a bulky young man who seemed to prefer wearing his baseball cap backward, which was an asinine thing to do in the Florida sun—straightened up from where he was huddled with a group of people, and clapped his hands. "All right, all right, let's get busy!" he yelled. "Somebody get Whitney in position! And you two, out of the way!"

He meant me and David, of course. Whitney winked at us, and blew David a mocking kiss as one of her makeup staff swooped in to swirl a brush over her face. David and I withdrew to a point outside of the cameras, behind the crew, and he stood there with his feet planted and arms crossed, looking stubborn and worried as he watched them pose Whitney like a life-sized doll, adjusting her for just the right sparkly angle against the Bugatti.

"Who the hell is she, David?" That probably sounded just a little insecure, but Whitney had rattled me. More than any other female (or female-appearing) Djinn I'd ever met, she seemed interested in direct, sexual competition for the attention of my lover, and I didn't like it. I didn't think he particularly did, either, which was a relief, but still.

"I told you, she's very young," he said. "She's—unusual."

"Yeah, I get that."

"No, you don't," he said. "She became Djinn in a way nobody else we've seen has been able to accomplish. Whitney died alone. Not with others, not in some mass disaster or slaughter. She died alone, and she became a Djinn."

That was *not* the way it worked for the New Djinn (or the Old Djinn, for that matter). Djinn could make the leap from human to superhuman only when there had been enough lives lost to trigger some kind of energy exchange . . . people dying alone, or even in small groups, wouldn't do it. David had made me a Djinn once, but he'd cheated, using his own power to sustain me. That hadn't gone over well, and it hadn't been sustainable, for either of us.

"She didn't have another Djinn helping her?"

"Nothing. She just . . . died, under traumatic circumstances, and then transformed. Jonathan was studying her to find out why, but she's difficult to control, and I don't think he got very far with it be-fore—" He didn't need to continue. We both knew that Jonathan had given his life so that David could live, after our disastrous attempt to keep me Djinn. "She's extremely powerful. More than any other New Djinn, except me, and that's only because I'm the Con-duit." David was the direct plug-in for the New Djinn to the powers of the Earth—the center of the spiral. Whatever his normal power level might be, he could draw on the strength of the Mother, and that trumped Whitney or any other New Djinn.

It didn't look to me like Whitney was the type to accept that with-out pushing the issue, though.

"She's—not like the other Djinn I've met."

"More human? She is that. In human life, she was savagely ambitious, and she's carried that over to life as a Djinn. Whitney's never seen a challenge she didn't want to take, or believed she couldn't win." He sounded as if he almost admired that—from a distance. "She was a thief and a con artist as a human. She's carried that over as well. No matter how many times I tell her being Djinn isn't a license to cause chaos . . ."

The primping apparently had concluded, and now the still photographer was having his day, having Whitney pout, pose, and lounge with the backdrop of the sports car. She was, I had to admit, good at it. I wished my best friend, Cherise, was at my side; surely she would have had some good, snarky asides to make me feel better.

Especially since Whitney kept glancing at David between shots, as if all her pouting, sexy posing was personal.

If it affected him, he wasn't showing it. He watched her with a cool, intense stare, arms folded, clear warning in his body language.

The photos went on for a while, but they were finally done, and a round of applause sounded around the crew.

"Get her set for the video," the director ordered, and ran over to check focus on his two high-definition rigs, much to the bored chagrin of the camera operators. "Come on, people, the light's going to go soon!"

"Well, this is exciting," I said. "And our champagne is getting warm in the car, you know."

"I know," David said. "But she's not here for the chance to look pretty."

"Then why *is* she here?"

"She's a sociopath and a thief, and as far as I know it could be anything. The thing is, if I leave, there's nothing to stop her."

Whitney must have heard him, because she straightened from a casual lounging position against the shiny Bugatti, smiled with blinding intensity, and said, "Oh, *honey,* please. There's nothing to stop me *now!*"

In between one breath and the next, she opened the Bugatti's door, slipped inside, and fired up the engine, which caught with a full-throated, intimidating roar. The director jerked upright, staring, utterly astonished, and dug in his pockets. He came out with a set of keys—the car keys, presumably—and stared from that to Whitney, who was playfully gunning the engine. "How—"

Whitney held up a finger. Her middle one. White bolts of electricity sizzled around it and reflected in her purple eyes. "Greed is bad," she said. "I'm just helping save all those people who'd see this ad and feel all inadequate about the size of their cars, that's all."

And then she put the Bugatti in gear, and arrowed it straight for the cameras.

Somehow, the people managed to scramble out of the way—David probably helped propel them, actually, from the way they were tossed around—and one of the cameras was blown into junk by a leading wave of invisible force before the car's bumper could touch it. The other was just knocked over like a big, ungainly insect. There was screaming. Some of it, I realized, was coming from a suited man who'd been sitting off to the side. From the horror on his face, he was the owner of either the Bugatti or the diamond bikini, and his insurance had just lapsed.

"Crap," David sighed, and turned to me. "Would you mind . . . ?"

"Do you really have to ask? Of course I'll do it."

I raced for the car, and David took the faster route, blipping directly through the aetheric from where he stood into the passenger seat. Fast as I was getting settled and the engine started, I knew that seconds were ticking. I didn't think the car I was driving, sweet as it was, had a hope in hell of chasing down a Bugatti with a Djinn driver, but what the hell.

I like a challenge too, Whitney. Let's play.

I wasn't the only one on the trail of the fleeing Bugatti. Behind me, the state troopers had finally gotten their act together and were blaring a siren in the distance, trying to make up distance. They'd never make it. Even their fastest car wasn't going to catch me, much less Whitney.

"They'll block her in," I said as I shifted, pushing the car faster around the next turn. The curves would get worse, and I knew I'd have to shed speed soon, but for now I had to try to make up as much road as I could. "She'll never make it past the first crossroads."

"That's a long way, and she can do a lot of damage before she gets there."

"Can't you just—you know—blip over and stop her?"

"Not without destroying the car," he said. "I thought you wouldn't want me to do that. I'm trying to disable the engine, but she's already put a shield around everything I've tried."

He was frowning, and I could see something was bothering him. "What?"

"Whitney's crazy, but she's not stupid. She knows this is a no-win chase. The police will block her in, or I'll find a way to stop her without hurting anyone."

"Maybe it's just a joyride."

"She's a *thief*. Not a joyrider. She has a reason for doing this—watch out!"

I saw it just as he did—an alligator, charging out of the swamp and onto the road. A gigantic one, ancient, and definitely nothing to be messed with under the best of circumstances. I didn't think for a second that the poor gator was doing this of his own accord, though—she'd thrown him in front of us as a living speed bump, with armor and teeth. We'd kill him if we hit him. We'd also damage the car, probably so badly that we'd have to abandon the chase.

"Hang on," I said, and reached out with Earth powers to literally drag the gator off the road to the other side. Earth powers are not my strong suit, and it felt like picking up a safe with one hand—painful, and all but impossible, but I'm not one to let a little thing like pain and impossibility stop me, and the confused reptile waddled/slid safely out of our path just in time, with his scaly tail flicking to boom against David's door as we whizzed past. I'd gone as far over to the left as I'd dared to leave plenty of room, and even then, it had been close. Very close.

I looked back. The gator was already disappearing into the muddy swampland, grateful to be out of our affairs, I suspected.

I caught a flash of metal up ahead. The Bugatti was still just barely in sight, which meant that even Whitney couldn't—or didn't want to—violate the laws of physics. We still had a chance.

Behind us, I heard a crunch of metal. The police car had come to a bad end, presumably, from the disappointed wail of its siren that quickly tailed off into silence. "See if they're okay, honey," I said to David. He nodded and blipped out, and I was left alone, steering my roaring Viper at its absolute limit along the narrow, curving road. I was taking turns race-car wide, and I hoped nobody would come bumbling along in a pickup truck for me to sideswipe, but I figured if the Bugatti had managed, I would, too.

The radio in the Viper suddenly let out a loud burst of white noise, and then Whitney's honey-dipped voice said, "You're just full of spice, little bit. I can see why David thinks you hung the moon. But just between you and me, I think you're a little bit out of your depth, sugar."

The radio wasn't a two-way, but I told her where she could shove it. It made me feel better. "Language," she said reprovingly, which meant she could hear me. Or could guess how I'd reply, anyway. "I'm *shocked,* Joanne. You should slow that pretty little car down before you get hurt. Honestly, why do you care what I get up to? I can see why *he* cares, and he's a funny old thing, isn't he? But you shouldn't. You and me, we're a lot alike. We both like fast cars, right? And shiny things."

"Oh, are we sorority sisters now?" I shot back. "Bite me, Bayou Barbie. What are you doing? Where do you think you can go? That car doesn't exactly blend in!"

"Doesn't have to," she said. "You know, if we *were* sorority sisters, that would be one kick-ass ball of fun, don't you think?"

"Whitney, what are you *doing*?"

"Having fun," she said, and there was a second of silence. When her voice came back, it sounded different. "Until it's time not to have fun. And that's coming up quick."

"You know, Bikini Spice, you might try being a little less vague and a little more informative, if there's something important going on."

"Where's the fun in that? Oh, by the way, heads up. Incoming!" She giggled, and then the static washed over it, and she was gone.

In the next instant, I saw something hurtling out of the sky into the path of my car, rolling out limply and lying flat on the pavement.

This one was no gator.

This was a man.

Instinct took over, and I slammed the brake and clutch, screaming rubber and pulling the emergency brake for added force. I didn't want to drag the guy out of the way—for one thing, I wasn't sure what kind of injuries he had, but they had to be pretty grievous, considering the height from which he'd fallen. "You *bitch!*" I panted, and managed to skid to a sideways stop with the smoking tires about three inches from the fallen body.

I scrambled out, legs shaking from the adrenaline rush, and fell on my knees next to him. The pavement was scorching hot, and the humid air felt suffocating; a swarm of mosquitoes instantly found me and started in on the bonanza. I blew them away with a pulse of Earth power and carefully put a hand on the man's forehead. I didn't know him. He was, as best I could tell, some stranger who'd just gotten caught up in things. I had no idea what he had to do with any of it.

David had described Whitney as a sociopath. This was real evidence that he was right.

The guy was alive, but he was unconscious and pretty badly hurt—internal injuries, a couple of broken bones. I was no expert at healing, but I did what I could, and as I did, I reached deep inside and tugged on the connection that existed between me and David—a kind of permanent cord binding us together. It didn't take long for him to blip back in, landing at a run on the pavement and kneeling next to me.

"The officers are okay," he said. "Shaken up and bruised, but no significant injuries." His face set like stone as he put his hand over mine on the stranger's forehead. "This one's different."

"You noticed," I said. I had already expended a lot of energy, and now I felt waves of warm, thick, golden power flooding into me, through me, speeding relief to the injured areas of the man's body. It burned, but I took it without complaint. If Whitney hadn't felt compelled to stop me, this wouldn't have happened. A little discomfort was the least I could do. "Okay, I think he's stable now. Thanks."

David nodded and eased off the flow of power, which stopped being a painful burn and settled into a gentle mist that soaked into every fiber of my body. It felt glorious, and I took in a deep breath as I savored it. He knew how much power I'd already spent, and this was his way of evening the scales.

"I need you to go back," I said. "Get him help. I can't take him with me—there's no telling what else Whitney will try to pull, and he could get hurt or killed if I put him in the car. Would you?"

He kissed me lightly and faded away in a golden blur on the hot, still air. I crouched down and grabbed the man—whose name I still didn't know—under the arms and dragged him across the road to a narrow strip of shade, as far out of the way as I could get him without moving him into the swamp. Then I put down a layer of protections around him that soaked into the ground, a kind of keep-away perimeter for all of the biting insects and bigger, more predatory killers that lurked out here, including the snakes. It wasn't perfect, but it would keep him safe and comfortable for a while.

Best I could do. Whitney had hoped to weigh me down with responsibility, but that was the advantage of having David—we could split the responsibility. He'd return in only a few moments, and I could keep moving.

I got back in the car, geared it up, and took up the chase. The Bugatti was, of course, well out of sight, so I let myself slide out of my body just a little, taking advantage of the aetheric to get a look at the power signatures at work in front of me. It was a kind of supernatural heads-up display, in a confusing array of colors and patterns that didn't necessarily reflect the real world I lived in, but I'd learned how to process the information as effectively as anyone born human could.

She was ahead of me, still driving, and the Bugatti was a hot silver scar on the riot of color and life around it. Djinn were difficult to see on the aetheric, but the Bugatti had its own signature, and a distinctive one at that. She wouldn't be able to slip away quite that easily.

And, frankly, she wasn't even trying. Maybe she was just enjoying the chase.

I concentrated on making up for lost time. In a sense, I was a little glad she'd brought this chase on, selfish as that was; I loved being so tightly bonded with the machine I was driving, feeling the power of the engine and the press of acceleration thrumming through my whole body. It gave me a sense of purpose, of control, of fierce joy that wasn't like anything else I did. Not even working the weather.

The weather.

I was an idiot. David would have every right to say so when he caught up to me. Of course, working the weather patterns *and* driving like a bat out of hell on treacherous roads, in pursuit of a supernatural enemy, was a bit of a stretch, but what the hell. Whitney and I had a lot in common when it came to ambition.

As part of my consciousness handled the necessary mechanics of the road, I split off part of it to do something that sprang from instinct, aptitude, and power—reading the flows of energy that moved through the air, the currents of disturbance and calm. Today was a beautiful day in Florida, which was (now) a little unfortunate; there wasn't a lot of potential energy to work with. Not impossible, though. Never impossible, in a world where action always brings a reaction, and if you're clever, you can create a storm out of a breeze without destroying the entire balance of the system.

I didn't say it was *easy,* okay? Just *possible.*

Once you get a certain amount of air disturbed and bouncing off of other, less excited air, you get energy. Every collision of molecules creates energy, and that energy has to go somewhere—in the creation of heat. Heated air pushes on cooled air. Wackiness ensues.

That's an obvious simplification, but if you've ever seen a storm form from the collision of a warm front and a cold front, seen those clouds boil up and turn dark and tower up into the heavens . . . well. That's how it works.

And you can start a forest fire by rubbing sticks together, if you're using the right kind of sticks and the right amount of force. The trick is being able to contain the beast you create, because once you get enough energy together, the dynamite is going to go boom. All you can do is direct the force the way you want it to go.

Needless to say, this is not a job for the timid.

The other complication was that Whitney could have known what I was doing . . . but then again, if, as David had implied, she was *really* young for a Djinn, she wouldn't think of everything. She couldn't. Someone like David on the run . . . that was something that was a much harder target. Whitney, in her see-me-from-space bikini and one-of-a-kind sports car? Not so much.

But *damn,* I hated the idea of hurting that car. Which was why my first lightning strike came down on the road in front of the Bugatti, as close as I could nail it without actually hitting it, and I watched in the neon energy trails of Oversight as the sports car wavered, skidded sideways, and then started to straighten out again. That was okay. The lightning had been a diversion, anyway.

What I was *really* doing was blowing out her tires with needle-sharp shards of black ice lined up on the road like shredder strips.

Whitney hit them at a reduced speed, thanks to my lightning feint, which saved her from a fiery matinee-worthy crash. I zoomed in on Oversight and saw the wheels explode—both front tires, then both back. And the Bugatti instantly went from a precision racing machine to a hunk of metal clumsily trying to plow the pavement.

Ouch. That was really going to hurt, but it was better than the alternatives.

My radio spit static, and Whitney said, surprised, "You *bitch*! You are so sneaky!" She laughed, long and loud, and then said, "I think I like you."

Right about then, David blipped in on the passenger seat of the car. "The guy on the road?" I asked.

"Safe in the hands of emergency help," he said. "He's stable. You blew out her tires?"

"Had to try something. Are you ready to spank this little brat before she gets somebody killed?"

"I'd better let you do it. You'd accuse me of enjoying it too much."

David knew me all too well, and it made me laugh as I pressed the accelerator and gained ground on our fleeing Djinn.

She was trying all kinds of tricks now, including forming new tires out of random shreds of rubber left on the side of the road by other luckless drivers, but David was focused entirely on undoing whatever she was up to, and I was completely locked into the car, the acceleration, the chase. Overhead, the weather darkened, and clouds formed to block out the hot sun. We were going to get rain, as a consequence of my actions, but it was a good rain. A washing shower, not a flood.

Suddenly, the Bugatti stopped. I could see it now, the silvery gleam of it unreal against the violent greens and dull browns of the swamp, like some crash-landed alien spacecraft. "What's she doing?" I asked.

"She," said my radio, "is thanking you very much for completely following the script, sugar. Hang on, now. It's going to get interesting."

And then everything changed, completely, because Whitney was not an idiot, a compulsive thief, or a sociopath after all—or if she was those last two things, she certainly wasn't the first. Because Whitney had been taking us somewhere, and we had just arrived.

I coasted the Viper to a stop behind the tire-less Bugatti—the shreds of rubber had fallen apart again—and David and I jumped out to check inside. No sign of Whitney. David turned in a circle, scanning, and then pointed off into the swamp. "There," he said. "She's there."

It's useful to have a Djinn along for a run through the Everglades . . . there's no good footing, but plenty of stinging, biting, and eating things to take an interest in your passage. I was an Earth Warden in addition to my Weather and Fire powers, but Earth was definitely my weakest skill set, and I was relieved I didn't have to manage it on the run. David simply created a firm, dry path out of the swamp, straight as an arrow, and made sure that any creatures with an eye to taking offense at our passage were kept otherwise occupied. I saw a couple of alligators eyeing us coldly from the water, but they stayed as motionless as floating logs. The hot, humid air felt like running a treadmill in a sauna, and I was soaked with sweat and gasping for breath in a humiliatingly short time.

We ran into Whitney about five seconds before I was sure I would drop of heat stroke and exhaustion, and I bent over, bracing myself on my knees, gasping and coughing. Whitney, of course, looked perfect. She was still wearing the diamond bikini, which just could *not* be comfortable on a cross-country trek; I was getting chafed, and nothing I was wearing came in measurements of carats.

Whitney put her hands on her barely clad sparkly hips, and gave me a superior look that made me want to throw up on her high-heeled shoes. "Sweetie, you're gonna want to pace yourself," she said. "We ain't there yet."

"Where?" It came out as a cross between a howl and a whine, which wasn't very heroic, and I blamed it on the urge to vomit. I swallowed, straightened up, and clawed hair away from my damp face to try again. "Where are we going?"

"There." Whitney nodded.

"I don't see anything."

"You will."

David, who'd been about to say something that I was fairly sure would scorch Whitney's exposed buttocks good, checked himself and spun around, staring upward. I didn't know why, but then I heard it.

The abused whine of jet engines, getting louder.

David shouted something in a language that I didn't recognize, but there was no mistaking the command in it, and Whitney lifted her hands to the sky along with him.

A four-engine jet burst out of the clouds, trailing smoke and fire from one wing. Way too low for where it was, which was miles from any decent airport capable of handling an emergency landing. It was an enormous plane, and as I launched myself up into Oversight I saw the black buzzing cloud surrounding it.

Impending death. Terror. The fear of more than three hundred souls, all preparing for the end.

The two Djinn were grabbing hold of the plane, straightening its flight, and I warmed air beneath its swept-back wings, trying to provide lift. It was a huge, ungainly weight without the right balance of physics to support it, and I could sense the terrified but determined pilots trying everything they could to keep it in the air.

"Clear a landing strip!" I yelled to David. "We can't keep it up!"

He and Whitney had already determined that. Whitney kept her arms up, channeling power to the plane, but pieces were breaking off of it now as the structural flaws began to shatter along fault lines. One of the engines imploded, streaming metal and fire that plunged down toward us. Whitney didn't flinch, so neither did I. I felt the impact of the twisted metal like a physical shock as it slammed into the water not ten feet from us, sending a tsunami of muddy green toward us. I didn't bother to stop it. We had more important things to do than stay pretty.

David's power was breathtaking and precise, and he wielded it quickly—dangerous, for a Djinn, because like Wardens, they had to be concerned with balance. He formed a solid pack of earth, a berm that ran straight through the Everglades, and knocked down enough of the cypress growth to provide a window for the plane's wings.

"Coming down!" Whitney yelled, and I felt the hot burn of the exhaust as the jet roared right over our heads, so close that I swear I could count the treads on the landing gear, which was winching its way down. The plane wavered, slipped sideways, and Whitney and I clasped hands instinctively and merged our powers, applying force to the side that needed it, bringing the jet back into a semistable glide.

Twenty feet.

Ten.

Down.

The tires hit the packed earth with more force than normal, and I saw one of them blow out in a mist of rubber and smoke. David flung out a hand and kept that side of the plane up as the pilots applied brakes.

Whitney and I changed the thickness of the air flowing along the flaps, adding to the drag, burning off speed at about twice the normal rate, until the plane was coasting, then a smoking, scarred wreck sitting motionless on the makeshift runway.

Whitney took a deep breath and closed her eyes, and the doors on the plane popped open. Yellow emergency chutes deployed. I could hear screaming from inside, but there was also shouting, people imposing order onto chaos.

I turned toward Whitney. "How did you know?"

She opened those eerie purple eyes, and for a second, I saw the woman she'd once been . . . infinitely tired, frightened, and burdened under all that glitter and gleam. "Once you've died that way, you know it's coming," she said. "It's just how it is."

I said, "I thought you died alone."

Whitney studied me for a few silent seconds, then nodded. "I did," she said. "I was in a plane that went down in the water. I lived. I lived a long, long time. And nobody found me. Nobody ever will." I was still holding her hand. She glanced down at our linked fingers. "This don't make us engaged, you know."

I let go, feeling a little off balance after all of this craziness. It wasn't often that someone threw me, but Whitney had, in every possible sense. She wasn't at all what I'd expected.

"Why didn't you just tell us about this, if you knew it was coming?"

She shrugged, which set off lots of glittering waves from the diamonds. "What kind of fun is that? I got you here, didn't I? I just did it my own way."

"Your way is insane. Go do something useful," David told her. "Send up a flare for the emergency rescue parties. They'll be on the way by now."

She gave him a smart little military salute, which was *very* weird considering her outfit, and executed a perfect turn to march away.

"Wait!" I said. "The guy you threw in our way on the road. Who was he? Why did you do that?"

She glanced back at the plane. Smoke blew away from the fuselage, and I saw a long, ragged hole, with the fragile metal skin peeled away. "He's the man who put the bomb on board," she said. "I didn't think you'd care if you didn't stop in time. I wouldn't have."

And then she vanished in a mist of diamonds. Gone. I looked over at David, who was shaking his head.

"What?" I asked.

"She took the bikini," he pointed out. "And nobody's going to get it back. That's her price for altruism."

I laughed. I could hear emergency sirens back toward the road, and I could just see Whitney standing out there glittering like a diamond convention, pointing the way for all the rescuers.

"I think I like her style," I said.

David rolled his eyes. "*You* don't have to be her boss," he pointed out. "Now. Let's see to the wounded."

In the end, there were remarkably few, and most of the injuries were minor. MIRACLE FLIGHT, they called it on the twenty-four-hour news channels, which featured interviews with everybody possible: people who'd been anywhere in the flight path of the plane, the crew, the passengers, and the director of Whitney's failed commercial shoot, who somehow managed to take high-definition footage of the aircraft on its dramatic flight and landing. He did a documentary. It won an Emmy.

The Case of the Missing Million-Dollar Model occupied headlines for many months, along with positively drooling pictures of Whitney leaning against the Bugatti Veyron with just enough diamonds on her lady parts to make her legal. She was spotted in Rio de Janeiro, and then in Cannes, and then in Argentina and—on the same day—in Shanghai. I think she enjoyed playing Where's Waldo.

David and I never got our beach picnic, but back home, many hours later, we made do. We moved the furniture out of the way, put down the blanket, and had wine and cheese and bread and each other, and somehow, that was still utterly blissful. As we lay there wrapped in each other's arms, lit by candlelight, I felt the rumble of suppressed laughter in his chest.

"What?"

"I was just thinking," David said. "Whitney. She's just insane enough to make a good second in command for me, don't you think? If Rahel can't do it?"

Rahel was a longtime friend and a very formidable Djinn. I couldn't imagine any set of circumstances under which Rahel wouldn't be able to step up to the plate, so I shrugged. "I suppose," I said. "She's certainly not the obvious choice."

He kissed me, long and sweetly. "That's what everyone said about you," he told me, and traced his thumb across my damp lips. "I think my instincts are pretty good."

"And I think you have a weakness for girls in bikinis."

"You're not wearing one now."

"I'm not wearing *anything*."

"Oh yes," he agreed soberly. "I *do* have a weakness for that."

And he showed me, all over again.

IN VINO VERITAS

Karen Chance

The bottom half of my longneck shattered, splashing golden liquid all over my jeans and the bar's floor. The mirror in front of me, already pockmarked with chips, now also had a hole courtesy of the bullet that had drilled through to the wood. The cracks spidering out from the center showed me back my own short brown hair and startled black eyes, and the joker with the gun back-lit in the doorway.

I couldn't see him very well, just a dark silhouette against the rusty evening light spilling down the stairs of the basement bar. But I wouldn't have recognized him anyway. Most of my varied acquaintances wouldn't have taken the shot, and the rest would have made damn sure not to miss.

"That's gonna cost you five bucks," I said, swiveling around. My own gun was out, but I didn't return fire. The guy hadn't taken the second shot, which meant he wanted to chat. Since I was still recovering from a near death experience all of two days ago, I was up for it. And if my vampire sense was anything to go by, a handgun wasn't going to be much use against this joker anyway.

"You want to stay out of our business," I was told, as everyone else scattered to the four winds. The large shape moved into the bar and resolved into a good-looking Asian guy in khakis and a brown leather jacket. The ensemble looked more weekend-in-the-Hamptons than biker chic and clashed badly with the orange and black tiger tat prowling around the right side of his face.

The tat told me a lot, none of it good. The Chinese don't like tattoos. In ancient China, they were used as punishment, branded on criminals before exile to ensure their easy identification should they ever return. They are still seen by many as a defilement of the body and a sign of generally poor taste. That attitude is changing among the young, but despite the glossy black hair and unlined face, this guy hadn't been young in centuries.

Of course, there was one group in China who had always liked tats.

"I don't have any business with the Chinese mafia," I told him, walking behind the bar to get myself a new drink. "Particularly not the vampire kind."

"Then how did you know what I am?" he demanded, coming closer.

The light inside the bar mostly came from the small TV flickering overhead, but it was enough to show me that I'd been right. The facial design was new, but it hid an old secret. I could still see the lines of the original tat, infused with magic so as to be irremovable, flowing under the newer, brighter colors.

"The artist was good, but magical tattoos are a bitch to hide, aren't they?" I asked with a smile.

The man's right hand twitched, like it wanted to cover his face. Or maybe rip off mine. "Like my teeth marks in your throat!"

"Not on the first date," I said, baring my own small fangs. "And I know who you are because I recently met your boss." As I recalled, Lord Cheung and I had parted as . . . well, not friends exactly, but I hadn't expected him to send an assassin after me.

Even one as inept as this.

"You're dhampir."

It didn't appear to startle him. And it should have. The children who result from a coupling between a vampire and a human vary widely in appearance and abilities, with some looking scarier than the creatures who sired them. But not in my case. Except for the vestigial fangs, which aren't noticeable unless I'm pissed off, I'm pretty much human standard. On first sight, most people think I'm sweet and innocent.

Most people are wrong.

But it looked like Tiger boy had known who he was shooting at after all. And then he confirmed it. "They say you're almost five hundred."

"A lady never tells her age."

He leaned on the bar, like we were having a nice, normal chat instead of planning to kill each other. "If you're that old, you should know how to avoid trouble."

"Guess I haven't been paying attention." I glanced over his shoulder. Was I being set up somehow? Because he just couldn't be this stupid. But there was no one there.

I glanced back to find him looking annoyed, like I wasn't keeping to whatever script he'd worked out in his head. Annoyed, but not afraid, despite the fact that I had one hand below the countertop. That told me he wasn't that bright. Well, that and the fact that he'd deliberately sought out one of the few things on earth capable of killing him.

"You aren't clinically depressed, are you?" I asked. "This will be no fun if it's some sort of suicide-by-dhampir."

He looked confused for a moment; then his face rearranged itself into a sneer. "I saw one of your kind once. A master I know keeps him on a leash. Like a *dog*."

"I doubt that."

"He didn't look like much." He took in my less-than-impressive height, my slender build, and my dimples. His lip curled. "Neither do you."

"Looks can be deceiving."

"So can little girls who have been surviving on their reputations for too long!"

Okay, maybe he could be that stupid. "I deserve my reputation," I said mildly.

"Sure you do." His eyes went roaming again, sliding over the black leather of my jacket until they fixed on the vee of my red T-shirt. "Prove it."

So I did.

"Damn it, Dory." Fin scurried up as I walked around the bar and knelt by the still smoking corpse. The owner was a Skogstroll, a kind of Norwegian forest troll, although to my knowledge the closest he'd ever gotten to the land of his ancestors was a PBS documentary. But it meant he didn't have to bend down to examine the damage the shotgun he kept behind the counter had done to the bar. "That's going on your tab!"

"No problem," I said, showing him the contents of the guy's wallet.

"No way." He started backing up, but tripped on his beard. "I'm not touching Tiger money! Not if the whole place burned down!"

I frisked the guy, but of course, there was no ID. Assassins didn't carry it, as a rule. I did find one thing of interest, though.

"Raymond," I said, with feeling.

"Is that his name?" Fin asked, staring at the book of matches I'd found in the not-so-recently deceased's coat pocket.

"No. Tell me about—," I began, when the body started twitching. So he wasn't just a regular old vamp, who would have been killed by that shot as sure as a human. Dumb as a rock or not, he was a master. Cheung really wanted me to get the message.

Whatever the hell it was.

"Don't do it, Dory," Fin warned, his tiny blue eyes worried. "You kill one, and they'll all be hunting you. That's how these guys operate."

"I'm not planning to kill anyone," I squawked, because the vamp had grabbed me around the throat. So I stuck a knife through his, pinning him securely to the wood.

Fin's glare intensified. "Dory!"

"Relax, it won't kill him. I'd have to take the whole head for that." I sat back on my heels. "And when did you become so squeamish?"

"I'm not! But you don't want to mess with these guys."

"I haven't been," I said, exasperated. "I had a run-in with his boss recently, but we cleared that up." Or so I'd thought.

Fin didn't look convinced. "He sent a master to screw with you for no reason?"

"Let's find out," I said, wrenching the knife out.

But even though I'd taken care to miss the vocal cords, it looked like the vamp had lost interest in conversation. An arm sent me skidding on my back into the forest of tables, reducing a few of the battered old pieces to kindling. I leapt back to my feet, but the vamp didn't press his advantage. He was gone between one blink and the next, out the door and up the stairs, despite the fact that, in vamp terms, sunlight + major blood loss = bar-be-cue.

If I was lucky, anyway.

Fin hopped about, contorting his body to avoid the shaft of light spilling over the old boards. Older trolls could withstand direct sun, and even those Fin's age didn't actually turn to stone. But he said it gave him hives.

"And stay out!" he shouted, flipping the door shut with his toe.

I picked myself up and assessed the damage. Other than for some bruised ribs and a jacket full of splinters, I was unharmed. The same couldn't be said for my cell phone, which had been in my back pocket. I fished out a few pieces of plastic and some metal innards, extracted the memory chip, and threw the rest in the trash.

It could have been worse; it could have been my head. And maybe next time it would be. Because it was a little hard to stop doing whatever was pissing Cheung off when I didn't even know what it was.

I walked back over and retrieved the guy's wallet. "You going to tell me what you know?" I asked Fin.

"It isn't much," he said, eyeing the fat sheaf of banknotes peeking out of the natty eel-skin cover. "They call themselves Leaping Tigers, and they're new. The first of them showed up about a month ago, but they operate out of Chinatown, not here. I heard they pretty much destroyed a couple gangs over there, setting up house. They're bad news."

Tell me something I don't know, I thought cynically. "And this house would be where?"

He licked his lips. "You, uh, you gonna need all that?"

I fanned myself with the fat stack of bills. "I thought you wouldn't touch Tiger money." He gave me a limpid look and I sighed. "You're planning to tell everyone I took it, aren't you?"

He looked pained. "You can take care of yourself better than me. And you *did* shoot him."

"So give."

"I already did. Nobody knows where they hole up during the day. It's like they just vanish."

"You mean nobody wants to know."

"That, too. Anyway, they've made a big impression pretty damn fast. You're better off staying away from them."

"Yeah. But will they stay away from me?"

"Just take care, Dory."

"I always do." I fished out a five and tossed the rest on the bar. "Drinks are on him."

Raymond Lu was a disreputable nightclub owner who had recently become a disreputable snitch. He didn't have a tiger tat, probably because he wasn't important enough to deserve one, but his boss just happened to be Lord Cheung. And the last time one of Cheung's guys had taken a shot at my head, it had been due to my association with Ray.

His club's logo had been emblazoned on the matches I'd found in the hit man's coat, so I decided to see if anything interesting was happening. It wasn't. Of course, that in itself was interesting.

The club usually did a pretty good business, despite being wedged between an acupuncturist and a cut-rate electronics store on a back-street of Chinatown. Not tonight, though. The jazzy neon sign was dark and the usual bouncer-and-rope combo was missing from the front door.

Instead, a large guy leaned against the dirty bricks, in the process of lighting a cigarette. The glow of the flame into his cupped palm highlighted a familiar craggy face. Zheng-ze, aka Scarface, Cheung's right-hand vamp and a first-level master with power to burn.

He and his boss were in the process of challenging for seats on the senate, the ruling body for vamps in North America. From what I'd heard, they'd been doing pretty good. I silently cursed and shifted a little closer to the Dumpster that was providing my cover. The fact that Scarface was standing guard duty cut down my chances of getting in by at least half.

A moment later, he finished lighting up and relaxed against the wall. And grinned at me. I gave it up and crossed the road.

"Haven't you heard that stuff'll kill you?" I asked as he took a long drag.

He laughed it back out. "You look like shit," he told me cheerfully, his eyes on the not-yet-faded bruises under the pancake I'd slathered on before leaving the house. "I heard you got yourself blown up."

"You heard wrong." Although it had been pretty damn close.

"Good. Once I get the Challenges outta the way, you and I gotta square off." He showed me some big white teeth. "See who's best."

"I know who's best."

"That's the spirit," he said approvingly. "There's no sport in it when they just give up and die."

I ignored that in favor of nodding at the building behind him. "So what's going on?"

I hadn't really expected an answer, although I got one—sort of. "Lord Cheung's trying to clean up his image. He's jonesing for a senate seat bad and thinks some of his activities might not look too good if they're brought up in the voting process."

"I thought combat decided the new senators."

"Combat narrows the field," he corrected. "But once we're through, we got to be confirmed. And your senators are going to be looking for any possible reason to turn us down."

"They're not my senators," I said flatly.

The senate employed me to clean up its messes from time to time, but the fact that I occasionally proved useful hadn't made me any more popular. The only one who might not hate me was Mircea, second in command to the consul, the senate's leader. Most vamps treated him like he was scary with a little scary on top, which I'd always found puzzling. He sparked a confusing tangle of emotions in me, but fear had never been one of them.

Of course, that might be because he was also my father.

"Look, I don't care who does or does not get on the senate," I told Scarface. "I just want to know why your master sent a hit man after me."

"You'd have to ask him about that."

"Is he in there?" A brief nod. "Then get out of the way and I will."

He blew smoke at me.

"I'm going in there," I informed him.

He dropped his cigarette to the stained concrete and ground it in with his toe. "I was hoping to wait until you recovered to beat you up," he said regretfully. "It won't be nearly as much fun this—" He broke off as I turned on my heel and headed down the sidewalk. "Hey! Where you going?"

"The side exit."

His booming laughter followed me around the building.

The short alleyway stopped after half a dozen yards, ending at another brick wall. Three steps went up to a door, steps that were occupied by another bored-looking vamp. He didn't seem surprised to see me, having heard my conversation with his buddy out front, and he didn't even stand up. I decided that was rude and started rooting around in my big black duffel bag.

"What are you going to do?" he asked, amused. "Mace me?"

"Good idea."

The heavy iron-headed mace caught him upside the head and

sent him crashing through the rusted railing and into the river of slime flowing down the center of the alley. I didn't wait around to see what mood he'd be in when he picked himself up. I threw open the door and sprinted inside, pausing only long enough to see that the sole source of light was on the balcony, one level up.

I heard a faint foot-scrape behind me and slammed the heavy old door in the vamp's face. He cursed and staggered backward, and I took off across the dark dance floor. I reached the curving iron stairs to the balcony and took them two at a time.

I was halfway up when the guard's foot hit the bottom step—and then abruptly fell away. He was soon joined by the rest of Cheung's men, but they bunched at the bottom, making no effort to follow me up. That didn't make sense until I burst out onto the catwalk and realized two things: there was already a vamp up here and he didn't need any help.

He was standing in front of the manager's office, halfway down the balcony. What he really looked like was anyone's guess, of course, most of the older masters found it useful to present an attractive appearance. In this case, that meant bronze skin, high cheekbones, dark, almond-shaped eyes, and a hawklike nose with a proud tilt.

I didn't know Cheung's background, but he looked like the kind of guy who should be wearing heavily embroidered silk or possibly warrior leathers. Something exotic and powerful, anyway. So he appeared a little out of place in a double-breasted pinstripe tailored so tight he could have cut paper on it.

The elegance of the outfit made the large orange and black tiger tat prowling around his smooth olive skin that much more noticeable. Of course, the movement helped, too. I watched it stalk around the back of his hand before returning to the concealment of the shirtsleeve, tail slowly swishing. It was beautifully done—all long, sleek muscles under a rich blanket of fur, with watchful emerald eyes and an occasional flash of sharp white teeth.

Its expression wasn't so nice. At the moment, both tiger and man wore the same one—of barely concealed impatience. "I thought I had warned you off," Cheung said, without preamble.

"Was that what you were doing?" I moved forward, since it wasn't like I could go back. "I guess the bullet grazing my ear must have confused me."

"The fact that it missed should have told you as much."

"Oh, I'm sorry." I stopped a yard or so away, close enough to smell his cologne, far enough away to have a chance to reach my weapons. "Maybe next time you could shoot me an e-mail instead?"

Cheung ignored that. "I know your father's power, dhampir. I have no wish to return you to him in pieces. If you swear to cease interfering in my business, you may go."

"It would help if I knew what your business is," I pointed out.

Cheung's eyes narrowed. "You do not?"

"Would I be asking if I did?"

His expression darkened, but he didn't reply, possibly because the front doors took that moment to slam open, allowing a dozen more vamps to pour into the room. It was starting to look like Cheung didn't have anybody on staff lower than master level; either that, or he'd left the riffraff at home. These radiated enough power to ruffle my hair, even this far away, which made it a little ridiculous that they were dragging one short, pudgy guy.

He wasn't halfway across the floor when I recognized him: Raymond, looking a little the worse for wear. He was trying to struggle but not managing it too well considering that neither of his feet was actually touching the floor. A tall vamp with Asian features but a pale blond buzz cut had him by the back of the neck, like an errant puppy.

I crossed my arms and got a grip on the stake up my sleeve.

Cheung noticed but didn't do anything, other than roll his eyes. He looked past me as Raymond was dragged up to us and forced to kneel. Or maybe his legs just gave out. He looked pretty damn terrified.

"You appear to make enemies wherever you go, Raymond," Cheung said, looking at him with a slight curl to his lip.

"I g-guess I'm just lucky like that," Raymond said. It sounded cocky, even with the stutter, and won him a cuff upside the head from the blond. But I didn't think it had been meant that way. Raymond was at the stage of terror where the mouth is on autopilot because the brain has retreated somewhere inside the skull in order to gibber quietly. If he'd been a human, he'd have soiled himself by now.

"Are you going to tell me what is going on?" I asked Cheung.

"I believe I shall let Raymond do that," he said, looking with distaste at his cowering subordinate.

Ray looked from me to the boss and back again, but didn't appear to find anything helpful. "Well?" I prompted.

He swallowed. "Uh. I might have, you know, mentioned that, uh, that the senate had appointed you as my, um." He stopped, looking at me pitifully. His usually beady blue eyes were suddenly large and soulful, like the aforementioned puppy's.

Or an albino rat.

"Your what?" I demanded.

"My bodyguard?"

I pinched the bridge of my nose and thought about saving everyone a lot of trouble and staking Ray right here. But I doubted he'd told the senate all he knew yet. And without his information, we had pretty much a zero chance of shutting down the smuggling ring he'd been running. Not to mention that the little guy had done me a few pretty big favors recently.

I was going to have to figure a way to get him out of this.

I could always stake him later.

"Then he *was* lying," Cheung said, looking satisfied.

I glared at Ray, whose eyes were still doing the huge and pleading thing. He clearly thought this was it. It didn't help that I was pretty sure he was right.

I sighed and accepted the inevitable. "Not exactly."

Cheung's forehead creased slightly. "You are assuming responsibility for him?"

"I am saying I already have it." I reached down and jerked Ray over to me by his collar. His eyes bugged out a little, but he didn't protest. If nothing else, that told me how serious this was. He usually whined nonstop. "He's mine."

"Yours?" One dark eyebrow rose. "You did not sire him. By vampire law, he is my property to do with as I wish. And I doubt the senate will flout thousands of years of tradition, even to save the life of their favorite . . . what is the word? Canary?"

"Your vocab's a little out of date," I said sourly. "And that's not how I remember it."

"I beg your pardon?"

"The last time you, me, and Ray were all together, you gave him to me."

The crease grew into a frown. "I did nothing of the kind."

"In exchange for me helping to cover up the fact that you'd kidnapped a senator's brother, threatened him with death, and trashed his new and very expensive car. Ring any bells?"

"There was no formal transfer made. You misinterpreted a casual remark."

I had done no such thing, and he damn well knew it. "I guess we can let the senate decide that." They'd have to support Ray, like it or not, or lose all that lovely information he still had locked in his fat little head.

Scarface came up the stairs and Cheung glanced at him. "Careful," he told him, looking at me narrowly. "She is dhampir. I don't know what she can pick up."

Not a hell of a lot, I didn't say. Vampire mind-speak had never been my forte. Especially not if it was in Cantonese.

But Mircea had spent some time in the East, and for all they knew, so had I. I decided to capitalize on the moment. "May I speak to Ray privately?"

Cheung hesitated for a moment, but then he nodded, probably wanting his own private confab. I didn't give him time to change his mind, but dragged Ray through the door into the office and slammed it shut with my foot. "Are we private?" I demanded.

He sighed morosely. "There's a privacy spell on the room; they can't hear us. Not that it matters. They're going to kill me."

"You should be more worried about me at the moment," I hissed. "Why the hell did you tell Cheung I was your bodyguard?"

"Well, you should have been," he said spitefully, suddenly growing some backbone. "Or somebody shoulda been. What did you think was gonna happen, as soon as I started spilling my guts? The master was gonna give me a medal?"

"He knew I was going to take you in. He had to expect—"

"What he expected was that I'd die before the senate could question me. I was a little under the weather, if you remember?"

The sarcasm was understandable. Ray had been sans a head at the time Cheung and I had cut our deal, and the body parts he'd had left had been pretty beat-up. Vampires are sturdy, but what he'd been through would have killed many at a higher power level than he was ever likely to reach. Cheung's conclusion had been reasonable.

But Ray was tougher than he looked, and he'd had some supernatural help Cheung hadn't known about. He'd not only lived, but once all his parts were reattached, he'd sung like . . . well, like a canary. And what a song it had been.

"Why didn't you ask the senate protect you?" I demanded. "You've given them enough information already to shut down half the illegal smuggling in Manhattan."

"I did!" he said indignantly. "But this challenge mess is all anyone can think about. And I don't think they believed the master would move against me, not with him vying for a senate seat and all. He's supposed to be on his best behavior."

"Yes, he is," I said hopefully. "Maybe we can use that. He's risking a lot."

"He's risking nothing! When I disappear, the senate might suspect him, sure. But I also could have lost my nerve and run. I thought about it, you know. I got a lot of contacts among the fey, and they can hide anybody. If they didn't creep me out so damn much . . . Anyway, without proof, they can't move against him. And since

Lord Cheung is my master, nobody else can trace me." He slumped onto the edge of the desk. "I'm toast."

I thumped him. "And thanks to you, so am I! I'm the only one who can tell the senate you didn't go on an extended vacation!"

"Then I guess you better figure us a way out of this," he told me resentfully, rubbing the side of his head.

I'd have thumped him again, but I didn't have time. I glanced around, but things weren't looking promising. As I'd already noticed, there was no phone, and mine was still in pieces. There was only one door in or out, and the only window was merely a paler square of brick in the wall behind the desk. Ray's place wasn't exactly up to fire code, having been designed for the convenience of the vampire owner and staff, not ease of egress.

"I don't suppose they left you a phone?" He just looked at me. Of course not. And his penny-pinching ways had led to him skipping the usual magical escape routes.

"I bet you wish you'd invested in a few emergency exits now," I said harshly.

"You don't need 'em when you got a portal," Ray commented, and my eyes jerked to the blank stretch of wall across from the door.

"That's right. You have a portal," I said, brightening.

"Had. The senate's goons were here yesterday. I guess they wanted to plug my link to Faerie before they started on the smaller stuff."

Typical.

"Then the only exits are in the main room?"

Ray nodded bleakly. I stared at the door and faced reality. As usual, my duffel contained a few surprises, but no way was I carving a path through all that. Not on my best day, which this definitely wasn't.

I was going to have to come up with something else.

The door opened and Lord Cheung leaned against the sill, looking considerably more upbeat. "I have been reminded that, in a case of disputed ownership, a duel is the common remedy."

I stared over Cheung's shoulder at Scarface's smug grin. I didn't have to ask who had done the reminding. He'd just seen me walk away from a challenge outside. I was in no shape to duel a kitten right now, much less a first-level master, and he damned well knew it.

"That's not going to get us anywhere," I said, trying to keep my voice even. "If you leave me alive, I'll tell the senate you killed Ray, ruining your chances at a seat. And if you kill me, Mircea will return the favor, for pride if nothing else. Then we're all dead."

Cheung's face gave nothing away, but I didn't need expressions to know what he was thinking. Mircea could take revenge only if he knew Cheung was responsible for my death, which he might never find out. But then, Cheung couldn't know who I might have told where I was going. Or, for that matter, what kind of a bond Mircea and I had.

In the end, he decided not to risk it. "You have a better solution?"

"Yeah. You want Ray; so do I. So we'll gamble for him."

"You wish to flip a coin?" The sarcasm was palpable.

"Coin tosses can be rigged. I'd prefer something where we both have an even shot, where no one gets dead, and where the outcome is sure."

"What, then?" Cheung asked, looking wary.

So I told him.

"Okay," Ray said, coming in from the storeroom flanked by two babysitters. "This is the lot; this is all I got."

He carried a cardboard box over to one of the club's small tables, which had been placed in the middle of the dance floor. Cheung had chosen the location, I guess to give his boys a chance to crowd around and see him kick my ass. Ray pushed through the throng, but then just stood there, the glass bottles inside the box chiming against each other because his hands were shaking.

"Put it down," Cheung told him impatiently.

"Th-there's not room on the table."

Cheung looked skyward. "Then put it on the ground." Ray obliged, and peeled back the cardboard top.

"That should be enough," I said drily, eyeing the stash that was revealed. There were twelve bottles, each holding maybe a pint. That didn't sound like much, unless you knew what was in them.

Fey wine wasn't really wine. It wasn't much like anything else found on earth, either. A distillation of plants, mostly fey in origin, plus some herbs, spices, and God knew what else thrown in for taste, it could put a bull elephant on his knees. That much would drop the whole damn herd, only they weren't going to be drinking it.

We were.

I'd have preferred something else, since my metabolism neutralizes regular old alcohol almost faster than I can drink it. Unfortunately, the same is true for vampires. If I wanted to win, Cheung had to end up under the table. And that meant hauling out the hard stuff.

"Is it not customary to cut this?" Cheung asked as Ray poured clear liquid into a couple of shot glasses. A little sloshed onto the table. I was slightly surprised it didn't eat on through.

"If you feel the need," I told him sweetly.

Cheung narrowed his eyes at me and tossed back his first shot. He didn't do anything so unmanly as choke, but his eyes widened perceptibly. And then it was my turn. I'd proposed a drink-till-you-drop challenge for two reasons. Physically, it was all I was up for at the moment. I was in no condition to take Cheung, and even if I somehow did the impossible, no way was Scarface letting me walk out of here after killing the boss. But it was reason number two that I was betting the farm on. Or at least Ray's continued existence.

One of the interesting facets of life as a dhampir is frequent rage-induced blackouts. They are a natural result of the vampire killing instinct mixed with an excitable human nervous system, but tell that to the people who've encountered one of us on a rampage. Not that there are usually any left.

Because of the scarcity of my kind—and the fact that we aren't on most people's Christmas card list—nobody had ever bothered to devise anything to control the blackouts. But after hundreds of years of questionable sanity, I'd recently discovered a remedy on my own. It wasn't a perfect solution: it kept me more or less sane, but it severely reduced my ability in battle—something that, in my line of work, was considerably less than ideal.

It also had some interesting side effects.

I picked up my glass, hoping one in particular was going to kick in. Because otherwise, I didn't have a much better chance at this contest than I would at a duel. I might drag it out longer, but my half-human metabolism was almost certain to be more susceptible to the wine's effects than a full vampire's.

I slammed back the shot, and felt my eyes start to water. Fey wine varied a lot in type and potency, depending on what exactly went into the mix, and this particular batch ought to have been illegal. Of course, come to think of it, it was.

"You okay there?" Scarface asked, looking amused. I nodded, my throat burning too much to speak, and sat the glass down beside Cheung's. Ray immediately refilled them, while I concentrated on my version of a Hail Mary pass.

I had not inherited the vampire ability to mind speak. But I had found that if I drank the feys' favorite beverage in enough quantity, I could pick up bits and pieces of what others were thinking. And I could speak to the mind of one vamp in particular.

This had led to some awkward situations, as the vamp in question, Louis-Cesare, was also my . . . well, I didn't know what to call him. We weren't lovers, exactly, at least not yet. And we were only friends in the way that we yelled at each other a lot. But there was definitely an attraction there. And for a few intimate, wine-fueled moments, I'd felt closer to him than to anyone else I'd ever known.

I didn't know if he could pick up my thoughts from this far away, as we'd never done any actual experimentation with our connection. But a long shot is better than no shot at all. I downed the second shot and thought, *Hurry up, hurry up, hurry up!*

Fifteen minutes and a full bottle later, it became obvious that Louis-Cesare was not hurrying. I licked numb lips and decided there was a silver lining. At this rate, I wouldn't be able to feel it whenever they got around to shooting me. "You owe me," Ray hissed into my ear as I sat staring resentfully at my tenth or fifteenth or twentieth shot. I'd lost count. But it basically added up to too many.

"Nowhere near this much," I muttered, trying not to slur my words.

"Oh, so now we're putting a price on friendship?"

"We're not friends," I told him darkly. I'd just seen Cheung toss back another shot. He'd lost his suit coat and loosened his tie, but other than that, he looked exactly the same as when I'd come in. The damn vampire wasn't even sweating.

"Don't talk," Ray said, putting a glass in my hand. "Drink."

I wasn't aware that I'd been talking. That probably wasn't a good sign. But at least I was still sitting straight. Cheung had started to list a little.

"That's you," Ray said, hauling me upright and handing me another glass.

"Hey!" I protested. "He has to drink first."

"He just did."

"I didn't see."

"It's difficult to see anything when one's eyes are crossed," Cheung said. And then he giggled.

I know I wasn't imagining it, because his vamps' heads all swiveled in his direction, expressions of incredulity on their faces. Scarface scowled at them and they quickly looked away. But a few were coughing and one had to abruptly leave the room.

I downed another shot and grinned at Cheung. "I c'n do this all night," I told him. "And you're already drunk."

Cheung gave me a superior look and tried to pick up his glass. He missed.

"He may be drunk," Scarface said, "but you're about to fall on your ass. And as soon as you do, that son of a bitch is ours." He scowled at Ray, as if his boss's loss of dignity were all his fault. Ray must have interpreted it that way, too, because he quickly sloshed some more liquid into the glasses.

"I am not even close to being on my ass," I said, offended. "And Ray's gonna be fine."

"That's right," Ray said staunchly.

Fifteen minutes later, I'd decided Ray really was toast.

"It's okay," he said, massaging my shoulders. "You're doing great. Just really, really good."

"How many more bottles are there?" I asked blearily. The way I felt, we must have gone through most of the case.

"Nine."

"Nine?" I did a little mental arithmetic, which was way harder than it should have been. "We've only been through *three?*"

"Three and a half," he said, and refilled my glass.

"That wasn't so bad," I decided after downing the shot. Maybe I was getting my rhythm.

"Because you threw it over your shoulder," Scarface told me, looking smug.

"Did not." I looked behind me, only to see an outraged vamp with fey wine dripping down his face. "Oops."

"It was for luck," Ray said defensively, wrapping both my hands around a glass. "Drink!"

I drank.

An indeterminate time later—my eyes couldn't seem to focus on my watch anymore—someone slapped me across the face. "Big, bad dhampir, remember?" Ray said, his face looming large in front of mine. It appeared agitated.

"Big, bad dhampir wan' go sleep."

"They're laughing at you," he said, grabbing my chin and turning my head toward Cheung's men. "Look at them. They're laughing!"

It took me a moment to focus, but when I did, they didn't look like they were laughing. Mostly, they looked bored and a little nervous. Apparently, the novelty of seeing the boss shit-faced had worn off, and a few of the smarter ones had started to wonder just how much they were going to pay for having witnessed this.

One look at Cheung, and I didn't think they needed to worry.

His tie was gone, his shirt was open halfway down his chest, his bangs had all flopped into his eyes, and while he might not have been sweating, he was looking pretty damn green. I wasn't sure how much he'd remember tomorrow, which was just as well, since he also appeared to have developed a fascination with Scarface's hair. He kept reaching up to poke at the spikes, and appeared amazed when they weren't sharp.

"You can take him!" Ray whispered in my ear.

"Damn straight."

The next thing I remember, Ray was fishing me out from under the table. Or at least he was trying to, but Scarface's foot was in the way. "On. Her. Ass," Scarface said proudly.

"She just slipped," Ray said, sounding frantic. "Anybody could slip. She's fine!"

"Like hell she's fine. Look at her!"

"I am," someone said, from somewhere behind us. "Would you care to explain to me what is wrong with her?"

Scarface slowly straightened, his foot sliding off Ray's wrist. Ray seized the opportunity to drag me upright. "I love you, man," I told him blearily, catching one of his hands.

"God. Just. Shut. Up," he muttered.

The room appeared to be spinning anyway, so I followed it around to where a handsome auburn-haired vamp was standing by the main entrance. He had a sword in either hand and appeared miffed. Louis-Cesare, my brain supplied helpfully, after a minute. I was pleased to see him, although I couldn't exactly recall why. But I sent him a sloppy smile anyway.

"She has not been injured," Scarface said, stepping away from the table to give himself room to maneuver. And as soon as he did, his boss slowly slipped off his seat and into a well-dressed lump on the floor.

"On his ass! On his ass!" Ray said, letting go of me to point.

"So is she," Scarface hissed, as I flopped facefirst onto concrete. "And she was first."

"Only because you were holding him up! You were cheating!"

"No, this would be cheating," Scarface said, and smashed a bottle upside Ray's head.

And then things got a little confusing.

Scarface lunged at Ray, who stumbled back, squeaking. But he tripped over me and slammed into the case of fey wine, crushing it beneath him. Thanks God for large favors, I thought fervently.

And then I remembered why I was happy to see Louis-Cesare.

"Love you!" I yelled encouragingly, which caused him to start suddenly. Then, for some reason, he scowled. And then the sprinkler system got turned on, although that might have been later, because when I looked around, I was by the bar.

Someone was trying to pound the butt of a shotgun through my skull. So I yanked it out of his grasp and brought it down on his kneecaps. He screamed in pain and grabbed for the weapon, we struggled, and it went off, blowing a hole the size of a basketball through the fake wood paneling separating the club from the bar.

We both stared at it for a second before he grabbed for me—at the same time that another vamp brought a club down, trying to crush my hand. I rolled out of the way and he hit his buddy's instead, with a crunching sound that indicated a broken bone or three. The first vamp screamed again and reflexively kicked out, knocking his buddy back into a nest of bar stools. The stools scattered, the vamp fell backward, and my hand closed on one of my guns.

I didn't even try to aim, since I was the only one there who could be killed by a stray bullet. I just sprayed them everywhere. I don't think too many connected, but it distracted my attackers long enough for me to reach the hole in the wall. One of Ray's boys looked through at me, his bright black eyes wide.

"Scotch?" I asked as a chair was slung across the room at my head. I ducked and the bartender handed me a bottle, just as the chair tosser lunged at me. I broke it over his head, staggering him. "A light?" My lighter was in my jeans, and no way was I coordinated enough to get it out.

I was passed another matchbook embossed with the bar's logo, and a second later, the vamp went up in flames. He could have stopped, dropped, and rolled them out, but most vamps aren't that levelheaded about fire. This one proved to be no exception. He panicked and crashed into his buddy, and they fell to the floor, screaming Cantonese invective at each other.

I looked around for the next threat, but all I saw was Louis-Cesare standing over a pile of vamps, none of which appeared to be in proper working order. It would have been cause for celebration, if it hadn't been for the boots hitting the street outside. Deciding to get out before Cheung's reinforcements ruined the odds again, I tossed a potion grenade at the front door and jumped out the side.

Louis-Cesare was right behind me. We landed hard in front of the puddle of water that spanned most of the alley. It reflected the explosion in the club behind us, flames shooting upside down, livid and wavering, until a screaming mass of panicked vamps came pouring out of the door. They scattered in all directions, some splashing through the water and turning it into a rippling mass of flame.

One of the last to emerge was Scarface, with the boss draped inelegantly over one shoulder. "You." He pointed at me. I blinked at him. "Later."

I nodded and waved him off as Ray came scooting out the door, the seat of his pants smoking. "Now who owes who?" I demanded as he hightailed it down the alley. He paused at the corner to shoot me the bird, before disappearing in the opposite direction from Cheung's vamps.

"He'll be okay," I told Louis-Cesare. "He'll run straight to the senate, and now that they know there's a danger, they'll have to—"

Somebody started shaking me, which was not a good idea under the circumstances. "Don' do that," I said, grabbing hold of Louis-Cesare's jacket.

"You're drunk," he accused. But he did stop shaking me.

I pondered that for a moment. It was undeniably true. And then

I remembered that there were extenuating circumstances, some of which involved him. "Well, you were late."

"I was in Brooklyn!"

"You went to see me?" I grinned happily. And then stopped, wondering if he'd had some other reason for making the trip. It wasn't like we had a Thing. Not an official Thing, anyway. He didn't *have* to visit, although I couldn't think of any other reason he'd be in Brooklyn. Louis-Cesare was definitely more of an uptown kind of—

"Why are you out of bed?" he demanded, looking like he wanted to start with the shaking again.

"I just wanted a quiet drink," I said defensively. That and I'd been going crazy with boredom.

"It appears that you found one," he said drily.

"Well, I don't know how quiet it was—" I broke off, because something in his expression was wrong. It took me a moment, but I finally sorted through exasperation, fondness, and relief to something that looked like hurt. And that didn't make sense.

"We won," I said distinctly. "At least, I think so. . . ." I looked around. The alley was quiet again, except for the crackling fire and the distant sound of sirens.

"Yes, we won," he affirmed.

I looked back up at him, fuzzily. "So why the long face?"

He took a deep breath. "I was hoping that the first time you expressed affection for me, it would not be in a room full of strangers. And that you would not have just said it to a sniveling creature like that Raymond!"

"I expressed affection for Ray?"

"Yes!"

"Man, I really must be drunk." Louis-Cesare just looked at me. I blinked politely back, until I realized that he expected a response. "Uh. Sorry?"

"Isn't there anything else you wish to say to me?" he asked impatiently.

I swallowed. "Yes. Yes there is."

Warm arms suddenly engulfed me, pulling me in, and one large hand tucked my head into his chest. "What is it?" he asked softly.

"I'm about to yak all over your shirt."

Vampire reflexes got me to the side of the road instead, and then he crouched there, brushing my hair away from my sweaty cheeks as I made good on the first part of my threat. He sighed. "One day, you will say it to me again. You will be sober. And you will mean it."

I was actually terrified that I already meant it. A guy just might be a keeper if he hears your cry for help in his head. And comes into a den of thieves to get you out. And then holds your hair while you throw up for ten minutes.

Then again, I was in no condition to judge. But that old saying kept rattling around in my head. *"In vino veritas,"* I whispered, faintly appalled.

"What?"

"Nothing." I looked up at him as he pulled me back to my feet. "Let's go home."

# HUNT

Rachel Vincent

The forest was singing, and its song was all mine. The others couldn't hear it, with their human ears. They heard only the crackle-roar of the campfire and their own voices. Huddled in down jackets and sleeping bags, they thought they owned the world, by virtue of their ability to tame it, and that was an understandable mistake. But they'd never *really* seen the world. Not like I saw it.

Soon I'd have to go back to the campfire. To their idea of "roughing it" with battery-powered radios, canned food, and no-rinse bathing wipes, guaranteed to keep you fresh, even days into a showerless camping trip. Soon I'd have to put on my human skin and put away my feline instincts, so I could be Abby Wade, normal college sophomore. I could do that. I'd been hiding that part of my life for a year and a half, and my secret run was just a temporary reprieve from all things human.

Still, the next few moments were mine.

My paws snapped through twigs and sank into underbrush, pushing against the earth to propel me faster, higher. I was a streak of black against the night, darker than the forest, yet a part of it, as I hadn't been in weeks. Small animals fled just ahead of my paws, scurrying through tangles of fallen leaves and branches. The scents of oak, birch, maple, and pine were familiar comforts, relaxing me even as they pushed me for more speed, greater distance. Thorns caught in my fur. Cold air burned in my nose and stroked the length of my body as I ran, like a caress from the universe itself.

I was welcome in the woods. I belonged there, at least for the next few minutes.

When I'd run fast and long enough to satisfy that initial need for exercise, I slowed to a gradual, soft stop, huffing from exertion. It was time to eat and replace the energy I'd burned during my Shift.

My ears swiveled on my head, pinpointing the sounds I needed to hear. Werecats can't track by scent, like a dog, so we hunt with our ears and our eyes. On my run, I'd smelled mice and a couple of weasels, both of which stay active in the winter, but I was holding out for a rabbit, or even a beaver. No use wasting a deer with only me there to feed on it.

Something scuttled through the underbrush several yards to the southeast. Too fast and light to be a raccoon. Probably a mouse or a rat. Too much effort for too little meat.

I slowed my breathing and listened harder. From the north came a soft, rapid, swooshy heartbeat, but no movement. Whatever it was, it knew I was close and hungry. I turned my head and sniffed toward the north—I could pinpoint it with my ears, but would have to ID it with my nose. A rabbit. Perfect. Its fur wouldn't be white yet—not in mid-October—but my cat's eyes would still spot it. As soon as I flushed it out of hiding.

I pounced. The rabbit sprung from the underbrush and landed three feet away. I got a glimpse of brown and white fur, and then it was off again, racing through the woods and jumping over low shrubs and fallen logs.

I ran after it at half speed, reluctant to end the chase too soon—who knew when I'd have another chance to hunt? But seconds later, a scream shattered the cold, quiet night with a sharp echo of pain and terror.

A sudden spike of fear glued me to the forest floor. I knew that scream—that voice. Robyn. My roommate, and for the next three nights, my tent-mate.

No!

I turned and raced through the woods toward the campsite, my lungs burning, my heart trying to beat its way through my sternum. I had no plan, no thought beyond simply getting there, and only the vaguest understanding that if I burst into the camp in cat form, I'd scare her far worse than whatever had made her scream.

But I'd gone only a few yards when a second scream split the night again, followed by two deeper, masculine shouts of fear and pain. What the hell was going on?

I pushed myself harder, my brain racing now. Bear? There was no growling or roaring, and I hadn't smelled anything even slightly ursine. Besides, black bears typically shy away from humans. As do bruins, though to my knowledge, no one had ever spotted a bear Shifter in the heart of the Appalachian Territory.

So what the hell was happening?

I flew through the forest, retracing my own path with no thought for the living buffet scurrying all around me this time. The screaming continued, terror from Robyn and Dani, sheer agony from their boyfriends. I'd seen a friend murdered once, and I recognized sounds I'd hoped never to hear again—my friends were being slaughtered.

My clothes hung on branches ahead, but I raced past them. The screaming was louder now, but there were fewer voices—Mitch had gone silent. I was too late for Dani's boyfriend, and before I'd gone another few yards, Olsen's screaming ended in a horrible, inarticulate gurgle.

My lungs burned and my legs ached—werecats are sprinters, not long-distance runners—but I pushed forward, demanding more from my body than I'd ever had reason to expect from it. This couldn't be real!

Robyn's screams intensified with her boyfriend's silence, then suddenly stopped, and for a moment, my heart refused to beat. *Not*

Robyn. I couldn't lose my roommate of more than a year. The girl who left her toothpaste open on the bathroom counter and made me hot chocolate in the middle of the night, when nightmares woke me up.

Then in the sudden quiet, the forest produced a new voice, and my next steps were fueled by simultaneous terror and relief.

". . . mouth shut, bitch, or I'll slice you wide open. Her too."

Robyn and Dani were alive—so far, anyway. But who the hell was with them?

A few steps later, I cringed as the scent of blood rolled over the forest, overwhelming my senses and shredding my heart. The sheer volume was horrifying, and the thought of how much Mitch and Olsen must have lost made me sick to my stomach.

I slowed as I approached the campsite, logic and caution finally catching up to the terror that had propelled my dash through the woods. I couldn't help the guys, and I'd be no good to the girls if I burst into the clearing and got shot by some psycho backwoods hunter. So I snuck the last thirty feet or so, silent and virtually invisible in the dark, as only a werecat can be.

The campfire flickered through a tangle of branches. I blinked, edging forward slowly, hidden by a thick, fat bush. I saw Olsen first, and had to swallow the traumatized whine trying to leak from my throat. He lay on his back in the clearing, his shadow twitching on the ground with every lick of the orange flames. His blue eyes were open; his mouth was slack. His coat was unzipped, his shirt completely drenched in blood, which now soaked into the ground beneath him. He'd been gutted.

Mitch lay in the same position, a quarter of the way around the campfire, his face forever frozen in a grimace of agony. His stomach and chest had been sliced up the middle, but unlike Olsen's, Mitch's coat and shirt had been spread open, showcasing the full extent of the damage. So the girls would know the same thing could happen to them.

Nausea rolled over me for the first time ever in cat form. I'd seen a lot of slaughtered deer—I'd even brought down a couple myself. But these weren't deer. They were friends.

My vision blurred until I couldn't keep the bodies in focus, yet when I glanced away, my focus returned, as if my brain didn't want to interpret the images of carnage my eyes were sending.

I blinked and forced the image back into focus, determined not to punk out. If I couldn't even look at the corpses, how could I hope to save Robyn and Dani?

Maybe I couldn't. I wasn't a cop. I wasn't even an enforcer. My summer training sessions with Faythe had included neither rescue missions nor hostage negotiation. But I had to try. I was all they had.

My roommate and her best friend knelt on the ground on the other side of the fire, and watching them through the flames sent chills through me. Like I was already seeing them die. They cried and huddled together, alternately staring at their butchered boyfriends and cringing up at their captors.

Three men stood between them and the campfire with their backs to me, each dressed in hunter's camouflage. Two of them held hunting knives, still dripping blood onto the packed dirt. They were human, based on the scent, but every bit as monstrous as the cruelest Shifters I'd ever met. And one of them smelled vaguely familiar, though I couldn't quite place his scent.

I backed carefully away from the bush concealing me and began to circle the clearing slowly and silently. I needed to be within pouncing distance before I made my move.

"Where is she?" the man in the middle demanded, and my heart actually skipped a beat. Did he mean me? Had they been watching us? Or had they simply seen five hiking packs and deduced an absence? Had they gone through my stuff to determine my gender?

"Where's who?" Robyn said through chattering teeth, loyal to a fault. She would keep me out of this, even if it cost her last breath. But I couldn't let that happen. They were scared and defenseless against men with knives, and I remembered being scared and defenseless. I remembered way too well. . . .

The man in the middle backhanded her, and Robyn fell over sideways, unable to right herself with her hands taped together in her lap. It took all of my self-control to hold in the growl itching at the back of my throat as I rounded the halfway point of the clearing. Drawing attention to myself before I was ready to fight would only get us all killed. That was one of the first things Faythe had taught me.

The tallest of the men hauled Robyn upright by one arm as I continued to circle silently, aching inside while she cried. "We know Abby was with you," he said, and I froze in midstep. I recognized that voice. A few more feet, and my eyes confirmed what my ears already knew. Steve . . . something. He'd transferred into my psych class a week into the semester and had sat in the desk behind me ever since, trying to make conversation while I only nodded.

What the hell was going on? Had he followed us?

"Where'd she go?" the second man demanded, and I noticed as I edged along that the contents of both tents had been dumped in a pile about three feet from the campfire, including my sleeping bag and purse. Was this a robbery, or were they looking for me? Neither possibility made sense—college students don't carry much cash, and I barely knew Steve and had never even met his accomplices.

The third man stepped forward, silently threatening Robyn and Dani with the knife when no one answered. My blood boiled, even as fear spiked my veins with adrenaline demanding to be used.

Robyn cringed, tears pouring down her cheeks. But Dani answered, staring at the blade now inches from her throat. "She went for a hike!"

"In the dark?" Steve crossed bulky arms over a bulkier chest, the tip of his knife tapping against the waist of his thick camo pants.

Dani shrugged, and I saw a spark of the stubborn defiance that made her fun to debate—and might soon get her killed. "She likes nature."

"And she took a flashlight," Robyn added, shaking violently, either from the cold or from shock. "Please, you can have anything you want. My purse is over there." She nodded toward the pile of supplies. "Just take it and let us go."

"Oh come on, this is a party!" Steve glanced at his friends with a look of anticipation that chilled my blood. "But we're one girl shy. You have her number?" Robyn nodded slowly, and Steve glanced at the third man. "Tim, give her a call."

I'd circled to within feet of my roommate by the time Tim—shorter and thicker than Steve—hauled Robyn to her feet. She whimpered when his hand slid into the front pocket of her jeans, and fresh tears rolled down her face. My claws curled into the underbrush, itching to rip through his flesh instead.

I watched Robyn and Tim, waiting for my opportunity to pounce, but in my head, I saw something else. Another man. Another place. A bruising grip on my own arm. A cruel, unwelcome hand, followed by pain, and screaming, and humiliation.

The bastard leered at Robyn until she closed her eyes; then he shoved her down again and flipped open her phone. He was already scrolling through the contacts list by the time she hit the ground. He pressed a couple of buttons, then held the phone to his ear, and they all waited.

But I already knew what would happen, and sure enough, a couple of seconds later, my phone rang out from inside my purse, on the edge of the pile of sleeping bags and hiking packs.

"Damn it, she didn't take her phone!" Steve kicked my purse across the clearing without bothering to open it, as his dark-haired accomplice hung up Robyn's phone.

Of course I hadn't. My cat skin suffered an obvious and bothersome lack of pockets.

"Fine," Steve said at last, having resigned himself to some inconvenient conclusion. "She'll come back—where else could she go?" He shrugged. "We'll just start the party without her."

No . . . I recognized that tone. That slimy, hungry grin. I knew what would happen next, if I didn't stop it.

Tim dragged Robyn away from Dani and closer to me. Robyn screamed and kicked, trying to twist free, but none of it fazed him. He dropped her on the ground and her head hit a fallen tree branch. Robyn moaned, dazed, and I could practically see the fight drain out of her.

"Get off her!" Dani shouted, struggling to get to her feet without the use of her hands. Her cheeks were dry and scarlet, fury eclipsing her fear, at least for the moment. She would fight them. And it would get her killed.

The third man glanced at Steve, brows raised, silently asking for permission. He hadn't said a word so far, but his clenched fists spoke volumes.

Steve nodded and gestured toward Dani with one open hand. "She's all yours, Billy. I'm holdin' out for the little redhead."

Me of course. Boy, wouldn't he be surprised to see me sporting black fur and claws instead? One hundred and four pounds was only a scrap of a woman but added up to one hell of a cat. Not that he'd ever know it was me.

Billy shoved Dani down, then kicked her in the ribs before she could roll away. Bones cracked. Her shout ended in a grunt of pain, and then he dropped on top of her, his huge, bloody hunting knife pressed into her throat. "One more word, and I'll cut your fucking head off."

Silent tears rolled down Dani's face, and each breath was a pained gasp. Her eyes closed and her head rolled to one side as he fumbled at the waistband of her jeans, and suddenly I couldn't move.

Bars. Tears. Pain. Blood. Terror.

No, that was all over. All but the terror. It had been two and a half years, yet the terror came back like a fucking razor-tipped boomerang. My heart beat too hard. The whole world began to go gray beneath memories of my own helplessness and humiliation.

No! This can't be happening. . . . Not again. Not in the human world. Not while I cower in the bushes.

Run! the voice inside my head shouted, as each breath slipped from my throat faster than the last. *They'll do the same thing to you if they find you. And you can't survive it again.*

But that was a lie told by the scared little girl still huddling in a dark corner of my mind. I'd grown up. I'd moved on. I'd learned to fight. True, my skills were unproven, but they were there, and they were a game changer. And beyond all of that, I was in cat form. They'd never recognize the Abby they were looking for in my current configuration of flesh and bone—and fur.

I *could* survive this. I could prevent this. I could *end* it.

"No!" Robyn screamed, trying to shove Tim off with her bound hands. "Stop, please!"

And that was all I could take.

I leapt out of the bushes, fury now pulsing through my veins, hotter than blood. A growl rumbled from my throat and rolled across the clearing. I slammed into Tim's side, knocking him off Robyn and onto the ground. My front paws pinned him to the dirt.

Around me, everyone froze. For one long second, they didn't even breath, and several hearts actually skipped beats. Then Robyn took a single, shallow breath, and began edging away from us slowly, pushing herself with her feet because her hands were still tied. She was as scared of me as she was of him, and terror had now driven comprehension from her eyes. For the moment at least, Robyn had checked out.

Tim was sweating in spite of the cold, and the scent was part fear, part adrenaline. But not enough fear. I leaned in closer, and the huff of breath from my nose blew his dark hair back. I sank my claws through his thick camo jacket and into flesh. He flinched, and when his mouth dropped open in surprise, I saw blood staining his teeth.

I sniffed while he shook in terror beneath me. The blood was Robyn's. The bastard had *bitten* her.

The entire world bled to red. I lunged, and the next few seconds were a series of unfocused, disconnected sensations. My teeth sank through something firm and warm. Tim jerked beneath me. I tossed my head, and flesh tore with a satisfying *ripping* sensation. Warm, fragrant blood sprayed my face, my shoulders. The form beneath me jerked one last time, then lay still.

Someone screamed.

I backed off the body, cleaning my muzzle out of long-term hunting habit, and looked up to find Robyn staring at me, huddled against the side of the nearest tent, shrieking uncontrollably. Her jacket lay on the ground to her left and she clutched the remains of her torn shirt to her chest, but the bloody bite mark on her right shoulder was exposed.

Without thinking, I stepped toward her, confused by my simultaneous human need to comfort her and my cat's inclination to first clean the fresh blood from my fur.

Robyn screamed harder at my approach, going hoarse now, so I stopped, physically shaking myself to clear my head. To fend off encroaching bloodlust and cling to my ill-fitting human logic. She was bitten, but otherwise unharmed. She'd be fine, physically.

I turned away from Robyn, forcing myself to ignore that small part of me that wanted to chase her, just because she wanted to run. My roommate wasn't prey. But the men who'd hurt her were.

Steve stood where I'd left him, his back to the fire, his white-knuckled fist still clenching a bloody knife. He watched me carefully, steadily, blade held ready, and again I saw too little fear to suit me. He'd have to be either stupid or insane to openly challenge a giant cat, and frankly, I was hoping he was both.

I growled, and for one surreal moment, I wondered if he could see the other me peeking through my greenish cat eyes. The human me, who'd once suffered what he and his friends had tried to deal out. That Abby couldn't fight back, but this Abby could and would.

Steve's blood whooshed rapidly through his veins. His eyes were bright and glossy with exhilaration. His arm tensed. He raised the knife for a strike, but I saw it coming.

I swatted the blade from his hand with my front paw, and my blow swung him around. He went down a foot from the campfire, but was up in an instant.

"Good kitty . . . ," he whispered, his voice low and steady, both hands spread in a defensive posture as I growled. He glanced over me, and a sudden scuffle at my back made my fur stand on end. I leapt to the side, but was too late to completely avoid the blow. Billy's huge knife slashed across my front right leg, several inches from my shoulder.

I hissed, and suddenly the blood-scent on the air had a new flavor. My flavor.

Dani scooted away from Billy. I took a step forward, trying to drive the men closer together, where I could see them both, but my injured leg half collapsed beneath me. I couldn't walk on it. Not for long anyway.

Steve noticed the limp, and I could see him assessing his chances. He had a real shot at survival now, and he knew it. He backed slowly toward the tent and hauled Robyn up by one arm. She screamed again. I limped forward, hissing, but before I could attempt another pounce, he glanced behind me, at Billy.

"We can't bring them both," he said. "Do her."

"No!" Dani shouted, and her shuffling grew frantic. She understood before I did.

I whirled to see him haul Dani up by one arm. She dug her heels into the dirt, trying to pull free. I stepped toward them, and my leg folded again. Billy shoved his knife into her stomach and dragged it up through her flesh. Dani's eyes went wide, and her mouth fell open. I roared in grief and outrage. He let go, and she collapsed onto the dirt, blood pouring from the gaping hole in her torso.

"Stay, kitty . . . ," Steve said, slowly pulling Robyn toward the woods. Robyn glanced from me to Dani, then to Billy, whose bloody knife glinted in the firelight. But she didn't make a sound this time, nor did she fight his grip.

Billy circled me slowly, leaving plenty of room between us. He held his knife ready, and though I growled the whole time, I didn't pounce again. And he didn't expect me to. A natural-born cat—they probably thought I was a melanistic jaguar—would never chase three healthy humans into the woods on an injured leg, when there were three fresh bodies to eat right there in the clearing. And there would soon be a fourth.

Dani was still breathing, but it wouldn't be long, and I couldn't let her die alone. Especially since I couldn't reasonably rescue Robyn. Not in cat form, anyway. Not when I couldn't put weight on my injured front leg.

Steve backed into the trees, pulling a shocked-silent Robyn with him, her face streaked with tears, her shirt streaked with blood. Billy stepped slowly out of the clearing on his side of the fire, and moments later, I heard him clomping through the underbrush toward Steve and Robyn. Then they headed through the woods together.

The last thing I heard before their footsteps faded from even my sensitive cat hearing was Billy's whispered question, and Steve's even softer reply.

"So, we're giving up on Abby?"

"No way. We'll regroup at the cabin."

I huffed softly through my nose as I limped toward Dani. There was a cabin. And they were obviously expecting me—the human me, the only one they knew—to come back to the campsite. If they were planning to come back for me, the cabin must be close. I could track them. I could get Robyn back. But not until Dani was gone. And not until I'd made a phone call.

Triple homicide in a werecat territory, involving a werecat tabby, was definitely a notify-your-local-Alpha situation.

Even mortally wounded, Dani tried to scoot away from me as I approached. She was dying, and she knew it—I could see mortality gleaming in her eyes, along with reflected flames from the campfire—but she wasn't eager to speed up the process by being eaten alive. And she had no reason to think I wouldn't do just that.

I dropped my head as I limped forward, whining softly, trying everything I knew to look unthreatening. To show submissiveness and concern. But she didn't stop struggling until I dropped onto the cold ground beside her and laid my chin on her leg.

"Wha—?" she began, but lacked the strength to finish even that one word. Her heartbeat had already begun to slow, and her chest was rattling. I didn't want to leave her, but I couldn't afford to let Robyn get too far away. And I still had to make that call. So I licked the back of her left hand—still bound to its mate—then scooted away from her to begin my Shift. And for the first time in my life, it didn't matter that a human was about to witness the entire process.

My injured leg bent to spare it, I stood three feet from the fire, and its warmth was my only comfort in the face of exhaustion, grief, fear, and ever-deepening rage. The last time my life had been in danger, I'd been too scared to Shift, even for my own safety. Even with Faythe there to talk me through it.

Not this time. This time, the changes came almost too quickly to bear, my Shift fueled by an intense need to save Robyn and avenge my other friends. To unleash justice on men so like the ones who'd brought a violent end to my adolescence, robbing me of peace and security, along with my virginity.

My muscles tensed, bunching and stretching as they took on new shapes. My joints popped in and out of their sockets as, in my memory, I screamed "No!" over and over, until the weight pinning me to the ground stole my breath.

My paws flexed uncontrollably, aching as they stretched and reformed. My claws retracted into the tips of my fingers as, in my head, I clutched at my clothes, at the bars, at the edge of the bare mattress, desperate to make it stop. To hold myself together as long as possible.

My muzzle began to shorten, my gums throbbing as my teeth broadened, the feline points smoothing into rounded human edges. My jaws ached, as they'd once ached from screaming, then from trying not to scream, desperate not to give him the satisfaction.

My flesh began to itch as my fur receded, and in my mind, my skin burned—scalding water from the shower. I'd scrubbed and scrubbed, but couldn't wash them off. Couldn't clean down to the real me. The me I'd lost. The me they'd killed in that basement, in the shadow of the bars I still saw sometimes when I closed my eyes.

When my Shift was over, I sat on my bare knees on the frigid ground, panting from exertion, crying over old ghosts. If I didn't hurry, it would happen to Robyn too. These men didn't have bars and a basement, but they had knives, and no reason to let her live.

As soon as I could move again, I crawled over to Dani. Danielle Martin, with her big mouth and her kind eyes, who'd invited me to come on their couples' weekend. Who'd insisted I wouldn't be a fifth wheel. But Dani's kind eyes were open and empty now, staring into the woods. Her bound hands still lay over her stomach, like she'd tried to hold the blood in until the last second. And I'd missed it. She'd died alone, and scared, and in pain.

Steve and Billy—whoever the hell they both really were—would pay for that. They would pay, and pay, and pay. . . .

Tears ran down my face, scalding my frozen cheeks as I pushed myself to my feet and jogged across the clearing. The fire was hot, but not hot enough for me to preserve my body heat without clothes. Yet I went for my purse first, dropping to my knees beside the pile of brush it had landed in when Steve kicked it.

My teeth chattering, I pulled back the zipper, praying my phone hadn't broken. When I flipped it open, the screen was bright in the flickering firelight, the battery charged and ready for use. I shivered as I stood and scrolled through the contacts for my Alpha's number, then pressed CALL as I dropped to the ground again next to the careless pile of our belongings. I'd just spotted my hiking pack beneath the portable charcoal grill when he answered the phone.

"Abby? What's wrong?"

"Jace, I need help. Fast." My teeth were chattering, and I sniffed back a choked sob. "How soon can you get here?"

Springs creaked as he stood, and I heard him walking. "Where are you? What happened?"

I hauled my pack from the pile and peeled back the flap, already digging for my change of clothes. "I went camping with some friends, and now they're all dead. All except Robyn, my roommate."

"Wait, first of all, are you safe where you are?" His voice was solid and steady, a vocal cornerstone for me to build on.

"For the moment. But I don't have much time." I stood with the phone pinned between my ear and my shoulder and stepped into my underwear, my teeth chattering so hard I could barely talk.

"Okay, start from the beginning. You went camping . . . ?"

"Yeah. Just a sec." My shirt was next, and I had to set the phone on the ground to pull the material over my head. "We're in Cherokee National Forest, just south of the Tennessee border." I gave him the coordinates we'd used to find the campsite, forever grateful for GPS technology. "I went for a run—the private kind—and while I was hunting, my friends started screaming. When I got back, there were three men at our campsite, carrying big hunting knives. They'd gutted Mitch and Olsen and tied up the girls."

"Wait, you walked in on a murder? In cat form?"

"They didn't see me. I was in the bushes." Like a coward.

"Good. They're human?"

"Everyone but me." I stood and shook out my insulated cargo pants, phone pinned to my shoulder again while I stepped into the fuzzy inner lining. "It doesn't make any sense, Jace. I know one of them. He sits behind me in psych. He's always so friendly, but now he's . . . *crazy*."

I sank onto the cold ground and swallowed another sob, trying to speak slowly and clearly, and to give him just the facts. Anything else would only slow me down and put Robyn in more danger. But Jace saw through my false calm.

"Abby, are you okay?"

"No! They know I'm out here too. I don't know if they followed us or what, but while they were waiting for me to come back, they tried to . . ."

The words froze in my throat, the edges sharp, like I'd swallowed glass. I coughed, then started over. "They had knives, Jace, and the girls were so scared. Robyn was screaming, and she couldn't stop him. The other one held his knife to Dani's throat. I couldn't just watch, and I couldn't leave them there. . . ." My explanation trailed into fragile silence, but for the crackle of the fire.

"What did you do, Abby?" Jace still sounded calm, but now his voice held a dark note of dread.

"I killed one of them. The one who was on Robyn. I just wanted to get him off her, so I pounced on him, and he smelled like her, and he'd bitten her, and everything just went red after that. But then Steve slashed my front leg, and the other one stabbed Dani. Then they took off into the woods." My tears were a mercy, smearing the carnage all around me. But they couldn't blur the overwhelming scent of blood. "I couldn't chase them. Not with my front leg sliced up and Dani dying."

"Of course not. You shouldn't have shown yourself. You could have been killed." Jace sighed, the sound a mixture of worry for me and rage on my behalf. "Just stay there. We're coming to get you. We'll call the cops on the way back." I heard voices in the background, as other toms volunteered for the emergency mission. Save the damsel in distress—one of those moments every enforcer lives for.

Only I didn't have time to be rescued. "I can't stay here, Jace. They're coming back for me. And they have Robyn. I have to get her back before they hurt her."

"No!" A car door slammed and Jace's engine roared to life. He was already on the go, no doubt with his three best enforcers. "Abby, do *not* go after them. That's an order."

"Jace, they're gonna kill her!" And by the time they got around to that, she'd be begging for it.

"And if you go after them, they'll kill you too."

"I can handle myself. I've been training with Faythe."

"Sounds like you picked up more than just her left hook," he muttered, and in the background, another tom chuckled. "Faythe's an Alpha, and before that, she was an enforcer. You're an elementary-ed major with two summers' worth of self-defense. Sit tight. We'll be there in an hour."

"She'll be dead by then!"

"But you won't."

I hesitated. I honestly did, because disobeying an Alpha was serious shit. Even a young, hot Alpha I'd known my whole life. But Robyn was the priority. "I'm sorry, Jace," I whispered, digging through my pack again for an extra set of thick socks. "You can kick me out of the Pride if you want, but I have to help Robyn. I'll see you in an hour."

"Abby, no——!" he started, while his enforcers went apeshit in the background. I flipped the phone closed, put it on silent, then slid it into my pocket.

The phone buzzed as I pulled my socks on, then again while I dug Olsen's pack from the pile. He had a hunting knife. I'd seen it. And in human form, I would need it.

I slid the knife into a loop on the right leg of my pants, then crossed the clearing and grabbed the insulated jacket they must have made Robyn take off before they tied her up. Her small folding knife was in the right pocket, and the material was still warm from her body heat. I couldn't believe how fast everything had happened.

Armed, dressed, and now fairly warm, I knelt next to Dani, avoiding looking at the guys. "I'm so sorry," I whispered, as I un-laced her hiking boots. Mine were a quarter mile away, in the oppo-site direction. "I hate to leave you like this, but I have to help Robyn. I swear they'll pay for what they did to you."

Fortunately, she had small feet, so the boots were only half a size too big, and with an extra pair of socks, I could barely tell.

Finally as ready as I was gonna get, I put on my hiking pack and stepped into the woods with only a single glance back and a fleeting bolt of sympathy for the forensics team which would soon be con-fused over her bare feet, the paw prints, and the drops of blood from the cut on my arm.

I headed in the direction I'd last heard Steve's, Billy's, and Robyn's footsteps, mentally crossing my fingers that they would stick to that heading——that they'd actually known where they were going from the moment they'd left the campsite. My human form kept weight off my injured arm, but for that advantage——that necessity——I'd sacrificed most of my enhanced feline senses. My nose and ears were still more sensitive than a human's, but they were nowhere near the advantage they would have been in cat form. And the flashlight I carried was no substitute for feline vision, a huge benefit in the dark.

After a quarter mile, I was freezing, exhausted from Shifting without eating, and reeling from the trauma of what I'd seen. Reality had finally hit me, and shock was like a cold blanket wrapped around me so tight I could hardly breathe, let alone think.

My arm throbbed with each beat of my heart, and by the time I'd gone half a mile, blood had soaked through both my shirt and Robyn's jacket. That one Shift hadn't been enough to completely close the wound, and moving my arm had kept the blood flowing. Frustrated, I turned the flashlight off and shoved it into the side pocket of my pack, then used my free hand to apply pressure to my cut. But then I couldn't see.

Damn it! How was I supposed to save Robyn when I couldn't even find her?

You're not cut out for this, Abby. Jace was right. You should just sit down and wait to be rescued. Again.

But if I did that, Robyn would die, scared, alone, and in pain. Just like Dani. And I'd be the coward who'd damned her.

You're not using your resources . . . a new voice in my head said, and she sounded for all the world like Faythe. *You're not human, and you're not helpless, so why pretend on either count?*

I closed my eyes, and the memory came back in full. We were training in the barn, at night, with the lights off. I could hear her when she spoke, but the others were silent, and I couldn't see any of them. Because then, like now, I wasn't using my resources. My senses.

The partial Shift. Standard procedure now, for all enforcers patrolling in human form, and one of the first things Faythe had taught me.

I squeezed my eyes shut tighter and forced everything else from my mind. The cold, the dark, the pain in my arm . . . None of that mattered. Robyn mattered. Finding her. Saving her.

Avenging the others.

Pain shot through my right eye, followed by an answering spear through my left. The pressure was enormous, like my eyeballs would pop right out of my head. But they didn't, and when the pain faded, when I finally opened my eyes, I could see. The colors were muted, of course, as they were for me in cat form, but the woods were clear, each tree crisply outlined by the little available moonlight.

I grinned. This was going to work.

My ears were next, and they were a real bitch. Shifting them was more complicated, and the pain was like needles being jabbed through my eardrums and into my brain. But when it was over the difference was unbelievable. I hadn't realized how much I was missing in human form until I could suddenly hear like a cat.

Rodent heartbeats. Wind rustling branches far over my head and half a mile away. An owl, halfway across the damn forest, swooping on its prey with a rush of air unique to that particular wing formation and dive pattern.

And beneath all that, the steady, low-pitched hum of machinery. A generator.

Steve's cabin. It had to be.

I let go of my injured arm and took off through the woods, easily avoiding fallen logs and jutting branches now that I could see them. Cold air burned my lungs, but I barely felt it. I was buoyed by the hope blooming in my chest. I could save her. I could make up for failing to save Dani. And maybe in doing that, I could prove to myself for good that the cowering, helpless Abby was gone. The men in the cage had killed her, but from her ashes, this new phoenix was born, and she was ready to unleash justice on their brothers in crime.

Justice and pain. Lots of pain.

Half a mile later, the cabin came into view, its generator growling now, in my sensitive ears. It drowned out any sounds I might have been able to hear from inside, and it was almost too much for my pounding head to take, so I Shifted my ears back as I watched the cabin, crouched behind a shelter of tall, thick ferns. But I kept my cat eyes. Feline pupils would adjust to the light inside the cabin. Once I got in.

The cabin was small—why did they need such a big generator?— and I couldn't see any movement through the windows. So after several minutes of nothing, I eased my pack off my shoulders and onto the ground, then ran hunched over to crouch beneath the un-covered front window, painting a square of untamed forest floor with light from within.

A couple of minutes later, when no one charged out of the cabin wielding a knife, I dared a careful glimpse through the glass—and nearly melted with relief.

Robyn lay on the floor against the back wall of what looked like some backwoods hunter's private retreat, bound with duct tape now, but still fully clothed. And completely alone, except for the half dozen disembodied deer heads staring down at her from the rustic paneled walls.

The trophies were grotesque and gratuitous, a horror only hu-mans would find tasteful. At least werecats ate what they hunted.

Robyn didn't see me—her eyes were closed—and I couldn't hear anything over the growl of the generator, but there was only one door leading off the main room, and it was closed. Surely if Steve and Billy had still been there, they'd have been watching their prisoner—or worse.

Maybe they'd already gone back for me. They'd never expect me to find them—or even to know who they were—and they probably wouldn't expect Robyn to escape, considering that her ankles were taped together. But I could fix that.

I pulled my knife from the loop on my pants, and crouch-walked to the front door. The knob didn't move, but it was secured with only a twist lock. I turned it hard to the right. The lock snapped, and then the door creaked open several inches. I froze. It was louder than I'd expected, even with the generator's constant grumbling. But when Robyn didn't wake up and no one stormed into the room, I took a deep breath and stepped into the cabin, then closed the door softly at my back so I could listen.

The generator was quieter inside the cabin but still covered both my heartbeat and Robyn's. My cat's pupils narrowed, adjusting quickly to the influx of light. And there she was, only fifteen feet away. She was unconscious—obvious, now that the generator and my B and E had failed to wake her—but with any luck, I could haul her far enough away to risk trying to wake her up. Werecat strength was the only advantage that translated fully into human form. Thank goodness.

Eager now, and more than a little nervous, I raced across the room toward Robyn—then fell flat on my face when my feet slipped out from under me.

What the hell?

Stunned, I lay on the floor on my stomach, still gripping the knife in one hand. I was too surprised to think, my mouth open, trying to drag in the breath I'd lost. My empty hand curled in the carpet, and I froze.

It wasn't carpet; it was a rug. A very *familiar*-feeling rug, which had slid out from under my feet as I ran.

No . . .

Horror filled me like darkness leaking into my soul. I closed my mouth and drew in a deep breath through my nose

Nonononono! The rug was fur. Smooth, soft, solid black fur.

Werecat fur.

I shoved myself to my knees and scrambled away from the morbid accent piece until my back hit the wall. I inhaled again, my hands shaking, my knife clattering into the hardwood over and over again.

I didn't recognize the individual scent. If I had—if I'd known the tom who died to make that rug—I might have lost it right then. As it was, I was still shaking in Dani's boots when the front door opened a second later, and Steve walked in, carrying my hiking pack.

"Hello, Abby." His knife glinted in the overhead light as he dropped my pack at his feet and closed the door. "We've been waiting for you."

My fist clenched around my own knife, but I was no longer sure it would do any good. The truth tapped at the back of my brain like a woodpecker on a really tough trunk, but I couldn't let it in. It didn't make sense. It wasn't possible.

The door on my left creaked open, and Billy stepped out of a darker room, bringing with him the scents of blood, and fur, and some harsh, acrid chemical. Did they stuff the deer heads here? In the cabin? "For now, we just want your company. But soon, we're gonna need you to Shift. That's what you call it, right?"

He raised his knife, still stained with Dani's blood, and pointed to the far end of the room. My gaze followed reluctantly, and that's when I saw what hadn't been visible through the small front window.

I gasped, then choked on my next breath. I blinked, but the horrible images didn't go away. They wouldn't even blur mercifully, as Mitch's body had. Instead, they stared down at me, through eyes too much like my own. Four werecat heads, mounted in a row on the far wall, on identical wooden plaques. They had their mouths open, lips curled back as if they were hissing, but the pose was artificial. Arranged postmortem. I could see that, even if they couldn't.

Three of them were strangers. Probably strays, based on the fact that I hadn't heard of that many missing Pride cats. But the fourth, the last one on the right, was Leo Brown, one of Jace's enforcers. He'd gone missing during his vacation a few months earlier, and no one had ever found a single sign of him. Until now.

"I . . ." I closed my eyes, then forced my gaze back to Steve. "I don't know what you're talking about." Denial. It was instinct, if not exactly flawless logic.

"Oh?" Steve raised one brow, glancing at my bloody sleeve, then back to my face. "How's your arm?"

And that's when the truth became too much to deny. They knew what I was. They'd known all along. They'd followed me into the woods, and my friends had paid the price.

Wood creaked on my left as Billy squatted next to me, evidently unfazed by my knife. Or maybe he couldn't see it, held so close to my opposite thigh. "You're the first girl Shifter we've ever found. Been watching you for weeks now."

"Psych 204?" I whispered, glancing up at Steve, who now leaned against the front door.

"A stroke of genius, if I say so myself. That's also how I met your girl Robyn, and good ol' Mitch. When he mentioned you all were going camping, I was happy to suggest a good, private campsite. Not many people know about this place."

Which was why it had seemed perfect for my solitary run.

I couldn't breathe. I couldn't think. I couldn't push beyond the fact that they knew. That they'd lured me there to be butchered, stuffed, and mounted. And I'd fallen for it. "You're hunters?"

"Of the highest caliber," Steve said, one side of his mouth turning up into a creepy grin. "You didn't really think no one knew your little secret, did you?"

Actually, I had. I'd always assumed that if anyone knew we existed, *everyone* would know. But exposing our existence would have put an end to their private safari, and they were obviously unwilling to risk that. Sick bastards.

"Damn, Steve, look at this!" Billy grabbed my chin, and I gasped as he turned my face toward the light. My fist tightened around the knife handle, but I was biding my time. I couldn't afford to miss. "She's got cat eyes. Never seen that before. Maybe we should just cut her head off and mount it like this."

"Hmmm. Dramatic . . ." Steve ambled closer for a better look. I jerked my chin from Billy's grasp, seething on the inside. Waiting for the perfect moment. It would come. *Please* let it come. . . . "Especially with all those pretty red curls."

When he was close enough, I closed my eyes and sent up a silent prayer. Then I dropped from my heels onto my rump and shoved my left leg out, grunting as I swept both of Steve's out from under him.

Steve shouted as he went down. Billy blinked, surprised, and reached for Steve, but my arm was already in motion. I swung Mitch's knife underhanded, as hard as I could. It slid into his stomach, up to the hilt. Warm blood poured over my hand. I pulled up, and the knife ripped through flesh toward his sternum.

Billy grunted, but never screamed. Steve scrambled backward and leapt to his feet. Billy fell over. His skull smacked the floorboards. Steve pulled his own knife from the sheath snapped onto his belt. And finally, I stood.

We faced off, circling slowly, as I tried to edge him away from Robyn, who still breathed shallowly on the floor. Now I could see the lump on the side of her head. She was bait, good for nothing more to them.

"You should probably know, guns are the most effective way to hunt a cat," I said, wishing I could wipe blood from the hilt of my knife. It was getting slippery.

"Didn't think we'd need them for a little girl. You're more trophy than challenge."

"And you're all monster." I circled toward the couch and a rickety-looking end table.

He rolled his eyes, sidestepping toward me. "Says the girl with fur and claws."

"Says the woman who's gonna spit on your corpse in about three minutes."

"Yeah, I'm scared of a five-foot-nothin' scrap of meat in borrowed boots. Your luck has run out, and in a couple of days, your pretty little head's gonna be mounted on a plaque in a cabin in Mississippi, where the next cat monster will get one fleeting glimpse of pointed pupils and red hair before we nail him up right next to you."

Mississippi was free territory, crawling with strays, most of whom wouldn't be missed. He obviously knew at least a little about our culture. Had he questioned his other victims before killing them?

I edged to the right, glaring at him with all the force of my hatred. My right foot hit the leg of the end table. I tripped and went down on my ass. Hard. I dropped the knife, and let it slide across the floor.

Steve dropped on top of me, blade ready. I shoved my right hand into the jacket pocket. He grabbed a handful of my curls and pulled my head back, exposing my throat. I grinned up at him and pulled Robyn's folding knife from her pocket. Steve's eyes widened. I pressed the button, and the blade popped out even as I shoved it forward.

The three-inch blade slid between his ribs.

Steve grunted. I shoved him off and stood, Robyn's knife sticky in my hand. He lay on the floor, blood pouring from his chest. I'd hit the heart, and his eyes were already glazing over. "But girl cats don't fight," he whispered, as blood trickled from the corner of his mouth.

I arched both brows and pulled my phone from my pocket. "Welcome to the new regime."

Jace got there twenty minutes later, armed with three enforcers and everything necessary to clean up my mess. Robyn was still unconscious, but breathing, and with any luck, she'd sleep through everything she shouldn't see.

When the cabin was clean, I would "find" Robyn and call the police, while Jace and his men watched from the treetops. Robyn would tell them what she remembered, but the cops would find no sign of the murderers, or of their morbid hobby. Jace and his men had already reclaimed all the cat trophies and would give our dead brothers a proper burial. And even if a forensics team found my blood at the campsite, they'd never piece together what had really happened. They'd think their samples were contaminated.

But for now, I sat with Robyn, watching the enforcers work, wearing clothes one of the toms had retrieved from where I'd left them. Jace knelt next to me on his way across the cabin, bulging trash bag in hand. "You okay?" he asked, for the fourth time in an hour.

"Yeah." Better than I'd expected, considering I'd just killed three men and seen three friends murdered.

"Good." He nodded, but his blue-eyed scowl was dark and angry.

"You ever disobey an order again, and I'll send you straight back to your father. Understood?"

"Yeah." I stared at the floor, feeling guilty, but not guilty enough to apologize. I'd done the right thing. The only thing I could do. The thing he would have done, in my position.

"Now that that's over . . ." Jace lifted my chin by one finger, so that I had to look at him, and this time, he was grinning. "Good work. If teaching kindergartners doesn't hold the same appeal after this, let me know. I'll have a job waiting for you, if you ever want it."

My brows arched in surprise. "For real?"

Jace nodded, eyeing me carefully. Admiringly. "It's in you now. I can see it."

I smiled slowly. Because it was. It was deep inside me, like it had been inside Steve, until I'd cut it out of him. "It's all about the hunt."

MONSTERS

Lilith Saintcrow

Leonidas held court in a nightclub, a cliché come to life. I do not ever make the mistake of thinking such bad taste makes him any less lethal. The place was full of walking victims, predators, and the Kin. The guards at the door barely nodded as I stepped past, wild-haired and in a bedraggled blue velvet that was last fashionable when Her Majesty reigned. And the boots, heavy-soled and more expensive than a human life in this day and age.

Though mortal life has ever been cheap.

An assault of screaming and pounding noise met me. It was what they call music nowadays. No doubt there are Preservers who will cherish it as I cherished the liquid streams of beauty from my Virginia's piano.

But I doubt they will be half as enchanted as I was. And Virginia's song was gone forever. Even her recordings were lost in last night's fire.

More smoke, of cigarettes. The taint of burning on my clothes and hair went unnoticed. Fragile warm bodies bumping against me on every side, islands of hard brightness that were Kin, the swelling nasty cacophony pumped through electronic throats buffeting the crowd. The bar was a monstrosity of amber glass, dark iron, and mahogany, the mortals behind it scrambling to slake various thirsts.

And there, across the wide choked space, red velvet ropes holding the crowd back. The baroque horsehair couches arranged in intimate little groups were exactly what they appeared to be—emblems of a king's receiving room. Leonidas lounged on the largest, draped across it like a boneless toy. White-blond hair, the left half of his face a river of scarring, he watched his little sovereignty avidly. Behind him, a shadow moved.

Sallow, unsmiling Quinn. *Tarquin*. The only ugly thing Leonidas allows in his presence. The White King does not even allow a mirror in his domicile, lest it somehow show him his own shattered face.

The ropes parted. I do not stand on ceremony, even among Kin. Nevertheless, I inclined my head to Leonidas as I stepped onto the dusty red rug.

"Eleni." His lips shaped my name, pleated ridges of scar tissue twitching. The noise swallowed us whole, like a whale.

And Leonidas looked *surprised*. It is not often a Preserver seeks out a Promethean in his place of power.

"I seek vengeance." My tone cut through the wall of noise. "*You* will provide it."

His fingers flicked a little, dismissing me. "What nonsense are you speaking?"

The noise was overwhelming. It sent glass spikes through my head. The smell of burning hanging on me spurred my fury.

Virginia. Zhen. Peter. And Amelie, my own heart's child. All mutilated and burned. "My house." I could barely speak. My fangs were swollen with rage. "My house, burned to the ground last night. My charges murdered. We had a Compact, Leonidas!"

"And we still do," he murmured. The "music" came to a crashing halt, and static filled the entire building. My rage, Leonidas's amused bafflement, and Quinn's unblinking attention.

I should have been pleased that Tarquin paid such attention to me. He must have considered me a threat. Me, a lowly Preserver.

I did not begin as a Preserver. We all begin as something else, each and every one of the Kin.

"Come," Leonidas said in the almost-silence, before the music started again. "Let us solve this mystery."

Upstairs in a private office, he arranged himself behind a mirror-polished desk. I stood before him like a supplicant, but I was past caring.

"They killed Zhen on the stairs." My throat was full. "My beautiful dancer. And Virginia in the library. She fought back. The young ones were in the cellar. Peter, and Amelie." I swallowed grief like a stone. "They were burned. And *mutilated*. Stakes through their hearts."

"Ah," Leonidas said, and nothing more.

"What do you intend to *do*?" My hands were fists.

He shrugged, a loose inhuman motion. "What can I do? I am no Preserver. And your charges are not the first to fall. The hunters are mortals, and they take only easy prey."

So he knew of this. *Easy prey.* I stared at him. What mortals could kill even the youngest and slowest of us? And yet.

Tarquin, at his shoulder, looked steadily back. His shoulders were tense. Another indirect compliment.

"Then I shall trouble you no further." I turned on my heel. My boots left black streaks on the creamy carpet.

"Eleni." Tarquin's voice, flat and heatless. "Try the Hephaestus, downtown."

I paused. Inclined my head slightly. Leonidas's anger filled the room, but what was his anger to me?

"I am in your debt, Tarquin," I said softly, and stalked away.

I did not venture downtown often. For one thing, it was dangerous. For another, it was . . . confusing. The bright lights, the crowds, the cars . . . it was easier and safer to gather what I needed for my little family elsewhere. I am a Preserver, I preserve what would other-wise be lost in the deep waters of time. Each of my charges was a gem, skilled in an art that could reach its highest expression when freed from the chains of mortality.

All that, gone. Lost in a nightmare of fire and screaming. Only I remained. And the thin bright trail of bloodscent—the weakest male attacker had been bleeding as he left my home. Without Tarquin's hinting, I might have lost his scent.

But no. At the corner of Bride Street I found the golden thread. It turned at corners, flared and faded, drifted with the wind. It is a predator's instinct, to bring down the weakest in the pack first.

Besides, the weakest break more easily.

The Hephaestus was a slumped brownstone building, weary even though the night was young. It reeked of desperation. I passed through the foyer like a burning dream, the proprietor not even glancing away from his television screen. I expected the smell to take me up into a room, but it did not. A hall on the ground floor led to a fire door that did not make a sound as I pushed it open. I stepped out and halted for a moment. Greasy crud slid under my bootsoles.

The blind alley was old, close, and dank. Refuse filled its corners. At its end, a single door. The blood trail led to it, but there was a heavier reek filling the air.

I approached cautiously. There was no outlet, this was a remnant of an earlier time. I wondered if the bricks underfoot were as old as Amelie.

My heart, that senseless beating thing, wrung in on itself. I ghosted to the door, every sense alert as if I were hunting for my family. My chest ran with pain at the thought.

I laid a hand on the door. It was solid, vibrating slightly as all matter does. It was locked and barred, I *sensed* the iron of the bar, metallic against my palate.

If I have learned one thing as a Preserver it is this: Strength does not matter. The *will* matters.

I gathered myself, stepped back, and kicked the door in.

A foul stench roiled out. I plunged into its depths, skipping down a set of sloping concrete stairs—my fist flashed and caught the mortal before he could even lift the gun. He flew back, hitting the wall with a sickening crack.

I hit him too hard. Then the *smell* hit me in return—I dropped down into a crouch, recognizing it, atavistic shivers running through ageless flesh. The *lykanthe* hung on the far wall, a writhing mass of fur held fast in silver chains, ivory teeth wired together by a muzzle cruelly spiked on the inside with more silver.

It was no threat, but still. For a moment I hesitated. Then I turned back to the human, who was making a thin high whistling sound. One of his arms hung at an odd angle.

They are so breakable.

My fingers, slim and strong, tangled in the front of the mortal's black turtleneck. There were leather straps too, holding knives and other implements. He was still trying to gain enough breath to scream.

I selected one knife, slid it free. Broad-bladed, double-edged, it gleamed in the cellar's gloom. Would anyone hear him? It was not likely; the alley and the blind walls above would mock his cries.

Good, I thought, and rammed the knife through his shoulder. He whisper-screamed again.

I closed off the scream with my free hand, clamping it over his mouth. Hot sweat and saliva greased my cold hard palm. I found words, for the first time since I had left Leonidas's nightclub.

"I will ask you questions." My voice was soft, my native tongue wearing through the syllables. "If you answer, I will not hurt you more."

It was only half a lie.

I did not drink from the filth. I was still gorged from last night's hunting. As fitting as it would have been to drain him, no cursed drop of his fluid would pass my lips.

His scarecrow body hung against the wall, twitching as the nerves realized life had fled. The *lykanthe* on the other wall moved slightly, silver chains biting its flesh. But it made no sound, not even whining through the muzzle.

I should have left it there. Their kind is anathema.

But I am a Preserver, and the waste of anything irks me. Especially any part of the twilight world where I fed and sheltered my charges.

There was a long table full of silver-plated instruments, gleaming in the low sullen light. The ones closest to the thing on the wall were crusted with blood and other fluids. I allowed myself a single nose-wrinkle. The stews I had found Virginia in had smelled worse.

A glimmer of eye showed between puffed, marred lids. It was madness to consider letting the thing free. There was probably nothing human left inside that hairy shell.

As much or as little was left human inside my own hard pale shell, perhaps.

The silver-coated metal of the manacles crumpled like wet clay in my fist. Raw welts rubbed the hair from the skin everywhere they touched. They are dangerously allergic to the moon's metal, a goddess's curse. Or so I have always heard.

I twisted, and one collection of bright amber claws dangled free. One hand. I bent and soon the legs were free as well, hanging bare inches from the floor. I glanced up—yes, the hook in the ceiling, there, they had hoisted it to deprive it of leverage. It hung like a piece of Amelie's washing—she had not yet lost the habit of cleaning her clothes after every night's rising, though her body did not sweat or secrete.

Now that body lay in perishing earth. A sob caught at my throat. I denied it.

My voice sounded strange. "I hope you can understand me. I am not your enemy. I hunt those who did this to you. Go to ground and sleep until you become human again, if you can."

It made no reply, merely hung there and watched me. Or perhaps it was dying, and the gleam of eyes was a fever-glitter. The shoulder looked agonizingly strained, sinews creaking.

"Mad," I muttered. "I am mad."

But I freed the last manacle anyway, the silver-plated trash bending and buckling. By the time its heavy body thudded to the ground to lie in its own filth, I was already gone. Straight up the brownstone's wall and over the rooftop.

Behind me, a long inhuman howl ribboned away. So it was alive, after all.

Uptown. I climbed carefully, fingers driving into the spaces between bricks where putty crumbled. The street below was deserted, and in any case, who would expect to see a woman in a dress going directly up a brick wall? Human beings do not see what they do not *wish* to see.

Each floor held a comfortable ledge right under the windows, as if the building were a lunatic belted tightly against himself. Or as if it were a worm, each segment caked with exhaust grime, rising above the ground before it dove.

Zhen held that the ancient world smelled better. I disagreed. Even with the reek of smog, there is no contest between my city and, say, Rome or Paris in their ancient, fouler days. Mortals have at least grown cleaner.

In some ways.

The fourth floor. My boot-toe gripped the ledge, I pulled myself up. Eased along it, weight balanced, velvet scraping brick. There was a smear of dried blood on the back of my left hand, other crackling bits on my face and neck. I would not wash until vengeance was complete.

It wasn't hard to find the window. It was half open, and the reek of adrenaline and bloodshed billowed out like red dye in water.

Nine-man teams, he had told me, choking as my fingers tightened on his throat. *Three Burners, three Fighters, a Sensitive, and the captain and his lieutenant. That's all, I swear.*

After I had cut off three of his fingers and he still swore, I believed him.

At the very edge of the window, I held my skirts back. Leaned forward and peered in.

The room was dark. A table stacked with odd shapes, a chair, a television blindly spewing colored light. On the bed, a stabbing motion, buttocks rising and plunging down.

The Burner had company.

A slightly acrid scent—the reek of a slightly dominant male. Cheap perfume mixing with aftershave and sweat, the musk of sex. The window did not creak as I eased it wider, wider. My shadow moved on the floor, I hopped down light as a leaf while the rhythm of creaking bedsprings became frantic. Softly I stepped across the thin carpet, avoiding a pile of clothing. Smoke-scent rose in simmering waves.

He had not even washed the stink of murder away. Loathing choked me. I glided to the bedside and looked down just as the man stiffened, his head thrown back. The woman's eyes were closed, her long pale hair spread on the pillow and her painted face garish even in the dark.

My claws sank into flesh and I ripped him up and away, viselike fingers clamped at the base of his neck. Just like a mother cat chastising a kitten—or a Preserver teaching a new charge to control the Thirst.

He flew across the room, hit the television on its low dresser. Glass shattered, wood splintered, and the woman inhaled to scream.

"Shhh." I laid my finger against my lips. She swallowed her cry, staring. My eyes would be glowing yellow by now. "Gather your clothes, child, and flee."

Her raddled face crumpled, but she did not make a sound. I turned my back on her and found the man crawling for the table and his weapons—I saw hilts and ugly penile gun-shapes. I caught him halfway there with a kick that threw him into a flimsy chair he'd set in the corner, the sweet sound of ribs snapping echoing off every wall. The tank settled in the chair toppled, liquid splashing, and the cap on its top bounced away. I smelled petrol and that same odd cloying additive.

The Burner lay moaning. Short dark hair, a hefty build. He was probably light on his feet, though, he would have to be. If they hunted anything other than a Preserver's helpless charges, they needed speed and ruthlessness.

Not that it would help him.

I was on him in a moment. Naked flesh, veined and crawling with the incipient death every mortal was heir to. One arm cracked with a greenstick snap. He howled. The tank glugged out a small lake of cold liquid. Soaking the carpet, splashing. I grabbed his short hair and ground his face down. That cut off the howling, and I do not deny a savage satisfaction. His hands flapped, long white fish.

My arm flexed, I pushed harder. His skull creaked, and I had to restrain myself. I didn't want to, but breaking his head open was too quick and easy.

The door opened as the woman fled. She had not stopped to clothe herself, and she was screaming as well. A slice of golden electronic light from the hall narrowed. I flexed again, dragging the man's face along the sodden carpet. Then I pulled his head up and rose, claws digging. He screamed, scrambling to get away, and I flung him across the room again. He hit the wall over the bed with a sickening crack, dislodging a forgettable, mass-produced painting. Not like Amelie's exquisite color-drenched canvases.

Fury poured through me. I leapt on the bed almost before he landed, broke his other arm. He could not get in enough air to scream, was making little whispering hopeless sounds.

Had Amelie made those sounds? Had she pleaded for her life?

The smell—petrol and that additive, and the bright copper of blood—maddened me. I thrust my hand into his vitals, another layer of stench exploding out, claws shredding. I was aiming to pierce his diaphragm, tear through lungs and hold his beating heart in my palm before I crushed it.

The door to the hall burst open, and the little pocking sounds around me were bullets plowing into the bed. I felt the stings and hissed, fangs distended and hot streams of stolen life I had meant to bring home to my charges tracing little fingers over me.

Instinct took over. I am a Preserver, not a Promethean. I leapt for the window, leaving the Burner choking on his blood, his body twitching as his comrades' bullets plowed through it. Down I fell, landing cat-light on the street and bolting.

Two dead, seven to kill. I could find them again with little problem, but now my prey would be wary.

I retreated across the street, black blood and other liquids fouling the dress Virginia had made for me. On a rooftop with a good view I crouched, and I watched.

I did not have to wait long.

Sirens rose in the distance. Exactly three and a half minutes after I'd fled through the window, four men carried the body of a fifth out of the brick hotel. None of them held the scent of dominance, but all of them reeked of petrol and fear. An anonymous navy blue minivan accepted the body as cargo, and they crowded in after it. One, a slim dark youth, took the driver's seat. He paused before opening the door, his curly head cocked, and I had the odd thought that he could feel my gaze.

That was ridiculous. No mortal could possibly . . .

And yet. *Sensitive*, the first man had said. I had not questioned further. Now I wondered if I should have.

I became a stone, sinking into the rooftop, my vision gone soft and blurring as I pulled layers of silence close.

The youth shook his head, opened his door, and hopped nimbly in. The vehicle roused from its slumber, and I shook off the silence just as a soft footfall sounded on the stretched-tight drumhead of the roof behind me.

Quinn? I turned, my ragged skirt flaring.

It was not Tarquin. Of course not. *He* would be silent.

The shaggy-haired man crouched, naked except for a rag clout the color of dirt. His torso rippled with lean muscle and scars glinting gray-silver. The reek of wildness and moonlight hung on him, like the brief tang of liquor before a Kin's metabolism flushes through it.

I dropped down into a crouch. They do not usually run by night, and I had never glimpsed one without clothes or fur. My claws slid free, and I hissed, baring fangs. It would distort my face, I would not have done so in front of my charges. Now, I cared little—except he was interrupting. My prey might well go to ground, I could possibly lose them if I was delayed here.

The *lykanthe* did not snarl. He merely cocked his head. His eyes were bright silver coins, the pupils wavering fluidly between cat-slit and round. He made a low sound, back in his throat.

An *inquisitive* sound.

I straightened, slowly. My claws retracted. The purr of the mini-van retreated, almost swallowed up in the hum of traffic.

I pitched back, grabbed the waist-high edge of the rooftop, and plummeted. It is no great trick to land softly from a height. The sound of cloth tearing was lost in the backwash of sirens as the mortal authorities arrived to wonder at the damage caused.

When there were no traffic laws, sometimes a vehicle could escape. They were lumbering-slow, true, but the flux and pattern of other crowding carriages sometimes provided cover. Nowadays, though, if you stalk a metal carriage through the streets, there are only certain choices at each intersection. If you can keep the sound of the engine in range, even better.

I did not worry about the padding-soft footfalls behind me. If the *lykanthe* had meant to attack, he would have. I cared little about his intent, as long as he did not rob me of my revenge.

The van was aiming for the freeway, a cloverleaf looping of pavement. It slowed, straining and wallowing through a turn. I leapt, catching the overpass's concrete railing, velvet snapping like a flag in a high wind as I soared.

Thin metal crunched as I landed hard, claws out and digging through the van's roof. It slewed, wildly, more predictable than a frightened horse. I am small and dark from childhood malnutrition even the Turn could not completely erase, easier for me to curl in tightly and hold on.

How Zhen had laughed at me. Tall lean Zhen with his grace. I was *gymnastic,* he told me in his mellifluous native tongue, not a *dancer.* I laughed with him, for it was true. But it was I who brought home stolen life each night, to fuel his leaps and turns in the mirrored room given over entirely to his dancing. Shelves of CDs and the equipment to transfer music from one form of storage to another, all burned and dead now, and dance was an evanescent art. He would never discover another movement, another combination, inside his long body now.

The van slowed, still swerving wildly, and I held, wrists aching where the spurs responsible for claw control moved under the skin. When I had the rhythm I would lift one hand and tear the top of the minivan open like one of Amelie's cans of—

Pain. Great roaring pain.

I flew, weightless, the egg in my chest cracked as my heart struggled to function, its bone shield almost pierced. The thudding was agony, I twisted as I rolled, glare of light and horrific screaming noise before I was hit again and *dragged,* the stake in my chest clicking against the road. My arm was caught in something, mercilessly twisted and hauling me along, shoulder savagely stretched.

A heavy *crunch* and a snarl. The dragging stopped short. Little hurt sounds, I realized I was making them. And bleeding, a heavy tide of stolen life against unforgiving stone.

Not stone. Concrete. Bleeding on concrete. A stake. I ached to pull it out, but my hands were loose and unresponsive. My claws flexed helplessly, tearing at the road's surface.

Footsteps. "Be . . . still." Halting, as if the mouth didn't work quite properly. "Not . . . *hrgh* . . . enemy."

Twisting. Wrenching. Each splinter gouged sensitive tissue as he *pulled* it free. A gush of blood, steaming in the chill night air. Too much, I was losing too much, I would not be able to feed them when I returned—

I remembered they were dead just as the stake tore free and was tossed aside. Then I was lifted, limp as a rag doll, and the night filled my head.

Daylight sleep is deep and restorative. It is a mercy that it holds no dreams. Though I could swear I saw them all printed inside my eyelids. Each one of my charges, my wards, my war against Time.

My battle to *preserve*.

The older you become, the incrementally earlier you rise. Purple and golden dusk filled the vaults of heaven, a physical weight as I lay on my belly, flung across something soft and smelling of dry oily fur and musk. There was weight curled around me, heavy and warm. As if Amelie had crept into my bedroom again, but it could not be her. It was too big. Zhen, perhaps? But he was past the time of needing reassurance. Virginia? No, she prized her solitude. It had to be Peter. If he had finished a miniature, or broken something, he would want comfort.

I rolled, slowly, sliding my arm free. My fingers rasped against fur—no, hair. Shaggy hair, not Peter's sleek silken curls.

The *lykanthe* lay half across me. His face was buried in my tangled hair. His throat was open, chin relaxed and tipped up. He was much heavier and bulkier than he looked, or he'd had a chance to eat. How long had the humans had him, torturing him in that dank hole?

The throat was inviting. And blood from another denizen of the twilight would strengthen me immeasurably.

His eyes opened, and he tensed. But he did not drop his chin. Finally, he spoke. It was the same halting slur as before. And he used only one word.

"Fr . . . Fr-friend. *Friend*."

I swallowed. My throat was dry. It was not the Thirst. His kind was an enemy. A pack of *lykanthe* could destroy many of the Kin during a daylight hunt.

And yet, he had pulled the stake from my chest. What had it been? I had to know.

"The stake?" I whispered.

He thought this over. Finally, a light rose behind his silver-coin eyes. His pupils were still flaring and settling. How much damage had they caused him?

"Gun," he finally said, and flowed away from me. The bed creaked. I blinked. My hair was wild, a mass of dark smoke-tarnished curls. I had cut my braid, it was buried in Amelie's . . . grave, behind the charred hulk of my house.

My house no longer.

I pushed myself up on my elbows. The windows were dark, blankets taped over them.

It was a small efficiency apartment. There was a large white fridge. The *lykanthe* opened it and stuck his head in. He made a snuffling sound of delight. I sat up and looked at my hands.

I would need to hunt. Then I would track them.

"What is your name?" I did not know why I asked. A *lykanthe's* name would mean less than nothing to me.

And yet.

He stiffened. "Don't. Know."

"You need more food. And rest. I must hunt."

He slammed the fridge door. A ripple ran through him. "Hunt. Good."

I muttered a word that had been ancient—and obscene—when Augustus was but a child. "No. Not you. You eat *human* food."

His chest swelled. He'd found a pair of jeans somewhere, thank the gods, but the fabric strained as he bulked, the change running through him like liquid.

"No," I said, sharply, just the tone I would take with a new, inexperienced fledgling.

The growl halted. He dropped his shoulders, expressing submission with a single graceful movement.

What was I to do now? We studied each other, *lykanthe* and Preserver, and I felt the weight of responsibility settle on me. And the hateful machine inside my head decided he could be useful.

"You can track." I slid my legs off the bed. The boots were sorely the worse for wear, and my dress was merely rags. "You can track *them*."

He nodded. His pupils settled, cat-slit now. Which was a very good sign. *Lykanthe* are pack animals, and they need to know their place in the hierarchy.

What would happen when he remembered what he was?

I decided I would answer that question when it arose. For now, he was watching me carefully. And I might well need his help, since they had some infernal invention that could hurl a stake through my chest. I was grateful it had not been hawthorn: the allergic reaction might well have sent me to join my charges before vengeance was complete.

"Very well." I straightened. "I need clothes. You need food. And you need a name."

He thought this over, his pupils holding steady. Then, slowly, he lifted one hand, pointed to his chest. "Wolf."

I nodded. "Of course." Pointed at myself. "Eleni."

It was a start.

The marks of my claws were fresh and glaring on the freeway's surface. We waited for traffic to clear, crouched in the shadow of the overpass. He had no feminine clothing in the efficiency, but I'd found a pair of jeans to cut down and a belt that served with a few extra holes delicately claw-punched. A none-too-fresh white tank top—laundry had evidently never been his specialty, if this was indeed his apartment—and a too-large brown leather jacket completed my oddest sartorial statement ever.

He watched with no sign of impatience or disgust as I hunted, and when my victim—a drug dealer in one of downtown's less savory quarters—was dispatched and I rifled the pockets, Wolf stayed wide-eyed and calm. No fur had rippled out through his skin.

The roll of cash was sticky with God alone knew what, but it was serviceable. Twenty minutes later, at a street vendor's stall, Wolf swallowed several slices of pizza; at another, he ate at least five gyros and washed everything down with a large soda. Empty calories, certainly, but better than nothing. He stared longingly at a soft-pretzel vendor, but I drew him away and he followed without demur.

Traffic roared past, a cavalcade of glaring white eyes. I heard a dead spot coming and rose. The *lykanthe* crouched easily. "Do you have the scent?" I asked again.

He nodded, lifting his shaggy head and sniffing. Fur crawled up his cheeks, spilled down his broad chest. Now I knew why *lykanthe* rarely wear shirts—tearing them in the change must be annoying. "Run," he said, his mouth moving wetly over the word as his jaw structure changed, crackling. "Run them *down*."

"Good boy." I could not help myself. But he shivered as if the approval was pleasant, and launched himself into a leap. I followed, and a double sound—the cloth-tearing sound of the Kin using inhuman speed and the howl that burst from him—echoed under the orange-lit city sky.

The mansion was several miles from the city limits, a graceless mushroom-white thing with a colonnaded porch, the grounds extensive but overgrown. Wolf skidded to a stop and crouched, snarling; I curled my fingers in the thick ruff at the back of his neck. It was an instinctive move, because I sensed the thread-thin wire strung between once-ornamental and now shaggy trees, metal humming with ill intent.

"Easy," I whispered, under the deep edge of his snarl. "Easy, young one."

Chill night air touched my cheeks. Wolf's growl stopped between exhale and inhale. He remained thrumming-tense, muscles bunched and ready.

I kept whispering, though there was little need. "They are on their guard now. Hopefully they are stupid enough to think their stake-gun disposed of me, but we cannot depend on that. We must go carefully, and quietly. Come back to your other form."

Shudders ran through him in waves, but I waited. The moon, half full, was a bleached bone in the sky, above the orange stain of the city. The night was young.

"Come back," I insisted. Fur melted, and soon I clasped the nape of a crouching young man in a loose corduroy jacket and torn jeans.

"Hear them," he whispered. "Five, six. Maybe more." The sibilants faded into mush, but I was better at deciphering his words now. The muzzle had damaged something, and he would be a long time healing.

"Good." My fingers moved, soothingly. It was a cross between petting a restive animal and soothing a child. He finally relaxed. "Now. You will wait here. Do not disobey."

He shivered. "Go. With."

"Wait here. Should I need you, I will call. I promise."

"Go with," he insisted, tilting his shaggy head back as if to trap my fingers. "Need. Go *with*."

My claws pricked. "You will wait here, *lykanthe*. Until I call."

He subsided. Became a statue. I petted him absently as I considered the tripwires. When I could see them clearly in my mind's eye, I took my hand away. The *lykanthe* made a faint whining sound, but he stayed put.

I backed up three paces. Four. Plenty of room.

"Eleni," Wolf whispered, haltingly.

I leapt. Caught the tree branch I was aiming for, rough bark against my palms, a squeaking sound as force transferred.

Yes, Zhen had told me I was gymnastic, and it was his training I drew on now. Body flying, legs flung wide then pulled in, twisting and turning with inhuman speed and precision as I tumbled through the gaps in the tripwires. They had covered the likely angles of approach—if the threat was *human*. A Preserver trained by one of her charges in the use of inhuman flesh and bone? It was almost child's play. I could almost see Zhen's narrowed eyes, hear his shouted encouragements. *Pull your knee up . . . think up, up! It is the center all movement flows from, Eleni! Arms straight, they are the fulcrum!*

Twisting, spinning, my smoke-tainted hair flying, a fierce joy filled me. For a moment I could pretend they were all still alive.

I landed, rolling, on the gravel drive. Leapt again, soundless, and caught the edge of the porch roof. *Pulled,* a silent gasp of effort turning my face into a rictus, and spinning weightless . . . before landing soft as a cat's whispering paw on the main roof, kneeling, arms held out to my sides in an approximation of one of Zhen's movements. *It is not enough to begin well and do well,* he would say. *You must also finish properly.*

"I will," I answered softly, and rose. Listened, head cocked.

Five pulses. No, six. Each human heartbeat is unique, echoing through muscle and bone, the differences like clarion calls to a Kin's ear. They were familiar, distinctive. I had heard them galloping along inside the van as it tried to shake me free. One was directly below me. Young, and suddenly speeding up.

The Sensitive. Sensitive to *me,* perhaps. Or to any denizen of the twilight. Was that how they had found my charges?

I leapt for the edge of the roof, turning in midair and catching the gutter. It ripped free, but not before it provided me with another angle, and my filthy boots smashed the window. The rest of me followed, straight and slim as a spear, and the youth was stumbling for the door, screaming in a girl's high terrified voice. I was on him in a moment, smelling the agony of fear as he lost control of bladder and bowels, right before my hand splintered ribs and I pulled the still-beating heart free. My hand closed convulsively, and the tough muscle splattered. Tiny droplets of flung blood dewed my face.

The body dropped. I cocked my head.

Two of the other five pulses scattered through the house quickened. A faint electronic buzz touched the edges of my hearing. Their security system, of course.

Good.

This was a monk's bedroom, with only a narrow cot and a cross on the wall, lit only by moonlight streaming through the broken window. I pushed the door open with my toe, stepping over the still-twitching body, and smiled.

I do enjoy hunting.

Their method of driving a stake through the heart was a modified crossbow. The disadvantage of a crossbow is that it takes a certain time to reload, and it flings a heavy object like a wooden stake far too slowly for a forewarned Kin. By the time the second stake had bisected the air where I was standing a moment ago, I was on the first shooter. Cupping his face like a lover, smelling his terror and the stink of petrol, giving the quick sharp yank that broke the neck like a dry stick. My foot flashed out, catching the one next to him in the ribs and flinging him across the room before he could bring his guns around to catch me.

Then it was a leap aside, another bolt singing through space I'd just vacated, and I collided with another shooter. He was screaming as I hit him, and blood flew from his mouth as kinetic force transferred. He hit the wall *hard,* slid down in a boneless lump.

I turned on my heel. Two left. One stank of petrol—the last of the Burners. The other held the crossbow, staring at me slack-mouthed, and he smelled of dominance under a bald edge of roaring fear. The lieutenant.

Both were stocky, short-haired, and well trained. But they were only human. I bared my teeth as the lieutenant raised the crossbow again, and their fear was sweet tonic to me. It was not enough—my charges had suffered more.

Which one should I keep to tell me where their captain was?

I took a single step forward, still smiling, my fangs aching with delight and my jaw crackling as the Thirst sang in my veins. I would need to hunt again before this night was out, the use of speed and strength taking their toll even on one so old.

The Burner dropped his guns and bolted. I leapt for him, and the world exploded with a roar.

The *lykanthe* leapt on the lieutenant, his teeth sinking into flesh as the man let out a high rabbitscream. It was too late to pull back, I collided with the Burner, my nose full of the reek of death, pain, and fuel. Bones snapped. He was dead before he hit the floor.

I spun. Wolf growled again, hunched over the body hanging in his jaws.

"Drop him!" I commanded, sharply.

He shook the limp form, fur standing up, alive and vital. He had lost his jacket, and his fluid form rippled with muscle. Bits of drywall and slivers of wood clung to his pelt. He looked a hairbreadth away from tearing flesh free of the body and swallowing it, and if he did that . . .

I know enough of *lykanthe* to know the taboo. *Thou shalt not eat human flesh.* I did not know quite what would happen, but I was certain I did not wish to find out here.

"Drop him," I said again, softly but with great force. "Wolf. *Drop* him. Now."

His eyes were mad silver coins. He stared at me, chest vibrating with the growl, and if he attacked me I would have to kill him. It is no large thing to kill mortals, but another of the twilight? A blood-crazed *lykanthe*?

That is altogether different.

His jaws separated. The body thumped down, and his growl faded.

I put my wet, bloodslick hands on my hips. "If he is dead, I will not catch their captain as easily. Did I not tell you to stay?"

He merely watched me. Narrow graceful head, the snout lifted a little, blood marking his scarred muzzle. His clawed front paws tensed and relaxed, as a cat will knead a pillow or its owner's thigh.

There was no pulse echoing from his victim's body.

I sighed, though the tension did not leave me. And I waited. The air still reverberated with their screaming, blood and death and terror.

The fur receded gradually until he stood there bare-chested, his jeans painted with spatters of blood, and shook drywall dust out of his shaggy hair. He hunched his shoulders, as if he expected a repri-mand.

It would do no good. To chastise the uncomprehending is cruelty.

It took effort to speak softly. "Come. We shall search this place, and then we shall burn it."

His head dipped in an approximation of a nod. "S-s-sorry." He could not even force his mouth to shape the simple word correctly.

A great pointless rage flashed through me and away. "It is of little account, young one. Come. Help me."

There was a bank of computers, the monitors glowing. Crates of ammunition, stacks of those odd canisters of petrol. The additive was in gelatin form, a large box full of premeasured packets of the stuff set carefully away from the tanks of fuel. There was a filing cabinet as well, and I opened both drawers, reading swiftly and col-lating information as Wolf touched the glowing screens with his blood-wet fingertips, fascinated.

More of them? I memorized dates and locations, a sick suspicion growing under my heart. Humans have hunted us before, piecemeal and never very successfully. They usually focus on Prometheans.

But this group hunted Preservers. Or their helpless charges. Not *utterly* helpless, but there is no reason for a ward to learn combat or hunting. It is the Preserver's function to learn those things, so the ward may focus on his or her art, whatever that art is.

Somehow, incredibly, these humans found Preserver houses in cities. Was it the Sensitives? I would have sensed human surveil-lance; I have moved my charges many times, when notice or war seems likely. Still, what could—

I opened another file, this one red and marked CLASSIFIED. Gasped, shock blurring through me.

Pictures. Of my house. Of Amelie in the garden, her heart-shaped face turned up as she studied the oleander tree. A blurred shot of Zhen through the windows of his dance studio, arms out and face set in a habitual half-smile. Virginia at the piano, her head down and her long dark braids tied carelessly back. Peter, standing on the front step with his mouth half open, caught in the act of laughing, probably at one of Amelie's artless sallies. No picture of me—of course, I was more careful, out of habit. But there was something else.

A heavy cream-colored card, with the address of our house written in rusty ink, a fountain pen's scratching at the surface of the paper. Ancient, spiky calligraphy, but still readable enough. It reeked of him, the perfume of a Kin.

Dear gods.

I closed the file. Brought it to my chest and hugged hard, the heavy paper crinkling.

Wolf whined low in his throat.

In a few moments, I had the other information I needed. Three locations, one of which was certain to hold this captain of theirs.

There was enough of the night left to accomplish that part of my revenge before I found the traitor who had given pictures of my family to these monsters. And I would make him *pay*, no matter how old, powerful . . . or Promethean.

I stared at the petrol canisters for a long moment before shelving my rage once more. There was work to be done.

When the house was aflame, we left.

The first location—an anonymous ranch house in the suburbs—was empty, but I found evidence of their presence. It was the second, a slumping tenement in the worst sink of the city, that held the prize. The entire place smelled of despair, urine, fried food, and the burning metal of poverty and danger.

I had rescued my Amelie from a place such as this. My hands made fists, loosened, made fists again.

I slid down the hall, crushing the cheap stained carpet under my fouled boots. My hair reeked of smoke again, and my fingers stung with splashed petrol. Wolf padded behind me, his head down. He would need more food before dawn, and a safe place to sleep.

Soon. Very soon.

We rounded the corner, and I saw the door, number 613. It was open a crack, spilling a sword of golden light into the dimness. I halted, and Wolf almost walked into me. He stopped, and tension sprang up between us.

A soft growl, far back in his throat. *"Vrykolakas."*

Even through the slurring, I had no trouble deciphering the word. I did not know whether to be saddened or relieved. My own answer was a whisper. "As I am."

For I sensed him too.

I pushed the door open with tented fingers. Stepped inside. Had he wanted to kill me, I would never have scented him. I would never have heard his strong, ageless pulse.

The apartment began as a tiny hall, a filthy kitchen to the right, a foul bathroom to the left. At the end of the hall, a single room with only a bed and a chair crouching on the colorless carpet.

The narrow bed held the captain's body, facedown. The dried, shriveled things hanging outside the slits between his ribs were his lungs. It is an old torture—the suffocation is drawn-out and excruciating. His wrists and ankles were lashed to the bed with cords, probably from the cheap blinds covering the window. Or brought to this place, because a careful killer is a successful killer.

Perched in the other chair, his back straight and his sallow face expressionless, was Tarquin.

Wolf snarled and lunged forward. I caught him by his hair, and he folded down to the floor, his knees hitting with a thump that shook the entire room. "No." I yanked his head back, exposing his throat. *"No,* Wolf. He will kill you."

He might very well kill us both. I met Quinn's flat dark gaze, his jaw set and a muscle ticking in his cheek. His hair was cut military-short, as ever, and he wore boots to match mine. No spot of blood fouled his leathers. The room could have been a charnel house and still he would have been pristine. Only once had I seen him covered in blood, and screaming.

I shuddered to remember.

"I am not here to kill you." Flat, as usual, each word with the same monotone weight.

Wolf surged forward. I tightened my grasp in his shaggy hair and pulled him back. Quinn watched this, and a shadow of amusement fluttered in his dark eyes.

"Then what?" The enormity of the treachery threatened to choke me. "*He* did this. Your precious White King. He gave over his own kind to mortals!"

"Eleni." Tarquin's gaze dropped to the *lykanthe*. "You were a Promethean, however briefly. You were a prize for *him*. When you left, he took it ill."

"No more ill than *you* did?" Old hurt rose.

That garnered a response. His face twisted briefly. It was shocking, a break in his customary immobility. "I made you. I do not wish to see you unmade."

He said it as if it would be so easy. I did not doubt that for him, it would be.

Then why had he not done it already? Why wait here, with the last victim but one of my vengeance dead on the crusted sheets of the narrow bed? *"Why?"*

"Because Leonidas is my King. I cannot stop him." He paused, considering. "Not yet."

Somewhere in the tenement, a baby woke. Its shrill faraway cry spiraled into an agony of need. In the street, gunfire echoed.

"But you will?" I did not credit my ears. His name was synonymous with loyalty, and had been for far longer than my own long lifespan.

He nodded once and rose, smoothly. Wolf tensed, and now Quinn looked faintly amused. "Only you would preserve a *lykanthe*." One corner of his mouth pulled up, a millimeter's worth. On him, it was as glaring as a shout.

I opened my mouth to tell him what he could do with his amusement, and his master. But he forestalled me.

"Take your dog and flee. I will tell Leonidas you are dead. Preserve what you can elsewhere, and stay away from the White Court and the Red." He indicated the bed with a swift, economical motion, and I dragged Wolf back as if his hair were a chain. "Some day, Eleni, I will avenge *all* his victims. Then I will need your help." He stopped, hands dangling loose and empty by his sides. "Do we have a bargain?"

I considered this. "Why should I trust you?"

"You are still breathing, are you not? And so is he." This time it was a flash of disdain as he stared down at the growling *lykanthe*. Sooner or later my hold on Wolf would slip. Then what?

"Very well." The words were ash in my mouth. "Make him suffer, Quinn. He must suffer to his last breath."

"Have no doubt of that." Quinn pointed at the bed again. "I am not merciful, Eleni. That is why you left me."

"No—"

But he was gone. The window was open, and the cloth-tearing sound of a Kin using the speed slapped the walls. I stared at the body on the bed, the dried lumps of the lungs. Exquisite, and I could be sure Quinn had done it with no wasted motion, not a single wasted drop of blood.

"I left because you did not love me," I finished, because it must be said.

Wolf sagged, and I realized my hand was still cramped in his hair. I let go with an effort. He caught himself on splayed hands, crouching, shaking his head as if it hurt.

"Bad." He peered up at me, craning his neck. "Bad *vrykolak*."

"Yes." There was no reason not to agree. "Now we must leave. It's too dangerous to stay here."

But before we left, I examined the body on the bed. The face was left intact, in a mask of suffering, the eyes stretched open but clouded by death. I put my face near his hair and inhaled deeply. Underneath the mask of death, yes. The smell of male, dominance, gunfire, and a faint fading tang of smoke and petrol. It was indeed one of the mortals who had been inside my house.

My vengeance was—mostly—achieved. But all I felt was emptiness.

The long gray of predawn found us miles away from the city limits, in a north-facing hotel room. The Rest On Inn was cheap, but it was safer than staying in the city. Stealing a car was easy, as was changing the license plates; I had also stopped in an all-night bazaar and bought another jacket for Wolf as well as a load of groceries. Simple, high-carbohydrate and high-protein things, either easily heated or good to eat cold. The *lykanthe* did not demur.

He crouched by the door, eating cold beef stew out of a can with his fingers. I used the duct tape to fasten the cheap curtains down, the weight of approaching dawn filling my entire body with lead.

"Don't open the door," I said, again.

He nodded vigorously. "No housekeeping. No visitors. No no."

I did not bother to take off my boots. Tomorrow we needed more money, a different car, more travel. There were other cities. They all held Prometheans, true, but Leonidas would not look for me if Tarquin said I was dead. And I had no fame among the Kin. I was merely an anonymous Preserver, working to hold back the tide of time.

I watched the *lykanthe* as he dropped the empty can in the rubbish bin and selected another one. A quick deft slice of his claws took the top off neatly. "Eleni." He half-sang my name, happily. Just as Amelie was wont to sing as she painted. "Eleni. Pretty Eleni."

I pulled up the blankets. Bleach, industrial-strength detergent, and the ghosts of mortals lived in the cloth. I arranged the flat pillows and lay on my back, hugging the red file folder to my chest. Evidence of Leonidas's treachery. Even Prometheans were not supposed to turn on their own kind. How long had he been planning this? How many other Preservers had died, or lost their charges to this malice?

Did it matter? I am immortal too. I could keep this evidence for a long, long time. If there was ever a chance, I could find a way to make the viper sting the White King.

And Wolf? Did Leonidas have a reason to hate him as well, or was he just the victim of mortal cruelty? Where were his kin? Destroyed? Still living?

Did it matter? He was my ward now. One more thing to save. Perhaps I could do a better job of it now.

"Pretty Eleni," he slurred. "Good *vrykolak*. Good Eleni."

Our kind does not weep. So why were my cheeks wet? I shut my eyes and called up their faces, each printed on the darkness behind my lids.

Zhen. Virginia. Peter. Amelie. Vengeance did not give them a heartbeat again. It did not salve the wound.

Another empty can hit the pile in the bin. I breathed steadily, wishing for the unconsciousness of daysleep. The sun was a brass note hovering at the edge of my hearing, ready to climb over the horizon and scorch the earth once more.

The sun drew nearer, and my body became unresponsive. The bed creaked. Wolf climbed up and settled against me. The file's heavy paper crinkled, but I freed one arm and he snuggled into my side, his head heavy on my slender iron shoulder. He made a low, happy sound.

I fled into darkness as the sun rose, and wept no more.

VAMPIRES PREFER BLONDES

P. N. Elrod

My weeklong singing engagement at the Classic Club was over, and my hard-earned pay was safe in a grouch bag hanging from my neck. All I had to do was trade my stage gown for a traveling suit, then get to the station to catch the milk train heading home to Chicago.

I was just dropping on a slip when my dressing room door crashed opened.

Being a damned pretty girl with a head of carefully tended platinum blond hair, guys "accidentally" blundering in on me has been a common occurrence since my first night onstage. As the star of this week's show I had the luxury of a private room, kept locked against such interruptions. This door's hook-and-eye latch was enough to discourage the casually curious, but not a meaty shoulder banging against it with serious force.

The latch snapped, one piece flying across to *ding* against the lighted mirror. I yanked the slip down and swung to face the invader, thinking it was a thief after my money. I put one hand in my open purse on the dressing table, fingers slipping around the grip of the .38 Colt Detective Special inside.

Four men crowded the opening, staring. I don't mind when I'm onstage, but this was my sanctuary. Had they burst in two seconds sooner we'd have been arrested by the vice cops.

"What?" I snapped, ready to fight. Just how drunk were they, how had they gotten past the bouncers, and how much belligerence would be required to get rid of them?

The closest was the biggest and apparently the muscle behind the breaking-in. He was unshaved; his clothing was seedy; his eyes were puffy, bloodshot, and oddly calm. The others were similarly unshaved and red-eyed, but one was in a new suit and looked like a respectable banker, another wore brown pants and a blue coat over just an undershirt, and the third was fully dressed but had no shoes, just filthy wet socks.

Collectively an alarming sight, but my intuition said to stand my ground and act tough.

"What is it?" I demanded, prepared to cut loose with a healthy scream if they made a move. I could shoot, but preferred having the club's bouncers deal with this . . . whatever it was.

The banker said in a flat voice, "She's not the one."

No-Shoes said, "She's blond, it's the right hair."

"She's not the one," the banker repeated. He had something in one hand that might have been a photograph and held it up for the others. Sluggishly, they looked at it, then back at me, while the skin on the back of my neck went tight and cold. Whatever was wrong with them was an unnatural kind of wrong, yet weirdly familiar.

"She's not the one," they finally agreed in identical flat voices, then turned and went down the backstage hall to the next door along.

Same operation: Seedy Guy forced the door open, and they looked inside.

The other headliner, a ventriloquist, was surprised as hell and more talkative, angrily asking questions, getting no answers.

"Not a girl," said the perceptive banker. This time they didn't check the photo.

I'd tiptoed over to watch, ready to duck, but none of them paid me further notice. I was shaking, fuming, and scared as I tore down the hall yelling for the stage manager and anyone else handy.

A couple bouncers appeared, offering friendly leers, since I was wearing just a slip, but they shot past to earn their keep when shrieks started up in the chorus girls' dressing room.

The strange invaders had a bad time of it because I didn't stop raising the roof until they were outnumbered by club employees three to one. Half measures are silly in some situations.

The backstage area was quickly packed with struggling bodies, punches were thrown and caught, clothes ripped. The confined area heard thumpings, glass breaking, men cursing, and girls squealing for what seemed like an hour, but was probably less than a minute. The bouncers knew their business and appeared to be enjoying the exercise. The four men made a good effort to defend themselves, though they moved like players who had overrehearsed and lost their spark.

But if you're going to have a fight, this was the best kind: brief, brutal, and with the home team victorious.

The men got the bum's rush. The bouncers and a few other guys who had joined the battle carried things to the back alley, and probably would have rolled into the street, but the club manager stopped them.

"No trouble with the law!" he bellowed, which halted the diehards. It was an advantage to any business not to have police cars roaring up and down the block, scaring off customers. The Classic Club, with illegal gambling in the basement, was particularly considerate of the feelings of its patrons.

The manager stormed into the backstage hall, scowling at the chorus girls who had cautiously emerged from their lair. "All right—who started it?"

With five of them in various stages of dress, undress, outrage, and agitation, he should have known better. They all started talking at once.

He should also have counted. Last I looked there were six girls in the line. While he tried to make sense of simultaneous stories, I eased into the dressing room.

It was like mine, drafty and poorly lighted, but with a lot more stuff confined to roughly the same space. A clothing rack took up the wall behind the door, near to collapse with gaudy taffeta, spangles, and feathers. Onstage the outfits were magical; here they were musty with sweat, sagging, sad—and twitching.

I shoved aside still-warm costumes. Katie Burnell, the sixth girl, crouched behind them, tying a scarf around her head. She gaped up at me in sheer terror for a startled second, then wilted with relief. Her exaggerated makeup had been spoiled by flowing tears. Black trails from her too-thick mascara cut through the supposedly water-proof pancake and greasepaint. She was a mess, a scared-out-of-her-mind mess.

"Those guys are gone, but the boss is hopping mad," I said. "Stay here a minute."

She gulped and nodded.

I returned to the hall. The manager—who really wasn't a bad sort, just upset—had worked out that none of the girls knew any of the guys.

"So they wasn't nobody's boyfriends?" he asked, his eyes sharp for the least hint of a lie. Male visitors were not allowed in this part of the club, only stage talent and other employees.

"Oh, please," said Big Maggie, who wasn't big, except for her loud, fluting voice. "I can do better than those mugs. Ask me if I can do better."

He declined the invitation. "You girls never seen 'em before?"

"They weren't in the audience," I said from the back. "They were dressed too strange." On weekends the Classic Club was a high-hat joint. Patrons had to put on the Ritz or find some other place for drinks and a show come Saturday night.

The other girls supported my observation, nodding, agreeing, and comparing notes now that the excitement had died down.

The manager turned toward the bouncers and guys who'd found an excuse to continue loitering at their end of the hall. You'd think they'd be used to seeing half-dressed females, but apparently not. The ventriloquist and even his dummy had come out for a gander.

The manager gave someone hell about the back door being unlocked, but it was like holding back winter: people were always leaving it open after sneaking outside for a smoke.

I kept my lips together about the men looking for a blonde like me.
Katie Burnell had dark hair, but it was a recent and poorly done
bottle job. No woman goes from traffic-stopping platinum to a mousy
shade of brunette without a good reason.

"Break this up and get back to work," said the manager. "No
need to call the law if no one's hurt."

"I broke a nail," Big Maggie informed him, showing her left ring
finger, the rest of her digits in a loose fist. She was too much a lady to
use her middle finger, which made the gesture all the more amusing
to everyone but the boss.

He grumbled about smart alecks as the girls went back to their
room. His gaze fell on me as the guys whistled and hooted apprecia-
tion. I straightened, having bent over to pick up some trash. The
only thing covering my behind was the pale satin slip. They'd focused on that, not on what I'd snagged from the floor and held
behind my back.

"You know anything about those mugs, Bobbi?"

"Nope," I answered truthfully. "They broke in on me, looked like
trouble, so I thought I better yell."

"You thought right." He turned to make waving motions to my
admirers. "Awright, you cake eaters, show's over. Walk around the
building. Make sure those crashers don't come back. Discourage 'em
if they do, but don't get caught."

Though the men were worse for wear with blackening eyes and
cut lips, they brightened at the possibility of another donnybrook.

"Has this happened before?" I asked as the troops moved off.

He shook his head.

"Maybe at another club?"

That got me a suspicious squint. "What do you know?"

"Nothing, it just seemed a good bet."

He snorted. "Next time play the horses."

"What happened at the other place?"

"Same as here. Four bums bust into the dressing rooms, only they left before they could be thrown out. My brother runs the Golden Rose and called about it. I better phone him back. This is an epidemic."

"What about the other clubs in town?"

"This is Waterview, not Cheboygan. The only entertainment is this place, the other place, a movie house, and a skating rink. Oh, yeah, the barbershop got in a Whiffle Board. If it wasn't for that colony of swells from Mackinac Island supportin' our slot machines, we'd be kissing cousins with a Hooverville."

"Bet it boomed during Prohibition."

"Nah, the rumrunners from Canada went to the next town over. Faster boats. You sure you don't know nothing?"

"I wish I didn't know this much."

"You an' me both, sister." He moved off, scowl intact. I checked on the girls. Their door leaned crazily on one hinge. Big Maggie stood guard while the rest finished changing. Everyone talked a mile a minute, but subsided when they noticed me.

"What's goin' on?" Maggie asked, buttoning her dress.

"Boss thinks it was drunks after a free show. They tried the same thing at another club."

"Huh. Creeps."

"Men," said another girl knowingly.

"Men-creeps," agreed a third.

"Damn," said a fourth, reacting to a run in the stocking she'd been pulling on.

"Where's Katie?" I asked, my heart sinking. Enough costumes had been shifted from the rack to show she was no longer there.

"Washroom."

I crossed to it, knocked, and called before pushing in. The window was wide, the room empty. The alley outside was also empty. Katie had made a clean escape.

Well, I'd *intended* to offer help.

I looked at the item I'd plucked from the floor. It was the photo the banker type had carried. Though crinkled with abuse, the image was clear, showing a much younger Katie Burnell. She couldn't have been more than sixteen at the time.

It was a bridal portrait; she was radiant, smiling, and had platinum blond hair.

The cardboard back bore the stamped-on address of a photography studio in Sheldon, Ohio. An elegant copperplate hand had written on the white space under the photo: *Mrs. Ethan Duvert on the Day of Her Wedding.* The date was under it.

The picture was less than a month old.

Good God, what was she doing to herself? The heavy makeup she always wore made her look years older. She'd also been *scared*. That could pile on the years.

"Hey, you done in there? I gotta go." One of the girls slipped by.

I went to my dressing room, donned my traveling suit, and arranged to get my trunk hauled to the train station. It wasn't a *big* trunk, not like the one my boyfriend sometimes sleeps in, but I'd checked inside in case Katie had gotten a bright idea. My clothes were there, but no runaway bride. I'd seen too many movies.

Yes . . . that is correct. My boyfriend sleeps in a trunk. During the day. But only *sometimes*.

I'll get back to him shortly.

One of the guys drove me and the trunk to the train station two blocks away. He offered to stay, but the stationmaster and a porter were there, and I had my .38. It made my purse heavy, but I didn't mind. I was safe enough. Those badly dressed creepy guys weren't looking for me, after all.

The porter took care of the trunk, the stationmaster took care of my ticket. It was three in the morning in Waterview, Michigan, and I had nothing to do for the next three hours, which was exactly perfect. I parked on one of the long benches and pulled an apple and a movie magazine from my purse. Both gave me something to do while I thought about Katie Burnell and whether there was still some way to find her.

I wanted to know what had her so scared, why those guys were after her, and to help if I could. I could call a cop, but if this was the kind a problem the law could solve, wouldn't she have already gone to them? Maybe she was at the police station even now.

She was a good dancer, keeping pace with the others, never missing a cue, smiling when required, but quiet. Not that she was snobbish, more like she wanted to be invisible. Some girls were like that, able to perform onstage, but shy the rest of the time.

Katie kept to herself and the hotel room she shared with two of the girls. I'd stayed at the same place and gotten to know everyone. Some headliners don't mix with the chorus, but not me. They always know the best gossip. Show a little respect and you've got friends for life.

Last Friday Katie had turned down going to the matinee showing of a Clark Gable picture with us, even after I said the tickets and popcorn were my treat. The girls and I had a great time, but no one wondered much about Katie. For that I felt a touch of guilt, but how was I to know scary lugs were looking for her?

A tall young man marched purposefully into the station. He was shaved, dressed well, and alert, which was wrong for the hour. Early risers and nighthawks were never so brisk at three in the morning. I decided to ignore him and hope he'd not notice me. Fat chance of that, since I was the only other person there.

He went to the stationmaster's window, rumbled a question, got a head shake in reply. He repeated things with the porter, and then it was my turn. It would have been silly to continue to ignore him, so I put the magazine aside, but not the apple.

Damned good-looking fellow, I thought as he approached and touched his hat. His features were as lean and sharp as his tailored suit; his beautiful dark eyes were impossible to ignore.

"I'm sorry to bother you, miss, but have you seen this lady?"

He tipped a fresh, uncrinkled copy of Katie's wedding picture toward me.

I'd taken a big bite of apple and put on my dumbest face, speaking with my mouth full. "Ain't she that actress?" I asked indistinctly, an apple crumb and juice slipping down my chin. I'd not planned it, but felt proud of the effect, swiping it away with one finger. "That one from the new Clark Gable movie?"

His face tightened with effort to ignore my lack of eating finesse. "No, her name is Katherine Duvert. She's my sister."

And I was Minnie Mouse. Katie's skin was pale as a Swede's in winter; his was a Mediterranean olive tone. Her eyes were a transparent gray, his were nearly black. Different brows, chins, noses—neither of them had any relatives in common unless it went back to Roman times.

He wore a gold wedding band. I'd noticed it when he held the picture. It glinted, new and shiny, in the dim station lights.

I pegged him as the jilted husband, so why sell himself as her brother?

I hate liars. If Katie wanted to run away from this pretty boy, then she must have a good reason. "No, I ain't seen her. I'd have remembered another blonde. We stick together, y'know." I fingered some of the hair not covered by my hat, smiling like a cheap flirt, certain there were apple bits sticking to my gums.

Something flickered behind his eyes. Distaste and disbelief. He'd not bought my act. I couldn't blame him, having laid it on too thick. If I ever got to Hollywood, I would definitely need an acting coach.

Then something flickered inside me, a twinge of unease that this guy was eerily familiar. I was certain we'd never met. I would have remembered someone so striking. He had not been in the audience back at the Classic Club or he'd have come backstage himself instead of those four guys.

"I was wondering—" he began hesitantly, unsure and apologetic, which was also an act. This was a guy who was supremely confident every day of the week. He must have thought hiding it would make people more willing to help him out.

I don't like manipulators any more than liars, but smiled encouragingly. "What?"

"Would you mind terribly checking the ladies' lounge for me? I'd do it but—" He made a small motion with his long fingers to indicate the necessity for female help given the circumstances.

"Yeah, sure, I guess so."

He stepped back, not crowding me as I stood. By then I'd come up with a reason why he posed as a brother, not husband. People might side with a runaway bride, and not help a deserted groom on the chance that he could be a wife beater, but a worried brother was someone else again.

He stayed put as I went to the door and looked in.

Lounge was a grand overstatement: three stalls, drab paint, drab tile floor, wire-meshed window—one of the half-open stall doors moved ever so slightly. "Sorry, mister, nobody's home."

He looked at me a few heartbeats too long for comfort, his face somber. "I see. Thank you." Then he remembered to smile, and the look in his eyes just then made my tummy flip over in a bad way. He left the station.

I let my breath out fast, feeling shaky. That mug was a hundred times creepier than the four crashers, and I'd figured out why.

He was like my trunk-sleeping boyfriend. Not *like* him, because Jack is a sweet, wonderful guy and never gives people the creeps unless they truly deserve it.

This one was like my Jack in a way that made my .38 with its ordinary lead bullets useless. I cast around for a reasonable substitute: anything made of wood, preferably with a point. The porter's broom and dustpan were propped in one corner by a trash can. The broom handle had potential, but *why* couldn't he have left a spear or baseball bat lying around?

I dropped my apple in the trash, grabbed the broom, and went into the lounge.

"Katie, it's Bobbi Smythe from the nightclub. I can help, if you'll let me."

A soft sob came from the middle stall. I gave her a moment, then looked in. She stood unsteadily on the toilet seat, doubled over with her head below the divider. She clutched a small suitcase in both hands, which hindered her balance. *Now* she looked very young indeed.

"He's gone for the moment."

"He?" she whispered, shivering head to toe. I'd never seen a face more lost or lacking in hope.

"I assume you're trying to avoid a handsome young husband?"

She came down so fast I had to catch her, and then I had to keep her from tearing out in sheer panic.

"Slow down, girl, you'll run right into him. Let me help you."

Katie shrank from my touch until stopped by one of the sinks. "You can't, you don't know what he can do."

"Tell me later. First we get you out of here."

"You don't understand."

"Actually, I do, a lot more than you'd think. Trust me a minute, would ya?"

While she thought that over I figured out how to improve my new weapon.

Under the window was a cast-iron radiator, bolted to the floor and tall enough to give me leverage. I forced the brush end of the broom into the narrow space between the radiator and wall, jamming it far enough in so that it wouldn't twist or slip free. The handle lay at a steep angle on top, resting between two of the accordionlike columns.

It took two good tries, yanking down with all my weight, to break it. I had four feet of pine dowel that might pass as a walking stick if no one looked too close. No point on the end, but more useful than a .38.

Next, I planned to get the window open and sneak us out, but plans change.

Something was coming *in* that way.

The window was shut, but a nebulous gray shape was impossibly pushing right through the glass and wire mesh like smoke through a screen door. For a second I was fascinated by the sight, but then my heart jumped to my throat. Once it got inside—

Young Katie put a fist to her mouth as she stared, able to see it, too. She froze in place, eyes popping as the grayness thickened and took on definition. A man's tallish shape began to materialize two feet in front of her, his arms spread wide, ready to grab her.

I scampered behind him, too scared to worry about consequences.

The instant he was fully solid, I swung and slammed the broomstick into the side of his head as hard as I could. The temple bones are thin there, more easily broken if hit with enough force.

The shock of impact twanged painfully up both arms. It was like hitting a metal flagpole. Only this pole had some give to it. Not much, but the wood in my hands made all the difference.

It was terrifying how fast he dropped, making a thud as his body hit the tile.

Katie stifled a scream, staring down in horror, not breathing.

He wasn't breathing, either, but that didn't bother me. I hadn't killed him, being far too late for it. Goodness knows when that had originally happened or how.

I went to Katie and made her look at me. "He's out for the count. Wood does that to his kind. You're okay."

She shook her head. "He'll come back. I've seen it."

"I bet you have, kid. Splash water on your face."

While she pulled herself together I went through the guy's pockets. My boyfriend and his partner do private detecting work, and I'd picked up some useful bad habits to add to a few of my own.

An ancient, long-expired driver's license identified him as Ethan Duvert. No surprise.

I *was* shocked at the thick wad of money casually folded into one pocket. The bills were twenties with half an inch of crisp C-notes keeping them company. I'd bet it had come to him the easy way; he'd have floated invisibly into a bank vault and taken it, leaving some hapless accountant to try to explain the loss. I put the money in my purse for safekeeping. Honest. I'd find a way to give it back somehow.

Then—a policeman's badge, a *real* one.

I nearly had a heart attack. If my boyfriend could be a private eye, then there was no reason why Duvert couldn't be a cop, and I'd just clobbered him. Oh, God, I'd gotten everything *wrong*. . . .

"It's something he uses," said Katie, drying her face. "He made our chief of police give it to him to get out of tickets."

It also gave him instant legitimacy with any cop between here and . . . "Sheldon, Ohio?" I read from the badge.

"My hometown. Used to be. Before *he* came." Her face started to crumble and she hiccuped like a toy machine gun.

I knew the signs and stood, hands on my hips. "Hold it, sister," I ordered in my harshest tone.

That derailed her. She gulped back a sob.

"Listen up, you can bawl like a baby later, but I need you to be a grown woman for the next three hours. Can you do that?"

She hiccuped again, but nodded. "Three hours?"

"The sun will be up by then."

Katie looked like I'd smacked her with a wet fish. "How do you *know*?"

"You first. Sheldon, Ohio—your family's there?"

"Everyone is. It's small, but we have a Carnegie library and there's a private college on the other side of . . . oh, that doesn't matter."

"Tell me what does. Tell me about *him*." I didn't have to point at the body.

"He came to town last spring. He seemed to be everywhere. Everybody liked him. They'd just look at him and *like* him. First he was at the mayor's house, then with the chief of police, then the minister, then my parents. My father's a judge, and he and all the men who run the town know each other, and Ethan met them all."

"And they liked him. No one thought that was strange?"

"If they did, he'd hear about it, then he'd meet them and change their minds."

"I bet he did. How did you meet him?"

"I was at the movies with my friends, and that was when he noticed me. We'd seen him with our parents, and he was so handsome, all us girls had crushes on him, even the ones with boyfriends. He started coming by the house to see me and I was so excited that he'd picked me from so many others. At first Father and Mother thought he was too old for me, but he talked with them . . . and things changed. My parents started agreeing to ideas they'd never think of in a hundred years."

"Like what?"

She swatted at her hair. "This."

"You used to be blond like me."

"I was already blond, but it was . . ." Her cheeks went red.

"A more natural color?" I said helpfully.

She nodded, relieved. "*He* wanted it like yours. One day my mother took me to the town beauty shop and told them what to do."

"You didn't have a say?"

She shrugged. "I don't know why I didn't fuss. I wasn't even surprised when Mother did that. She and I acted like it was the most normal thing in the world for me to get my hair bleached out like Jean Harlow."

Maybe that was normal in Hollywood with a stage-obsessed mother looking to land her willing daughter a part in the movies, but *not* for a judge's respectable wife and daughter in a small town in Ohio. "Anyone tease you at school about it?" Schoolgirls who dyed their hair were "fast" and instant outcasts. I should know.

"I stopped going. My parents didn't mind, the principal and teachers didn't mind—*I* didn't mind."

"Down deep you must have."

"It wasn't important. There was just Ethan. My whole life was for him . . . and it was wonderful. Absolutely *perfect*. I'd never been so happy. Every day I just loved him more and more and more. He had clothes sent to me—grown-up gowns from New York, real silk stockings, real gold jewelry. He—"

"I get it. Then he proposed?"

"It's a blur now, like a dream. A wedding gown arrived, and I was fitted for a trousseau."

"He had pictures taken." I showed her the one I'd recovered.

"I look so happy, but it's wrong. It has to be, the way I feel now."

"You married him."

"*He* married *me*," she said sharply.

That anger was sweet to hear. Anger was good for her. She'd earned the right.

"My own father performed the wedding on my sixteenth birthday. But I was always going to marry George Coopley from across the street. We've been going steady since ninth grade. First I'd go to that private college and come back and be a teacher, and George was going to work in his dad's bank, and it was like everyone forgot, even George. *He* was the one who gave me away to Ethan."

I looked down at the still form of Ethan Duvert. Words clogged my throat, most not fit for Katie's ears. I needed release, so I smacked him in the gut with the broomstick. I hoped he felt it.

Katie gasped at the violence. I didn't apologize.

"He had it coming," I said, debating whether to hit him a third time.

Her face twitched. It might have been a smile trying to break through her misery.

That was encouraging. "So you were married and living happily ever after in Sheldon, Ohio?"

"In the mayor's house. It's the biggest in town and the best. He moved his family to that horrible old drummers' hotel by the tracks. Ethan said that was funny and everyone laughed."

"Including the mayor?"

"More than anyone else. Did everybody go crazy?"

"No. They were hypnotized. You, too."

"But—"

"Think about it. Ethan looks everyone square in the eye and next thing you know he's running the whole town—except for drunks and the crazy people, and they didn't matter. Right?"

"Were you there?"

"No. But I know what he is." I started to say how, then thought better of it. If I told her about my boyfriend she'd lose confidence and assume I was another hypnotized victim. That kind of work gave my Jack a nasty headache, so he avoided using it. Duvert must have thought the pain worth it if the result allowed him to own a whole town and everyone in it. "So do you."

She stared at Duvert, then at me, and whispered, "He's a vampire."

"More than that, he's a dirty, low-down, manipulative, thieving bastard."

"Thieving?"

"He stole your town, didn't he? Not to mention your life."

"More." Her eyes glittered as fresh tears formed. She touched her throat. "He . . . fed from me."

I couldn't see the marks. They tended to fade fast and not leave scars. "Did he make you feed from him in turn?" It had to be asked.

She couldn't speak, nodding instead.

"I bet it felt good, though." I knew that from my own experience with Jack. It was always intense for us, but even more so when he and I . . . *well*.

Katie blushed to her now-dark roots. "I couldn't help myself."

"Don't let it bother you, honey, it's what *he* arranged, like it or not. He got your body to do what it's made for. It's completely different when you do things with the *right* guy, one who doesn't have to hypnotize a girl into loving him."

Oh, boy, was it *ever* different.

But that part aside, my having Jack's blood in me enabled me to see Duvert sieving through a closed window. Whenever Jack pulled his vanishing act I could follow his otherwise invisible movements while others could not. It was spooky, but he was my man, and some guys had worse habits. There was another advantage, too.

"Be glad he did it," I said. "*That* was Ethan's big mistake."

"What do you mean?"

"Once his blood was in you it gave you immunity from his hypnosis. He couldn't control you that way anymore. He must not have known." Vampires don't wake up dead knowing all the ropes about the condition. They're only as good as their teacher—if he or she bothered to say anything. Jack was still learning.

"It was like waking up," said Katie, "but I was alone. The only one awake in a town of sleepwalkers. No one else . . . I couldn't talk to anybody, not even my mother. She'd have told him."

"Don't blame them. It's his fault."

"I do blame them. *Why didn't they wake up?*"

I reminded myself she was barely sixteen and feeling betrayed by those who were supposed to protect her. "Is that when you ran away?"

"First thing in the morning. I got a bus to Cleveland, then Toledo, then I ran out of money and had to do something. The only job I could get that paid right away and kept me moving was chorus-line work. I had tap classes when I was in school. I lied about my age, and Big Maggie and the others looked after me, but I couldn't tell them anything or they'd think I'd lost my mind."

"You're awful darned lucky, kiddo."

"Lucky?"

"That you fell in with Big Maggie and not white slavers."

"What are those?"

"Never you mind. Who are those guys who came to the club? Did you see them?"

"The man in the suit is the mayor. I don't know the others, but they'll be from Sheldon. After I left, that picture of me, and a reward offer, appeared in all the newspapers. I changed my hair and wore lots of makeup and hats with veils, and it worked till now. Someone must have recognized me and sent word to Ethan."

"This might be the first time he's left Sheldon since his arrival."

"So?"

"The town will wake up, given time. The hypnosis wears off unless he reinforces it, especially if it goes against what a person would normally do."

"How do you *know* this?"

I had to bend the truth. She was in no shape for my life story. "I used to know a vampire. He was *not* like Ethan. He was a real man, good and decent. He helped me out of a jam and told me things. I wish he was here, because he'd kick this four-flushing dewdropper into the next state."

Hefting the broom handle, I wondered if Duvert was due for another crack on the noggin. Vampires could recover fast from otherwise fatal injuries and not give a clue until it was too late to do anything. Even weakened and half conscious he could snap us in two a hell of a lot easier than I'd snapped the broom.

"Decision time, Katie. We can get on the train and head south or—"

"He'll keep looking for me. What if he goes back to Sheldon and hurts my parents? What if he finds another girl and makes her do things she doesn't want?"

"You've been thinking about this, huh?"

"Ever since I ran away. I want to go home. I want to be me again, not his puppet."

"There's always a Reno divorce," I said, making a joke before raising a far more serious alternative. Katie beat me to it.

"Or I could be a widow," she said in a low, steely voice. Her pale eyes were too hard for a sixteen-year-old's face. "I thought about that. A lot."

"Yes . . ."

"It's better than killing myself. I thought of that, too, but he'd go turn someone else into a puppet, and I'd be dead."

"There's no advantage to it," I agreed.

My tummy did another queasy flip. We were talking murder. Just thinking about the actual, physical act of killing someone, anyone, made me sick. I'd shot a man dead once, in the heat of a white-hot rage and to save others, but it bothered me. Every day it bothered me—I kept busy so as to not think about it.

But I knew people who weren't bothered by killing. One of my gangster friends would help out gladly as a favor, but he was miles away down the tracks in Chicago. It would take time to get him here, but if need be I could keep Duvert out for the count.

I'm no movie heroine. I'm just Bobbi Smythe, a blond chicken who's happy to let someone else do her dirty work. If you can't bring yourself to go down in the sewer, call a rat.

"Katie, I'm gonna get us help. We'll have to hole up. With him. It won't be bad during the day but—"

For the second time that night someone crashed through a door to what I thought was a private place. Katie yelped and scrambled toward the window. I faced the threat.

Threats: badly dressed hometown guys. The banker looked punch-drunk, and I couldn't tell if it was from his beating or months of forced hypnosis.

The four men stared at Duvert, silent.

Was now a good time to scream? It would bring the porter and stationmaster. But cops would get involved, because Duvert was a dead body, and here I was holding the murder weapon. They'd never believe anything about him being a vampire. They'd toss me in the tank, and I'd be a sitting duck for Duvert if he decided to invisibly float in to teach me a lesson.

I pulled the .38 from the purse still hanging from my arm. I didn't want to kill them, but a shot in the foot would slow them down. "YOU! Listen to me!"

Their heads moved my way in unison, their eyes utterly empty. I'd half recognized it back in my dressing room. The people Jack hypnotized got that same look. On one person it was disturbing; four at once was intimidating as hell.

"Out of here. *Now.*"

Oh, my goodness. They were *leaving*. Shuffling out backward.

"Stop."

They stopped.

"What are you doing?" Katie squeaked.

"I think I'm directing traffic, honey. Maybe all you need is a firm voice. *Pick him up.*" I pointed at Duvert's body.

Each of them grabbed a limb, and then awkwardly they got through the door.

"Take him to the car," I ordered. I didn't know if they had a car, but they'd gotten to town somehow. It seemed a good bet.

They carried him across the station while Katie and I hung back. The porter lay on the floor, feebly moving. Oh, hell. I went to the ticket grill. The manager was likewise abused. I urged Katie to grab her little case, and then we slipped out to the street.

Duvert had a paneled truck. A smart choice: he could ride in back during the day, protected from the sun.

His minions had the back open to lift him in. Sure enough there was a trunk, looking uncannily like the one Jack used when he went on out-of-town trips.

I abruptly saw a problem about to happen. Duvert could not have contact with his earth or he'd recover quicker. I shot forward, Katie at my heels.

"Get in the front cab," I told her, and poked at the mayor of Sheldon with the broomstick. "Stop! Put him inside, but not in the trunk." I repeated that until it got through, then ordered them to climb in and shut the door. We had to get clear and fast. The two men in the train station would set the law on their four attackers when they woke up. Waterview cops would notice a truck with Ohio plates and check it.

Then I hoisted into the cab, pushed the stick and purse at Katie, and fumbled for the key. The last driver had thoughtfully or—being unable to think—thoughtlessly left it in the ignition.

I found the starter, then coordinated things until the motor rumbled alive. The gears were just bigger than I was used to; we jerked into first and rolled south on Route 23, heading for Cheboygan, about six miles away.

"What'll we do if someone catches us?" Katie asked.

"They won't." I shifted again and floored it. The truck was almost new. Trust Duvert to help himself to the best. We shot down the road at fifty, then fifty-five. I liked Cheboygan; I liked saying the name and did so, repeating it like a chant. This was great, nothing but tall trees on the right, Lake Huron on the left, and clean night air.

"What about Cheboygan?" Katie demanded, her voice high over the roar of the motor.

"Bigger town, easier to hide in."

It had been a few years since I'd played there. I wouldn't remember much; all I'd have seen would have been the stage, the hotel, and cheap eateries, but every town had places where a truck could park unnoticed until sunrise. With Duvert safely dead for the day, I'd call my friend in Chicago. Heck, I could probably drive there; this wasn't so hard.

Icy gray fog flooded the cab.

Duvert materialized between us.

He damned near broke my foot slamming his own on the brake pedal. He shoved me from the steering wheel. It was like being swatted by a giant, he was that strong. I cracked my head against the window and saw sparks.

Katie screamed and screamed, but none of it impressed Duvert. He quickly and efficiently brought us to a halt and cut the motor. She ran out of voice, falling silent except for trying to catch her breath. I couldn't move. Too stunned.

Duvert's good-looking face loomed into view. This close all I saw was his nose going in and out of focus. There's a reason why I close my eyes when I kiss.

He reached around me and opened the door. I tried not to fall out, feebly grabbing at anything, slowing the drop to a woozy slither. I sat hard on damp pavement, rubbery legs every which way, my back to the truck's muddy running board. Duvert dropped lightly next to me, bent, and looked me straight in the eye.

"Sleep, you dirty little trollop," he ordered. "You will *sleep*."

My lids shut all on their own, but I didn't go out. My head hurt too badly to be bothered, though Jack's blood in me had something to do with it.

It was too much for Katie. She'd been so brave, but her only friend was down for the count. She began making that awful toy machine gun hiccuping. In another second she'd cut loose, but all the tears in the world wouldn't save her from the handsome vampire here on the side of the road by the dark, dark woods.

"Be quiet," he snarled.

She gasped and shut down, probably staring at him.

"What the devil did you do to your hair?" he demanded. "You're ugly now, and after I made you so beautiful—"

"Shut up," she said in the steely tone she used when talking about becoming a widow. "You just . . . *shut up*."

He thought that funny to judge by his brief laugh. "You're not the first to show a little spirit, sweet Katherine. I'll bring you around. I like my girls calm and quiet. Keeps them prettier longer."

"Who cares what you want, you—you four-flushing dewdropper." She put enough acid into the borrowed slang to make it sound like real cursing.

Atta girl, I thought, trying to think of options. I was in no shape to run and hide in the woods. He'd spot me, night was day to him. But across the road—yup, Lake Huron. Miles and miles of it stretching into a black forever. He couldn't come after me. Vampires and free-flowing water don't mix. I could outswim his helpers.

It would leave Katie in a tough spot, but I had to look after myself in order to come back to fight another night.

All I had to do was get clear until dawn. If his hypnotized gang drove them back to Ohio, so be it. I'd find a way to follow. Thinking about killing no longer made me sick. For him, I'd do it with a grin.

He wasn't done scolding Katie. "What have you been doing all this time? Dancing onstage like a drunken harlot? How many men did you let—"

The flat, businesslike crack of my Detective Special interrupted his ego. She'd found it in my purse. Oh, good girl.

It cracked again. Duvert staggered, looking surprised at two spreading patches of blood in the center of his chest. Point-blank range made it easy for her. She fired a third round, hitting his shoulder. Lead wouldn't kill him, but it did hurt like hell.

He vanished. An agitated gray maelstrom spun in the air where his body had been.

Seconds, just seconds before, he returned. He'd come back, healed and hungry.

I lurched up, determined not to be his first-aid nurse. Blood hammered the top of my skull. My damned eyelids did not want to stay open. I leaned into the cab. Katie was backed against the passenger side, my gun in her shaking hands.

The broomstick was on the floor, within reach. I yanked it clear and turned toward him. The grayness was beginning to thicken as he eased back to solidity.

I sagged, dizzy and sick, no strength in my arms. I was barely able to hold the damned stick, much less knock him silly with it.

Katie, I need help, I tried to say, but weird mumbling drivel spilled out instead.

He was halfway back, taking his time. You could see through him. He waved tauntingly at Katie, and she wasted the last three bullets. They zinged harmlessly through his ghostlike form. He went back to being a gray cloud.

It drifted toward the truck cab, oozing inside. She moaned disgust as the chill grayness covered her. He'd re-form on top of her, perhaps to feed, and drain her into a blood-exhausted stupor.

I reeled toward them, leading with that broomstick, hoping to buy time until I could recover enough to do him real damage.

He went for another instant materialization. I stabbed in just before he was fully solid—then, oh my God, the shriek he gave knocked me right over.

The wood skewered him in midchest, front and back, like a pinned bug. He screamed and roared and clawed at the makeshift spear, finally falling from the truck. He slammed hard on the pavement, thrashing violently, trying to pull the thing out, but he'd re-formed right around it, and it was firmly stuck.

And *wood* kept him from vanishing.

Strangely, there was no blood. Just as well, this was bad enough.

But he might force it out . . . yeah, he was trying to do just that, lifting up and dropping on his back. He howled each time, but it pushed a few inches of wood along, and he was desperately pulling with his hands.

I looked for a rock or more wood to stun him with . . . nothing. Maybe there'd be a tire iron in the back of the truck.

Katie came sliding out, her face determined. She had her little suitcase in hand.

She swung it low like a croquet mallet, hitting him square in the head. She used so much force that the handle broke, the case popped open, and her things scattered.

But it got quiet again. Duvert lay sprawled and still in the middle of the road. Maybe there was wood in the sides of the case. I wondered why vampires were so vulnerable to it, but no matter, so long as it worked.

Katie came and dropped next to me and had herself a good long blub. I joined her; it had been a hell of a night. When I felt better we'd clear up the mess and drive into Cheboygan, and I'd have her call her mother.

But for now we leaned on each other, not speaking, and sometime later we watched the sun come up over the lake.

Rapid aging shriveled Duvert's features. Jack had once told me what he knew about the slow process of dying for vampires, not giving much detail. With good reason.

Duvert must have been *old*. He went from beautiful young man to dried-out mummy, and by full sunlight he was a shrunken husk with blackening skin and bones.

Soon not enough was left of his rib cage to hold the broomstick in place, and it swayed and fell over into the growing pile of dust.

I grinned and hoped, really hoped, that it had *hurt*.

NINE-TENTHS OF THE LAW

Jenna Black

Nothing good ever comes from private citizens visiting my office. Which was why I looked up from my pile of paperwork and scowled when a middle-aged couple stepped through my office door without knocking.

I guessed the man's age at about fifty, though it was a well-preserved fifty. His neatly trimmed hair was a dark blond that camouflaged a hint of gray, and he had rounded apple cheeks that would always give him an aura of boyishness. The woman was considerably younger—late thirties, early forties—and beautiful enough to qualify for trophy-wife status. Both were impeccably dressed, and obviously tense.

"Are you Morgan Kingsley?" the woman asked tentatively, looking me up and down with a little frown tugging at the corners of her mouth. All right, I don't dress like a corporate clone; so sue me. It was hot as hell out today, so I'd gone for a clingy camisole top and low-rise capris. Just as well Ms. Stick-up-her-ass couldn't see the drugstore flip-flops that graced my feet.

"Yes," I said, smiling tightly. "That's me. What can I do for you?"

"May we sit down?" the woman asked.

My knee-jerk reaction was to tell them to call for an appointment and then ignore the phone calls. I don't much like being sneered at.

You need the money, Lugh chided gently in my mind.

You've got to love the irony of an exorcist possessed by the king of the demons, don't you? Once upon a time, ours had been a silent partnership, Lugh residing deep within the recesses of my mind, able to communicate with me only when I let my mental barriers down in sleep. Now, he was my constant companion. And, apparently, my business manager.

He was right, though. Ever since he'd possessed me, my life hadn't been my own, and the day job had been on the back burner. In a separate house. Ten miles outside the city.

Long story short, it would be beyond stupid for me to send potential clients away, whether I liked them or not.

"Please, have a seat," I invited with a wave of my hand.

They sat in the chairs in front of my desk. The man was fidgety, and seemed disinclined to make eye contact. I suspected that wasn't a good sign.

"What can I do for you?" I asked again.

"I'm Patsy Sherwood, and this is my husband, Scott," the woman said. Her husband nodded a greeting, but still didn't make eye contact. "We have reason to believe our daughter is possessed."

"Against her will you mean?" I asked, just to clarify things. If their daughter was a legal, registered demon host, then there was nothing I could do to help them.

The woman's eyes flashed dangerously, and her hands clenched in her lap. "She would never accept the Spawn of Satan into her body," she said with a curl of her lip.

O-kay. Not a big fan of demons. Having been a champion demon-hater myself once upon a time, I knew where she was coming from.

I was constructing a tactful reply—tact not being one of my strong suits—but Patsy continued before I came up with one.

"She's only eighteen."

"Ah," I said. The legal age of consent for demonic possession is twenty-one. If the girl really was possessed, then her demon was an illegal, and I could lawfully cast it out. "What makes you think she's possessed?" Usually, it's hard to tell that a person is possessed if the demon doesn't want you to know. When a demon takes a human host, it has access to all the host's thoughts and memories, and can mimic its host's behavior to a tee. The legal ones don't bother, since it's a matter of public record that they're in residence. The illegal ones, however, have every reason to hide, especially in Pennsylvania, which is one of the ten states that executes illegal demons that can't be cast out.

Patsy frowned deeply. "Melanie's been acting strangely for a long time now."

"Almost a year," her husband put in.

Patsy shot him an annoyed look, and a hint of red colored his cheeks. Apparently, this was Patsy's show, and she didn't appreciate the interruption.

"She's been sullen and rude," Patsy continued. "She started swearing— she's never sworn before in her life! And the way she dresses . . ." Patsy shuddered.

"She's going through a goth phase," Scott said, earning himself another glare.

"It is *not* a phase," she snapped. "It's a demon!"

"Sounds like a typical teenager to me," I commented. I think I managed to keep a straight face.

Patsy shook her head vehemently. "It's more than that. She has refused to join us in m—" Patsy forced a cough. "—church."

I raised an eyebrow. "Church? What were you about to say before you changed it to church?"

She waved the question off. "It doesn't matter. It doesn't matter if you believe me, either. I want to hire you to examine her aura. Surely you're willing to do that even if you think I'm imagining things."

I sat back in my chair and thought about it. Based on her reference to demons as the Spawn of Satan, I suspected her dislike of demons ran to the fanatical. Had the word she'd stopped herself from saying been "meeting"? As in a God's Wrath meeting? My gut instinct was yes, and that was a serious cause for concern.

If the girl was possessed, then I had no problem with casting the demon out and sending its ass back to the Demon Realm where it belonged. But if Patsy was a member of God's Wrath, she would be unlikely to accept exorcism as a solution. According to the wackos in God's Wrath, those who host demons must be "purified" by fire. As far as they're concerned, demons cannot possess the pure of heart. Therefore, if you're possessed, you're corrupt enough to justify being burned alive.

Was Patsy the kind of God's Wrath wingnut who would burn her own daughter? I had no way of knowing, but just the *suspicion* made me want to refuse.

She'll just find someone else to do it, Lugh reminded me. *And that other someone might not care what happens to the girl if she's possessed.*

Once again, Lugh was right. I was far from the only exorcist who had ever hated demons. Generally, you didn't get into this profession if you thought they were here for the good of mankind. I balked at the idea that any of the exorcists I knew would look the other way while God's Wrath burned a young girl to death. But there were plenty of exorcists I didn't know.

"All right," I said, trying not to sound as reluctant as I felt. "How do you want to do this?"

As a general rule, I deal with the police, casting out rogue and illegal demons that have already been judged guilty and sentenced. Those ceremonies are conducted in the demon containment area beneath the courthouse, with the demons thoroughly restrained and fitted with stun belts. Those who try to resist are given a good jolt of electricity, which fucks up a demon's ability to control its host's body. If Melanie really *was* possessed by an illegal demon, I couldn't see her holding still long enough for me to examine her aura.

Patsy reached into her fussy little purse and pulled out a business card. The address printed on the card was crossed out, and another one was handwritten off to the side.

"Come to the house tonight at ten," Patsy said, putting the card on the top of my desk and sliding it toward me with one finger.

That sounded suspiciously like an order. I don't take orders well. "Sorry, but I only operate during normal business hours."

She gave me a schoolteacher glare. "Naturally, you will receive a bonus to make up for the . . . inconvenience. Would double your usual fee do?"

"Depends. How do you plan to convince your daughter to hold still for the exam if she's possessed?"

"Leave that to me. She'll hold still for it."

I didn't like the sound of that. But, as Lugh had said, if I didn't do this, someone else would. And double my fee was undeniably tempting.

Feeling sure I was making a big mistake, I agreed to the deal.

The Sherwoods lived out on the Main Line, which was the border between Philadelphia proper and its suburbs. I'd known the Sherwoods were well-to-do based on their clothes, so their enormous house—big enough to hold my apartment three times—came as no surprise. I parked by the curb, thinking they might not want my junker cluttering up their driveway.

Patsy met me at the front door before I had a chance to ring the bell. Being my usual contrary self, I hadn't bothered to change into anything more formal, and I could see it bugged her. But hell, it was still hot and muggy, and the air conditioner in my car hadn't worked since the previous century, so she was just going to have to deal with my outfit.

For a moment, I was sure she was going to shut the door in my face, but she somehow resisted the urge.

"Come in," she said, her tone of voice telling me I was about as welcome as a door-to-door salesman.

The house was refrigerator cold, and goose bumps peppered my sweaty skin the moment I stepped inside. I'd hate to see their electric bill. The decor was almost as cold as the air, everything blue or beige or white.

In the living room, the furniture had all been pushed to the walls, and a large circle of white pillar candles had been laid out. A white

blanket emblazoned with a stark black cross had been neatly folded
in the center. Scott Sherwood sat on one of the chairs against the
wall, his elbows resting on his knees, an empty highball glass in his
hands. He looked up and gave me a brief nod, then left the room—in
search of more booze, if I read his expression correctly.

"We're operating under the assumption that you will perform an exorcism once you're satisfied that Melanie is possessed," Patsy explained.

The words should have soothed me. After all, if they planned on
having the demon exorcised, that meant they weren't going to burn
the poor girl at the stake. Right? But my feeling of unease persisted.
I would be glad when this was all over and I could get the hell away
from Patsy and company.

I nodded. "And where is Melanie?"

"Follow me," she said, and then led the way upstairs.

The stairs were not carpeted, and the house was eerily silent. The
clack, clack, clack of Patsy's heels echoed as she climbed, as did the
thwack of my flip-flops. I paused briefly to look at a stiff, formal family
photo on the wall. Scott and Patsy stood behind two pretty blond girls.
The younger girl, who looked about twelve, smiled brightly at the
camera, but the older one—Melanie, I presumed—looked bored and
resentful.

When we reached the top of the stairs, Patsy reached under her
jacket and pulled out a Taser.

I came to a screeching halt, wondering if I would be better off
charging forward and tackling Patsy to the floor, or leaping off the
side of the staircase in hopes of avoiding her first shot. But she didn't
turn the Taser on me, instead arming it, and then holding it down
by her side.

"I put enough chloral hydrate in her cocoa to knock out a horse,"
Patsy said, apparently not having noticed my double take, "but just
to be on the safe side." She held up the Taser.

I gaped at her. "You *drugged* her?"

Patsy looked surprised. "Of course. How else would I get her to
submit to the examination?"

I took the remaining stairs two at a time. If Patsy'd given the girl enough chloral hydrate to affect a demon, then it was probably enough to kill her if she *wasn't* possessed.

Patsy followed more slowly. She didn't look at all worried that she might have just killed her own daughter. "The demon won't allow its host to be harmed," she assured me.

I wanted to grab Patsy by the shoulders and give her a good shake. "Where is she?" I demanded.

Patsy gestured to one of the closed doors down the hall, and I sprinted for it. I had visions of bursting through the door and seeing a dead or dying teenager. But when I shoved the door open, I saw nothing but an empty twin bed, looking forlorn in a barren room.

The white walls were stained yellow in places, and little patches of paint had been peeled off here and there. The stains and patches tended to form rectangular patterns, and I had a hunch the walls had once held posters that Mommy Dearest had not approved of. The bed was rumpled as if slept in, and in its center sat a sheet of yellow legal paper.

I stepped into the room and heard Patsy follow behind me. She gasped when she saw the bed.

I picked up the paper, read the note, and handed it to Patsy.

FYI, the note read. *Whatever you put in my cocoa tasted like shit.*

Patsy crumpled the note and hurled it at the wall with a furious snarl. Belatedly, I noticed that the open drawers of the bureau were empty. I pushed open what I correctly guessed was a closet door. The hangers were empty, except for a suit, a conservative navy blue skirt, and a couple of prissy white blouses. On the floor were two pairs of sensible pumps, one black, one blue. I suspected this was what Patsy considered acceptable attire for a teenage girl.

Behind me, Patsy kicked the bureau, her face an unappealing shade of red, the Taser clutched in a white-knuckled fist. Call me crazy, but I got the feeling she was a little annoyed her daughter had chosen to fly the coop instead of drinking the proverbial Kool-Aid.

I suspected anything I said would just piss her off more, so I kept my mouth shut, half expecting smoke to come out of her ears.

Little by little, she regained control of herself. I had to wonder what she did with all that rage when she wasn't in the company of strangers. Maybe Melanie had more than one reason to run away from home.

"It appears your services won't be needed after all," she said eventually. "Naturally, I'll pay you for your time."

At least the trip wouldn't turn out to be a total waste, I consoled myself. "If Melanie comes home and you'd like to reschedule, give me a call," I told her, my feet already itching to be out the door. I handed her my card, and she took it by reflex.

"Of course," she replied in a flat tone that told me I wouldn't be hearing from her again.

That might have been the last of my involvement with the Sherwoods, if I hadn't received a disturbing phone call the following day.

I went into my office and was balancing my books—fun, fun, fun—when my phone rang. I checked the caller ID, and saw the name Elizabeth Sherwood. I stared at the name for a moment before I picked up the phone and uttered a cautious greeting.

"Um, hi," said a girl's voice from the other end of the line. I had never asked Patsy about her other daughter, but I guessed this was the smiling child from the family portrait. "Are you an exorcist?"

"Yes," I confirmed, trying to keep myself from speculating about why she was calling. My Spidey-senses were telling me I was about to get dragged into something I'd be better off staying out of. "Can I help you?" I tried to keep my voice gentle.

"I don't know," she said. "Maybe. My name's Beth Sherwood, and I think my parents hired you to examine my sister's aura last night. Is that right?"

Her voice was kind of quavery, like she was on the verge of tears.

Ordinarily, I wouldn't have answered a question like that, figuring it would be some kind of violation of client confidentiality. But too many aspects of this case had given me the willies, and I couldn't in good conscience put the girl off.

"Yeah, that's right. I was supposed to examine Melanie's aura last night, but she was gone by the time I got there. Has she come home?"

"No," Beth said. Her voice dropped to almost a whisper. "I think my mom is hiring a private investigator to look for her."

There was an awkward silence on the other end of the line. I got a feeling Beth wasn't used to reaching out for help.

"Is there something I can do for you?" I asked, hoping I didn't sound impatient. I've never been the nurturing sort, and I have a tendency to be abrasive, even when I don't mean to be.

Beth took a deep breath, then let it out with a whoosh. "I think Melanie's in danger," she said, her voice even softer now. "My mom is convinced she's possessed, and she . . . doesn't like demons much."

"Yeah, I noticed that. Is your mom a member of God's Wrath?"

She seemed taken aback by my question, but she rallied quickly. "There's no law against that."

I smiled, glad she couldn't see me. The kid might not like her mother's fanatical leanings, but she was quick to leap to her defense. "Of course there isn't," I replied. "But you said Melanie might be in danger."

Beth hesitated for a long time, then decided to level with me. "Mom hired you as kind of a concession to my dad. He's God's Wrath, too, but he's not as into it as my mom is. I think if she finds Melanie, she's going to get one of her cronies to do the exam, and I . . ." She cleared her throat. "I don't trust the guy."

I thought about this for a moment, rolling the implications around in my head. "So what you're telling me is you think this guy is going to declare her possessed whether she is or not?" There was no answer from the other end of the line, but I took that silence as a yes. "And you think they're going to burn her?"

Beth let out a choked sob, and I felt like a heel. My bedside manner could use some serious work. "I'm sorry," I said. "I shouldn't have been so . . . blunt."

She sniffled. "No, it's okay. I'm worried about what will happen if they find Melanie."

"Do you think she's possessed?" I asked. If Melanie really *was* possessed, then she'd be harder to find. A sheltered teenager might not have the means or the smarts to remain hidden, but a demon . . .

"She's not possessed!" Beth said sharply, then sighed. "Mom would just rather blame a demon for everything than admit Melanie's got . . . a problem."

"You mean a drug problem?" I prodded gently.

"Yeah. She started going out with this guy last year." I could hear the distaste in Beth's voice. "I don't know where she met him. He's too old to be in school. Anyway, that's when she started to change."

I remembered Scott Sherwood mentioning that Melanie had been acting strange for about a year. I also remembered how Patsy had shot him down when he mentioned it. My guess was she hadn't appreciated the reminder that her daughter's "possession" had coincided with her new relationship with a human man.

"The madder Mom got about stuff, the more Melanie changed. She was doing it just to make Mom mad, but Mom saw everything she did as proof that she was possessed. But it's not a demon that's making her act like that! It's her sleazebag boyfriend!"

I sat back in my chair and wondered what I was supposed to do with this information. Technically, it was none of my business.

Yeah, and that was going to make me feel much better when Melanie Sherwood's "purification" by fire made the evening news. I wasn't sure what I could do to help. But at least I could try.

"Do you have any idea who Melanie might have gone to for help?"

"The only one I can think of is Rick the Prick." She coughed. "Um, I mean her boyfriend."

I couldn't help smiling. "Shall I look him up in the phone book under 'the Prick,' or do you have a last name for him?"

Beth gave a little snort of laughter, quickly cut off. "You have to swear on your life you won't tell my parents. I told them I didn't know his name, because I don't want them to find Mel."

"I swear on my life I won't tell them," I promised.

Beth took a deep breath—for courage, I supposed. "He says his last name is Bull, but that could be, you know, *bull*."

"It's a start, at least," I said. "I have a friend who's a PI. We'll see if we can locate Melanie." Before Patsy and friends did.

"And can you help her? If you find her, I mean."

"I don't know," I told her with complete honesty. "But I promise I'll do everything I can."

Barbara Paget was the kind of woman I usually disliked on sight. Petite, blond, curvy, and stunningly pretty, she looked like an adult version of the cliché vapid cheerleader from every teen flick I'd ever seen. I'd started calling her Barbie when we'd first met, and I'd been unable to break myself of the habit even now that I saw through the pretty packaging to the sharp, driven woman beneath. (Not that I'd tried very hard.)

She was a private investigator, and she'd been drafted to be a member of Lugh's royal council when her investigations had led her to uncover forbidden knowledge. She'd turned out to be quite the valuable asset—and a decent human being, to boot. I was counting on her good nature to convince her to help me find Melanie Sherwood.

Barbie did not disappoint. After I told her about my meetings with the Sherwoods and Beth's phone call, she volunteered to do a little digging—I didn't even have to ask. Within twenty-four hours, she had unearthed an address for Richard Bull, aka Rick the Prick, and had put together a dossier that proved Beth was an excellent judge of character. I read through that dossier when Barbie brought it over to my apartment early Friday evening.

Richard Bull had been arrested five times since he'd turned eighteen—which was six years ago. The charges were all drug-related, but apparently nothing that would keep him off the streets for any extended period of time. The mug shots showed a scrawny, hollow-cheeked thug with greasy hair, bad skin, and soulless eyes. I couldn't imagine what Melanie saw in him.

"Do you think Melanie is staying with him?" I asked Barbie doubtfully as I looked at the address. Bull's apartment was in one of the city's less attractive neighborhoods. "I have the feeling a white goth girl would stick out like a sore thumb around there."

Barbie nodded. "I'm sure she would if she showed her face, which she's probably not doing if she thinks her family's going to burn her if they find her."

I grimaced. Too true. "Of course, *we're* not going to blend into the crowd, either."

Barbie shrugged. "I've gone into worse neighborhoods and lived to tell about it. And our friend the Boy Scout is our best shot at locating Melanie."

I had to concede the point, which explains how Barbie and I found ourselves standing in the dingy hallway of a seriously nasty apartment building, knocking on Rick the Prick's door while the floor beneath our feet rattled from the rap music blasting from the next-door apartment. The hall had the vomit-and-piss stink of a sub-way station, and I wondered how a girl brought up on the Main Line could stand the place.

Repeated knocking was getting us no results, and the longer we loitered in the hallway, the more apt we were to draw unwanted attention. We'd been stared at and propositioned a number of times as we'd made our way into the building and up the stairs, but so far that was it. I wanted to keep it that way.

I reached out and gave the doorknob a good rattle, testing the strength of the lock. It felt pretty flimsy—I could probably bust it even without having to let Lugh take over my body and use his superior demon strength, something I would allow him to do only under the most dire circumstances. I was never going to get used to the utter lack of control that went with having a demon driving my body, or the sickness I often experienced when he once more receded into the background.

Barbie must have seen the direction of my thoughts. She put a restraining hand on my arm, then reached into the pocket of her black cargos—part of what I liked to call her "Stealth Barbie" outfit—and pulled out a set of lock picks. Some of her methods as a private investigator were somewhat less than ethical, but I wasn't about to complain.

Barbie knocked on the door once more. "Come on, Rick," she said loudly. "I'm not in the mood to pick this lock, but I will if I have to. It'll be a piece of cake."

When there was still no answer, Barbie shrugged and inserted her tools into the lock. I wasn't sure I liked the idea of us bursting in on the guy—the chances were good he'd be armed, and he might shoot first and ask questions later if he felt threatened. I was about to mention the possibility to Barbie, but was interrupted by a voice from behind the door.

"Who the fuck are you, and what do you want?"

Rick the Prick, I presumed.

Barbie and I had agreed in advance that she would do the bulk of the talking, seeing as she had the tact and patience I so obviously lacked. So I bit my tongue and let her answer.

Barbie removed her tools from the door and smiled up at the peephole. Her looks and that smile were enough to stop traffic, and I bet Rick was thinking impure thoughts about her the moment he got a good look at her. Myself, I stood a little off to the side, where he couldn't see me. I have a tendency to intimidate people—a tendency I'd honed and perfected over years of being the queen of attitude—so it was best to have Rick's attention focused on the harmless-looking Barbie instead. Never mind that she wasn't nearly as harmless as she looked.

"We're looking for Melanie Sherwood," Barbie said, still smiling. "We thought you might have some idea where she is."

"Don't know her. Get the fuck out of here."

Barbie was unperturbed by his response. "Of course you know her, Rick. You've been dating her for about a year. My friend and I really have to talk to her. It's very important. Like, life-or-death important."

"Fuck. Off."

"You think tossing off an f-bomb every sentence makes you into a tough guy?" I asked, unable to resist. Barbie gave me a reproachful look, and I tried to look innocent.

"I guess I'll have to pick the lock after all," Barbie said with an exaggerated sigh.

"I ain't tellin' you nothin', bitch," he growled. "Don't matter if you're inside or out."

In went the lock picks again.

"You come through this door, I'm gonna bust you up!" he warned, but there was a hint of fear in his voice.

"You can try," I told him as I reached into my purse and withdrew my Taser, arming it. Usually, I'd only use it on demons, but I'd be happy to make an exception for Rick.

A woman's voice, too soft to make out beneath the echoes of rap music, spoke from the other side of the door. Rick snarled something indistinct at her, but moments later, the door swung open, Barbie's picks still stuck in the lock.

Whatever goth phase Melanie Sherwood had been going through, it seemed to be in the process of passing. Her hair was dyed black with purple streaks, and if you looked closely, you could see the holes around her eyebrows, nose, and lower lip where various jewelry had once pierced her face. But she was dressed in a perfectly ordinary pair of blue jeans and a faded baby blue T-shirt, which was a serious violation of goth uniform.

Rick the Prick hovered behind her, his face set in a sneer that I suspect was supposed to be menacing. I was more threatened by the persistent twitch in the corner of his eye and by the size of his pupils.

Melanie looked grim and maybe even frightened as she opened the door wider and invited us in. I wasn't sure accepting the invitation was wise, but Barbie waltzed right in as if she didn't have a care in the world. I followed more slowly behind her.

I'd been too busy indulging my paranoia to remember that I was still holding the Taser down by my side—until I stepped through the doorway and heard Melanie's gasp. Not the best way to set the tone for a friendly interview, I must admit. I started to put the Taser away, but I guess Rick the Prick didn't like seeing the weapon move.

"Rick, don't!" Melanie cried, too late to stop his fist from slamming into my jaw.

Even though I saw the punch coming, I didn't move fast enough to avoid it. Pain exploded through my brain, my head snapped back hard enough to cause whiplash, and I went down hard. There was some scuffling and some shouting around me, but I hurt too much to pay attention to it. I sure hoped Rick hadn't just broken my jaw.

He didn't, Lugh's voice said soothingly as I put my hand to my aching face. *You'll have a nasty bruise, but I can fix it next time you go to sleep.*

My own internal medic, that was Lugh. He couldn't use his supernatural healing powers unless he took control of my body. Luckily, he could take over control easily while I slept, and I didn't suffer the nauseating side effects that way.

I blinked to clear my vision and saw that my situation had not improved. Rick loomed over me, pointing a gun straight at my head. A few feet to the side, Barbie had her own gun out, pointed at Rick. He was wide-eyed and panting, his hands shaking ever so slightly—I wondered if he'd ever actually pointed that gun at anyone before. Too bad he was so close he couldn't miss if he tried. Lugh could fix a lot of injuries that might kill a normal human, but he couldn't fix a bullet to the brain.

"Put the gun down," Barbie ordered, her voice cool and full of authority, her aim completely steady. I knew it was a front—despite what you see on TV, PIs don't as a general rule go around getting into gun battles with the bad guys—but it was a *good* front.

I lay as still as possible, not wanting to make even the tiniest motion for fear it would startle Rick into shooting me. Hell, if I could have kept from breathing entirely, I would have.

"Everyone just stay calm," Melanie said, and her voice was even cooler than Barbie's.

I blinked and focused on her. She was standing just a couple steps to Rick's left, her hands up as if to prove she was unarmed. There was no fear in her eyes, and her breathing was slow and steady as she eased a little closer to Rick.

"Put the gun down, Richard," she said in that same calming tone.

"They're working for your fucking parents!" he said, hands now shaking even more.

Melanie took another step closer. "Even if they are, shooting them isn't going to help anything."

I was frozen in place by Rick's gun, my head throbbing in pain, but I had enough functioning brain cells to come to the obvious conclusion that Melanie Sherwood wasn't alone in that body after all. There was no way a teenage girl—especially one with her upbringing—would stay this calm under fire. I guessed I should be happy she wasn't encouraging Rick to shoot me. Illegal demons aren't known for their great humanitarianism.

Melanie's hand came to rest on Rick's arm, and he flinched. Luckily, the gun didn't go off. At her urging, he lowered the gun slowly, still looking way too twitchy for my taste.

"Now put it away," she said, and with a shuddering sigh, he tucked it into the back of his pants and took a step backward.

Barbie had not relaxed her stance, and her gun still pointed steadily at Rick's chest even as he backed away. "I suggest you tell your boyfriend to leave the room," she said, and Rick's gaze flicked from the gun to Melanie. Her chin dipped in a slight nod, and with a last withering glare at me, he turned around and stomped out of the room, heading down a hallway and out of sight. Moments later, a door slammed.

Barbie let out a slow breath and lowered her gun, flicking on the safety. I noticed, however, that she didn't put it away. And that she was eyeing Melanie with a fair amount of suspicion. She must have come to the same conclusion that I had.

Melanie reached a hand out to me, and I saw no reason not to take it and allow her to help me up. My head spun for a moment when I got to my feet, but the feeling quickly passed. Too bad the same couldn't be said for the pain. Keeping a wary eye on Melanie, I picked up the Taser I'd dropped when Rick hit me.

"Let me get you some ice for that," Melanie said as she shut the door to the apartment and locked it.

"Never mind," I told her. "I'll be fine."

I wasn't being stoic—it was just that I didn't want to have both my hands full, and there was no way I was putting away the Taser. Melanie blinked at me, then nodded and gestured to a ratty mustard yellow couch with sagging cushions and frayed arms.

"Please, have a seat."

Barbie and I shared a look. I shrugged, and we both sat down on the couch without ever taking our eyes off Melanie. She made no hostile moves. I was pretty sure if she'd meant us harm, she'd have attacked already. But not sure enough to put away the Taser.

Melanie sat in an easy chair and clasped her hands in her lap. She gave Barbie a quick once-over, then turned her full attention to me.

"You're Morgan Kingsley," she said.

I raised my eyebrows. "Have we met?" I knew I'd never met Melanie Sherwood before, but I had no idea which demon currently resided in her body.

She shook her head. "No. But your reputation precedes you." Her lips curved in a wry smile. "Only the best will do for my parents."

I decided to lay my cards on the table immediately. "You mean your *host's* parents, don't you?"

Melanie pressed her lips together into a thin line, then sighed, her shoulders sagging slightly. "Yes, my host's parents. I suppose there's no point in denying it."

I was pretty damn surprised at that attitude. It seemed like the threat of execution would be a pretty good reason to deny it. "Melanie's too young to host a demon legally," I said, a master of stating the obvious.

The demon nodded. "Yes. But it is unlikely she would have survived long enough to become a legal host, even supposing the Spirit Society would accept her as a candidate."

"What do you mean?"

She glanced at the hallway down which Rick had disappeared. "Richard, as you may have gathered, is a drug addict. When he and my host started dating, she picked up his habit. At first, it was just a way to rebel against her parents, but it turned into way more than that. What she didn't know was that Richard was infected with HIV."

I winced.

Melanie shook her head. "He didn't know." Again she glanced at the hallway. "He'd never been tested. But as you've no doubt guessed by now, my host was also infected."

"HIV isn't an automatic death sentence these days," Barbie said, echoing my thoughts.

"No, but her parents would have kicked her out the moment they found out, and she had no means of supporting herself. Not to mention the drug habit, which was only getting worse. The combination of circumstances would have turned it into a death sentence."

I eyed Melanie skeptically. "So what you're trying to tell me is that you illegally possessed her, but I should look the other way because you're an angel of mercy, saving her life?"

"Something like that. She is far better off with me in residence than she was before. And while the transfer might not have been technically legal, both she and my original host were willing participants."

"Your original host?"

Melanie nodded. "My original host was legal and registered." Her face twisted into a grimace. "And our relationship was the opposite of love at first sight."

I'd known other demon/host relationships of that ilk. The hosts did not fare well under those circumstances. Demons just had too much power and were bound to come out on top in any conflict.

"If I'd had to reside in that host for my entire stay on the Mortal Plain . . . It would have been hell for both of us. So we agreed that we would try to find someone else to host me. Meanwhile, Melanie had decided that her only chance of survival was to find a demon who could manage her disease." She smiled slightly. "She doesn't like to admit it, even to herself, but part of the reason this solution appealed to her was that her parents would disapprove so badly. Another teenage rebellion."

I almost smiled back. I'd gone the opposite direction myself. My parents were devout Spirit Society members, who'd always hoped I'd volunteer to host one of their "Higher Powers," as they called demons, when I came of age. Instead, I became an exorcist.

The smile faded before it took root. "This story sounds great," I said, "but you've broken a lot of laws." Possessing an unregistered host was a capital crime, as was changing hosts. The only legal way for a demon to possess a host was through a sanctioned summoning. "Not to mention that it could be total bullshit."

I watched Melanie's face closely, searching for a reaction that would give me a hint as to whether she was telling me the truth. I didn't get one.

"I understand your skepticism," Melanie said, "and I don't blame you. But consider that I had many options when you presented yourself at this doorway. If I were the kind of immoral creature you suspect me of being, my choice would not have been to sit down and talk to you. I could have killed you both like that," she said, snapping her fingers. "The problem is there's no way for me to prove that I'm telling you the truth. I can produce the results of Melanie's HIV test, but that would only tell you that she's ill, not that she's hosting me of her own free will."

"No," Barbie said, "we'd have to hear it directly from Melanie herself to be sure it's the truth."

The demon frowned at her. "But you know that's not possible."

"Actually," I said, catching on to Barbie's train of thought, "it is. All you'd have to do is temporarily move out of Melanie and into Rick. Just long enough for us to have a word with her."

The demon froze, the look on her face one of mingled wariness and confusion. "But Richard might not survive the process."

"You'll just have to make sure he does," I countered. We then engaged in a short staring contest. Usually, a host is left catatonic when a demon moves out—hence the law against demons changing hosts— but one of the secrets I'd learned since becoming possessed myself was that the catatonia is caused by abuse. If the demon wanted Rick to stay intact, he'd be fine.

She lost the staring contest, her gaze dipping quickly down to the floor as she chewed her lip in thought. Then she seemed to come to a conclusion, for she met my eyes once more.

"Richard might not be willing to take the risk," she said. "He is not exactly an altruist. Would you have me take him against his will?"

That question made me squirm. I made my living exorcising demons who took unwilling human hosts. How could I in good conscience allow such a thing to happen right before my eyes? True, the demon was unlikely to go through with the transfer if it wasn't telling the truth, and if it was telling the truth, it was unlikely to harm Rick in the brief time it possessed him. But still . . .

"If you feel you must exorcise me, then you'll have a fight on your hands," she said. "I would do my best not to harm you, but I can't make promises. I *have,* however, made promises to Melanie, and I will not abandon her."

I gritted my teeth against a sharp reply. The threat was uttered with no heat, and the demon's body language was relaxed and not even remotely hostile. Slowly, Melanie pushed to her feet. Barbie and I both stood up considerably faster, though still Melanie made no hostile move.

"Let's settle this without violence, shall we?" Melanie suggested. "Come with me."

She headed toward the hallway down which Rick had disappeared. Barbie looked at me for a decision. I momentarily longed for the good old days, when no one looked to me to make difficult decisions.

Do you think she's telling the truth? I asked Lugh.

She's not human, Lugh reminded me. *If she were human, I'd say there's a good chance she's telling the truth. But demons are better at lying than humans are, so I can't be sure.*

And wasn't that a comforting thought! Unfortunately, it put the burden of decision-making firmly back on my shoulders.

Melanie had disappeared from view—which if she was a bad guy was not a good thing. I headed down the hallway after her, Barbie just behind me. Melanie stood in a doorway two doors down, her mouth set in a frown, her arms crossed over her chest as she stared into the room. With a shake of her head, she stepped inside. Barbie and I followed.

It was a squalid, nasty little room, with grimy walls and cloudy windows. Rick lay sprawled across a sagging twin bed, its stained sheets shoved off onto the floor. An empty syringe lay on the mattress beside one hand, and a rubber tourniquet was still banded around his left arm. His eyes were closed, and I'd have thought he was dead if it weren't for the slight rise and fall of his chest.

Melanie stood at the bedside and looked down at him. "He will destroy himself even faster than my host would have," she said. "He was already high as a kite before you came. I suspect he'll need medical attention." She turned to look at me, her eyes flicking briefly to the Taser and away. "If you let me move into him while you talk to Melanie, I can repair whatever damage he's just done to himself."

"Can you cure the HIV?" Barbie asked.

Melanie shook her head. "I can stop it from causing any harm while I'm in residence, but I can't outright cure it. Shall I transfer?"

I didn't have to let her, not now that I had the Taser. I could just shoot her full of electricity and send her back to the Demon Realm. But despite my notable lack of faith in both mankind and demonkind, I found myself wanting to give her the benefit of the doubt. Maybe I was going soft. . . . Or maybe I just didn't like Rick and wasn't as worried about protecting him as I should have been.

"Do it."

Melanie sat on the bed beside Rick. She untied the tourniquet, then picked up the empty syringe and tossed it onto the bedside table. The look in her eyes said she genuinely cared about him, but maybe she was just a good actress. She reached out and brushed an errant lock of hair off his forehead.

Melanie's body language changed subtly, her shoulders slumping as her hand fell away from Rick's face. His eyes opened, and I knew immediately that the demon was now in the driver's seat. His pupils were no longer dilated, and the expression on his face was too . . . serene to belong to the angry, drug-crazed asshole who'd hit me.

Melanie looked up at me, her eyes a little too wide as she chewed her lip. "How did you find me?" she asked.

Something had clearly frightened her. My first thought was that the demon had threatened her before it moved out, but she was pressing close to Rick, as if seeking his protection.

"Was the demon telling the truth?" I asked. "Are you a willing host."

"Yes. Tell me how you found me!" She was breathing hard, her hands clenched into fists in her lap.

Rick sat up and put a soothing hand on her back. "Don't be afraid," he said, though of course it was the demon talking, not Rick the Prick. "Whatever happens, I'll protect you."

I felt like I'd somehow missed a part of this conversation. "What's the matter, Melanie?" I asked. "What are you afraid of?"

Instead of answering me, she turned and practically flung herself into Rick's arms. He held her tightly, tucking her head under his chin and looking at me over her head.

"The only person who knew Rick's full name was her sister," he explained. "She thinks you found her because Beth betrayed her. And that you're going to hand her over to her parents."

"No way in hell I'd do that," I assured him. The little hairs on the back of my neck were prickling.

Maybe it was naive of me, but I was dead certain Beth had told me the truth, and that she was very, very worried about Melanie's safety. Worried enough that there was no way she'd have given Rick's name to her parents, not when that would have helped them track Melanie down. Worried enough to reach out to a stranger and ask for my help—and risk telling me Rick's name.

I turned to Barbie as apprehension settled in the pit of my stomach. "You didn't happen to check to see if we were being followed when we came here, did you?" I asked.

Barbie muttered a curse under her breath. "No. It never occurred to me."

Damn it! It had never occurred to me, either. How had Beth known I was the exorcist her parents had hired? Maybe because they had "carelessly" left my card lying around for her to find? And if they knew Beth wouldn't give them Rick's name, what better way to find it than to trick her into telling someone else? Someone else who would conveniently lead them right to their wayward daughter.

Melanie cowered in the demon's arms, and he rocked her like a baby. I met his steady gaze.

"They wouldn't really . . . ?" I started, then found myself unable to finish the question. I'd had a pretty sucky relationship with my parents, and they'd never protected me in the way parents should protect a child. But even *they* would have balked at killing me, much less torturing me to death with fire. I knew there were people out there who were capable of that kind of cruelty, but my very soul rebelled at the idea.

"Her mother has ambitions within God's Wrath," the demon said. "What better way to prove her loyalty and commitment to the cause than to sacrifice her own daughter? Besides, I think she truly believes she'd be saving Melanie's soul."

There was a loud knock on the front door, and we all froze. Melanie let out a bleat of terror, and I couldn't blame her. Sure, it could be just a neighbor asking to borrow a cup of sugar—does anyone really do that?—but I wasn't counting on it. I checked the charge on my Taser, and Barbie drew her gun, flicking off the safety.

Rick shook his head. "They've done this before, and they know how many people are in this apartment. There will be too many of them for us to take. And no one in this building will stick their neck out for us."

Of course, Rick didn't know that he wasn't the only demon in the room. I had a feeling Lugh would even the odds.

Not against a mob armed with Tasers, he reminded me.

The knock sounded again, more firmly. A male voice shouted something authoritative-sounding, though I couldn't make out the words.

"Call the police," Rick said. His voice was still calm, but his eyes were wide and frightened-looking, and he was holding Melanie so tight he was practically crushing her. "Tell them what's happening, and tell them if they don't get here in time, they'll find us at Melanie's house. God's Wrath has what they call a 'facility' in the basement."

There was a loud crash from the front of the apartment. I had a sinking feeling that was the sound of the front door being broken down. "Hold them off as long as you can!" I ordered Barbie as I whipped out my cell phone and hit speed dial.

If I had to go through 911, I'd never get through an explanation before it was too late. However, Adam White, the director of Special Forces—the branch of the Philly PD responsible for demon-related crimes—was a member of Lugh's council, and I could enlist his aid with a minimum of bullshit.

Barbie, standing in the bedroom doorway, fired off a warning shot down the hall, and Melanie screamed.

"Don't come any closer," Barbie yelled to someone out in the hallway. "The police are on their way!"

Yeah, well, sort of.

I figured that from her defended position, Barbie might be able to hold the bad guys off for a couple of minutes. What I hadn't counted on was the canisters of tear gas said bad guys lobbed our way. It wouldn't have a whole lot of effect on demons, but it would take Barbie and Melanie out of play in no time.

I didn't hesitate to let Lugh take control—I wouldn't be able to tell Adam diddly-squat if I was coughing up a lung, as Barbie was starting to do. She fired off one more shot blindly, then was overcome by the gas.

It seemed like a century before Adam answered the phone. He started in on some sarcastic greeting—I never called him with anything resembling good news—but Lugh cut him off.

"Get to 125 Oak Grove Court, fast," he gasped, the tear gas making his breath come short even if it didn't incapacitate him. "Basement. God's Wrath is taking us—"

A masked figure suddenly appeared out of the cloud of gas. Lugh tried to dive out of the way, but twin Taser probes latched onto his chest and stomach, and fifty thousand volts of electricity short-circuited his control of my body. The phone fell from his limp fingers as he collapsed to the floor.

Put me back in control, I ordered him, though I dreaded what would happen when he did. With him in control, I didn't feel any of the pain or misery that the gas and electricity were causing my body. However, humans and demons respond differently to Tasers, and the last thing I wanted was for God's Wrath to figure out they had more than one demon they could throw on the bonfire.

Lugh faded into the background of my mind, and I lost myself to misery.

I must have passed out somewhere along the way, because the next thing I knew, I was in a moving vehicle. My hands were tied brutally tight behind my back, and I was practically suffocating under a heavy hood that blocked my vision. A cloth gag sucked all the moisture from my mouth and bit into the bruise on my jaw. My chest ached from coughing, and my eyes burned so badly I doubt I could have seen anything even without the hood.

It was not looking good for the home team. God's Wrath never hesitated to take responsibility for the demons they killed, but they were never willing to give up the individual members who'd participated in the murders, making it almost impossible for anyone to be prosecuted. Unfortunately, since Barbie and I would know damn well who to point the finger at if Melanie turned up dead, I suspected we were about to become collateral damage.

I really hoped Adam had enough information to work with and was even now speeding to the Sherwood house to enact a rescue. Too bad Lugh hadn't been able to communicate that we were up against an armed, organized mob. If Adam came alone, he could end up roasting right beside Rick or Melanie.

The ride to the suburbs took forever, but at the same time didn't take long enough. The vehicle in which I was being transported came to a stop, and the sound of doors sliding open told me I was in a van. Rough hands grabbed me under my arms, and when I tried to struggle, I was rewarded by a blow to the head that took all the fight out of me.

I was only semiconscious as I was dragged out of the van and then slung over someone's shoulder. My captors didn't speak, but I could hear some more scuffling, then the muffled sound of sobbing. My heart squeezed in sympathy for Melanie, even though my own situation wasn't looking much brighter.

I heard a series of locks being opened, and then my captor began to descend, his feet pounding down a set of wooden stairs. I suppressed a whimper as I caught the reek of old smoke.

I was unceremoniously dumped onto the cement floor with a teeth-rattling thump. The hood was pulled from my head, and I opened my still-stinging eyes to a sight every bit as horrifying as I'd imagined.

I was in a barren, unfinished basement, lit only by a series of thick pillar candles that lined three of the four walls. An enormous blackened fireplace was set into the fourth wall. My guess was it was supposed to look like one of those medieval castle fireplaces, where you could roast a whole deer on a spit. Unfortunately, it wasn't a deer they were planning to roast tonight. A thick iron pole rose from a bed of concrete at the back of the fireplace, wood and kindling piled at its base.

I struggled to sit up—not easy when you're bound hand and foot. No one helped me, but no one tried to stop me, either. Glancing around, I saw Rick, Melanie, and Barbie, all similarly bound and gagged. We were surrounded by figures in black hoods and robes, at least ten of them crammed into the small basement. Several of them held Tasers pointed at us, and one of them had a gun. Not good odds.

Melanie was sobbing so hard she was having trouble breathing around the gag. Barbie was pale and wide-eyed with fear. But Rick's eyes were alive with calculation as he took stock of the situation. The demon had clearly not transferred back into Melanie during the attack, and I wondered if we could take advantage of the fact. God's Wrath were expecting Melanie to be possessed, but they weren't necessarily expecting it of Rick.

One of the Taser-wielding loonies stepped forward. Before I had a clue what was about to happen, he'd shot Melanie full of electricity. She screamed from behind the gag, her body collapsing to the floor, where she lay twitching spastically.

"She is free of the Spawn of Satan," the loony intoned.

Well, that was certainly one way to determine if someone was possessed. If Melanie's demon had still been in residence, she would not have been twitching. One of the other hooded figures suddenly rushed forward and grabbed Melanie, wrapping her into an embrace.

"Oh thank God!" Scott Sherwood's voice said from beneath the hood.

"What about that one?" another hooded figure asked, and this time I recognized Patsy's voice as she pointed at Rick. She sounded strangely hopeful. I supposed she was really eager to have someone to burn in that fireplace.

A lot of things happened at once then.

The demon burst free of its bonds and charged the man who was about to Taser him. The Taser went off, but its probes sailed harmlessly over Rick's head as he rode the homicidal nutcase to the floor.

I realized the shit was about to hit the fan, and that if we had any hope of all of us surviving until Adam could arrive with the cavalry, we couldn't afford to have any demons go down for the count. Which meant that, despite the unpleasant side effects that were sure to follow, I had to let Lugh take control again.

It was a calculated risk. If Rick and Lugh lost this fight—which seemed likely, considering we were badly outnumbered and the bad guys had Tasers—I was announcing to everyone involved that I was possessed, which would make me a candidate to join Rick at the stake. But though I'd once thought of myself as selfish and cowardly, I couldn't just sit there and do nothing while man and demon were barbecued.

Lugh's demon strength was easily enough to let him tear loose from the ropes on my wrists and ankles. My flesh got torn up pretty good in the process, too, but Lugh cut me off from the pain. I was now nothing more than an observer in my own body, seeing and hearing the action without actually *feeling* anything, at least not physically.

Rick's attack came as a surprise to the God's Wrath mob; Lugh's came as a total shock. I mean really, who's going to expect an *exorcist* to be possessed, of all people?

Lugh plowed into one of the Taser-wielding guys, his momentum carrying them both into yet another one. All three of us went down, with Lugh on top. The man on the bottom cracked the back of his head against the cement floor and didn't move. I told myself I hoped he wasn't dead, but I had to admit there was a spiteful side of me that didn't much care.

Lugh wrested the Taser from the hand of the man he'd knocked down, crushing the barrel with one strong hand. Without a Taser, the guy wasn't a threat anymore, so Lugh leapt to his feet.

Rick had taken down two of the hooded figures, but by the time Lugh was fully vertical, Scott Sherwood had shoved his still bound and gagged daughter behind him and lunged forward, jabbing his Taser into Rick's back. The demon collapsed. Between them, Lugh and Rick had incapacitated four of the fanatics, but once Rick went down, the remaining six were able to focus all their attention on Lugh.

Six against one is never good odds, even when you're a demon. But Lugh is a very clever demon. Plus, he knew he didn't have to defeat them—just delay them.

Several of our attackers had already fired their Tasers and missed, which meant they had to either stop and reload, or try to use the Tasers at close range as stun guns. No one seemed real eager to get close. Imagine that!

Lugh grabbed at the closest figure, his hand closing around an upper arm. The hood fell down, revealing Patsy Sherwood's face. Her teeth were bared in a snarl, her eyes narrowed with hatred, her cheeks flushed an angry red. She swung her Taser at Lugh, but Lugh hit her arm so hard it knocked the Taser from her grip and sent it skittering into the fireplace. He then pulled her up against him, using her body as a shield against the others.

I was almost beginning to feel optimistic about our chances. Unfortunately, I am nowhere near as petite as Barbie, and Patsy Sherwood's body was an inadequate shield for a woman of my height.

The fanatics who were still standing spread out, making it hard for Lugh to keep an eye on all of them at once. Two of them fired their Tasers at the same moment. Lugh used Patsy to intercept the probes from one Taser, but that left his back open. Patsy screamed, but neither Lugh nor I had time to feel even a flicker of satisfaction before the probes from the other Taser took us out of the action.

My optimism turned to bone-chilling fear as Lugh fell. I'd come damn close to being burned at the stake once before, and the situation was looking just as grim now. One of the wackos grabbed Rick's limp body under the arms and started dragging him toward the fireplace. Another bent to grab me.

Everyone—including me—was so focused on the upcoming bonfire that we didn't notice the arrival of the cops until Adam bellowed for everyone to freeze.

Turned out the Sherwoods had been on a police watch list as possible God's Wrath "enforcers," so when Adam had heard the address, he'd immediately had a good idea what might be happening. He'd managed to call in enough heavily armed cops to convince the entire gang to surrender without a fight. Scott Sherwood was too shell-shocked to talk as he was led away in handcuffs, but Patsy was practically foaming at the mouth, shouting disjointed passages of scripture while hurling accusations at me and Rick.

Melanie managed to shuffle her way over to Rick's inert body and brush her bound hands against his cheek before the cops dragged her away from what Patsy claimed was a dangerous demon. I knew that the demon had taken advantage of that brief contact to move back into Melanie. It wasn't a perfect solution, because the cops would be sure to examine us all for demonic possession before any of us was allowed to go home, and Melanie's demon still wasn't legal. But I was pretty sure I could convince Adam to give her a chance to "escape" before an exorcist got a chance to examine her aura.

As the rest of the cops ushered Barbie, Melanie, and Rick up the stairs, treating them with all the caution they were trained to use against potentially dangerous demons, Adam came to kneel beside me. He's capable of a world-class glower, and he was giving it to me full force at the moment. Funny how he always gets so testy when he thinks I'm endangering the life of his king.

The Taser shot was beginning to wear off, and Lugh was still in control. I felt him force my lips into an imitation of a smile.

"Don't be angry with Morgan over this," he slurred. "It's not her fault."

Adam narrowed his eyes, his glare becoming even more furious, which was an impressive feat. "How about you?" he growled. "Can I be angry with *you*? What the fuck did you think you were doing?"

And Lugh—brave, powerful king of the demons that he was— passed control back to me rather than answer.

DOUBLE DEAD

A NIGHT TRACKER NOVELLA

Cheyenne McCray

DEDICATION
To Daniel. All I can say is thank God for you.

Welcome to New York City's Underworld
PRESENT DAY

Dark Elves/Drow: We rock.

Demons: I am *so* through with Demons.

Dopplers: Paranorms who can shift into one specific animal as well as into their human form.

Fae: Should have paid attention during our last case if you wanted to know all of the different races.

Gargoyles: Freaking ugly. And dangerous.

Incubis: No Adonis could begin to compare to these paranorms. Stay. Away.

Light Elves: Mirror, mirror, how art we better than all?

Metamorphs: Slimy paranorms who can take on the persona and appearance of any human and almost any paranorm. And not in a good way. Metamorphs have *no* redeeming qualities. None.

Necromancers: Exactly what you think. They talk to and raise the dead. Creeeeepy.

Shadow Shifters: Paranorms with the ability to shift from human form into shadows.

Shifters: Can transform into any animal of their choosing as well as take their human form.

Succubis: Promise sex good enough to sell your soul for. One word: don't.

Vampires: There's something with these guys that we're missing. . . .

Werewolves: Can take wolf form almost any time, but at the full moon they go nuclear.

Zombies: I do not want to talk about Zombies. You can't make me.

CHAPTER 1

Like a metal ball in one of those old pinball machines Rodán kept at the nightclub, the earth spun. Whirled. Bounced. Pinged. Every time I thought I would rush down into oblivion, something hard would smack me back into a spinning orbit.

What was happening to me?

I couldn't think clearly. My mind wouldn't stop spinning like that metal ball. Where was I? Why did I feel like that tiny pinball had smashed me like a wrecking ball? My whole body was one big mass of pain. I felt fluid trickling from my nose and over my lips, and tasted blood.

"Look at me, Tracker." At the sound of the male's voice I started. Could a voice be hard and cold, yet amused at the same time? Apparently it could. "Now, *Tracker.*"

I opened my eyes and tried to focus on what I saw in front of me. The images of three human males were wavering and trying to merge into one. Finally they became one and my head spun a little less. The male was dressed like an NYPD officer, and he was holding a baton streaked with blood. My blood.

The smell of alyssum, like newly mown hay, meant there was a Metamorph close. The strength of the smell told me there was more than one. At least two, maybe three. Despite my muddled state, I was pretty sure the male I was staring at was a Metamorph. Or rather I was looking at the reflection of the human whose appearance the Metamorph had taken.

"Thought I'd get the beating out of the way." The male snapped his baton, then returned it to its place on his duty belt. "You'll be less likely to draw out a game that you'll lose . . . Nyx of the Dark Elves and Night Tracker."

Connect the dots, Nyx.

I knew I was in my human form because I sensed it was still daylight and I felt the differences in my body. How did the Metamorphs know how to find me during the day or even know that I was a Night Tracker?

Night Trackers patrolled their territories to make sure scum like Metamorphs who broke the laws were eliminated or taken off the street and put into the detention center. The Metamorph's or other paranorm's punishment depended on the severity of the crime.

Then bits and pieces of memory came back to me as my thoughts began to clear. Chills rolled through my body.

I'd been waiting in my apartment for Adam to drop by for a little afternoon recreation. But when he got there, something had seemed wrong, out of place. I'd been so excited to see Adam, thinking about his adorable tousled hair and his boyish smile, that at first I didn't notice that he didn't smell of coffee and leather like usual.

Without bothering to close the door, he grabbed me to him and kissed me—

He'd tasted like grass. Dry, dust-coated grass.

Not Adam. Not Adam!

I stared at the man while thoughts of how they had captured me flashed through my mind. My stomach churned.

When he kissed me, my first reaction had been to jerk away from the being that was not my Adam. I wanted to puke from kissing what I realized was a Metamorph.

Realized too late.

He had a gun to my temple before I could blink. The gun didn't faze me. Even in my human form I could have taken out a single Metamorph.

Eight more Metamorphs rushed through the open doorway. In my Drow form, with my Drow strength, my dragon-clawed daggers, and my elemental magic, I could have taken on all of them. Even in my human form I would have been hard to beat.

Right now I wanted to shake my head, shake off the memory. But my head hurt too much to move it. Metamorphs had gotten me. *Metamorphs.*

They'd caught me completely off guard, everything amplified by my shock and revulsion because I'd just kissed a being who was not Adam. A disgusting Metamorph. The fact that the being had managed to get that close to me, without my realizing what he really was, had added to the shock.

Before I'd been able to call the air to aid me, one of the Metamorphs slapped a cloth over my nose. That was the last thing I remembered before this moment.

The fog in my mind started to clear. Thoughts of how I'd been captured and what was happening now raced through my head so fast that I was almost dizzy from them. What were the Metamorphs doing? What did they want? Where was Adam?

I glared at the Metamorph. I wanted my hands around him in front of me so badly I could almost feel myself squeezing his neck. Feel it snapping. I attempted to lunge forward but my arms jerked against chains and metal cuffs bit into my wrists. The legs of the chair I was in scraped the floor as I struggled. I snarled and tried to lash out with my feet. They wouldn't move. Metal ankle cuffs dug into my skin.

When I looked down at my shackled ankles, my long, tangled black hair fell over my eyes. Blood dripped from my nose onto my

Dior pale cream blouse and slacks. My clothing was torn, bloody, filthy. My Pradas were missing, leaving my feet bare.

When I fisted my hands, the tension caused me to fully take in the fact that they'd beaten me while I was out cold.

The elements. I could take care of this whole situation and be done with it. A small cyclone would do.

My first shot at controlling the elements told me that the handcuffs that bound me were treated with elemental magic. My second attempt just reaffirmed that fact.

The specially made cuffs weren't supposed to affect Trackers. They'd all been altered to recognize every Tracker in New York City so that our magic wouldn't be affected. How had these Metamorphs been able to contain me? I couldn't use the elements at all.

I frowned in concentration. Maybe I had to shift into my Drow half before the cuffs would have no effect on me and I could use my elements again. I was Nyx Ciar, paranorm PI during the day. After sundown I would be Nyx of the Night Trackers.

It wouldn't be long now, though. I sensed that nightfall would be soon—none of them would be getting out of this place alive once I was through with them.

My hair was in my eyes and stuck to the blood on my cheeks when I raised my head.

Instead of some windowless interrogation room, we were in a large kitchen with peeling wallpaper and cracked and chipped laminated flooring. I was sitting in the middle of the cramped space. A dining table was shoved against one wall along with three brown wooden chairs, the varnish darkened with age and worn in places. Apparently I was in chair number four.

I almost smiled when I saw the stove three feet away on my right and the sink two and a half feet away on my left. Fire. Water.

If I could get out of these cuffs I'd be able to use the elements of fire and water and either toast or drown these creeps.

I was leaning toward the idea of toasting them.

"Hello, Tracker filth." The male crouched in front of me. Instantly, from his powerful alyssum smell, I knew that he *was* a Metamorph. "I'm Tom Smith. I'm going to let you watch me cut your boyfriend into itty-bitty pieces."

Fear for Adam along with instinct drove me to try to lunge for Smith's throat. The chair rocked but I wanted to scream with rage as my bindings held me fast.

"Underworld sloth." I glared at the Metamorph. "The pieces I cut off of you won't be so tiny if you dare hurt him."

Smith slapped my bruised face so hard that my head snapped to the side. The pain caused by gritting my teeth, to not cry out, was worth it as I turned slowly to glare at him again.

He scowled as he wiped his palm on his black jeans. "Detective Adam Boyd's life is getting shorter every minute you mess with me, Tracker."

"What. Do. You. Want?" My face hurt as I hurled each word at the Metamorph.

"I was misinformed about the whereabouts of tonight's Paranorm Council meeting." His question surprised me enough to cause me to blink. "The council gathers at sundown and my men are ready to greet them on my order."

"What do Metamorphs care about the Paranorm Council?" Disgust edged every word I spoke. "Metamorphs don't even have a representative."

By the way his hands shook, I was pretty sure Smith was holding back his anger, trying to control himself this time. "That will change."

"Yeah, right." I gave a hollow laugh. "Like that's going to happen."

He lost a good portion of that control and slapped the side of my head so hard my ear rang from the force of it. "Tell me now or you die, Tracker. So does your boyfriend."

I had to stall somehow. If I could keep him busy until sundown I would likely get my powers back. "How do you know if I'm a Tracker or not?"

"We have informants." Smith gave a casual shrug. "We know you are a human PI for the paranormal world during the day. By night you become a Tracker."

I narrowed my gaze. "Why me?"

"You are one of the very few paranorms who can come out in daylight." He grinned. "And you're predictable."

Predictable? As a PI, maybe I was. That was going to have to change.

I said nothing, just stared at him. I didn't know if he was bluffing about Adam, so I had to call his bluff. I almost groaned when he drew out his baton and snapped it to its full length.

"Carl." Smith looked up, somewhere over my shoulder, and made a slight motion with his head. By the smell of alyssum, I knew it was another Metamorph who moved in front of me. Also dressed in an NYPD uniform, "Carl" looked and walked like a flesh-and-bone version of Robocop. Built like a muscle-bound weight lifter, he was slow to move. "Get Detective Boyd," Smith said.

My heart pounded and my body radiated with tension. The bulky Metamorph headed through an archway of the place we were in, his boot steps loud against the tile floor before the sound finally faded.

Steps, sounding like high heels, came from the other side of the archway just moments after the Robocop Metamorph left. I continued to stare at the archway, and another Metamorph walked in.

With rich waves of mahogany brown hair and big gray eyes, this Metamorph was gorgeous—or at least the replica of the human or paranorm she mirrored was. And she knew how to dress. I'd give up my XPhone if she wasn't tottering in Ferragamo pumps and carrying a matching satchel.

Despite her sophisticated, beautiful looks, the fake innocence in her eyes and her pouty lips made her look like a spoiled, pampered brat.

"Becky." Smith went to the woman and hugged her in a way that made their relationship obvious. He kissed her before he pinched her ass cheek through the fine organza of her dress.

"Have I missed anything?" she said in a voice so squeaky it caused me to wince.

Footsteps again, only this time I heard two pairs—one stepping purposefully, the other shuffling unsteadily. I glanced back at the archway in time to see the muscle-bound Metamorph shove Adam into the room. The man I loved was shirtless, his body and face bloody and bruised.

Adam collapsed face-first on the tile.

And didn't move.

CHAPTER 2

Adam!" His name cut the air in an involuntary shout. I couldn't have stopped myself from calling out to my lover if I'd tried.

I lunged against my bonds again and this time I nearly toppled my chair. Smith grabbed a spindle of the chair and kept me from pitching forward.

My breath burned harsh and heavy in my chest. "You might as well start thinking up your last words." I turned my glare to Smith as I spoke with slow, deliberate malice. "You don't have very many left."

Almost imperceptible fear glittered in his black eyes before he laughed. A forced laugh that almost made me smile. He was scared of me, and I had to give him credit for not being stupid enough to make the mistake of totally disregarding what I might be capable of.

Adam groaned, and a tempest of emotions whirled through me as I swung my attention in his direction: relief that he was alive, followed by anger that he'd been hurt so badly, shifting into fear as Robocop Carl aimed a handgun at Adam's head.

"It is a very important council meeting tonight." Smith crouched so that he was eye level with me. "What location has the meeting been changed to?"

A trickle of blood rolled down the column of my throat from an open wound on the side of my head. "What are you going to do?"

Smith scowled. "What do you care, Tracker? You treat all Metamorphs like scum."

I pulled against my bonds so that my body was a fraction closer to him. He looked like he wanted to shrink back. "You're so slimy the only thing you're good for is greasing machinery. But you'd screw that up, too."

The Metamorph's complexion turned a really odd shade of taupe. Smith unsheathed a dagger from his cop duty belt. The sharp edge gleamed in the kitchen light. He grabbed a handful of my hair and jerked my head back so that I was looking at the ceiling, which was yellowed and dirty from years of cooking in a cramped space.

"Tell me, or we can use the human cop's brains to grease the floor." Smith bared his teeth in a freakish smile as he leaned over me, blocking my view of the ceiling. I felt the cold, sharp edge of the dagger's blade as he pressed it against my throat. "Where has the meeting been moved to?"

I didn't dare swallow, knowing the blade would slice into my throat. The feeling of helplessness I experienced was not one I'd faced often. I heard a round being chambered in a handgun, and my heart started pounding hard enough that the sound of it throbbed in my ears.

"Now, Tracker." Smith jerked my hair harder. "Tell me, or that's it for both you and your human playtoy. After all, that's what the human is to you, isn't he?"

Sundown was approaching and I would be shifting within twenty minutes. I couldn't think of any way to stall without getting myself or Adam killed. I'd just have to take care of the problem then. But for now what choice did I have?

"It's still at the Paranorm Center near the northern end of Conservatory Water." I couldn't help swallowing and gasped as the dagger bit into my flesh. "Below the Alice in Wonderland unbirthday party sculpture."

The Metamorph narrowed his gaze but released his grip on my hair. "We were told the location had changed."

"It was a ruse." I raised my head as he backed up. "There were rumors that some kind of interruption might happen, but the council members didn't want to move the meeting. So to make sure no one would try to barge in, they put out the word it had changed."

My gut churned as I glanced at Adam and he groaned and rolled onto his side. Carl still held his gun with its sights aimed right at him.

I didn't feel my own aches and pains. Instead it was as if I felt every bruise on Adam's body as I stared at him.

"I actually believe you." Smith turned and walked away from me. He glanced over his shoulder at me. "Now to put my plan into action."

"Metamorphs won't be screwed around with anymore." Smith drew a Glock from his cop's duty belt and aimed it at Adam's head. "And I'm finished screwing with you, Tracker." Smith leveled his gaze on Adam. "If you lied to me, here's what will happen to your friend DeSantos."

"Olivia?" I said, but then my mind spun as Smith's aim followed Adam's movements as my lover shifted and groaned again.

Smith squeezed the trigger.

A loud report echoed in the kitchen.

I screamed.

Blood splattered the kitchen walls.

Horror and shock made my head spin as Adam's body slumped facedown in a lifeless mass on the floor.

"You—" I gagged on useless words as I stared at Adam's body. In my mind spun thoughts of *You promised* and *You lied*. Stupid, worthless words.

"Have your fun, Carl," I heard Smith say, but his words were muffled by the emotions flaring in my mind.

Fury grew inside me along with the pain I felt at Adam's murder. The feelings were so great, so intense, that for a moment I thought I might be able to break free of the elemental cuffs now and make Smith pay for what he'd done.

I fought my bonds and snarled as I turned to look back at Smith. He was gone.

"Aw." The female Metamorph, Becky, moved toward me like a sleek cat. Her high-pitched little girl voice made me want to strangle her. "Did your human playtoy go bye-bye?"

The Drow curse words I let rip the air would have cut her to pieces if they had been knives.

"Tom is a brilliant male." Becky smiled as she toyed with a heart charm bracelet on her slim wrist. "After tonight, not only will Metamorphs have a place on the council, but Tom will be elected by the council as chief."

"Have you taken your delusional pill?" I said as I stared at her. "Because you're not in any existing reality."

"His plan is perfect." She maintained her amused smile. "All he needed to know was the exact location before sundown because everyone is ready to play their part."

For now I had to ignore what had happened to Adam and try to figure out what was going on so that I could stop the Metamorphs. Whatever it was, it wasn't good. "Play what parts?" I asked.

Becky sat on one of the chairs near me and crossed her legs at her knees. "As each council member arrives at the entrance to the Paranorm Center, a Metamorph will be waiting to take his or her place. The only one who won't be replaced will be the chief. She's needed to conduct the meeting and to report our victory afterward, you see."

Robocop Carl looked nervous. "Miss Becky—"

The female waved him off. "The council guards will also be replaced. Counsel Chief Leticia and the Dryads will never know the difference."

Chills turned into goose bumps that prickled my skin. "Then what?" I asked very slowly.

She gave a delicate shrug. "The meeting will be held and votes will be cast as to whether to allow Metamorphs on the council. The meeting was already set to include determining whether or not Witches can be represented on the council. Allowing Metamorphs on will be like letting the Witches have a representative." She gave a triumphant grin. "It's a perfect plan."

"Why do Metamorphs even care?" I asked. "Metamorphs have never been interested in or adhered to paranorm rules."

I was already thinking she was one eraser short of a pencil, and that was made even more clear by the giddy expression on her face. "Respect!" She punctuated the word as she pointed at me, and I winced from the shrillness of her voice, which grated on me like gravel beneath the tires of my 'Vette. "And we want Trackers to back off. When the replacement council votes that we are not to be touched, nothing can stop us from taking over human lives." She stroked her Ferragamo purse. "Like those of the wealthiest men in the city. We can mirror anyone and take over his life."

"And kill the real human," I said, disgust filling me. "Then not only are you leeches but you are murderers, too."

Then my eyes widened and my jaw dropped. I don't know why it hadn't occurred to me earlier. Shock, incredulity over the whole situation—it didn't matter. "You're going to kill the real council members, aren't you?" I said it with disbelief, yet with the realization that my conclusion was true.

"Took you that long to figure it out?" Becky laughed as she stood and looked at Robocop Carl. "Tom did say you could have your fun with her."

Carl grinned at me in a way that made my stomach curdle.

It was then that I sensed the sun was going down.

And Robo-Carl was going down.

Becky would be taken care of, too.

Then it would be Smith's turn.

As I sensed the sun disappearing and the city become immersed in the night, the cuffs fell away from my ankles and wrists. The clatter on the floor startled Carl, who aimed his Glock at me. Becky stumbled back in her high heels.

The sleeves of my blouse tightened slightly around my arms and at my shoulders as my body grew stronger and the muscles in my slender arms became more defined. I wished I had my leather fighting suit as I rose from my chair. I ripped the sleeves from my shirt so that my arms were bare and less constricted.

My body continued to transform into my Drow appearance as I jerked each sleeve off. Expressions of shock and panic were on their faces as my once fair skin turned into a faint shade of amethyst. The tangled hair I pushed away from my face was cobalt blue now instead of black. My incisors lengthened into petite fangs.

Every ache and pain from the beatings vanished as my body healed during the transformation.

Fury built within me, and now I fed it with my elements. The room began to shake, windowpanes rattling as the earth beneath the building started to buck. Kitchen cupboard doors slammed open and closed. Ceramic plates, bowls, mugs, flew off shelves and smashed to shards on the aged linoleum.

Drawers rolled in and out. One drawer filled with silverware spilled every knife, fork, and spoon onto the floor. They rattled and clattered in tune with the pots and pans secured above the stove.

A sack of flour landed with a thud outside the pantry and coated Becky and Carl in white.

Becky let out a scream and landed on her ass on the linoleum, which was now cracking from the force of the earthquake I had created.

Carl swung his gaze around the room as he stumbled against a counter and dropped to his knees. His eyes were wide and filled with shock as he swung the gun from the archway to me and back again. His hands were shaking as he tried to hold on to the Glock. "If—if you're doing this you'd better stop it, bitch."

The room continued to rock and Carl had to brace one of his hands on the floor. Becky screamed again and huddled in a corner, her palms braced to either side of her in an effort to keep from rolling across the bucking floor. Dark Elves are lithe, our footing perfect, and I easily kept on my feet.

Loud snaps from wood cracking came from the door frame. I directed my air elemental magic at the frame. I used my element to rip a sword-length shard of wood. At my command, my magic propelled the shaft straight at Carl.

His gun clattered to the floor as he flung his hands over his face.

The jagged point of the staff pierced his hands and buried itself in his head.

Becky screamed again, horror on her face.

I ignored Carl's body as he collapsed onto the linoleum, and I ignored Becky's continued screams. I released my control of the elements. The ground beneath the building settled and everything went still.

Keeping Becky within sight, I moved toward Adam. I dropped to my knees beside his body.

My heart felt like it had cracked like a wooden plank, then burned to cinders. If Dark Elves could cry, my face would have been flooded with tears. My eyes ached, and with everything I had I wished I could cry. I grasped Adam's shoulder and moved him just enough so that I could see his precious face—with his sightless eyes. My hand shook as I reached for him and started to close his eyelids.

I went still. The smell of alyssum was so strong I almost gagged. The moldy odor of wet, ruined hay rushed over me, a smell given off by a dead Metamorph. This wasn't Adam. This was a Metamorph who had taken on Adam's appearance.

Confusion, then relief, made my head spin. My thoughts raced. If this wasn't Adam, where was he? Had they killed him already? *Please let Adam be okay.*

"Nyx!" Olivia's voice came from the doorway, and I jerked my head up to see my partner there. More relief touched me as I saw her. She looked fine, and this dead male beside me wasn't Adam.

"Come on." She cocked her head in the direction she had come from, and the kitchen light caressed her skin, which was like flawless brown silk. "We need to hurry. Something big is going down at the Paranorm Center."

I registered four things at once in a rapid flash.

Olivia was human and didn't know about the Paranorm Center.

Olivia didn't talk that way. She would normally have told me I looked like hell and to stop screwing around and get my ass down where I was needed.

Olivia was wearing a plain T-shirt. Just a plain black T-shirt. She *never* wore plain shirts. Ever. The shirts always had sayings like the one she'd had on this morning—

I sometimes go to my own little world, but that's okay. They know me there.

And this female smelled like alyssum.

No way in all of the Underworlds was this Olivia.

I dove for the pile of silverware that had scattered across the floor. I grabbed a steak knife and rolled onto my back.

I flung the knife across the room. It flipped end over end and then buried itself in the fake Olivia's heart.

CHAPTER 3

Becky's screaming was like a shrill alarm clock in the background. I was tempted to shut her off, but she was nothing more than an ignorant pawn, who hadn't tried to kill me, which meant I had to return the favor. Still, I kept her in my peripheral vision just in case.

I started toward the archway where the not-Olivia had crumpled to the floor. I automatically reached for one of my dragon-clawed daggers when I realized I was still in human clothes and wasn't wearing my weapons belt. I ground my teeth. It wasn't likely they'd had the courtesy to bring my handbag along with me, much less my leather fighting suit and weapons.

Rodán and the other Trackers needed to know what was going down, and I needed backup.

"Give me your handbag." I held my hand in Becky's direction. The flour-coated simpleton stopped screaming as she grabbed her purse from off the floor and clutched it to her. Idiot. Facing her possible demise and she was protecting her Ferragamo purse from me. She had only one of her matching heels on; the other was near Carl's body.

With my hand still extended, I scowled at her. The floor started to rock again and Becky screamed and threw her handbag at me.

I caught it and she yelped as I jerked the purse open in a not-so-delicate manner. I dug through it, found her cell phone, then dropped the purse on the floor. Becky started to scramble toward it but stopped when she got a good look at my expression.

That's right, lady. Don't mess with a pissed-off blue-haired amethyst female Tracker.

A sense of urgency made my skin feel like ants were crawling over me. I flipped the phone open and called our Proctor, Rodán, who was also my mentor and former lover.

It didn't take me long to explain everything to Rodán. He pinpointed my location by the cell phone signal and would send the Paranormal Task Force to clean up the mess and take care of Becky.

I would have called Adam, who was an NYPD detective, or Olivia, but both were human and couldn't enter—or know about—the Paranorm Center. Chills prickled my arms. I didn't even know if Adam was alive. Or Olivia for that matter. Had the Metamorphs gotten to my lover or my partner?

I pocketed the cell phone, scooped Carl's gun up from the floor, then grabbed the elemental-magic-treated wrist and ankle cuffs. My eyes narrowed and my jaw set, I approached Becky.

"No!" Her high-pitched voice was a squeak. "Don't hurt me!"

"Shut up." I knelt in front of her, grabbed one of her wrists, and cuffed her to the handle on the door of the pantry. For good measure I cuffed her ankles, too. The PTF would be here in no time and take care of her.

I stepped over the dead doubles of Adam's and Olivia's bodies before rushing through the archway. Pictures had fallen off the walls, lamps had toppled from end tables, glass from broken picture frames had shattered on the carpet from my mini-earthquake.

From the looks of the place, the Metamorphs had taken over some human's apartment. The front door of the small place was steps away. I tucked the handgun in my waistband and was out that door within seconds.

I jogged down a set of stairs and pushed my way through a pair of double doors. Cool winter air filled my lungs as I ran around the building until I reached a fairly busy street. Amsterdam, close to West Forty-second Street. Now I had to get to the Paranorm Center which was below the Alice in Wonderland unbirthday party sculptures in Central Park on the Upper East Side.

I pulled a glamour, making myself invisible to humans—who might freak at an amethyst woman with blue hair—and ran. As my bare feet met slush and snow, I wished desperately for my leather boots. Dark Elves generally don't have a problem with cold, but having bare feet in polluted slush from melted snow was on the chilly side.

My air element helped push me faster than my already enhanced speed. I would have been a blur to humans if they could have seen me.

When I finally reached the unbirthday party sculptures, Angel was already there. She was walking the circumference of the sculpture counterclockwise, reciting the engraved nonsensical poem to open the door. " ' 'Twas brillig, and the slithy toves did gyre and gimble in the wabe.' " I had no idea what the poem was supposed to mean, but it would open the door beneath the toadstool.

Angel was a beautiful blond Doppler with corkscrew curls and was a squirrel in her animal form. She looked like a bubbly cheerleader but had graduated from Harvard and had been an intern with NASA.

"Have any other Trackers made it here?" I asked when I came to a full stop.

"Not that I know of." Angel was now at the back of the sculpture, and the door beneath the toadstool began to open. She scanned me with her brilliant blue eyes. "You look amazingly healthy considering your clothing is bloody rags. Kind of like you've been engaged in some one-on-one with a leopard and he got in a few good licks."

"We have to hurry." I didn't have time to go into anything but what we were here for. "If the information I was given is correct, they've already replaced the council members, and that leaves us with two tasks."

"Find the real council members," Angel said.

"And stop the charade going on now." I glanced into the darkened park. "We'll take care of this. Other Trackers will have to save the real council members."

We started down the winding set of stone stairs. "How did the Metamorphs find out that the council meeting is really being held here and not at another location?" Angel asked.

"Long story." Inside I groaned. The Metamorphs had tricked me by making me believe that was my Adam they'd had as their captive. I'd spilled it out of fear for him—but I'd also been sure I would have the opportunity to escape come sundown. And I would stop the Metamorphs.

The Paranorm Center was a throwback to the Otherworld most of us originated from, some centuries, if not thousands of years, ago. Everything reminded me of home in the belowground realm of the Dark Elves . . . so *medieval*.

Torches flared to life to light the way into the darkness as the door slid shut behind us. Dark Elves have incredible night vision and I didn't have to watch my step as I took the twisting turns of the rock staircase, which went almost as deep into the earth as the Realm of the Drow was in Otherworld.

When we reached the bottom we were in the enormous main foyer, which had five separate archways. We paused and then each took a side of the archway that would lead us to the main area of Paranorm Center. The massive hallway was empty. Quiet. The council chamber doors were closed.

"Some sentries they are," Angel said beneath her breath as we looked at the Dryads sleeping in their towering wooden columns. "Their sense of smell sucks or they would have identified the Metamorphs."

"I'd bet my cat that the guards that are usually inside the council chambers are Metamorph replacements, too," I said.

Angel rolled her eyes. "That's no stretch. I'm not even sure you like that blue Persian."

Very possible. Kali had shredded so many of my Victoria's Secret panties that I'd probably take a turtle in trade for the snotty cat.

The council doors were thick and heavy enough to completely mute any sound or voice inside. "I think they might consider backup security after this."

I was wishing for one of my dragon-clawed daggers when Angel said, "You could use this." When I turned my gaze to her, she carefully tossed a wicked-looking eighteen-inch-long dagger to me so that I caught it by the hilt.

With a quick nod of thanks, I slipped around the archway, wielding Angel's dagger in my right hand.

"Halt." A deep but musical bass of a voice sounded like thunder in the great hall and I came to a stop. "You are not allowed to wield any form of weapon here," an ancient Dryad said from one of the thick columns. "You know this, Trackers."

We didn't have time to argue. "Who passed this way most recently?" I asked.

The Dryad narrowed her brow. "I do not answer to you, Tracker."

"My apologies." I wanted to scream with frustration. "All we can tell you is that Metamorphs have probably taken council members hostage and their doubles are inside the council chamber in their places."

Dryad whispers echoed up and down the hallway at my words. The Dryads had no way of confirming this, because the Paranorm Council was *para*noid about any of its discussions being overheard.

Who knew—the mystery of the chamber could be that it was actually a spa where council members all got foot massages and pedicures. No one could really say what went on behind those doors, and council members kept their meetings secret. All we heard out of them was an occasional ruling, a new law, or a modification of an existing paranorm law.

The Dryad nodded, the creak of wood accompanying her movements. Angel and I hurried to the enormous council chamber doors.

"Open," bellowed the vibrating voice of the Dryad we had been speaking with.

The council chamber doors swung open.

Six male and female council members turned their heads to look at us.

I sucked in my breath. Now would have been a really good time to have employed a little stealth.

No thanks to the Dryad who had opened the doors to the chambers without giving us a chance to assess the situation. Dryads have no tact and no sense of battle strategy.

From the corner of my eye I saw that Angel wasn't there any longer. It was no surprise to see a blond squirrel's bushy tail disappearing beneath the council's draped semicircular table.

The strong odor of alyssum emanated from the room, which could only mean Metamorphs. How could the Dryads have missed it, even if they aren't known for their keen scent of smell?

Light flickered from wall sconces throughout the room. The torchlight cast shadows across the dim room, giving an almost eerie feel to the place. It smelled faintly of smoke and crushed rose petals.

I gripped Angel's dagger, and in a quick scan I saw two guards at the back of the room, and I saw that the Metamorphs had done well in replacing five of the six council members. If I hadn't known they were replacements. I wouldn't have known the difference.

Chief Council Member Leticia—the real Chief, not a Metamorph—looked both perplexed and upset at first glance, as if something wasn't going right. Leticia, a Doppler, perched on a throne at the center of the crescent-shaped table, and she also represented all others of her race; the Drow and Light Elves had one delegate who served on the council for both of our races; a Siren had been voted in by the Fae to represent all fifteen-plus races of Fae; a Shifter was in attendance for all Shifters; a Werewolf was the envoy for all Weres; and a Vampire represented his kind.

In the mere moment it took me to process all of this, I saw that to the side of the council table, in a chair beside a witness stand, was a black-haired Witch dressed in a white sparkling beaded dress. The sophisticated-looking Witch had a pensive, almost confused expression. No doubt she was the real deal and had been appointed to represent all Witches in their appeal to be on the council . . . and this council meeting was not going according to normal standards.

And on the witness stand—

Smith.

The head Metamorph flashed me a look of complete shock; blood drained from his face. So this was how the Metamorphs were planning to get Smith on the council. He represented his entire race to gain admittance, while all of the council members had been replaced by Metamorphs with the exception of Leticia. He couldn't lose.

But I was going to shut him down.

My rapid appraisal ended with my gaze meeting Chief Councillor Leticia's.

"Tracker." Leticia frowned from her center perch. "Leave at once. This session is not public."

"These aren't the real council members." My voice rang through the hall as I spoke. "They're all Metamorphs. They've kidnapped the real members."

A prickle raced up my spine. I caught a flash of silver in the corner of my eye. I ducked into a crouch. A Dryad screamed from inside a wooden pillar as a dagger buried itself in her midsection.

Damn. I had moved instinctively and hadn't realized a Dryad was behind me.

I turned to see two guards coming at me from the great hall. A low growl rolled from inside me along with my fury. The dangerous white light flashed in my eyes as the poor young Dryad sobbed and sap bled from her belly. I would kill the guards just for what they'd done to the Dryad.

One of the guards had a bow, a gold-feathered shaft nocked in it. The arrowhead glinted in the light cast from the chambers as the guard let it loose. I reached up and caught the arrow, then flung it back at the guard, my air element pushing it even faster than my own power.

I pierced the guard through the heart all the way up to the golden feathers.

"What in the name of—," Leticia shouted from her seat.

Angel transformed from her squirrel form and appeared behind the chief council member. She yanked Leticia out of her seat and pushed her under the table. "Stay down!" Angel shouted at the Doppler. "These Metamorphs will kill you."

I was aware of everything, but it all happened so fast it was a blur.

The guard who had thrown the dagger came charging forward, brandishing a sword. The floor rocked as I ordered my earth element to shift through the stone hall floor. A crack in the stone tripped the guard. With another command my air element twisted both the guard and the blade so that the guard landed on his own sword and severed his neck to his spine.

Angel battled three of the five Metamorph imposters. Her side kick sent one sprawling across the room. She grabbed the arm of a female Metamorph and flipped her onto her back. The third, Angel grabbed by the head and snapped his neck.

At the same time I was fighting off the two guards and the other two fake council members who came at me from inside the chamber.

One guard had a gun and I flattened myself to the floor. As he missed me, I rolled toward the other guard, tripped him, and gutted him with Angel's dagger.

A Metamorph jumped on me but I flipped onto my back, grabbed him by the head, and rammed my knee into his face. He screamed and blood and tears flushed down his face as I broke his nose and his jaw.

The fourth Metamorph had a gun, too, and he and the first guard began shooting at me.

I wrapped myself in a cocoon of my air element and called to fire.

Torch flames from inside the council chambers roared into fiery life. A dragon of fire swooped down and swallowed the guard and the Metamorph, burning them to ash as it carried them down the great hallway.

Another guard came out of nowhere.

Before I had a chance to do anything, a burst of green light came from the Witch. Plant tentacles wrapped themselves around the guard, taking away his ability to move.

A green Witch. I glanced up at her intense face. Witches never killed, but they would fight to protect themselves or others using whatever power they commanded. Hers obviously came from nature.

All thoughts and actions happened within moments.

Seven down. I glanced in Angel's direction. Her three were down. That left Smith.

I cut my gaze to the witness stand.

Smith was gone.

Warning chills scrabbled up and down my body.

Too late.

Fiery lead pierced my abdomen and then my thigh before I could react. Blood flowed from the bullet wounds.

Smith had slipped out of the melee and around to my side.

Pain seared me like my fire element had seared the two men.

I gritted my teeth and forward flipped twice toward Smith.

Shock was on Smith's face as I knocked the gun from his hand, grabbed his head, and slammed my forehead against his.

"Stop. Please." His begging only made me angrier. "We'll go away. You'll never see us again."

I jerked his head down with my fists full of his hair. I rammed my knee up and into his face just before I snapped his neck.

For a moment, silence filled the chamber and the hall. Dead bodies. Blood everywhere. Cracked floor. Destroyed furniture. Burnt clothes and bones. Stench of charred flesh. Odor of rotting, molding hay.

It was over.

As my eyes met Angel's, I started to feel dizzy. I looked down and blood was flowing freely from my abdomen.

Two Dryads left their columns and caught me from behind as I slumped.

Then passed out.

CHAPTER 4

What happened to you?" Olivia eyed me up and down as I pushed open the door to our PI office; the Fae bells jingled as the door slid shut. "Get sucked in through a jet engine this morning?"

"Feel like it." I'd taken a shower and dressed in fresh clothing, but I did feel like I'd gotten caught in a helicopter's rotors.

I grinned when I saw Olivia's T-shirt.

Where are we going and why are we in this handbasket?

The real Olivia.

I wanted to hug her but I knew she'd get even by shooting me with one of her eraser-loaded rubber bands.

Last night I'd made sure Adam and Olivia were okay by having a couple of other Trackers check in on them. After being shot, I couldn't do anything until I shifted back into my human form. To say I was relieved when I was told they were okay—well, we'll just keep it to "that's an understatement."

"So tell me why you look like you got chewed up and spit out in little pieces," she said.

"I'm fine. Just a rough night tracking." I smiled my way through my aches and pains. It's much easier to heal when shifting from human to Drow than it is shifting from Drow to human. I'd mostly healed from my wounds, but not totally. What was more important was that Olivia was here and well. "I am so glad you're okay."

Olivia gave me one of her *looks*. "And why wouldn't I be . . . ?"

That made me feel even better. If she didn't know, then nothing had happened to her at all. "Nothing."

Olivia frowned.

I set my handbag on my Dryad-made wooden desk and a pang went through me at the thought of the young Dryad who'd been shot last night. The Healers weren't sure she was going to survive.

"What happened?" Olivia narrowed her gaze. When I shrugged she grabbed an eraser from the stash on her desk and loaded it into a rubber band. "Tell me *now*."

I held up my hands in mock surrender. "Metamorphs. They went a little crazy last night."

"Metamorphs?" Olivia looked like she was going to laugh. "Since when did one of them grow a backbone?"

"They chose last night to do it." I drew my phone out of my handbag, and the worry that had been biting at me all morning snapped at me. "I need to call Adam again. I haven't been able to reach him."

"Hold on." Olivia pulled on her loaded rubber band. "Tell me everything first."

Fae bells tinkled and I cut my attention to the front door. "Adam!" I dropped my phone into my bag, ran to him, and flung my arms around his neck. His leather and coffee scent was so good, so familiar, that I breathed deep before I said, "You're okay. Olivia's okay."

"Hey." Adam caught me by my waist and I winced when he pressed one of his thumbs into my abdomen, right where the bullet had gone in. "Feeling better this morning?"

"What?" I looked up at him, confused. Adam didn't know what had happened. Couldn't have.

"Last night you said you weren't feeling well so you didn't want me to come over," he said. "We were going to watch *Body Double* before you went tracking."

I laughed even though it hurt my belly.

An eraser pinged off my backside and I looked at Olivia, who'd loaded another one. "Start talking, Nyx."

I told them both *most* of what had happened last night. No matter that they were two of the people I cared most about here or in Otherworld, I was sworn to secrecy about the Paranorm Center—humans were never to know about it.

"Why didn't you call us?" Olivia asked when I finished massaging my story to the part about getting shot. She put her hand on her own handgun. "I don't like it when you leave me out of things, and you know it."

"That's right, Nyx." Adam's voice was calmer than Olivia's, but it held disapproval, too.

"It all happened so fast that I didn't have time to call you," I said, looking from Olivia to Adam. "That's the truth." More or less.

Another eraser pinged off of me, this time off the back of my head.

"No wonder you were worried something happened to me and Olivia." Adam took me by my arms and ran his hands up and down them, causing a pleasant shiver to skim my body. "What happened to the real council members?"

"Two other Trackers—Ice and Joshua—located them," I said as I rubbed my scalp. "Wiped out the Metamorphs who'd kidnapped the council members, and saved the hostages."

"Thank God everything worked out all right." Adam brought me into his arms and hugged me. I winced again. I hadn't told them the part about getting shot.

"I know my job." I wrapped my arms around Adam's waist. "But thank you both for caring."

I knew another eraser was headed my way and I turned my head just enough to see it and catch it. She gave me one of her looks.

Adam cupped my face in his hands and brushed his lips across mine. "I think that what Olivia's telling you is that it goes without saying that we care about you."

A happy sigh filled me, and I breathed him in as I rested my head against his chest before rising up to kiss him.

"Give it a rest and get to work," Olivia said, and I turned to watch her shove another file on top of the ones teetering on her desk. "We got a call first thing. Something about a Succubus. I stuck a note on your desk. Check it out with Rodán."

"Succubus . . ." I kissed Adam one more time, then headed toward my desk, which was covered in pink sticky notes. "Now this ought to be interesting."

A ROSE BY ANY OTHER NAME WOULD STILL BE RED

Elizabeth A. Vaughan

Red gave a quick tug at her black leather gloves before she pounded on the ironbound wooden door. Her breath hung heavy in the cool, misty night.

Muffled voices came from within the guardhouse. She puffed out a breath impatiently, adjusting her black cloak to cover her armor.

"Try talking first." The High Baron had said. *"Use your blade only if words fail."*

A slot opened at eye level on the wooden door. "The slave market's closed," came a growl. "Come back at first light."

"Message from Swift's Port," Red said softly. That made the damn slaver pause, as she'd known it would.

The one eye she could see squinted at her. "Who be you?"

"What does that matter?" Red snapped. "Since I've never been here, and I've orders to deliver it direct? Open the damn door, I'm freezing my ass off out here."

The eye blinked, and then the slot closed. There were more muffled noises, talk mostly. Three of them, from the sound of it.

Good. She could handle three well enough.

A rattle, then the door opened just wide enough for her to slip inside the hot, stuffy room.

The place was dark, lit only by flickering oil lamps and the fire in the hearth. A table, a few chairs. Red wrinkled her nose at the smell.

Sweat, smoke, and underlying it all, the acrid scent that went with selling slaves.

There was a rope dangling from the ceiling in the corner behind the door. The warning bell, no doubt.

"Master ain't gonna like it, being disturbed this late," the man muttered as he secured the door behind her. His armor was open in front, as if he'd just shrugged into it for the watch. He was between her and the rope.

"Did the royal messenger come through before me?" Red demanded.

"Oh, aye." One of the men seated behind her chuckled. He was in leathers, a tankard in one hand, gathering up dice with the other. "Bearing a royal decree from Queen Gloriana about ending slavery." He rattled the dice in his hand. "Tried telling us that the High Baron of Athelbryght had returned, too. The Master gave him short shrift. He's naked, whipped, and thrown in with the worst of them."

"He'll not be so pretty come market day, if he lives through the night." The one against the fire laughed. He was also still in leathers, but with no weapon at hand. "Not with those monsters."

Well, that made her task that much easier, now didn't it? Red smiled, throwing her cloak back, clearing her leathers and weapons. "Your Master should have listened."

"How so?" asked the first one.

"Because," Red said, drawing one of her daggers, "I'm enforcing the Queen's command."

It was laughable, watching the muckers react to her blades. Damn fools, for letting her through the door in the first place.

The doorman went for the rope, but Red grabbed his collar as the others scrambled for their weapons. *"Give them a chance to comply, Red."* The High Baron had said.

She'd give them as much chance as they'd given their "wares."

Red jerked the doorman back and thrust her dagger deep into his thigh. He collapsed with a cry, and she spun to deal with the other two.

The one by the fire was quick, reaching for a sword. The dicer was still rising from his chair. She shoved the table hard with her free hand, sending him sprawling.

The faster one came at her, snarling. Not calling for help, the fool was intent on taking her on his own. She dodged, and scored his cheek with her dagger as he moved past. He cursed, starting to turn as he reached for his face. She rammed the short blade into his lower back, punching through the leather armor.

He dropped like a rock.

The dicer was on hands and knees, scrambling for the door. Red flipped the table aside. The dice went flying across the floor as she took two steps and drove the toe of her boot up between his ass cheeks.

He collapsed with a high-pitched squeal, grabbing for his "injuries," so to speak.

Red stood still and held her breath. There was no alarm.

"Damn you." The one by the door had his hands clasped around his thigh, trying to stop the bleeding. He glanced up, but the rope was well out of reach.

Red knelt before him, her dagger pointed at his throat. "How many guards?"

He stared at her, and licked his lips. "Eight, counting us."

"Near as I can figure, lady, there's about fifteen regulars." The innkeeper had said. *"There's always a crowd of them in here, drinking themselves stupid and harassing my girls."*

"One more chance," Red said softly, holding his gaze with hers. "How many?"

The man didn't blink. "Eight—"

Red shoved the dagger up through his throat, then yanked it free as he gurgled out his last. She cleaned it quickly on his clothes, sheathed it, and then dragged his body to a dark corner.

It took but a moment to set the table aright and get the other body slumped in a chair. With all but one lamp extinguished, the darkness helped conceal the details. She placed the dice on the table, rather pleased with that touch, then unlatched the door she'd entered through. Just in case. So far, so good.

She knelt next to the dice player, still wheezing, trying to catch his breath, his eyes wide.

"How many?" She asked.

"Who . . . who are you?" he croaked in a whisper, darting a glance at the bodies.

"A mercenary in the service of Lord Josiah, High Baron of Athelbryght." Red drew her dagger again, and tapped the tip of the blade on his cheek.

The man was trembling. Red was certain it was half pain, half fear. "Now," she said, pulling her dagger. "How many?"

"Guards, there's ten not counting us." He flinched back as Red shifted her dagger. "But there's a special shipment came in today with five guards. Their wagons are in the courtyard."

Muck. Red kept her face still, and her dagger point close to the man's face. "Servants?"

"None that sleep here." The man gasped for breath, staring at the tip of her blade. "Master uses slaves and they're chained at night. Even the ones in his bed."

Red tightened her grip on the dagger.

"Try not to kill them all. Most are just men, working for coin." The High Baron's voice echoed in her thoughts.

"On your belly," Red ordered with a sigh.

He swallowed hard and rolled over, his face making it clear he thought she'd cut his throat. She should. It'd be safer. More expedient. Muck.

She trussed the fool up fast and gagged him with a rag, then stuffed him back into the shadows and threw a cloak over him. She leaned over him and placed the edge of her dagger against his neck. "Don't move, don't make a sound, or I will return and gut you slow."

He quivered, but made no noise.

She eased open the door to the courtyard and slid through, closing it softly behind her. The cool air was a gift, the heavy mist falling on her skin. There was no sign of disturbance, no alarm yet. She pressed herself into the deep shadows by the wall.

Fifteen guards. Red considered that. She wasn't in so deep yet that she couldn't retreat at this point. Wait until the Royal Guard of Palins came through with fancy uniforms and more blades. They'd see to these pigs. But that would be months from now, what with the Queen fresh on her throne. That did nothing for the poor, miserable ones chained within. And a special shipment could be anything . . . including children.

Anger rose in her throat like bile, and her gloved hand tightened on her dagger.

"Rescue, yes, but not at the cost of your own life," The High Baron had said.

Eh. Fifteen. Easy enough, if they were of the same quality. It was worth a try. If the alarm was raised too soon, well, she'd get out and return later. But for now, she had the night. Besides, it wouldn't do for any to think that she'd gone soft, working for the High Baron, now would it?

Red grinned as she moved down the wall, staying in the shadows. Those men had been settling in for their watch, from the looks of things. So with any luck, there would be some asleep and some on watch and drowsy.

"They claimed the Mayor's manor house, lady. He'd a walled-in courtyard, and fine stables, and a deep cellar for wine. We was a prosperous town, once. Before . . ." The innkeeper had stopped, his voice breaking.

"Enough." The High Baron's voice had been gentle. *"Tell her what she needs to know."*

"I can draw it out for ya. The stables, the wine cellar. There's the main house. . . ."

Two torches burned at the main doors of the house. The stable was across the yard, and two wagons along the side. Prison wagons, with solid wood walls and the smallest of barred windows at the top.

Red wrapped her cloak around her, lifting it to hide her breath in the cold night air. She stayed in the shadows and watched and waited.

Patience was not one of her best skills, but time had taught her the need. She waited until she was sure, then waited a few moments longer. Better to be sure than—

There. By the wagons, in the deep shadows. One man stamping his feet and swinging his arms as if to warm himself.

Odd, that. Why guard the wagons?

Red kept still, watching. And was rewarded when the wagon guard went to the stable door and pounded on it. "Hern, give a man some kav, eh?"

The stable door opened, and light and noise spilled into the yard. "Gar, you've only been on watch for—"

"The damp goes clear to the bone," Gar replied. "Hand out some kav, or some of the damn gutrot you're drinkin'."

Laughter came from inside, and Red saw something handed out to the man. The door closed with a bang. Muck, from the sound there had to be at least a handful of them in there, all awake, damn them.

Still . . .

Nothing by the main gate. If there was a guard up at the house, it was inside and not out. So take out these six, and there'd be, what, maybe only nine left, and some of those had to be sleeping.

Oh, aye, and tomorrow would be paradise, with scarlets singing in the birches.

Gar had his bottle now, and he was walking around wagons, taking swigs, his back toward her.

Red grinned, and darted across the courtyard.

She ran right up to the front of the wagon and ducked down, crouching on the wet flagstones. Gar's feet paused for a moment, then continued on. She could hear him grumbling under his breath. There were other sounds too, quiet breathing and soft . . .

Muck. There was something in the wagons.

Red froze, but there were only seconds to decide. Gar was circling around. Attack? Run?

"Damn cold," Gar muttered. "Damn dice. Last time I dice for watch. Last time I—"

Her dagger was up before she drew another breath. She launched herself at him, aiming for the throat.

Her blade caught him in midswig, head back. The damn bottle fell and rolled away, but the man slid down, silent but for the gurgle of his dying.

Red dragged him over to the wagon and stuffed him under it. She crouched there, bloody dagger in hand, trying to listen over the beat of her heart. The bottle rolled to a stop in the center of the courtyard.

Silence.

There was a whine from within, questioning, and a snuffling noise as claws dug at the wooden walls of the wagon. Red's throat closed, expecting a baying at any moment. Dogs, it had to be, and slaver dogs would take a scent and run their prey to ground. . . .

Still, only silence.

Red dared to breathe, taking in cold air tainted with the strong smell of piss and wet fur. Whatever was in the wagon had not been cared for, that was sure. She ran her hands over the dead man's body, more from habit than anything else. Never knew what you might find—

Her fingers brushed over two keys on his belt. She held them tight so they didn't jangle, and cut them loose, tucking them into the top of her glove.

Then the faintest of whispers from the wagon. "Who's there?"

Slaves in with dogs? If there was a slave dog-handler in there . . . Red could not believe her luck would run that good. Still . . .

"You're not one of them." The sound was so soft that she had to strain to hear it. "They'd be . . . is it . . . are you?" The voice paused, then rushed on, heavy with hope. "Rescue?"

"Quiet," she breathed. The snuffling continued for a moment, the animals taking in her scent.

"We can help," the whisper continued, pained and excited. "Unlock the—"

"Gar?" The door to the stables opened, slamming against the wood. "You finish that—"

Light spilled out onto the courtyard. The bottle sparkled.

Then a muffled voice, from the guardhouse. "Help! A woman warrior. She's killed—"

Red grimaced. So much for showing mercy.

The guard in the doorway uttered his curse, and started to call for his fellows.

Red leapt up and ran for the door, both daggers in hand. She surprised the man standing there, peering out into the darkness. She lunged, going for his eyes, more to force him back then anything else.

The blade caught the bone, and sank deep within. He sagged, and she pushed his body back as it fell. She stood in the doorway, and brandished her two blades with a laugh as another charged.

She kept herself back just enough that the doorway hindered their movements. The man's sword swings hit the wood, and he was forced to use his sword to block her blows. Her blades were swift and small, and she didn't hesitate to go for any target he offered. The shouts from behind him were a relief; she'd feared another exit. If she could keep them coming at her one at a time . . .

But that mucking dicer was still yelling in the guardhouse. Then shouts came from the main house. From the corner of her eye she saw a door open and movement, and knew she was done.

She focused back in time to see a spearhead thrust at her.

She dodged, but too late. The blade sank deep into her shoulder, and the wielder twisted it as he forced her back, out into the courtyard.

Red clamped her jaw against the pain and pulled away, getting herself off the blade. The pain was bad, but she could still grip the dagger. She skipped back, conscious of the shouts and pounding feet from the main house. Her foe came after her, and the spearman right behind, all spilling through the stable door, spreading out.

Red charged right into them, using the daggers to feint at their faces, dodging the few that managed to swing swords. Her speed and their confusion allowed her to pass through the group. She'd some vague idea of running into the stables but the body in the doorway changed that plan. So she turned as she passed the last man and lashed out with her strong hand.

She caught the guard's upper arm and cut deep, enough that he cried out and dropped his weapon. But now the others were focused on her as their target, and they started to move, spreading out to surround her.

Breathing hard, Red ran for the wagons, and darted down between them and the wall of the stable. The shelter was fleeting; they'd box her in at any moment. She could go for the wall, try to get up and over—

"Stay safe, Red. Your life is dear to me." A small part of her remembered the High Baron's admonishments. But her blood sang of steel and death, and caution had no place in the moment.

She ran to the back of the last wagon, thrust the larger key in, and twisted. The lock clicked open, and she lifted the bolt.

The enemy of her enemy, with any luck.

The door burst open. Red fell, landing hard on her back, the wind pushed from her lungs. Her daggers went skittering away.

A huge *something* stood over her, growling, its teeth inches from her throat.

Red fumbled around, trying to find her daggers, staring at the jaws of the monster. It was as big as a bear; she couldn't see much past the teeth. Hot breath stung her eyes. It sniffed the air . . . paused—

—then spun off, charging toward the guards.

Red flipped onto her chest, grabbing up her daggers as a seemingly endless stream of the creatures jumped out of the wagon. Their huge paws were all she saw, landing around her and then past her, off into the darkness. Screams started then, of men fighting for their lives.

Red scrambled up to her feet, not questioning her luck. If the beasts could draw off a few, she could take down the rest.

She rounded the wagon on the other side and saw two men, their backs to her, fending off one of the creatures. Softly, holding her breath, she ran up behind the one, grabbed his hair, yanked back, and stabbed at his throat.

He screamed, blood spurting from his neck. She jerked the dagger free, letting him fall to the ground. The other guard was fending off the animal, shield high, eyes hard. "Here! She's here!"

Red snarled, pulled her blade free.

An arrow slammed into her shoulder, the pain driving her to her knees.

The flagstones swam before her eyes. Blackness swirled as well, but Red fought it off, forcing herself up, her one hand still grasping a blade. But two hits to the same shoulder—that hand wasn't going to grasp much of anything anytime soon.

"Bitch," one of the men growled as they started toward her. "Don't crowd, boys. Disarm her, then we'll have some fun."

Red grimaced, not really seeing much more than heavy boots, drawing close. Enough men to take her, that was sure. Provided they were willing to pay the price.

A scrabbling sound came then, of claws on stone. Deep snarls from behind the guards, who lost all interest in her, fast.

Red used the distraction to force herself to her feet. The arrow in her shoulder shifted as the tip grated on bone.

Dark, swift forms leapt out from the wagon's shadow, claws scraping on the flagstones.

"Vores," one of the guards cried out, no longer focused on Red.

The others cried out as the animals leapt forward, fangs gleaming white. Huge wolflike creatures, but these were no wolves. These were nightmares out of the darkness with teeth and fangs and savage fury in red eyes. No matter. The enemy of my enemy . . .

Red launched herself at the man who'd screamed, bringing her dagger into play. He was swift enough to parry her. She had a quick glimpse of grim eyes under the helm, and a sword swinging for her neck. She blocked, but not before the blade caught the arrow and tore the tip partway out of her shoulder. Red staggered back as her arm went numb and useless.

A big vore with silver on his ruff darted in behind her opponent. The man cried out as he fell, hamstrung. Red heard the beast growl, and then the screaming stopped.

Red kept moving back until she came up against the wall of the stable, the pain ebbing just enough so that she could see.

Blood covered the cobblestones until at last all was silent. The guards were down and those not dying had been torn apart, with flesh and blood scattered everywhere. The animals were around her, breathing heavily, growling under their breaths, their heads held low, their muzzles stained with blood. Odd though. They weren't eating the bodies.

Suddenly a few of the creatures lifted their heads and looked toward the manor house.

More men spilled through the doors, weapons and bows at the ready. Five, ten . . . Red snarled as she readied her weapon. That dicer had much to answer for.

The vores growled, their heads low, intent on the enemy. But Silver, the big one with the ruff, glanced off toward the wagons, and then back at the gathering force.

Red heard it then—the faint rattle of a key in a lock. She glanced over to see a pair of bare human feet at the back of the second wagon. And a larger dark shape leaping down and darting into the shadows. Followed by another . . . and another.

More vores. They had to be.

The growls around her deepened. Red turned and saw more bows being brought to bear.

"Scatter," she commanded, more from instinct than anything else.

To her surprise, the vores obeyed. The entire pack seemed to disappear, loping off into cover, under wagons, behind barrels, into the stables.

What were those creatures?

No time to worry about that. Red threw herself between the wagons and the stable, Silver at her heels. Arrows thunked into the wagon.

"Muck," Red grumbled under her breath as she pressed herself against the wagon. She rammed her dagger into the side of the wagon, then worked the arrow in her shoulder all the way out. It came free, at the price of pain. Red pressed her head against the wood, woozy and sick to her stomach.

More arrows thunked into the wagon. The guards were advancing.

Red swore. "Best I run for it now." She glanced down at the animal at her side.

Silver looked up at her, and the intelligence in those eyes struck her hard. It waited for a moment and then shook its head in a negative gesture.

Red's skin crawled. The movement looked unnatural and wrong. "You got a better idea?" she whispered.

Sliver moved his head up and down with an odd deliberation.

Her stomach clenched. "Fine," she snapped.

Silver barked and darted back into the courtyard. He—and Red had no doubt he was a "he"—moved fast.

Shouts from the men. They had crossbows now. Bolts clattered on the flagstones. Red heard cranking as the weapons were reloaded. She glanced around the wagon. The men were moving, slowly coming closer, the bowmen toward the rear.

Two more vores darted toward the men, then away. Bolts and arrows rained down, but none hit their targets that Red could tell.

Silver came across the courtyard at a run, then whined and half collapsed. Shouts rang out as he dragged himself toward her. Red reached out with her good arm and hauled him into cover. She knelt and ran her hands over him, searching for . . .

The big animal stood and shook himself. And gave her a toothy grin.

"Faker," Red growled in admiration. "Still, we—"

Screams.

Red was up and moving, but Silver was faster. They both broke out from cover to see that the new vores had come up from behind and targeted the crossbowmen.

Silver howled, and a fierce joy filled Red. She charged—

"Return to me, my Red," The High Baron's voice rang in her head. *"Don't let your bloodlust overrule your common sense."*

She took a few more steps, then stopped. No sense in being stupid. Besides, the beasts had them down. There was no need.

A slim man made his way down the side of the wagons, wearing a tattered tabard around his waist. The cloth bore the crest of the young Queen, the white dagger-star on a red background. "Are they all dead?" the young man asked, his ribs sticking out, with whip marks on his chest and face. "Are all the slavers—"

Red nodded.

The man sighed, and slowly lowered himself to the cobblestones. "Thank the Lord of Light."

Two of the creatures padded over and crouched next to him.

"What are these things?" Red breathed, watching as they finished the guards.

"I don't know." The young man shook his head. "The slavers stripped me, beat me, then threw me in the wagons, figuring I'd be eaten. The creatures hadn't been fed, the wagons hadn't been cleaned. They had to keep the snarling beasts back with spears when they opened the door. I thought I was dead when they tossed me in."

"But—," Red prompted him.

"But these creatures, whatever they are, I swear they knew I wasn't one of their captors. They understood me. They didn't hurt me, and slept with me, kept me warm. I've—"

"The High Baron of Athelbryght sent me," Red interrupted him; then a high-pitched screech interrupted her.

From out of the manor house ran a fat man, dressed in silks, fleeing the vores snapping at his heels. The dark animals chased after him, their tongues hanging out, and Red could have sworn they were laughing as they herded him in her direction.

The fat one screamed again when he saw the blood and the dead, but he threw himself at Red's feet, sobbing. "Call them off! Call them off!"

The vores stood there, hackles raised, growling. Staring.

Red looked down at the slave master. "If it was my choice, you'd be their prey and rightfully so."

Silver started stalking toward the fat man.

"But it's not my choice," Red warned.

Silver gave her a hard look.

"Into one of the wagons," Red ordered. "The High Baron will decide your fate."

"But . . ." The man gathered his robe tight around his body.

"Now," Red barked.

The fat man scrambled off the flagstones and ran for the wagon door.

"You're hurt," the Queen's man said to her.

"It can wait." Red managed to sheathe her dagger, and pushed the weakened hand into her belt. "We need to open the main gates, and send word to the High Baron. Then there's questions to ask, and slaves to free."

"Aye to that." The young one smiled. "And then there's them."

The vores were all seated, staring at them. Red could swear they were listening.

"True enough." Red looked around the courtyard. "We'll summon the High Baron, and see if we can find some answers. Can you get the main gate open by yourself?"

"I'll try." The young man pushed himself up with the help of the wall. "But what will you be doing?"

Red looked over at the guardhouse. "Oh, I've a promise to keep."

SUPERMAN

Jeanne C. Stein

PROLOGUE

My name is Anna Strong. I am vampire. It's been over a month since I fed. A month since the first anniversary of my becoming. A month since I assumed the mantle of the Chosen One. I've gone about my daily routine as if nothing has changed, when in reality, everything has changed.

I move out to the deck off my bedroom and sink into a chaise. The early-morning sun is hot on my face. It feels good. I can almost feel my blood warming, though I know that's an illusion. Only feeding and sex warm a vampire's blood.

I haven't had either in a while.

I sip coffee. A few blocks away, the ocean sparkles under a flawless summer sky. I live in San Diego, Mission Beach to be exact, near the boardwalk. I love it here. The sea is vibrant, alive. People drawn to it are vibrant and alive, too. Kids at play in the sand, surfers bobbing on the waves, sunbathers eschewing warnings of dire consequences to bake pasty skin to a toasty brown. All share a common bond. They are human. They belong.

I drain my cup, rise to go inside. I'm feeling the effects of lack of blood. Like a diabetic without insulin, my body is slowing down, my mind becoming sluggish. I'd better call Culebra and make sure he can arrange a host to meet me at Beso de la Muerte.

I can't afford to let myself become vulnerable—not anymore. Not to anyone.

CHAPTER 1

The guy waiting for me in Culebra's back room looks to be about thirty. He's lying naked on the bed, his clothes folded neatly on a bedside chair. He has a sheet thrown over the lower part of his body. He's lean, muscular, with the arrogant good looks of a guy used to having his way with women. He smiles when he sees me, a smile of relief and anticipation. I'm sure the relief is because I'm female (a host never knows) and the anticipation that because I'm female, sex will be a part of the deal.

I pull a wad of cash out of my purse and lay it on top of his clothes. "I just want the blood," I tell him. "Whatever you do while I'm feeding is up to you, but I don't intend to participate."

"Are you sure?" The guy pushes the sheet off his hips. He started without me.

If the size of his dick is supposed to impress me, my reaction must be a bitter disappointment. I flutter fingers in a dismissive gesture. "Yeah, I'm sure. Face the wall, please."

"Don't you want to know my name?"

"No."

He grunts and rolls over. I position myself behind him, spoon style, and pull his head closer. My body vibrates from need and the heady sensation that comes from watching blood coarse through an artery just a kiss away. His hands are busy between his legs and he groans before I break through the skin.

Then I'm lost in my own sensations. His blood is sweet and clean, his fitness the result of good diet and exercise, not pills or needles. Not that it would matter. Vampires are immune from human drugs and disease. Only the taste differs, like drinking vinegar or wine, and I'm pleased with this vintage. The first mouthful brings intense pleasure, my body now tingling with something other than hunger. There's a fleeting moment when I am tempted to roll him over, to mount him, feel him inside me while I feed.

But I resist.

The blood is enough. It awakens every cell in my body. It revives and restores. My skin warms. A flush of heat floods my cheeks. My senses become needle sharp. The feel of the host's skin against my lips, the smell of his arousal, the quickness of his breath, I experience it all. His heartbeat. Steady, rhythmic, until he nears climax. Then his heart begins to race until it reaches a crescendo and his body tenses. He moans, grinds against me, one hand clutches the sheet, the other moves faster and with more urgency.

I keep feeding until the last shudder of release passes and he is quiet beside me. I use my tongue to seal the puncture wounds, watch as the marks fade. He does not speak or move. In a minute, his breathing becomes deep and regular and I know.

He's fallen asleep.

CHAPTER 2

When I join Culebra at the bar, he looks past me toward the door to the back room. "Is he still alive?"

He hands me a bottle of Dos Equis with a lime wedge propped on the rim. He could be an extra in a John Ford western, lean, craggy-faced, and, at the moment, determined to get answers.

I squeeze the lime down into the bottle. "Why wouldn't he be?"

He takes another beer from a cooler under the bar and motions for me to follow him to a table. When we're both seated he answers. "You looked hungry when you walked in. How long has it been since you fed?"

I shrug. "A while."

He watches me drink. "It's been a while since we talked, too. A month to be exact. I have a lot of questions."

One of the reasons I've stayed away.

Culebra picks that thought out of the ether. He frowns. "I thought I was your friend."

He shuts me out of his head. He's angry or disappointed. Maybe both. I can't tell. But the result is the same. I give in with a sigh. "Sorry. You are my friend. I should have been in touch sooner."

I glance around the bar. It's almost empty this early on a Sunday morning. There are a couple of vamps sitting with two human women. The snatches of thought I catch from the vamps are that they're well fed and well sexed and are looking for a way to leave gracefully without offending the female hosts. They may want a re-peat performance down the line. The vibes the females give off tell me they wouldn't object. I watch them a few moments until Culebra is back in my head.

You're stalling.

I'm granted another reprieve when my host appears at the door. He grins at me with a look calculated to let anyone watching think I'd sucked more than his neck. I'm tempted to make a snarky re-mark, but don't. I simply let him swagger over to the other table. The females greet him, and in another moment, all five leave with a parting wave to Culebra.

We're now alone.

Culebra waves his bottle in the direction of the door. "I assume that look was a bit of bravado for the benefit of his friends."

I laugh. "You'll need to change those sheets."

The moment passes. I feel the intenseness of Culebra's eyes as he waits. I release a breath. "What have you heard?"

"The challenge. What happened with Lance. The way you han-dled Chael. Sounds like you did well for yourself."

Did I? What I didn't tell Frey, what I'm hiding from Culebra now, is that nothing was settled. Not really. Chael is still intent on pursuing his own course. A course designed to elevate vampires to the top of the food chain and relegate humans to nothing more than fodder, an expendable food source whose only existence would be to serve their vampire masters.

Culebra's voice breaks through my dark thoughts.

"What are you hiding from me, Anna?"

"Nothing." Everything.

His thoughts are like a laser, trying to bore into mine. *I know you better than that. What aren't you telling me?*

I raise the beer bottle to my lips, drain it. Rise. "Have to go, my friend. I'll be in touch soon."

Culebra doesn't answer. I feel the heat of his frustration as I start to leave.

"Wait."

I half turn, pause.

"I had a visitor yesterday. He left you a message."

"Who would leave a message for me here?"

Culebra crosses to the bar, reaches behind it for a folded piece of paper. "Somebody who is afraid you wouldn't return his calls if he tried to reach you directly."

He holds the note out to me. As soon as I see the signature, I understand why he'd go through Culebra. He's right. I wouldn't have returned his calls.

The note is from Max.

Culebra feels the anger build as I stare down at the note. Max is an ex-boyfriend. Human. Couldn't take off fast enough when he found out what I am, even though it's *because* of what I am that he's alive today. To make matters worse, he decided that sex with a vampire while acting as a host was a pretty damned good way to get his rocks off. So he comes here to enjoy fucking vampires. Anonymous vampires. It's me he doesn't want to fuck anymore.

My hand curls into a fist, crushing the note. "Why would you take this? You know how I feel about Max and his new hobby."

Culebra holds up a hand in defense. "Max hasn't come here to be a host for some time. Whatever he needed to get out of his system, he seems to have succeeded."

"You mean me, right? He needed to get me out of his system."

Culebra shakes his head. "Read the damn note, will you?"

I drag my eyes back to the note, open my hand, smooth the paper against my thigh. I can't imagine being interested in anything Max has to say to me. The bastard left without saying good-bye.

The handwriting is cramped, uneven. As if he wrote the note in a hurry.

Anna. I need your help. Call me. Max.

"Wow." I wave the note toward Culebra. "This makes me want to drop everything and ring him right up. He doesn't even say please. Christ. Why would I want to help him?"

Culebra lifts his shoulders. "It must be important."

"He didn't tell you?"

"Not exactly."

"Didn't tell you *what* exactly?"

"For Christ's sake, call him, will you?" Culebra's irritation flares, radiates outward from his thoughts and burns into my head. *Don't be so goddamned stubborn.*

I don't even know if I still have his number. A last whining excuse. *Of course you still have his number. In your cell.*

He's right. Not that I'll give him the satisfaction of telling him. Just like I won't give him the satisfaction of knowing that deep down I want to call Max. Only to satisfy my curiosity. Only to find out how Max plans to grovel his way back into my good graces. Only to enjoy turning him down no matter what he says.

His leaving was no laughing matter, but telling him to go to hell would be good for a laugh, not to mention my ego.

I turn my back on Culebra and stomp out, letting one thought drift back.

Fucking men.

CHAPTER 3

On the drive back home I debate with myself.

Do I want to call Max? It's been eight months since the last time we ran into each other in Beso de la Muerte under less-than-perfect conditions.

Why would I want to call Max? On the off chance that he wants to tell me what an ass he's been and to thank me at long last for saving his ass in Mexico?

Shit.

It irritates me to realize I'm curious. It irritates me to realize I want to know why he wants to talk to me.

It irritates the hell out of me to realize I know how long it's been since I've seen him without doing the math.

I'm sure Culebra knows more than he let on. Max is a drug enforcement agent. He spends quite a bit of time in Mexico, and has used Culebra as an informant. Not in an official capacity. Culebra has a lot of contacts on both sides of the law and the border. He and Max have a quid pro quo arrangement. Culebra helps Max when he can, and in turn, Max keeps quiet when he comes to Beso de la Muerte to ensure that those under Culebra's protection are not hassled.

At least that's the way it worked when Max and I were together.

A lifetime ago.

CHAPTER 4

I've been sitting on the bed staring at the telephone in my hand for fifteen minutes. Max's number is up on the screen, just waiting for my finger to press SEND. I'm not sure now why I'm so hesitant. There's only one reason I'd call him, and the only thing I have to decide is the number of expletives to insert before I tell him to fuck off.

So what's the problem?

I suck it up and punch SEND.

He picks up so fast, it takes me a second to realize he's on the line. "Max?"

"Anna." There's relief in his voice. "Thanks for calling. I need to see you."

"Why?"

"I can't talk about it on the phone. Can I come in?"

My grip on the phone tightens. "What do you mean, come in? Where are you?"

"Outside. On the boardwalk."

I cross the bedroom to the deck, look toward the ocean. The boardwalk is crowded. It takes me a second to locate him. Max is leaning against the seawall, staring up toward the cottage. He waves when he sees me. But it's not a cheery wave and he's not smiling.

I'm not smiling either. "What are you doing here? How did you know I'd call?"

"I didn't, but Culebra told me you'd picked up the note."

"Did he also tell you I don't want to talk to you?"

"Yes. I'm glad to see he was wrong."

"He wasn't wrong. There's only one reason I'd call you. To tell you to fuck off—"

"Anna, please." I see Max cup his hand around the phone. "If there was anyone else I could go to about this I would. You are the only one who can help."

"Jesus, Max." Irritation and anger crash like cymbals in my head. "Why so dramatic? You sound like you're jonesing for a fix. God. Is that what this is about? You tired of screwing anonymous vamps? You remembering what a good thing you threw away?"

"No. Anna." He bites off the words. "Everything isn't about *you*. I need you because I think I'm dealing with a vampire. A vicious vampire. And I don't know how to fight him. I thought you'd want to help. Culebra thought you'd want to help. Guess we were both wrong."

He snaps his cell phone shut, ending the conversation before I can respond. He doesn't look my way again, but heads up the boardwalk toward the parking lot. He shoulders are drawn up, his strides long, fast, stiff with anger.

Shit. A vampire? It takes me about a heartbeat to decide. I'm probably going to regret this, but I'm down the stairs, have grabbed up my purse and keys and reached the end of the boardwalk before he does.

Max isn't startled when I appear in front of him like a genie sprung from a bottle. He knows what I can do. But he doesn't look relieved or pleased either. He stares down at me from his six-foot-three-inch vantage point and waits for me to speak first.

"What do you mean you're *dealing* with a vampire?"

His shoulders hunch up even more. The lines of his face draw down, as if weighted. He looks tired. He looks stressed. The Max I knew—the one with lively blue eyes, a quick smile, and sun-burnished Latino good looks—has been swallowed up by this sallow-faced, sober, weary doppelgänger.

"Are you sure you want to hear this? Or are you waiting for another opportunity to tell me what a fuckup I've been?"

I close the distance between us and jab a finger into his chest. "Oh, I'm sure there will be plenty of opportunities to do that. Right now, I want to know what you meant on the telephone."

He looks around. "Let's walk. I don't want to risk being overheard."

The boardwalk teems with people. Skateboarders, cyclists, Rollerbladers, joggers. If we walk here, we'll spend most of our time dodging incoming. I'm not going to invite him to the cottage, either. I don't want him invading my personal space.

"Let's cross to the bay side."

He doesn't object. Neither of us speaks until after we've crossed Mission and headed for the sidewalk that runs along the harbor. Here the view spans the San Diego skyline on one side, row on row of condos and apartments on the other. There's a marina and a small park. We head for the benches in the middle of the park. We choose the one that faces a playground. The water is at our backs and we have a clear view of the sidewalk. It's much quieter here.

"So talk."

Max looks toward the sidewalk, eyes restlessly scanning the faces of the people moving at a Sunday-afternoon, warm-summer's-day kind of pace. I look, too. But I know I'm not seeing the same things he is. He's looking at them with cop eyes.

"I've been working a joint task force with the Mexican border patrol," he says at last. "Drugs mostly. But in the last month, we've been finding something else on our patrols. Bodies drained of blood. Entire families killed and dumped in the desert. No clue as to who is doing it. At first we thought it was some local drug lord's new and vicious way to intimidate."

"But now?"

"The victims all had their throats slashed. But there's never any blood at the scene. None. The tox screens we've run always come back negative for drugs. They're not addicts or dealers. The victims have no connection to local law enforcement either, always a favorite target of the cartel. We've traced some of the victims to places in Latin America and as far south as Ecuador. A hell of a long way to transport bodies just to dump them. They're from poor families. If they were carrying anything of value on them, it's gone by the time we find them. All that's left is the clothes they're wearing."

Max pauses, draws a breath. He hasn't looked at me since we sat down on the bench. He does now. "I think we're dealing with a coyote. I think he takes money from these people to get them across the border. Then he kills them and dumps them within sight of the border. Probably lets them know how close they are before he kills them."

It doesn't take much of a leap to know what Max is leading up to. "You think this coyote is a vampire."

"I do. The slash marks are clumsy. Because the bodies are found in Mexico, we haven't been able to do anything but drug sampling. But I'd be willing to bet if we could do the autopsies here, we'd find something under those slashes."

He would. When I worked as a Watcher, I used the technique myself. A vampire can erase puncture wounds from a live donor, but not a dead one. Slashing the throat is a way to hide the fact that a body has been sucked dry.

Confirming that Max is right about this and how I know that he's right is not something I want to share. I already know what he thinks of me. "What do you want from me?"

"There's a pattern to the killings. We find the bodies on our patrols on Tuesday mornings. Always in roughly the same location."

"If you know this, you don't need me. Set a trap."

"We did. Once. The guy slipped past us as if he were invisible. But not before leaving us another victim. A young girl. You have to realize, Anna, our emphasis is on stopping the drug trade. Not human trafficking. We don't have the resources to conduct another undercover op. That's why I'm here. To ask you to come with me tomorrow night. If I'm right, the only way we're going to stop him is by fighting fire with fire."

I snort. "You mean vampire with vampire."

Max's mouth tightens. "This isn't a joking matter."

"Do I look like I'm joking?"

His expression shifts, softens. "Sorry. I know I'm asking a lot. I don't know what else to do. If we don't stop him, he'll go on killing. He likes it. He's found an easy food source. And he takes money from victims desperate to make a new life."

He pauses, draws a breath. "Culebra told me you're some sort of *über*-vamp. Well, I need an *über*-vamp. I can't think of another way to stop him."

Über-vamp. Yeah. That's me, all right. Head of the thirteen vampire tribes. Only thing is, except for a few extra abilities, I don't feel any different than I did before. The only thing that's changed is that I have another *über*-vamp, Chael, gunning for me.

I push the thought out of my head. I can probably help Max. I'm stronger than other vamps. The question is, do I want to?

Stupid question. I choose my words carefully.

"I'll do it. But not for you. I'll do it because a vamp who acts like this is a rogue, a killer, a threat to all vampires. Sooner or later, what he's doing will come to the attention of vampire hunters. Then none of us will be safe."

Max lets his relief show in a tiny gesture of gratitude. He holds out a hand.

I let my feelings show by standing up and taking a step out of reach. The wound is still fresh. "Where shall I meet you?"

He stands, too, lets his hands fall to his sides. "The border crossing at San Ysidro. Tomorrow night. Ten o'clock."

I nod. Max stares at me a minute, waiting for the ice to melt, I suppose. It doesn't, and finally, he walks away.

For the first time, I notice.

Max was hurt in Mexico. A broken ankle. He's not limping anymore.

At least one wound has healed.

CHAPTER 5

It's a clear, quiet, moonless night. Max and I have tramped across two miles of barren desert. We're both dressed in dark camo, ski masks covering our faces. I have a .38 strapped to my waist. Just in case Max's coyote turns out to be human after all.

Max dons night-vision goggles. I don't need them. The creatures of the desert are as clear to me in the inky blackness as they would be in the brightest sunlight. I see more than Max ever can, down to the tiniest scurrying insects he crushes underfoot as we trudge onward.

I hear more, too. The faraway cry of a bird of prey. The squeal of a rabbit as the jaws of a coyote snap closed around its neck. The pebbles pushed aside in the wake of a slithering snake.

Then, something else.

I touch Max's arm. Signal him to stop. Point off to the north.

Too far away for him to see, there's a dim shadow against the darkness. Moving toward us.

Max doesn't question me. We seek cover behind the sloping bank of an arroyo, dry as dust in the summer heat. And hunker down to wait.

The shadow draws closer, divides into three. I probe, careful to keep my own presence hidden. The unmistakable psychic pattern of a vampire comes back like the blip on radar. At least one of them is vampire.

Then a feeling I've come to recognize swamps my senses. Revulsion. Rage. Bloodlust so powerful the vampire within bursts from its human cocoon with the gnashing of teeth.

Evil approaches.

Max seems to detect the change. He leans away from me, an involuntary, instinctive reaction to danger. "What's wrong?"

I strip the ski mask from my face, let it fall to the ground. It takes effort to speak, to form words and force them through a throat that wants to howl. "Stay away from me. No matter what happens."

I don't wait for his reply. I leap over the embankment and head out to meet the monster.

CHAPTER 6

She senses my approach.
        She.

Max's coyote.

We're still a mile away from each other, but she picks up the rage. I close the distance in seconds.

Then we're face-to-face.

I point to the man and woman at her side. They are stunned by my sudden appearance, by my vampire face. They are young, maybe twenty, dressed in dark jeans and hoodies that are tattered and stained. Each carries a small satchel. They cringe away, look to their guide.

I look at her, too.

Let them go.

The vampire tilts her head to one side, studying me. Physically, we are evenly matched. She is weighing her options.

You have no options.

She is cloaking her thoughts. After a moment she says, *Perhaps you are right. These two are of no consequence.*

Do they speak English?

A nod.

I drag my eyes away from her, motion to the couple. "The border is three miles straight ahead. There is a tear in the fence. You can make it on your own."

I am trying very hard to sound human. Even to my own ears, my voice is rough. It comes from my gut, not my vocal cords. A growl.

The humans are mesmerized. They can't look away from my eyes.

The vampire raises a hand, strokes the hair of the woman. *They want to stay with me*

She has not shown her true nature. The woman steps behind her for protection. The vampire laughs.

The fury in me builds. I realize her intention. Her mouth opens, her teeth gnash. She reaches behind to pull the woman forward.

I have her neck before she can grab the woman. I pull her away and spin her around, showing the cowering couple the true face of their savior.

They jump back, mouths open in astonishment.

The vampire laughs again. I force her to her knees. Reach into the pocket of her jacket. Pull a wad of bills from inside.

"Take your money. Go. Now."

This time, there is no hesitation. They circle around us in a wide arc, uncomprehending, fearful the creatures might change their minds. Then they're off, running across the desert floor.

I hold the vampire on the ground until the rustle of their clothes, the sound of their footsteps, are a distant echo.

You could have let me keep the money.

She is not afraid.

Why?

Do you know who I am?

Everyone of our race knows who you are.

Then you know I can't let you go.

Still no reaction. Her mind is closed. Mine is not. *Do you think because you are not resisting I will spare you?*

I think you will spare me because I have something to offer you.

I pull her to her feet. She faces me squarely. We are the same height. Her dark eyes have changed back; she still holds the vampire in check. She wears pants and a blouse that skims her shoulders, a denim jacket. Her hair is tied back from her face with a scarf. She looks like a woman of about twenty-five. Her thoughts are much older, much darker.

The creature before me radiates malevolence. She has killed for a hundred years. She has a taste for it. Lust for blood oozes from her pores like the foul smell of rotting meat. My instinct to kill her now and quickly battles with a desire to find out what a being like this thinks she can offer me.

See? You are curious.

I backhand her across the face. She flies fifty feet and lands on a barrel cactus.

She struggles to her feet. *Damn, bitch. That hurt.*

I'm at her side with my hands around her throat before she can finish whining.

She still has not released the beast. I can feel her fury building. She wants to. What is holding her back?

I have killed vampires before. Vampires more powerful than this sniveling female. It can be done many ways. This one, however, deserves to die slowly. The same way she has killed the helpless humans she's lured to this place with a promise of a new life. She will feel her life ebb away drop by drop until there is nothing left but an empty husk.

I am done with you.

For the first time, something besides sarcasm and confidence flickers in the depths of her eyes. Fear is there, too. She pulls away, her hands on my arms as she tries to break my grip. Her struggles are fruitless.

But I have something you want. Information I am willing to offer in return for my life.

You have recklessly taken human life. Left bodies to be discovered—

No one of importance. No one who will be missed. I have incited no threat against us. Why should it matter to you that I thin the ranks of the miserable? I do them a service, ending their pathetic lives.

Her attitude is like a red-hot poker in my gut. *Do you ask them first? Give them a choice? You kill for sport. You take their money. Worse, you offer hope, then snatch it away. You are an animal. You deserve the same fate as those you toy with, the ones you consider unimportant. I am here to exact vengeance.*

Then what Chael says about you is true.

The name makes me draw back a tiny step, to look into her eyes. *What does Chael have to do with you?*

She takes advantage of the momentary distraction to draw herself up. *Chael says you think more of mortals than you do of your own kind. I see he is right.* Her words drip acid. *Well, be warned. You may soon find yourself alone. There are many of us who are tired of hiding. The tide is rising.*

So this is why you are here? To deliver a warning? You have made a grievous mistake if you think killing innocents is the way to gain my support for your cause.

She shakes her head. *I am not here to gain your support. Chael told me there would be only one thing to tempt you away from the path you have chosen. Kill me now and you will never know how to achieve what it is your heart desires.*

And how do you know what my heart desires? How does Chael?

It is obvious. You wish to return the gift of immortality, to become human.

I make a guttural sound in my throat—half snort, half snarl. *You think you can forestall the inevitable with this foolish talk? The only reason you are not dead already is that I want to make sure the humans are safely away before I end your miserable existence. They have been traumatized enough.*

I may not be so easy to kill.

Finally. The beast is unleashed. Her right hand dips into her jacket. Lightning fast. She pulls out a small stake and lunges for my chest.

I am faster. A half turn and the stake strikes a rib. It tears flesh and opens a gash that weeps blood. The pain, the smell of my own blood, only strengthen my determination. Adrenaline propels me forward and I wrest the weapon from her hand, toss it away.

She makes her move. Locks her arms around me, intent on bending me backward; snapping jaws seek my throat.

I am stronger. It takes very little effort to break her grip. Our positions reverse. For a fleeting moment, I have a glimpse into her head. Hate boils in her blood, turns her thoughts red with rage.

And Chael is there, too. His whispered entreaties that she should seek me out. Tempt me with the secret.

Chael is there.

Who is this female to Chael?

What is the secret?

No matter.

The bloodlust burns too strong to pull back now. Nothing is more important than the hunger. I tear at her jugular. Her blood, hot and delicious, fills my mouth, my senses. She squirms and pounds at my chest with her fists. The blood from my chest wound seems to mingle with her own blood as the one flows out and the other flows in.

She is strong. Her will to live is not easily extinguished. She is kicking at me, her hands frantically seeking anything to use against me.

Too late to deflect it, I feel her fingers close around the gun clipped to my belt. She fires it without drawing it out of the holster. The roar of the gunshot rips the quiet fabric of the night. A bullet pierces my side.

The bullet moves inside me, scorching a path through muscle and sinew before it explodes out. It does not penetrate organ or impact bone. It does not weaken my resolve.

It does not stop me from snapping her arm.

We both scream in pain.

It's the last sound she makes. She is getting weaker. I regain my hold, lock my jaws tight once again. Her blood is no longer thick, but thinning out as the last drops are consumed. She no longer fights. She is no longer capable of shielding her thoughts. The atrocities she's committed, the victims she's tortured, the senseless agony she's inflicted. All threaten from the dark. There is no thought of loved ones or family. Like her victims, she has lived most of her second life alone. Only fear is left. Dread.

As I drain the last of her blood, feel the shudder as her soul leaves the body, my hatred ebbs. I rejoice.

It is just.

She has died like her victims, alone and afraid.

The metamorphosis begins the instant the soul leaves the body. The young woman I held in my grasp is an old, withered shell by the time she hits the ground. It is the way. Drained of blood, the vampire body reverts physically to its mortal counterpart. I stand looking down at an old lady well past her one hundredth birthday.

My metamorphosis begins, too. The human Anna comes back, slowly, reluctantly.

Slowly. Infusion of blood temporarily warms a body that is even now returning to its natural state. The warmth fades too quickly.

Reluctantly. With the return to human form comes rational thought. I will not forget what I have done.

I have killed.

I have no regrets. She deserved to die. I only wish killing didn't come so easily.

But what of Chael? What was this woman to him? His instincts were good. The fairy tale of regaining mortality is the one carrot he could dangle in front of me—the one prize I might be tempted to pursue.

But not at the cost of more innocents.

Never at the cost of more innocents.

With rational thought comes something else—awareness of the pain that racks my side. Slowly, carefully, I draw myself up, stretch gingerly, willing the healing process to move more quickly, to numb this ache.

CHAPTER 7

Anna!" Max's voice. "Where are you?"

I rouse myself and step over the vampire's body. I realize I never learned her name. Does it matter? Not now.

Max is fifty yards out, moving toward me at a run.

"Here."

I let him find me. He has his gun in his hand and he is breathing hard. When he sees the crumpled remains on the ground, he turns to me, startled, bewildered.

"Who is that?"

"Your coyote."

He kneels for a closer look. "She's an old woman. How could she possibly—"

"What you're looking at are mortal remains. You were right in suspecting a vampire was behind the attacks. She was with a couple when I found her. I let them go."

"I know." Max holsters his gun. "I saw them run by."

"Did they make it?"

"From what I could see."

"Good."

Max switches his gaze from the corpse to me. For the first time, he sees the blood soaking my shirt, on my thighs.

"You're hurt?"

"No." Not much anyway.

I don't think I'll tell him I let myself get shot with my own gun. "It looks worse than it is."

He nods. Luckily, he knows how it is with vampires.

"What should we do with that?" He points to the thing on the ground.

"Bury it."

Max swings his flashlight in an arc. "I didn't bring a shovel. What can we use?"

I spy a flat piece of rock and a long, sturdy branch kiln-dried by the sun. I retrieve them. "It will take work, but we can use these."

I hand him the branch to begin scraping away sand and follow after, scooping out a hole with the rock. My side screams in protest, but within fifteen minutes we have a hole big enough and deep enough to cover the corpse. I grab her by the arm and throw her in.

"She's really dead, right?" Max asks.

"You mean is she going to rise up in three days and come after us?" I prod at the body with my foot. "No. She's gone."

We set to work, shoveling the sand back in, tamping it down with our feet, setting a layer of rock and debris over the grave. To protect it from scavengers.

A flashback. Another vampire corpse. Another grave dug in the desert. Another pair of hands working beside mine.

Lance. Friend. Lover. Traitor.

Dead now. By my hand.

A shudder racks my body.

Max's shoulder is so close to mine, he feels my body jerk. He pauses. "Are you sure you're all right?"

The vampire answers from the darkest place in my soul. "It's nothing. I just walked on someone's grave."

EPILOGUE

Max recognizes one of the guards at the border crossing. They exchange a few words in Spanish and he waves us through. It's good because I'm not sure I want to try to explain the rust-colored stains covering my clothes.

Max drives me back to my car. He watches me climb gingerly out. "Can you drive?"

I massage my side. The scrape caused by the stake is healed. The path the bullet tore through my side is healed. Now it's just the skin pulling tight as it regenerates over the wounds that makes me wince when I move.

"Yeah. I'm a little stiff but by the time I get home, I'll be fine."

Max watches as I get into my car and crank the engine before he motions for me to roll down the window.

"Thanks, Anna. You did good tonight. I owe you one."

Okay, here's my chance to tell him what I planned to tell him. To go fuck himself. To never call me again. To go to one of his vampire whores the next time he needs help.

What am I waiting for?

Max is leaning toward the window, smiling. He looks more like the Max I remembered. Superman, defending truth, justice, and the American way . . .

Shit.

I smile back.

And drive away.

MONSTER MASH

A DELILAH STREET, PARANORMAL INVESTIGATOR, CASE

Carole Nelson Douglas

Sansouci, the main muscle for the Las Vegas werewolf mob, caught up with me at the neutral territory of the Inferno Hotel bar.

"Muscle" was no cliché when it came to Sansouci. I stand almost six feet in heels, and talking to him made me tilt up my chin, but then, I'm not afraid to lead with it.

"Delilah Street," he greeted me, or maybe purr-growled.

Everybody assumed Sansouci was a werewolf. Yeah, with the silver forelock in his jet-black hair, the forest green eyes, and a long, lean build, you could picture him chasing the full moon in a thick fur coat, a creature of ferocity and grace.

Except I already had my own really butch wolfhound-wolf-cross dog named Quicksilver, and Sansouci was a vampire.

Not everybody knew the truth about Sansouci. Just me, in fact. Taken either way, Sansouci sported extremely white and handsome canines, which now flashed at me like a fishing lure.

"And where's your boyfriend, the Cadaver Kid?" he asked.

"Ric's in Mexico," I reported, "rounding up demon drug lords and feral zombies in a multinational policing operation. And what have *you* done for the good of humanity and world peace lately?"

"Looked you up. Or down."

His glance slowly skied the curves of the sweetheart neckline on my fifties black velvet top.

"One spike heel to the kneecap and you'd fold," I pointed out.

"Maybe. But I'd take you down with me."

Flirting with Sansouci was dangerous, which was why I enjoyed it so much.

And I *was* dressed to kill. The velvet bodice topped a ballerina-length, full, dark gray taffeta skirt that made solid me look so Audrey Hepburn–girlish you'd want to take me to brunch at Tiffany's . . . until you noticed I was wearing silver-metal-laced gladiator-goth-style high heels that also worked well as weapons.

Sansouci had, and was looking even more lean and hungry.

"So," I asked, "why'd your mangy, murderous werewolf boss let you off-leash from headquarters at the Gehenna Hotel?"

You'd think a female human paranormal investigator like me would sympathize with werewolves. We shared that three-days-a-month temporary-insanity-and-blood thing.

Yet I liked Sansouci precisely because he hated his werewolf over-lord, Cesar Cicereau. Sansouci had been a hostage in the uneasy peace between the werewolves and the vampires that had lasted since Las Vegas's 1940s founding all the Way to Where We Were, 2013. That added up to seventy-five years. Good thing Sansouci was immortal.

And most vamps still suffered from that twelve-hour-a-day "impotency handicap," not that I'd dare use the phrase with Sansouci. Being an ex-reporter, accuracy was my middle name. Anyone who survived as a vampire gigolo was good to go 24/7. His breed of New Model Vampire had been in the making since the 1930s, a daylight vamp who sipped from a willing harem of female donors. Killing them softly with sex, not death, and they loved him for it.

Not I.

"Why'd you come all the way over to the Inferno," I prodded Sansouci, "where you're not welcome, from the Gehenna, where you're *really* not welcome?"

"We have a problem."

We? I lifted my eyebrows.

Nick Charles, the official Inferno barfly, rushed to my side. Yeah. *That* Nick Charles, the 1930s book and movie lush—detective with the witty wife and hyperactive terrier, Asta.

The entire trio was black-and-white and gray all over. They were Cinema Simulacrums, aka SinCims. Vegas throngs with black-and-white movie characters overlaid on zombies to give the tourists some semi-"live" entertainment they could not only gawk at, but actually talk to. Which was happening right now.

"Look here, my good man." Nick Charles accosted Sansouci with a hand on the concealed gun in his tuxedo jacket pocket. "You're not to pester our Inferno patrons."

Asta's teeth were tugging on one leg of Sansouci's black designer jeans while Nicky's sleek wife, Nora, was running a languid hand inside his jean jacket and down his firm pecs and abs to frisk him. Friskily. Face it, Nick Charles has a retro-cool pencil-thin mustache, a tipsy wit, and ace deductive ability, but he's not exactly buff in modern terms.

"You have the most annoying allies, Street," Sansouci said with an impressive shrug. "Get these reanimated vintage-film freakos off me. We have business to discuss."

"I'm okay, Family Charles," I assured my friends. Then I ordered Brimstone Kisses from the human barman and we adjourned to a table for two.

"I'm actually celebrating a private party here with some of my CinSim pals," I said, sipping the spicy cocktail of my own concoction. "What's going wrong at the Gehenna now?"

"Yeah," Sansouci seconded me, "Cicereau does seem accident-prone, particularly when it comes to the supernatural set." He slugged down my spicy liquor-loaded concoction in three gulps. "When are you going to invent a cocktail in my honor?"

"You don't claim the Vampire Sunrise?"

"I'm not that kind of vamp."

"The 'Sansouci' sounds comatose. Hardly you."

"More like Cicereau lately."

"You saying *he's* comatose?"

"That would be nice, if you could arrange it. I know a few dozen vamps who'd like to catch him snoozing and kill him without tasting a drop of his rotten blood. But, no, he's the same power-hungry, brutal, dumb mob boss as ever. Except he's been cursed."

"Cursed? Like bespelled?"

"Maybe that way. On the surface, it looks like a vengeful dead dame's got him on her radar."

"And I can help . . . how?"

"You got rid of the daughter he offed. He thinks you're the one to banish this new dame."

"What do you mean, *me*? I know what crimes against women Cesar Cicereau is capable of. He tried to force me into his Gehenna magic act when I first hit town, playing on my exact likeness to that hot *CSI V: Las Vegas* corpse, Lilith, but he gave up that idea."

"You weren't as cooperative as he likes his women to be."

"You mean alive and kicking."

"I do. Not a problem for me, though."

"Why can't *you* handle this?"

"He won't listen to any of his pack, and I'm the hostage help, so I rank even lower. You're the perfect undercover operative to figure out what's going on."

"But you're still his top enforcer."

"Because I can still outkick werewolf pack butt. Just because my . . . dining partners are voluntary doesn't mean I can't unleash the vampire bloodlust that kept me alive, so to speak, for seven centuries or so."

"A real Jekyll and Hyde."

Sansouci nodded. "The best . . . and worst . . . of both worlds. Don't forget that, Delilah, while you admire my designer sunglasses."

Sansouci had pulled out opaque black Gucci shades with titanium frames. Dark glasses began to be commonly used only during the Great Depression, when some vampires learned that keeping their eyes shaded allowed them to stroll around unsizzled by broad daylight. Once unhumans went public after the recent Millennium, the vampires were even more eager to live "normal" lives without being labeled serial killers, which tended to get them hunted down, staked, and beheaded.

"Let's take a trip down the Strip," he suggested.

"Cicereau's still got it in for me, and I'm not dressed for work."

Sansouci eyed my party getup. "The boss is so many decades behind the times, that outfit will lull him into thinking you're a nice girl. This looks to be another corporate exorcism job. He'll pay you well to get the freaks off his back."

"Like the teenage daughter he murdered back in the forties?"

"Like Loretta, yeah. With werewolves, alpha pack power is thicker than blood."

"I'll do a meet with Cicereau," I said, "but that's not saying I'll take the job."

Still, I wondered what fresh "ghosts" were bugging the Vegas mogul. And I knew my carotid artery was safe in Sansouci's company, if not much else.

"You want your *car?*" asked Manny, my Inferno parking valet buddy, as his goatish yellow eyes sized up Sansouci. "The visiting Gehenna Hotel fur-back owns wheels?"

"At least I don't leave scales on the leather upholstery." Sansouci eyed Manny's case of all-over orange psoriasis. "Off-black Porsche Boxster with terra-cotta leather interior," Sansouci spit out, handing Manny a claim ticket.

"Shallow and overrated," Manny sniffed. "Figures." He jumped into an idling Lamborghini and raced it up the ramp.

Vegas supernaturals can get edgy with each other. Being in an entertainment venue usually keeps that under control. I could charm or bribe the lower-order supers to my investigative causes. Manny, formally known as Manniphilpestiles, was a demon who'd made it all the way to "pal," like the Invisible Man CinSim, who'd also saved my skin. I wouldn't trust Manny with my soul, though, a recognizable commodity in Vegas long before the Millennium Revelation had brought the supers out of the closet.

"Minor-order demon punk," Sansouci muttered.

"A poor thing, but mine own," I agreed. "Your red-orange car interior color screams über-carnivore. Manny will certainly know whose name to shout around if I turn up missing."

Sansouci shook his head. "I'll get you back here in one untoothed piece, if Cicereau's newest problem children don't do you in."

The Gehenna was a sprawling hotel-casino that rose from the flat landscape, a dark, glassy tidal wave frozen in midcrash. It seemed poised to devour, like huge wolfish jaws.

Inside, an elegantly dark and menacing forest theme prevailed, interpreted in green marble, wood tones from black to gilt, and lurid lighting glittering like migratory flights of fireflies in the casino areas. There was where Theme Décor met Taking Care of Business.

Even in 2013 you can't enter a Vegas hotel without the raw sights, sounds, and smells of a casino assaulting your senses from the common business areas of the registration desk to the theater and restaurants.

More than drink glasses sweat in these dark, icy mazes of flashing lights and chiming slot machines spread across acres of puke-patterned carpeting. Greed is the color of money in Las Vegas. The overpowering smell is well-salted deodorant.

Over the clanging, chiming, whooping, coins-colliding noises programmed into the slot machines came a faint, high, sweet trilling that made me look up to find the source.

I backed out of the casino's clang into the aisle to hear it better, so mystified and eager to trace the sound that Sansouci had to jerk me out of the way of an oncoming luggage cart.

"So you've noticed it already," he said.

"Noticed what?"

"That's what you're here to tell Cicereau."

I also noticed that even slot machine patrons were looking up for the source of the singing after every button push, not staring at the reeling blurred icons that would tell them whether they'd won or not.

"That sound is . . . oddly angelic," I said, "for an enterprise sporting the hellish name of Gehenna."

Sansouci shrugged. "That sugary-sweet high pitch drives the werewolves crazy. Their hearing is acute and this stuff never stops."

"And you? You don't find it . . . mesmerizing?"

"*I* do the mesmerizing," he said with a modest smirk. "Besides, I dig smoky altos. Coo 'I've Got You Under My Skin' at me and I'll listen. Otherwise, it's all noise."

"I can't even pick up a tune as a hitchhiker," I said. "My tin ear tells me we're hearing a heavenly . . . soprano."

"Thin soup. Sopranos always sound to me like they're being throttled," he added.

"That's because most guys don't like opera."

"Do you?"

"Uh, no," I admitted. "But I have to admit I find this endless . . . aria-like perfume in the air addictive."

"Good," Sansouci said. "Find out where the sonic Chanel No. 5 is coming from and end it. You'll get Cicereau's eternal thanks—for about five minutes and a few thou—and I'll be glad to have him off my back, totally nonhairy, despite the demon parking punk's jibe."

"As if I'd care to know. This . . . sound isn't coming over the hotel sound system?"

"First place I looked. No. And I checked the security control room too. You pioneered those routes when Cicereau's daughter's ghost took over the hotel audiovisual systems until you exorcised her."

"Loretta had good reason to haunt her murderous father, and I'm no exorcist. I just figured out how to make some other supernatural gag her. That's what I am, a lowly human problem solver. Who is this . . . superb-voiced siren?"

"Someone or something that will shortly drive the paying customers away and the Gehenna's wolfpack mad. I wouldn't care, but the vampires aren't ready to move on Cicereau yet."

"Some are planning to?" This was hot news in the old town tonight.

Sansouci's grin was wicked. "That's for me to know and you to find out. You're the paranormal investigator. Investigate."

He gave me a little shove in the taffeta bustle, so I was propelled back onto the marble-floored hotel concourse. Sansouci. Always the gentleman vampire muscle.

I hopped into line behind another bellman-propelled luggage cart, protected from the milling crowds, and headed for the main atrium circled by elevators to the Gehenna's various hotel floors and condo towers.

The haunting soprano voice kept me gazing up and around like a geek at an electronics exposition, tripping over my own feet, even though being gauche enough to tangle your killer heels is a Vegas mortal sin.

Being tone deaf doesn't make for musical expertise, but this eerie, sweet as Heavenly Hash voice had me hooked. Since I'm also Black Irish, I was a Celtic woman deep down. I didn't even notice that I'd slowed to a stop to listen until a couple dozen tourists dragging wheeled bags jammed up behind me, screeching annoyance at my back.

Before the rude crowds could mess my crinolines, they suddenly stared upward too, shouting and pointing and hitting the marble floor all around until I was the only upright long-stemmed rose in the garden.

That's when I spotted a large, dark blot streaking down toward me. An ape in a Mad Hatter outfit wearing a fright wig of coarse hair instead of a top hat swung down on a bungee cord. Before I could duck away, a huge hairy hand snagged me around the corseted Audrey

Hepburn waist and swung us both up, up, up several floors to the sustained high-note accompaniment of the heavenly voice and my furious alto scream of protest. In seconds, my powerful captor used the upper-body strength of a circus strongman to perch us like gargoyles atop the highest railing of the Gehenna Hotel's towering atrium.

First, I checked his grip on the thick brass rail. His feet curved like talons around the metal, but wore soft leather shoes curled up at the toes and down at the heel, slippers Santa's elves would wear. My gaze inventoried the odd bits of wardrobe clothing his squat distorted body, then studied a pale bony array of bulbous cheeks and forehead and forked chin, every feature somehow pulled off center like a melted plastic mask. One eye was entirely missing. Rather than a mouth, the creature had a broken-toothed maw. A bushy eyebrow over that bright malicious single eye finished off a face twisted into a grimace a gargoyle would flee, shrieking.

Even at this suicidal height, I'd have pushed off from my captor just to avoid an inescapable double jeopardy of death by asphyxiation: the mixed reek of garlic and onion breath. While I calculated how to tip us backward onto the safety of the balcony fronting the elevators, the powerful arms spun me sideways to lift me like a trophy above the misshapen head.

While my stomach made an imaginary drop of forty stories and the siren's voice soared to higher melodic peaks up here, my captor's terrifying maw shouted something over and over to the crowd below.

"Sank you, Harry!" or some such gibberish spewed from his harsh throat. He snarled down at the gaping crowd below, repeating the word or phrase as boast . . . or challenge. I clung to the sleeves of his long arms as my personal King Kong shook my helpless torso like a weapon.

Then he swept me down again, clasping me doll-like to his barrel chest. In a moment his apelike feet had pushed off the railing as he swung us out over the gaping crowd on the hard marble hundreds of feet below.

My stomach did another swan dive.

Death by implosion was not on my adventure-travel wish list. I clung to the wide lapels of his organ grinder's monkey jacket. He seemed eerily at home swinging on a rope, and was still gabbling that guttural challenge to the gawkers below.

In times of unthinkable danger, the mind decides to sweat the small stuff. All I could focus on was that the crowd sure could see up my full skirts and crinolines to . . . my—good thing I'd been brought up to anticipate a sudden car accident and always wore underpants.

Only then did I see what we swung from . . . not a Cirque du Soleil bungee cord, but an . . . untethered . . . steel elevator cable. Oh, Lord. Were some innocent civilians also dangling from a broken steel thread in one of this row of a dozen elevator cars?

My position remained completely helpless, so, for motivation and an adrenaline surge, I ramped up the indignation of it all. I'd been swept off my feet before by far more attractive and supernaturally powerful forces than this scruffy tent-show acrobat.

I grabbed tight to the nearest long powerful forearm and twirled like a trapeze artist. That spun us into a tangled bundle. I hadn't expected the creature's response.

Instead of dropping us to the nearest balcony like any rational madman, he swung us back over the railing, past the exposed solid ground of the hallway . . . through a pair of open elevator doors . . . and into the naked elevator shaft. No enclosed car awaited inside . . . only empty space.

Screeching triumph, the creature swung from one rising or lowering elevator cable, ducking under or sailing over the stately sinking and rising cars, his rhythm sure and athletic. He Tarzan of the Apes, me Jane.

A distracting fantasy, but this still put me in mortal danger, and I was one of the few mortals still left around this town since the supernaturals had come out to play. Visions of imminent collision with the speeding elevator cars made me clutch the demented monster for dear, if questionable, life. . . .

At last we descended to the deserted equipment bays below the elevator shafts. Here, all was as dark and empty and cold as the hotel casino's public spaces had been bright and well lighted. The icy artificial air-conditioning up top had been replaced by a subtle subterranean chill.

Solid ground was the ancient limestone that underlies the desert sand.

As I caught my breath, I still heard the unknown siren's unearthly song, trilling madly. I now thought of it as a melodic scream for help. Soon I might be making such noises myself.

While rows of elevator cars clanked continually above us as they came and went, I spied some pine-scented Gehenna bed linens nudged into a nest on the hard ground, and room-service plates and food stockpiled by the same limestone wall.

"Safe. You. Here," the creature grunted. "Thank-you-very."

Thank-you-very. Was that the gibberish he'd bellowed from the peak of the atrium?

Somehow, I suspected that his mumbled signature phrase was a clue. This mind-boggling, impulsive creature must be a key to the mystery I'd been hired to solve.

So it was only a hunch. That's what I'm paid to follow.

Right now, he was shoving the trays of room-service leavings at me. I realized this was what he subsisted on, poor inarticulate thing. I eyed the fag ends of cocktail shrimps and the abandoned crescents of gnawed cheeseburgers and pizza crusts. I supposed other handicapped persons on the fringes of the Las Vegas Strip survived on such leavings of the rich and famous.

His huge hands thrust a tray of the "choicest" pieces at me.

I'd only just been kidnapped. I'd had no time to develop the hunger of the truly needy.

But I always had time to understand the generosity of the easily ignored.

"Thank you very," I said, smiling and nodding, as I plucked a couple brown-edged celery sticks from the array and nibbled politely.

The satisfied grin on that lantern jaw helped me gum down the rubbery stalks. Was I supposed to be his dependent? To share this marginal existence? Because I was what? Convenient? Or female?

My sympathies aside, this guy had to learn that I was not the swoop-up-able female of fiction and fable. And then I realized that my kidnapper was just that, a creature of fiction and film. He'd been so grimy and things had happened so fast that I hadn't realized I was dealing with a CinSim, a character from a movie given an extended life attached to the "canvas" of a zombie.

His . . . uh, one eye and skin tones and clothing were not just gray, but shades of cinematic black and white. My earlier "hunch" had been vague, but on the track.

Even as I realized this, I felt a cold snakelike uncoiling at my ankles. My snazzy silver shoelaces were undoing themselves.

The silver familiar, my version of a sidekick-cum-unshakable personal demon, made like twin garter snakes and twined free of my shoes' lacing holes. The familiar relished the drama of being spectacularly present as much as it enjoyed being overlooked. Kinda like any private eye since Sherlock Holmes.

Its twofold form coiled up between my rustling skirt folds and into my curled palms, gaining warmth and a supple strength from the blood pounding in my veins.

I watched a descending elevator glide to touch rock bottom just forty feet from the creature's makeshift camp.

My hands swung out in a sowing gesture, releasing and casting the silver familiar into a fifty-foot lariat lashing out to mate with a momentarily still elevator cable.

Within the coiled tension of my fisted hands, the links of silver shortened and pulled me atop the elevator car like a giant slingshot. I'd become used to its sudden shape-shifting, but the only witness to the operation remained below.

I gazed down ten feet at a jumping Rumpelstiltskin chattering away like Cheetah, Tarzan's clever movie chimp costar. Only from above could I see that my kidnapper hadn't been an ape or a monkey but a man. A hunchback. *The* Hunchback, I realized.

Now I could translate the sounds he had chortled from high in the hotel atrium while I'd been hefted like a trophy over his ungainly head. I had a silent movie script to go by, where the word had been shown onscreen. Not "Thank you very" but *"Sanc-tu-ary!"*

That's the word the Hunchback of Notre Dame had shouted as he swung the kindhearted Gypsy girl, Esmeralda, away from the stake where she was to be burned as a witch and up to the gargoyle-guarded stone heights of the famed Paris cathedral, where a hunchback was the humble bell ringer and where an innocent scapegoat like Esmeralda could find a triumphant "sanctuary" from the ignorant mob storming the church grounds.

This guy had mistaken the crowd of pushy tourists for a rioting mob and me for Esmeralda.

I could think of only two black-and-white-era CinSim hunchbacks, both consummate actors, both despising the Hollywood looks sweepstakes. One was Charles Laughton. The earlier, silent-film version had been Lon Chaney, "the Man of a Thousand Faces."

Something about this bizarre situation was ringing a bell in my head besides the endless vocalizations above, now segueing from the soaring hymn of "Ave Maria" to "Ah, Sweet Mystery of Life," which reminded me of my mission.

Thrilled as I was to have actually relived one of the most iconic moments in the early history of film, I had to lose this scenario and figure out why and how a woman with the voice of an angel would want to haunt a murderous old sinner like Cesar Cicereau.

I'd begun my escape swinging on a silver cord instead of a bell rope, and now was clinging atop a rapidly rising elevator car. Looking up, I saw enough cables to string a harp and a big dark flat nothing—the elevator shaft top—waiting to brain me.

I wound the familiar's shrinking silver cord around my palms. When I had just a garrote-length left, I looped it around the handle on the car's rooftop emergency escape hatch and pulled . . . only I wanted in, not out.

Moments later, just as the elevator shaft top loomed above like an iron hat, I jerked open the hatch to drop down into the brightly lit car, taking my weight on my bent knees. I straightened as the hatch overhead banged shut, smiling at the startled tourists into whose midst I'd so abruptly appeared.

"*Whew*. What a wild private party on the penthouse level," I complained. "Do *not* accept any of those slot machine invitations. It was ballistic." They eyed me with mixed suspicion and envy.

Meanwhile, I noticed the Muzak filling the now-plummeting car. More of that sweet and impossibly sugary soprano voice. What was she singing now? "Send in the Clowns"? No need to get personal!

"Oh, that voice is unearthly," a woman said as the elevator doors finally opened on the main floor.

Yeah! Probably a ghost.

At least I was back where I'd begun, even though my newly laceless shoes were useless after my catapult atop the elevator car. At least I was now wearing a silver charm bracelet dangling place-appropriate wolf heads.

I decided to restart my investigation on the main floor. First, a limping detour down the shopping wing brought me to a store called Two Cool Tootsie's. My dressy spike heels were buckling sideways, so I charged a pair of Steve Madden leopard-print flats with a rose on the toes to Cicereau's account.

Unfortunately, the gushing saleswoman took me for Cicereau's latest moll, not an employee whose wardrobe had suffered in his service.

"Shame about your mangled Jimmy Choos," she consoled me.

I'd explained I'd caught one high heel in an elevator door and broken the second while wrenching the first loose.

"Are you sure the boss will like you as well in flats?" she asked. "I hear he runs hot and cold."

"Oh, Cesar is quite a runner, but he dotes on anything that reminds him of dead Big Cats," I said. "That old Starlight Lodge hunting urge, you know."

She shuddered as she rang up the new shoes. "I've heard what gets chased down at that place. Just stay on his safe side, honey. Cringing is good."

Shod again, I cruised the main entertainment area with a fresh eye. The building's gigantic wooden tree architecture mimicked soaring Gothic cathedral columns. No wonder the Hunchback had replayed his best scene here with me as a stand-in.

Tourists strolled leaf-patterned parquet paths around forest scenes of ferns and flowering plants and thick clustered trees. The scale made you feel as small and helpless as a chipmunk skittering near the trickle of hidden streams, hearing the rustle of bird life in the leaves above. Sensing silently stalking wolves in the shadows. At least I did.

I was glad to break into the brightness of a skylight-illuminated mountain village square with a half-timbered inn called the Huntsman's Haven that broadcast scents of fresh-baked bread, beer, and bratwurst.

A Gypsy wagon and camp drew children to the tricolored wagon, ponies, and the music and color of juggling, knife-throwing, and fortune-telling attractions. I am not an outdoorsy girl. One enforced summer at a mosquito-ridden Minnesota camp during my group home days had been enough for me.

I really needed to check out the hotel's theater stage. The Gehenna's big contracted show starred Madrigal, the strongman magician, and his creepy pair of female fey assistants. Picture two-foot-high Barbie dolls with glitzy wardrobes, webs, and venom.

My captor had been an escapee from an old silent movie. Had the Gehenna been adding new attractions?

Sure enough. The slick marquee advertising Madrigal and his fey accomplices had a smaller satellite now, a film theater showing *London After Midnight*.

This was definitely a black-and-white silent film. As a vintage film junkie, I was drawn toward the marquee like a mesmerized bride-to-be of Dracula. This 1927 silent classic had been lost, burned in a fire in the sixties. How could *London After Midnight* be shown here?

Before I could get close enough to the booth to barter my shoes or my soul for a ticket . . . so much for refusing to carry a purse . . . a sinister figure, all in black, stepped into my path.

He wore a top hat over a clownish, frizzled, chin-length hairdo that framed a vintage gray face with popping eyes and an ebony-lipped mouth grinning to show every tooth filed into a point. I didn't know whether to scream with laughter or fear, and aren't those the yummiest theatrical moments of all?

Spotting me, he spun with a demonic grimace and lifted the arms of his calf-length cape . . . to display the bat-winged spines visible underneath.

Sinister or comic? Early films walked that very thin line.

"Wait!" I shouted, my voice lost in the echo chamber that is a casino concourse's everyday clamor. Tourists love the sounds of crowds and action.

The bizarre figure vanished behind a clot of fanny-pack-wearing sightseers.

I froze.

"Don't you look *sooo* darling, dear?" A grandmotherly tourist in a Jimmy Buffett T-shirt, Bermuda shorts, and varicose veins intercepted me.

"Love your vintage rag-doll look and Hello Bad Kitty shoes. Are you one of those living statues? You can't fool me! Where's the bratwurst bingo line?"

I wordlessly pointed in the direction farthest from where I was standing, and the troop of seniors trekked on past.

But my freaky vampire vision had disappeared just as I'd been about to put a few bizarre pieces together. I was beginning to feel like Alice in a Wonderland of horror films. Since when had Cesar Cicereau's Gehenna Hotel and Casino been anything but an old-style establishment with only one miserable Peter Lorre CinSim on site?

Since before Sansouci had been sent to get me. And where was the handsome nondog, anyway?

I sighed, audibly, surprised when a monocled English gentleman in a tweed suit, bearing a silver-headed cane, stopped to address me.

"Pardon me, miss. Perhaps you can help me catch and unmask a foul vampire. I'm a Scotland Yard detective, but I'm quite lost among all these odd, loud, milling people."

Would Sherlock Holmes hesitate? Could I throw him Sansouci?

He was all in subtle shades of gray from his eyes to his lips to his tweedy Norfolk jacket, another CinSim, yet *not* another CinSim if you knew the film. The vampire had been the detective in disguise. Lon Chaney had played a role within a role.

The scales were falling from my eyes (and also from the trilling woman's voice above all the Vegas hotel hullabaloo).

I needed to get to Cesar Cicereau, fast, which meant I had to snag a conventional elevator ride to the penthouse level. I streaked through the crowd, watching the top-hatted vampire offering to escort a troop of local Boy Scouts into the wood. Not good.

In the concourse in front of the elevators, people were pushing toward every lit Up arrow, chattering and checking their fanny packs for cash and credit cards.

The melee was so huge and loud that the haunting singer could no longer be heard. No one even noticed the Hunchback of Notre Dame grinning down at me as he swung back and forth against the bank of elevators like the weight on a grandfather clock's pendulum.

At last I'd battled my way into an up elevator all the way to Cesar Cicereau's forty-third-floor penthouse. And he was the one who wanted this appointment.

A carved wood tree design on the mirrored elevator car walls made riders feel claustrophobic, as if their reflected image and the frame of trees extended into infinity. Since I'd been known to mirror-walk, I kept a firm grip on myself to avoid being drawn into Wereworld.

The elevator opened on the foyer to Cicereau's penthouse.

This high, the soprano was coming in loud and clear, singing "My Blue Heaven." I rather doubted it, having visited here before.

Two half-were bodyguards bracketed the elaborately carved

wooden doors to Cesar Cicereau's personal lair. They had frozen at man height in transition to wolf. I imagined the chatty wolf from "Little Red Riding Hood" would look like them—hairy, predatory beasts with snouts like crocodiles standing on two shoeless feet but otherwise clad.

These weren't the fully human Cicereau pack members who usually faced the public. These were Cicereau's paw-picked bodyguards, the weres who never fully reverted to human for some reason, like the half-were biker gangs on the Vegas streets.

In fact, I wished I were facing a tormented, self-hating werewolf like the Larry Talbot persona actor Lon Chaney Jr. had pioneered. The 1941 classic horror film *The Wolf Man* portrayed the title character as all angsty dude, with my devoted CinSim and all-around character actor, Claude Rains, playing his father figure.

But, no, it was the big boss I needed to see. No one half human.

"The boss is expecting me," I said.

The guards eyed me for a long moment.

My adventures had finally made me look the part of the accused witch and Gypsy girl, Esmeralda. I was rumpled and bruised, with my ballerina-length taffeta skirt as ragged and bedraggled as my shoulder-length hair.

Their elongated lips curled. "The boss don't entertain skags like you."

"Skags like me can save his hairy ass. Tell him Delilah Street is calling."

They reared back as one recognized me. He clawed at his buddy's furry forearm to impart a fearsome message.

"This is the dame who killed that Frankenstein dude who plunged out the boss's windows."

"He was dead to begin with," I pointed out. "Unless you yearn for the same condition, either let me pass or announce me. I won't touch a hair on your matted bellies, but Cicereau wants to see me."

Their handlike forepaws clawed at their shaggy, upright ears as the soprano reached the top of her four-octave range and held the note for an eternity. I could see the fur around their jaws was scabbed with blood. The high-pitched sound of music really did torment the poor misbred creatures.

"Please," I added.

My alto-pitched voice must have been soothing. They panted in doglike relief and opened the doors for me. Or maybe nobody here said "please" without begging for his life.

"Forty-three stories, dude," one whispered to the other behind my back. "A wild-woman. Almost as merciless as the boss."

That was a bad rap, but any reputation in this town can't hurt. The creature I'd tricked into that suicidal leap had already torn apart several tourists and even a few werewolves. Like the real Frankenstein's monster, he had been more of a victim of his makers than bad to begin with. I'd done what was necessary to save lives, even supernatural half-lives. That didn't mean I wasn't sorry I'd had to do it. Hopefully, this assignment would have a happier ending, but I doubted it.

I knew the suite's layout from my previous visit, especially the paired guest bathrooms bracketing the entry hall like guard wolves, so that welcome and not-so-welcome guests could clean off blood and gore, coming and going.

Inside, I felt nervous. Outside, I acted like the Girl Who Had Offed Frankenstein's Monster. Inside, I was just another mob hireling.

Cicereau sat ensconced on a lavish spread of Swedish modern furniture, all woodsy and leather. He was wearing furry earmuffs and clutching an icepack to his head. The moon was recovering from being full, but Cicereau still looked like he had a hunting hangover.

I'd considered the Hunchback of Notre Dame a grotesque figure at first, but Cicereau, although totally human in his nonwerewolf form, was a sort of human toad whose broad, rapacious face lacked half the intelligence I'd seen glimmering in the mostly mute Hunchback's one eye.

"Street. So you're really here," Cicereau crowed. "And so is the screeching siren I want you to eliminate. About now the sound of your scream after my men hurl you through the window would be worth the momentary overriding of the screaming Mimi in my hotel."

"Wronged women do seem to have it in for you," I commented. "I need some information before I wrap up this case."

"Really? You plan to wrap up something besides your own life and career?"

"You recently invested in some new CinSims, didn't you?"

"Yeah, but none who sang. My accountants say I need to up the main-floor attractions. I'm old-school. I think a couple thousand rooms, a big theatrical show, a shopping mall, a bunch of bare boobs here and there, and a casino crammed with gaming tables and machines should do for the stupid tourists.

"And do you know what those CinSim things cost? They're leased, like freaking vending machines. What a racket. Worse than that freaking supernatural soprano. You pay over and over for the product, like any sucker who visits Vegas. Not Cesar Cicereau. I figured out how to beat the Immortality Mob at its own game."

"Let me guess. You leased the Man of a Thousand Faces."

"Well, that's exaggerating what the dead dude has to offer, but yeah, that particular deal was attractive. The CinSim people assured me that this Lon Chaney actor would be a freaking chameleon. At least ten for the price of one."

"I've never heard of a CinSim being leased to play multiple roles. It could turn the actor underneath the characters schizophrenic."

"Stop the schmancy-fancy words. 'CinSim' is hard enough for my electronic dictionary. I'm experimenting with the Gehenna's tourist attractions, okay? I happen to think this CinSim craze isn't here to stay, but I'll try something now and then if it seems to fit my theme. I mean, this guy is the whole freak show put together: the Hunchback, the Phantom, Dracula, the Mummy, the Wolf Man, whatever. He's got the monster chops down, and I like that.

"What I don't like," Cicereau said—leaning forward and pointing at me with the kind of big, dark, stinky cigar familiarly called "a wolf turd"—"is that girly high-pitched yammering whining like a bitch in heat all through my hotel. Her you get rid of, and I don't care how. Right?"

"Cicereau seems a bit confused about his CinSims," I pointed out after I'd washed off the cigar stink in the entry-area powder room and joined Sansouci in the hall outside the kingpin's suite.

"Cicereau hires people to know about things that confuse him."

"Do you smoke?" I asked.

"Only after sex," he joked. "Listen. Just do the job and don't overthink ole Cesar. He doesn't."

"Listen," I answered, leaning my hands on a brass railing related to the one I'd almost been tossed off earlier. "That woman has the purest, clearest vocal tone I've ever heard and is on perfect key. You can't say it doesn't move you. If I could sing like that—"

"If you could sing like that you'd be on Cicereau's death list." Sansouci looked up. "Besides, your job is to send her back where she came from. She'll still be singing somewhere."

I sighed. "I probably can do that, but something's wrong about Cicereau's SinCims purchases. Can you get me some info off Groggle?"

"Me? Look up something for *you* on a computer? Do I look like a male secretary?"

"I'll write it down for you. If you can read."

"I can read you. You're pretty desperate." He handed me a pencil stub and a Gehenna matchbook from the Hell's Kitschen Lounge.

"Yeah," I admitted. "I need a full report—pronto, puppy—from you on these two names, just like you were a private dick."

"I sort of am," he said with a gigolo gleam.

"I'll warn you that they're dead guys."

"Bros." The undercover daylight vampire nodded sagely as he pocketed his makeshift notebook. "This'll be an intriguing change of pace."

"And I'll need to know all about who they were, on and off the silver screen."

"You want a freaking book?"

"I think I've read part of it, but I need more. You know how to print out from online, don't you? You just flex your fingers and hit PRINT."

"Five-finger exercises are second nature to me. Where'll you be?"

"In the deepest pit backstage of the hotel theater, entertaining the creep who set *her*"—I looked up to where the encompassing voice seemed to be ensconced—"haunting *us*."

Was I aching for a reunion with the Hunchback of Notre Dame? Hell, no! I was hoping for a rendezvous with the Phantom of the Opera, though.

That was who had drawn the mysterious voice down from CinSim heaven.

I might welcome a bit of Internet intervention and detailed info from Sansouci . . . who would make an admirable private secretary, but I'd basically determined that the Gehenna's troubles were due to the eternal triangle. Man, woman . . . man.

You just had to picture the key elements as monsters, movie monsters.

Meanwhile, I was developing as extreme an allergy to sopranos as Cesar Cicereau. That we should have something in common was disgusting.

I had barely arrived back on the main floor, when Sansouci put the make on me again.

"Your printout, madam."

"That's an iTouchOften screen."

"Works for me."

I reached for it, but he held it behind his back, as if in a game.

"This really means something to you," he charged. "Not just the what and the how, the assignment and the pay, but the who and the why."

"Maybe. I doubt an ancient vampire like you could understand."

"Maybe if you knew my what and how and who and why, you would."

"Maybe that's a too unhuman place for me to go."

He considered, then shrugged.

"How do exploring the dark, deep crevices of the human heart, soul, and mind work for you?" I asked.

"My 'hood."

"Forgive me if I don't think that you have the depth."

"Try me."

I needed an assistant. I could use some muscle and I could provide the missing "soul."

"Is that main-floor maze through the woods populated by anything but naive tourists?" I asked.

"Cicereau was aiming at a walkway of fairy-tale victims."

"Fairy-tale victims?"

"You know. Toothsome females in supine positions, like Sleeping Beauty."

"And Snow White in her crystal coffin?" I wondered.

Sansouci grimaced. It didn't look anywhere near as bad on him as it did on the Hunchback. "She had that Lilith look he likes."

"My double. Right. That's why he hires me: look, but no need to touch. Just use me to save his ass."

"It's a job," Sansouci consoled. "Like mine."

"There are jobs and there are jobs. Are you willing to walk Little Red Riding Hood through the woods?"

"This hokey 'attraction'? If it will stop that woman ghost upstairs from howling, sure."

"She gets to you too?"

"Nothing gets to me."

"We'll see."

The woodland walk was too new to attract many tourists. No gaming, no glitz. We were alone.

"You realize," Sansouci said after a while, "you're Little Red, and I'm the Wolf."

"Not this time. And don't let my devoted wolfhound know that."

"He's not here."

"He could be in two seconds flat," I said with a grin.

Just then we heard a fierce canine growling in the woods. I shrugged complacently before rushing toward it. Sansouci held back a bit.

The growling ended with a piercing wail of surprised pain that rose up in a weird chorus with the ghostly soprano.

I crashed thorough the carefully planted underbrush to find a blunt-featured, perfectly respectable middle-aged man writhing on the forest floor.

"It bit me!" he cried. Then he spotted me. "Oh, are you all right, miss? You haven't been bitten too? I tried to divert the wolf from hurting you." He glowered over my shoulder at Sansouci.

I was no longer the accused witch Esmeralda outside of the great cathedral of Notre Dame, but the werewolf-threatened young woman Larry Talbot had saved from a werewolf bite in the forest, making himself the werewolf-to-be.

I knelt beside him, another CinSim, yet still wounded in spirit and fact. "I'm fine," I told him. "You saved me. What's your name?"

The distant trills above made him gaze up through the canopy of leaves. "What beautiful music I hear. It's like a lullaby."

"You mustn't fall asleep," I said, shaking him. "Concentrate. What's your name?"

"Name? Creighton. No, Larry now. Not Creighton. I was walking in the wood to visit the Gypsy camp and saw you. An enormous wolf was threatening to bite you."

"You stopped it," I reassured him.

Meanwhile, my mind was on overdrive. Something was wrong here. His name was Creighton? There went my house of cards of a theory. The movie hero, Larry Talbot, had been played by the son of the Hunchback and the Man of a Thousand faces, Lon Chaney. I was now comforting Lon Chaney Jr., CinSim.

I'd now met both father and son CinSims, both famed for playing multiple roles, multiple monster roles. I should be bringing these events to a conclusion, but the scenario and cast were just getting more confused.

And who the hell was the ghastly, ghostly soprano still commanding the upper reaches of the Gehenna Hotel?

I had no trouble persuading Sansouci to leave the troubled man in the woods to his own devices.

"What a wimp," Sansouci declared when we neared the main concourse. "I got 'bit' for eternity too and you don't see me moaning around about it."

"You're not the angsty protagonist of a movie classic."

He snorted derision.

"Scoff all you like, but Lon Chaney Jr. knew what his father knew, that a likable monster under the mask is much more intriguing than an evil being through and through. Cicereau would be more fully rounded if he'd actually regretted having his daughter killed."

"No sell," Sansouci said of his boss. "You can handle these schizophrenic CinSim shape-shifters?"

"I'll have to. Give me the printouts you made for me. Lon Chaney Sr. mistook me for his movie leading lady. Most CinSims are leased in a single role, but this pair were known for metamorphosing. Maybe I can convince Larry Talbot I'm his love interest."

"You'd do all this for Cicereau?"

"Heck, no." I snatched the folding papers Sansouci produced from his inner jean jacket pocket. "I'll do it for getting these helplessly entangled CinSims' house in order. Whatever's gone wrong has to do with the actors' private lives. You'd better leave me to it."

I stood there and listened after Sansouci left. The voice was still singing, although familiarity bred dismissal. It was becoming just more casino background music. Yet, Larry Talbot had been right.

She'd been singing a lullaby while we'd talked in the ersatz woods, Brahms's famous one, in fact, and it had almost put Larry Talbot to sleep.

Suddenly, I had a plan.

I headed back to the theater area. It was "dark" now, even during daylight, since only two evening shows played there. I knew my way around theaters, and had almost been an indentured attraction here, so I raced down the empty aisles and up the steps at the side of the stage, then into the dark and curtained wings at stage right.

Large light-board and special-effects layouts filled the area. Matching installments were set up at the back of the "house." I wanted under, not up, so I scrabbled around in the dark until I found a set of narrow, steep steps down to the subbasement.

Before I descended, I turned on the pinpoint light and punched the button on one of two dozen labeled sound and visual effects: lightning, thunder, parade . . . there! Just what I needed. Wedding processional.

Sansouci was right. I was making the ultimate sacrifice to pursue this case.

Glad for my flat-heeled shoes, I backed down the ladderlike steps into the dark. Above, I heard the house above fill with the thrilling notes of "Here Comes the Bride," aka Wagner's operatic Bridal Chorus from *Lohengrin*.

The music was ponderous, slow, churchy organ music. I'd never expected to waltz down the aisle to this famous, formal organ music, but it was crazy appropriate for the past and the present I needed to meld into one big postmortem family reunion to end the haunting of the Gehenna and put restless human spirits and silver-screen stars to bed in Lullaby Land. I hoped it would conjure the most famous monster of all.

And, with the vibrations of that thunderous march shaking the stone roots of the subbasement, I stopped and listened for the thin soprano trill that never stopped.

Yes! Faint, but still discernible.

I stepped forward to the march's beat, clasped my hands at my demure Audrey Hepburn waist, and mouthed the words "Here comes the bride, all dressed and wide." Well, those were the lyrics we had used at Our Lady of the Lake Convent School.

"Beautiful," a thrumming male voice added to the cacophony.

A face from a nightmare leapt in front of me. "You? You, girl. You sing like a chorus of angels emerging from one throat. I'll teach you, shape you, make you even more magnificent."

I simpered at the grotesque face with the eyes circled in black paint and the blackened and ragged teeth. I couldn't sing, but I could hear, and I mouthed along with the distant siren, while the Phantom of the Opera closed his lids over those mad, blasted eyes and swayed to the song echoing above. . . . "Think of Me," as it is sung at the Las Vegas Venetian Resort Hotel Casino performance of *The Phantom of the Opera* every night, by Christine, the beautiful soprano the Phantom loves and longs for.

Finally, the female phantom of the Gehenna finished a long, sustained phrase, and . . . stopped.

The automatic organ melody had died even earlier.

I stood alone in the darkened silence with the Phantom of the Opera, 1927-style, Lon Chaney's greatest transformation.

"My love. My Christine," the Phantom said, words Chaney had mouthed on the 1925 silent-film screen. He'd never uttered an audible word until his last film in 1930, and, dying, this son of deaf-mutes had not been able to speak at all. "Only you can sing my soul to rest."

Yes, that was true. To accomplish that, I had to lead him on a merry chase.

Up the stairs I sprang on my brand-new leopard-skin rose-toed flats, feeling the CinSim clutch at my ragged taffeta hem.

Onto the stage and up the aisles to the bright artificial light of the concourse I flew like Cinderella eluding her Prince. Tourists paused to observe and *ooh* and chuckle. Just part of the performing mimes

Vegas hotels are famed for. Then I ducked into the carefully land-scaped wooded area and hoped my high-pitched screams befitted a frightened girl fleeing a werewolf.

Larry Talbot, now fully furred and fanged, rose from the under-brush, growling, determined to stop my pursuer.

I stepped aside like a bit player trying to save her acting wardrobe as monster met monster.

The Phantom ruled his understage world, but he was an emotional and intellectual monster.

The Wolf Man bared his fangs and his wild, white-eyed look and pounced on the disfigured maniac opera buff.

I couldn't have the Immortality Mob's property tearing each other gray limb from black limb, so I jumped between them.

"You want to save me, noble suitors," I cried in what for me was close to a swooning soprano, "do not destroy each other. I love you both."

Well, there. I'd introduced a logical impossibility into the plot of every film either "man" had ever acted in.

In confusion, Lon Chaney Jr. morphed into his Mummy persona.

"Oh, Karis," I said, pressing a restraining hand on his blood-smudged chest wrappings. "He is but an old man, a figure of fun, not a rival."

At which, Lon Chaney Sr. obligingly changed into one of his de-mented clown personas.

This is when I discovered that the female love interest is the queen of the board, the key to every plot of every originally cheesy melodramatic script these film legends had appeared in. She was lovely, she was engaged, she was a swooning wimp, and they ached to own her love, but always lost out to a fine, stalwart, handsome, ordinary human man.

In some ways, the life and loves of Lon Chaney and his son

Creighton, who would resurface as Lon Chaney Jr., much to his embarrassment and shame, were as much at stake here as any misunderstood film monster's fate.

I was getting a lot of melodrama whiplash keeping these legendary actors and their roles apart when a woman's voice came to my rescue.

"Stop. Stop! I won't be caught between you! I won't be the maiden victim again and again. I won't be silent. I will sing. I'd rather die than be torn between the two of you. Monsters! I am a nightingale and I will not be caged."

A pretty woman wearing a pale, long gown now stood among us, a figure of hysterical anguish.

She threw back her slim soprano's neck and lifted an even slimmer glass vial to her gray silver-screen lips. A thin stream of mercury slid oysterlike down her throat. Then she screamed, screeched, writhed, clutching her vocal cords as they corroded and cracked, and vanished along with her ability to make any sound.

"You did this," the Wolfman snarled at the Phantom. "You told me she was dead, that I had no mother. But the mercury poison destroyed her vocal cords, not her life."

"Her vocal cords *were* her life!" How odd to see the Phantom of the Opera scorning a woman for using her gift, but the character had been a control freak too. "Cleva wanted to perform, and you were a young boy, Creighton," the Phantom argued. "You needed a mother with you, not one off in nightclubs singing for far less than emperors."

"Creighton. That was *her* surname," Larry Talbot remembered, "given to me as her firstborn. She tried to kill herself because of you."

"I had theatrical work, boy, a rising career! Cleva refused to give up her singing to stay with you."

"Others could have tended me. They already had."

"Yes, her voice was sublime, beyond incredibly sweet."

"And it never was so again. You cared nothing for her gift, her talent, so she seared it from her throat in front of you," the Wolfman said with a guttural whine of pain. "And then you told me she was dead. I was just a boy of seven. You kept us apart for years until she found me again."

"Once you knew of her existence, you left me, Creighton. You went off with her."

"Which was fine with you. You never wanted me to go on the stage, on the screen, as you never wanted her to sing. She destroyed her gift in her pain at your not valuing it. Or her."

"You called yourself 'Lon' and tacked a 'Jr.' on your name at the order of the studio bosses after I was dead."

"I didn't want to. I wanted to be my own man, as my mother wanted to be her own woman, but your legend mired us both in paths that hurt us."

"I didn't put the bichloride of mercury in her hand."

"You put the despair in her soul."

"Our divorce was overdue."

"As I was born prematurely. I guess," the Wolfman said, straightening into the sad, human, but familiar form of Larry Talbot, "I guess our timing was always off, Dad."

I held my breath, caught up in the family tragedy. Sure, they were all CinSims, so it was like watching ghosts play out some long-dead script. But the drama was true to life.

"I died young, Son," Lon Chaney admitted, "alone, before age fifty, from cornflakes, of all things, used to make snow on a set. I lost my voice at the end, as Cleva had, as my deaf-mute parents had before their births. A throat hemorrhage silenced me forever, seventeen years after Cleva's mad attempt at self-destruction."

"So why is she singing now?" Lon Jr. asked.

They turned to me, as if I were the image of Cleva. I was brunet, as the printout photo of her had been, but my hair was closer to jet-black. She'd looked high-hearted smart in a top hat and a monocle from some forgotten vaudeville or nightclub routine. We hardly resembled each other, but to the CinSims' eyes, we were the eternal woman, heroine, victim, mother, child, lover, supporter, opponent.

"She wanted Creighton to *hear* what she had been," I said to the Phantom. "And," I said to the Wolf Man, "she wanted to *see* what you had become."

"Yet," the Wolf Man said, "she lived to a riper old age than either of us."

"But . . . you'd never heard her sing," I pointed out. "Now you have."

The Wolf Man nodded. "The pack sings. It's part of our heritage."

"Are you the actor or the role?" I asked.

I gestured at the Phantom. "This is an inspired and impassioned instructor. You have a chance to replay all your roles over and over again, with Cleva as an invisible audience. I don't think you'll see or hear her again, except in your CinSim hearts."

Frowns. The moment had passed. They resumed their roles, utterly alien to each other except in being monsters. Phantom and Wolf Man. Larry Talbot vanished into his woodland arena. The Phantom limped back to the bowels of the theater.

I reported to the head monster in the penthouse soon after.

"So you're saying I leased a pair of CinSims with unresolved relationship issues?" Cicereau demanded. "What is the Immortality Mob pushing these days?"

"Leasing illusory surfaces of human beings is a dodgy business, even in these post–Millennium Revelation days," I told him.

"And the ghost of the Chaney wife and mother decided my hotel-casino was the place to sing bloody murder about stuff that went down a hundred years ago, when she and Lon Chaney got divorced? Women! They never give up. Why me?"

"Perhaps you own daughter's haunting created a channel for another woman who felt a trusted man had taken her life, one way or another."

"I didn't hire a psychoanalyst-investigator, Street. Out, out, damn Joseph Campbell! You quit the psychobabble and concentrate on being a babe and just guarantee that psycho siren is outta the Gehenna and my hearing for good."

"Oh, she's gone, and I will be too. Once you fork over what you owe me."

He pulled a wad from his pin-striped pants and peeled off Benjamin Franklins, snapping the hundred-dollar bills to the desktop like he was laying out playing cards.

At three thousand, he paused for my reaction.

"I banished one ghost and reunited two CinSims, not to mention tussling with the Hunchback of Notre Dame, the Wolf Man, the Mummy, and the Phantom of the Opera."

He resumed, slapping down hundreds until he reached five thousand. It made quite a pile.

"Tell me you don't sing," he asked with a beady eye on my throat.

"I don't."

"Fifty-two Benjamins for the whole deck of cards, covering a maintenance visit if the Chaney boys act up again."

Lon Chaney, the Man of a Thousand Faces and reluctant postmortem "Sr." to his son Creighton's studio rechristening as Lon Chaney Jr., had hoped his feats of grotesque disguise proved that "the *dwarfed, misshapen* beggar of the streets may have the noblest ideals and the capacity for supreme self-sacrifice."

Cleva Creighton had sacrificed her sublime voice in her tormented fight for the right to use it.

Lon Chaney had learned to "speak" so eloquently in silent films by growing up with deaf-mute parents, and then died speechless of throat cancer.

Creighton Chaney had rejected the father who'd deprived a young boy of his mother, but fate had turned him to walk in the same career shoes.

Speaking of shoes, I left the Gehenna with a couple months' salary, a satisfyingly "happy" ending for two icons of film history, and a kicky new pair of leopard-pattern flats with full-blown roses on the toes in honor of poor, deluded, but talented Cleva Creighton.

"Need a lift back to the Inferno party?" a voice asked as its owner fell into step with me as I strode through the din-filled Gehenna lobby.

"I've had enough unwanted transportation today, thanks," I told Sansouci. "I think I'll walk."

The daylight vampire might claim to feel no regrets for his centuries of survival on other people, but I guessed he had more in common with tormented Larry Talbot than a mobster like Cesar Cicereau would ever perceive . . . or believe.

Alone, I pushed open an entry door and walked out of the intense hotel-casino air-conditioning to mingle with the throng of tourists heading like lemmings for the Strip under the hot-syrup warmth of the Nevada sun pouring down.

Something was snuffling at my new shoes.

I stopped, looked down, and spotted a big black wet nose.

Quicksilver, my ever-shadowing wolfhound-wolf guard dog, was grinning up at me with fangs and panting tongue on equal parade display.

"All's well that ends swell, boy. We can head home to the Enchanted Cottage and the DVD player now. How'd you like to settle in with an Awesome Gnawsome chew stick, some jalapeño popcorn, and a couple of really prime vintage monster movies? *The Wolf Man* is a must, but, after that, do you go for heroic bell ringers or demonic organ players?"

His sharp, short bark indicated he was ready to eat up anything.

WANTED: DEAD OR ALIVE

L. A. Banks

Tanya took a deep breath, collecting her thoughts as best she could before speaking into the small, handheld digital recorder.

"Being dead sucks, especially if it happened on the job. Okay, true, I'm not what you technically call dead, but the fact is, I don't have a heartbeat. I'm this in-between kind of being, sorta the way I've lived my whole life: Really smart but couldn't conform to school. Really sexy, if I do say so myself, but hated that guys couldn't get past my rack to look me straight in my eyes. Stood up for justice at every turn and broke the so-called law every chance I got. Yeah, all right, I admit it, I'm complicated. And so what? Why would I think dying would be a straightforward two shots in the back of the head in a parking lot or something?"

Tanya clicked off the tiny digital recorder she held in her slender palm and then tossed it on her desk. "This is bullshit." Tears momentarily filled her eyes and then burned away as she stared out of her office window at the new moon. "What was I thinking? A book? Stop dreaming."

Leaving a legacy had never been her plan. Until last month, Live fast, die young, and leave a good-looking corpse had been her motto. *That* had been the original plan.

By twenty-nine, she was one of the best bounty hunters, and

sometimes hit woman, in the biz. She'd always thought that one day someone would get to her before she got to them, if she got sloppy. But she'd also felt that, if she did manage to live long enough to get old and sloppy, then having a faster gun put her out of her misery wouldn't be a totally bad thing.

But having a long-range plan that meant leaving some sort of legacy was never anything she'd dwelled on. Hell no. Life was too unpredictable for that. After her own disastrous childhood, trying to have a couple of kids and win the Mother of the Year Award would have been a disservice to the planet. No, rather than be a procreator she'd elected to be an eliminator, wiping the city streets clean of the kind of scum that had made her childhood hell.

Tanya hugged herself. It had been so easy to get into the business. Maybe too easy. Work with bail bondsmen was her entry point. It was good money, fast money. The bigger the fish she hauled in, the more side jobs would come in, until one of the casino boys realized that she had the body of a black widow. Most of her targets were male. All of them were dirty as sin, so she didn't get into the politics of justice. She just served it.

Regardless of nationality, her targets were always wary of other men casing them, but not of a female who looked like she did—five seven, satiny brown skin, mahogany-hued hair that swept her shoulders, intense Egyptian kohl-rimmed eyes, with thirty-six, twenty-four, thirty-eight dimensions. That was always good for a conversation opener. Slipping them a roofie made hand-to-hand combat a less likely thing, albeit she was prepared to go there if she had to.

Then in one night, the night that would have been her largest takedown, everything went wrong.

Dimitri wasn't like her other targets. He didn't drink. He didn't bend to her feminine charms. He did seem amused by her, though. That should have been her cue. But she'd gotten cocky. Had never missed her mark. Had become the thing she promised herself she'd never be while still young: sloppy. That would never happen again.

Even now thinking back on it, the memory gave her a chill.

Somehow Dimitri had gotten her to actually drink . . . and chat . . . and had turned her on. Now she knew why. There was something hypnotic about his dark, intensely piercing eyes.

Back then, it was all still a strangely exciting mystery. It was a shame that the people who'd hired her wanted him dead. The man was seriously fine, but had been fleecing their blackjack tables, and when they'd stepped to him, he'd killed several of their guards. The people who ran Vegas beneath the shimmering lights didn't want to wait for law enforcement. They wanted justice served the old-fashioned way: cold and immediately. They thought they'd be sending a message to the Russian mob and had no idea that it was an invitation to war with a seriously old vampire.

Tanya looked around the expansive Manhattan brownstone that she now owned, courtesy of her last job. Dimitri had old-world tastes, but had a fully functional vaulted crypt in the basement. At some point when she cared more, she'd have it all redone.

Still, the one thing that bothered her was how quickly the mission had gotten blurry and how she foolishly wasn't afraid of the interesting, dark-haired Russian. At that time he seemed like he was just a man. After sex, they all fell asleep. At some point, they all had to eat. Poison. A silenced bullet. Whatever. It didn't matter. She was patient. Unfortunately, so was he.

Tanya closed her eyes. This was the part that she wanted so badly to write about. This new awareness of a life beyond life was what she wanted to chronicle. That would be her legacy, the only thing that maybe she'd be remembered for.

But then she'd also have to tell how he'd toyed with her as though playing with his food. Humiliating, but true. She was human, then; he was not. He'd brought her back to his suite; she thought she was in a good position. He just smiled and remained the perfect gentleman . . . pouring her a merlot. And she found herself getting naked for him while he watched from across the room. His eyes held more fascination than desire—an enjoyment of the hunt that she'd recognized too late. And that's when everything began going badly.

Tanya unconsciously covered the side of her neck with her palm and walked away from the window. He'd tranced her to come to him and then he'd stood, caressing her throat with the softest kisses that instantly turned into blinding pain. Panic swept through her, but survival instinct kicked in and sent her hand clawing his groin. She was rewarded with a backhanded bitch slap that sent her sprawling across the room to shatter the small oval coffee table by the sofa.

Clearly enraged, he glowered down at her for a moment, her blood staining his mouth. He then cursed at her in a language she'd never heard, and then suddenly he laughed. That's when she saw his teeth. It was a cruel laugh of unchecked power. His eyes were no longer intense and darkly sexy; instead they were all black, no whites showing. The eyes of a demon. The eyes of certain death.

"You will die tonight, my lovely," he'd said. "Such a disappointment, I know—especially when you had come all this way to kill me. Ah . . . the vagaries of fate."

Tanya squeezed her eyes shut and rested her forehead on the wall, still hearing his voice echoing in her mind. Then he'd lunged at her; she'd used the broken table leg like a knife to defend herself and to ward him off. It gored his heart and left her beneath a pile of burning embers. Everything from that point forward became a blur. She knew she had to move, had to get out. Up in an instant, she covered her mouth to keep from screaming, found her dress and her purse with the gun in it, and was gone.

Fifty large they'd paid her, but that wasn't enough money in the world for what her life was suddenly to become. Others followed Dimitri, looking for his killer. At first they thought it was another vampire—she could feel them, hear their thoughts. All those he had made were looking for his heir apparent. Everything that Dimitri was and had learned bled into her mind over the days she lay dying in her dark apartment by the bay. Then one night her heart stopped, but her eyes opened. The hunger came, and with her first feeding came the knowledge that she'd never see daylight again.

Everything he'd owned, she inherited, even at times the way his words threaded through her mind and changed her normal patterns of speech. She now owned his made men, too. But in the vampire world that also meant that she owned the late Dimitri Andropov's problems as well, namely those who had wanted to wrest power from him for a long time. And that meant a nightly vigil against those who wanted to take her down and not knowing whom to trust . . . not that living that way was any different than her human life had been. But still. The constant paranoia was wearing and she was new to the vampire way of life.

In the vampire world, to the victor go the spoils. This was not the legacy she'd wanted. And for all its opulent, everlasting glory, when the time came for her assassination, all that she ever was would turn into a smoking pile of embers, her memories and knowing suddenly owned by her killer. But for the moment, membership did have its privileges.

Now she understood her kind's fascination with history and building monuments. She understood why they were so erudite in the arts. For beings that lived for an eternity, knowing that they would disappear from the annals of time by a simple assassination had to be maddening. To be both timeless yet ephemeral, therein lay the paradox.

Tanya glanced back at the small silver digital recorder and then up at the moon. She had to get out of here. Dinner and danger were on the streets.

"Pyotr, do not grow arrogant and lose your life for it. Dimitri was a centuries-old vampire and lost his life to a mere mortal."

"My friend, your words bring comfort that you have my best interest at heart, but this human *girl* is only a month old to the ways of Vampyre. We will find her. We will kill her. It is already decided and quite a simple task."

Pyotr stopped walking and leaned against a tree in Central Park for a moment, taking his time to light a cigarette and slowly exhale the smoke. "Do we yet know how many are still loyal to their bond to Dimitri?" When Vikenti didn't immediately answer, Pyotr stared at his ancient friend. "Just as I thought. There is no way yet to know."

"What is to know is that she walks this path every night, and for every night that we wait, she grows stronger. For every night that we linger in worry, another may beat us to our objective and claim his victory—then we would have to assassinate him. Not such an easy task."

"But we do not yet know of her numbers, those that stand with her."

"How many of Dimitri's loyalists will stand to be told they cannot procreate? What leader of a coven from the old world would have such an edict that no more of our kind could be made?"

Vikenti spat on the ground, his dark eyes narrowed with disgust. "Who will now change the way they once fed freely to accept her preposterous notions of drinking only from the wicked—no longer tasting the pure innocent? Ha? You have no answers."

Feeling victory in his grasp, Vikenti watched his friend take a particularly long drag off his cigarette before he pressed on. "And now she organizes them in vigilante squadrons to help humans. Dimitri's made men must spend their nights in service to their food? Where is the honor in that? It is madness—no, it is weakness. Her connection still to the human condition is an opportunity. But we must be quick, my friend, for her ranks will attempt a coup. Of this I am certain. It is rumored that they are already assassinating each other for the chance to be the first to go against her while she is still new."

"You know this rumor must be false or there is some element of this story we do not know. Her own made or those she inherited from Dimitri cannot kill her."

"But they can align with others not of her line and give them critical details to make it easy for them to assassinate her . . . so says our master, Aleksei. He was giving us a hint, giving us a clue to in-crease his territory without his hands getting dirty on this."

Pyotr pushed himself away from the tree he'd been leaning on. "And there are two of us. This inheritance of Dimitri Andropov can go to only one."

Vikenti smiled, allowing a bit of fang to show. "Then, my friend, I suggest you hurry at the task. May the best man win."

Winter wind cut at her face, but she didn't hunch against the cold. Leather coat wide open, she allowed it to billow out behind her, en-joying the sting of feeling halfway alive. Frigid temperatures bit into her arms and torso, ignoring her black sweater, and then wrapped around her black leather pants and boots, chilling her legs. The cold evening air was obviously in no mood for compromise tonight; but then again, neither was she.

Tanya watched dispassionately as humans bundled up against the elements walked quickly and kept their heads down. Cattle. The thrum of their heartbeats and blood was intoxicating, but she had to show restraint as she scanned dull minds when she passed warm bodies. The homeless had committed no crime beyond being poor and mentally ill. To her way of thinking, to feed on them and then kill them would be unjust. They'd already gotten the shit end of life. Same with the working girls on the streets, she thought as she passed a group of shivering prostitutes. Someone was already kicking their asses; someone was already sucking the lifeblood out of them, be it a pimp or their drug dealer or the johns that kept the trade going.

No. Her goal was the bastards that created the conditions. She wanted the men like Bernie Madoff, and bankers, and politicians, and corporate moguls who stole from the poor to give to the rich. Her best feeding grounds were on Wall Street or in the high-rent districts. They also ate a better grade of food and drank top-shelf liquors and wines. Their blood was all the richer for it.

Tanya crossed through the park to save time. Maybe she'd dine in Greenwich, Connecticut, tonight, or even scour SoHo. Tonight was going to be different. No more petty thieves and thugs. The cops could handle them. She'd go after the ones that had enough resources to buy their way out of prosecution. Yeah . . . it was time to upgrade. But a presence behind her gave her pause.

A tall, lanky man stepped out from behind a tree before her, smoking a cigarette. Although her focus was on him, she could feel a silent but deadly hulking form behind her. Instinct told her they were both vampires. Their feel told her immediately that they'd never belonged to Dimitri. They were enemies.

Seconds clicked by. No words were exchanged. The air around her suddenly became too still. She could feel the one behind her go airborne. She could smell the freshly broken wood he grasped in his sweaty palm.

Tanya went down on one knee as the assassin hurtled over her. She came up with two steel blades in her hands and caught him in the back. But the puncture wounds missed his heart entirely. The second one was on the move, charging her, as the first one pivoted with a snarl and came at her again.

Using the tree for leverage, she ran up one side of it, flipped over them, and caught the lean one in the center of his chest. The huge, burly one hissed his fury as his friend went down on one knee.

"Get up, Pyotr!" he yelled as he got out of Tanya's kill range. "Feed and it will all be better. Don't allow this human sympathizer to squander your existence!"

Before she could blink, the stake the thick-muscled nemesis had been holding whizzed toward her like a missile, but she sidestepped it and caught it in a firm grip, and then quickly relay-flung it into the chest of the vampire that was slowly standing up. An explosive plume of embers lit the night around her. Now the odds were even.

She watched the huge vampire before her give his friend's passing a moment of thought before he launched at her with visceral rage.

Taking him at hand-to-hand combat was out of the question. He seemed almost as ancient as Dimitri had been. But the question was, did he own anything close to Dimitri's old power? Only seconds would provide an answer. Tanya held up her hands in front of her and sent a black charge of dark energy out from them. The Russian hit it like he'd slammed into a brick wall. She jumped back, winded and feeling slower. The felled vampire looked up at her, eyes completely black as he scrambled to his feet to attack again, but then suddenly burst into flames as his head fell away from his body.

Tanya jumped back and snarled. A presence stepped out of the smoke and calmly tucked a large bone knife into his brown leather jacket.

"Who the fuck are you?" Prepared to battle yet another assassin, she waited, her every sense keen.

"I am Anastas. . . . It means 'resurrection' in my native language. So, you might say, I have come back to see if the rumors were true. And they are."

Still wary, Tanya circled him slowly, watching him turn with her in a counterclockwise direction. This vampire was definitely dangerous, but why had he helped her? There was no such thing as a free lunch, so what did he want? Maybe the chance to kill her for himself?

She drank in everything about him, trying to place him. He felt familiar, but he wasn't controlled by Dimitri at all. Odd. His intense dark brown eyes held a bit of a smile in them, and his auburn hair hung about his broad shoulders in an old-world way. His accent had that formal Eastern Bloc ring to it, but she couldn't place it. Strong chin, strong, solid features. Tall. Maybe six two or three. A hint of five o'clock shadow graced his jaw. Beside his brown leather jacket, he wore an ebony turtleneck, jeans, and scuffed, well-worn brown leather boots. If they both walked out of the park alive, she would not forget him.

Suddenly he stopped circling with her. "This dance is making us both dizzy. Can I buy you a drink?"

She stopped moving and stared at him. "What?"

"A drink. You have to eat, and so do I after expending so much energy."

She hated that he was right. "What do you want?"

"I needed to see for myself that Dimitri lost his life to the black Madonna. Or black widow, as the case may be. A centuries-old vampire taken down by a human hit woman on the payroll for the human mafia, who in death has grown a conscience and only wants her coven to kill those who she feels deserve that fate. Completely fascinating."

"So, you've seen. But that doesn't explain what else you want."

He shrugged with a casual smile. "I'm very old, too. I am not easily fascinated. I like being fascinated. A few centuries from now, you will be like me, a slave to intrigue and curiosity."

"Fall back. I don't know who you are or—"

"I already told you. I am Anastas Baranov, but to clarify, made in the sixteenth century in Poland. Sadly, that bastard Dimitri turned my father, who immediately came home and savaged my mother and sisters . . . and I was injured while trying to save them. I killed him, but I had already been badly bitten and lost a lot of blood. I think I survived three nights, but escaped my own funeral. In those days humans were wiser. They drove a stake through your corpse's heart or beheaded it if they even suspected . . . but I digress. That is unpleasant conversation for a lady. How about that drink?"

"And now you come to claim Dimitri's inheritance by assassinating me." Tanya stood her ground, immovable.

"No. I want nothing he owned. He took all that meant anything to me. But I have been systematically wiping out his line for centuries. It was an old grudge match between us. Haven't you wondered why none of his made have come to you?"

Tanya tilted her head slightly; the subtle gesture was all that she would allow right now as a possible concession.

"Correct," he said, giving her a slight nod in return. "Your lair should have been flooded by all whom he made. But you've only sent out telepathic desires, yes?"

"And?" Tanya could feel her hands balling into fists; the line of questioning was hitting too close to home. It made her nervous. She hated people knowing more about her than she knew about them, especially people she didn't know squat about.

Anastas gave her a broad, toothy grin. "Those loyalists are afraid because they know that having them does not please you. Fear makes them dangerous, but they cannot kill that which has made them once fully turned. It is vampire law. So they avoid you like the plague until you call them for a specific task. But do not make it a big task, as there are not so many of them left now." He chuckled and began walking away from her. "This last month I've culled the ranks. I had to act quickly while you were still learning."

"And you think now you can come for me!"

He turned slowly to face her. "I do not wish to kill you, but I will do so if you force me to defend myself. My complaint was with Dimitri, not you. Now he is gone, so I have no complaint."

"And you just showed up for giggles and grins after killing anyone who could help me."

"Or kill you," he replied calmly. "Dimitri was a cruel master. Many wanted him dead, but none dared to try. They couldn't. But who knows what pledges they have made, what bargains were out there in the streets? My killing them sent a message. I don't think they will attempt any more backroom alliances now for a while."

"And I guess your thugs will—"

"I work alone. I always have. I have never eaten from an innocent or turned anyone else into this abomination that you and I have become. If you do not understand anything else, know that."

She watched him lift his chin with dignity, scanning him in search of any deceit. "All right, then, how about that drink?"

They sat at a bar in an upscale sushi house, watching the ebb and flow of the human traffic with a merlot before her and a fine vodka before him, both drinking nothing.

"Did Dimitri ever come for you?" she said in a quiet tone, staring into the ruby liquid in front of her and wishing it didn't have to be blood. She missed wine. A lot.

"Plenty of times. That was the great game of it. I wanted to drive him insane with anger. I wanted to make him kill me as badly as I wished I could kill him. But he was stronger. So I had to chip away at his peace of mind and erode his borders."

"Gangsta," she said with a smile, and then looked up at Anastas. "So, you could kill his lesser made men because you were made by your father—not by Dimitri."

"Yes," Anastas said, and then brought the vodka to his nose to savor its scent. "Dimitri did not directly make me, so he had no direct control over me. He would have told my father to force me to come to him, as he controlled my father, and my father would have controlled me. The one problem Dimitri always had was that I'd escaped my father's control by stabbing that murderous bastard in his heart with a chair leg. That is how a rogue like me . . . and you . . . is created." Anastas clinked his short rocks glass against Tanya's long-stemmed wineglass. "This is also why you fascinate me so. You killed Dimitri much like I killed my father, through much good luck, and have now set edicts in place that go against every decadent principle Dimitri ever infested the world with. This I like."

Tanya gave Anastas another half smile, but this time she could feel a slight hint of fang beginning to show. "And how do I know this isn't bullshit?"

Anastas shook his head and chuckled. "You already know it is not. You have scanned me for fraud or you wouldn't be sitting here with me now. Do not try to bullshit an old bullshitter."

This time he made her laugh.

"Okay, but seriously, what do you really want?"

His smile faded. "Somewhere to go."

His sudden seriousness caught her off guard, but the intensity in his gaze told her that he'd spoken the truth.

"I don't understand," she said just above a murmur.

"My purpose is over. I have won," he said in a sad, far-off tone, and then looked out the window beyond her. "For hundreds of years my goal was to make Dimitri's existence miserable—taking sick joy from the vengeance. Then in one night, he gets careless and allows himself to get killed by a woman of dubious principles, but principles I admire nonetheless. So, now, where will I go? I have made no others to stand with me. The other covens shun me, for a rogue in their lair is a dangerous thing. Other rogues are few and far between. Most do not last as long as I have. And so," he added with a sad chuckle, bringing his gaze back to hers, "I am without a purpose. Shall I eat and exist for more centuries with nothing to do? Or shall I ask to be adopted by the one being that bested my nemesis . . . with a pledge of loyalty to protect you from other covens that may wish to annex power."

"You said having a rogue in your lair was a dangerous thing."

Anastas nodded and stood. "It is. But I can teach you how to elude other masters. The offer stands. We both have time to decide, but first I think we should have that drink." He inclined his head toward an Asian businessman speaking to what looked like an elderly Wall Street banker. "They have eaten well and have high blood alcohol content. Their souls are also dirty as hell . . . so?"

"I've never done it like this before—just picked them up at a bar."

"I suspect there's a lot you've never done before as a vampire, even though you own Dimitri's memories . . . and not all of it is bad. I will show you." He gave her a sexy smile, one so intensely erotic that she had to look away from him toward their targets.

"I've always gone for those in the midst of a commission of a crime—followed a robber or stopped a purse snatching or derailed a rape. I guess I just didn't trust myself beyond that right away."

"And yet you aspired to more. To reach the levels of the human masters, yes?"

She nodded. "But how did you know?"

"Everything you want resonates through every artery of your line down to the remotest capillary of it. This is how we know you still exist versus that time when your nights will become embers—and may that be an eternity from now, dear Tanya." He took up her hand and pressed a tender kiss to the back of it. "Our job is to know what you want and how you want it, if we are yours."

Tanya swallowed hard, feeling a pull to this man that she hadn't expected.

He threw down a wad of bills on the bar to pay for their untouched drinks and then held out his hand again to her. She accepted it, quietly taking in the feel of his broad, slightly callused palm and long fingers, and then stood.

Sated, they left the bodies in the limousine that had chauffeured the businessmen to the restaurant, with a stunned driver none the wiser. Anastas dabbed the corner of her mouth with his thumb, wiping away a tiny trickle of blood.

"Are you all right with what just happened?"

Tanya nodded. "They were bad men to the core . . . fleecing hard-working souls out of millions."

"Much worse than a poor junkie sticking up a convenience store, yes?"

"Yeah."

"You don't sound convinced."

"I'm doing math in my head, is all."

He stopped walking and looked at her. "Mathematics?"

"Anastas, how many bodies do you have on you after being around for hundreds of years?"

She stopped and turned to look at him when he didn't answer. "That's my point, man."

"It is unavoidable, unless you have human minions who donate."

"They do at the blood clubs."

"And now you're talking suicide to go there, unless your forces are extremely formidable—which at present, they aren't."

"Here's a safe bet," Tanya said with a casual shrug. "The masters dine on whatever they want and wouldn't have to show up at a blood club. They have private gorging orgies in their lairs and don't risk unnecessary exposure."

"But their made men and women would."

"Right," she replied quickly. "Now you're catching on. So, what better way to even the odds but to blow away a bunch of bottom feeders like the ones that just came after me?"

Anastas walked away from her in the opposite direction. "Now you are mad. I see how Dimitri was tricked. He thought he was dealing with a sane and beautiful woman only to be deceived!"

"No, think about it," Tanya said, jogging to catch up with him. "If I hit the local blood clubs, wouldn't that not only cull the other local masters' ranks to be about equal to mine, but would also let them know not to send any of their thugs my way trying to pull a bullshit coup? Not to mention, it would get a helluva lot of vampires off the streets and allow us to walk into a blood club with some solid street cred under our belts."

"And I supposed we'd just go in guns blazing?"

"No," she said, laughing, and keeping up with Anastas's long strides. "If you haven't noticed, regular bullets don't work, and I don't have humans that can load my clips with silver or hallowed-earth-packed shells."

He stopped walking and turned to stare at her. "Hand-to-hand combat so outnumbered is pure suicide."

"Puh-lease," she scoffed, and began walking again. "That's old-school. How about blowing a gas line beneath a building or something simple like that? Working for the mob boys did teach me a thing or two. Besides, the other masters have been sending their hit men out to smoke me ever since the night I died. I need to let them know two can play that game. So, are you in or what?"

"You *are* mad," he whispered, pushing a lock of her windblown hair away from her face.

"I've been called worse," she murmured. "Much worse."

"And if I go along with this insanity?"

"What's in it for you?" She smiled.

"No. That is not my entire question. . . . Well, perhaps it is, but it was poorly phrased."

She placed a palm gently at the center of his chest and watched him swallow hard. "My bad."

"This will not wipe out the species, Tanya. As long as we're left, as long as one is left, there will always be Vampyre. It is like a virus, just like polio still exists, the bubonic plague still exists. Evil still exists no matter how many dirty bankers and politicians—"

Her deep kiss stopped his words just as his full mouth and total embrace stopped her breath. "We can let tomorrow take care of itself and save blowing up a few blood clubs for another night."

"If you claim me, I will help you write this book."

He'd obviously gone into her mind searching for whatever pleased her, and that he'd even bothered to do so carved out a very special place for him within her eerily still heart. There was something impossible to resist in being wanted dead or alive.

She touched his cheek with trembling fingers. "You think too much, Anastas Baranov."

Only inches from her face he stared into her eyes. "No, Tanya . . . search and you will see that my mind is blank only for you now."

He was right to insist that they go down into the vault. Daylight surely would have caught them unaware. But as far as she was concerned, she'd already burst into flames. His touch was like hot embers, delicious long-awaited torture. Each kiss brought delirium, and yet he cried out as she planted more against his chest.

Slowly knowledge seeped into her brain; it was the reverb of her caresses echoing off his touch, trading pleasure back and forth down to the cellular level. His French kiss between her thighs left her weeping; warm, rough palms cradling the delicate skin of tightened nipples left her panting. Passion fusion. It was all too insane. Bodies fitted together as though welded. Sweat and sweet, pungent love essence was the lubricant that slicked all boundaries and made them move together like greased gears.

His hair in her fists, she watched him arch beneath her and give her his throat. The temptation was too great to bear; the deep knowledge rising within her, impossible to ignore. In a blinding flash of pleasure, he was marked as hers. Claimed and wanted, dead or alive. She bit him and came so hard that she was afraid she'd drain him dry.

Anastas's wail rent the air as his fists wound themselves in the crimson satin sheets while ejaculation spasms tore through him. Her name became a broken mantra panted out in two syllables as the tremors ebbed. She lifted her mouth from his throat and dabbed her blood-wet lips with the back of her hand. Tears filled his eyes and then he suddenly gathered her up, sheets and all, hugging her tightly and rocking her hard.

"Never have I been claimed," he said in a harsh whisper that fractured against her neck.

"Nor have I," she whispered back, fighting a sob. "I've never been here before either."

Tanya waited patiently as one by one, mind-stunned humans found an inexplicable need to exit the massive warehouse building. Pulsing music made the night air throb red. Some took a smoke across the street, staring out blankly at the water. Some walked around aimlessly trying to hail a nonexistent cab. A few claimed to be hungry for pizza and fare not served at the bar, and they squabbled with the huge vampire bouncers guarding the exit doors.

"You know after this there's no turning back," Anastas said grimly, staring across the street from the shadows.

"I know," Tanya replied, and opened her cell phone, then punched in the numbers that would detonate the charges they'd rigged in the tunnels beneath the building. "Call 911 to minimize the blaze and to keep it from spreading to other buildings right after I push SEND."

Anastas nodded and Tanya watched a slow smile creep across his face. She depressed the SEND button with a French-manicured nail.

The building exploded in an orange inferno. Windows shattered beneath glass-melting heat. Almost knocked off their feet from the force of the blast, they hunkered down against the adjacent building that protected them. Heat and flames licked at broken bricks and twisted metal. Shrapnel from the rubble whizzed by them, but Tanya wrapped them both in a dark energy shield as Anastas hugged her against him tightly. After a moment they both looked up to stare at their handiwork. Humans snapped out of their daze and rushed back and forth outside screaming, but no vampires had exited the building.

"You have sent a large message, I believe."

"They are gonna be so pissed."

"Yes . . . and now that we have visited the Russians, I know of this nice little Polish blood bar in Queens where we can also get a drink with no troubles. Shall we?"

Tanya just shook her head and laughed.

MIST

Susan Krinard

—an ax age, a sword age
—shields are riven—
a wind age, a wolf age—
before the world goes
headlong.
No man will have
mercy on another.

SAN FRANCISCO, PRESENT DAY

The sword sliced the air inches in front of Mist's face. She swung Kettlingr to intercept the blow, bracing herself and catching the blade in midstroke. Metal clanged on metal with glorious, discordant music. Her opponent bore down hard for several seconds, his furious gaze fixed on hers, and abruptly disengaged.

"One of these days," Eric said, his face breaking out in a grin, "I'm going to beat you."

Mist lowered her own sword and caught her breath. Perspiration trickled from her hairline over her forehead, soaking the fine blond hairs that had come loose from her braid, and her body ached pleasantly from the hard workout. She grinned back at Eric, who sheathed his sword and reached for the towel lying across the bench against the wall.

"You're good," she said. "Almost as good as I am."

He grimaced and scrubbed the towel across his face. "I outweigh you by eighty pounds," he said. "I don't want to think about what you could do to me if you were my size."

Size had nothing to do with it, though Mist hadn't yet found a way to tell Eric why he'd never be able to beat her. She'd even thought once or twice of letting him win, male pride being such a fragile thing, but instinct was too strong.

There had been a time when her kind had been no more than choosers of the battle-slain, bearing the trappings of war themselves, but never baring their swords. Ragnarök had changed Odhinn's handmaidens, as it had changed so much else.

Mist sheathed her own sword and stroked the runes engraved on the hilt. *She* had no right to pride of any kind. She had but one purpose in Midgard, and it had been her only reason for living after everything she had known was gone. The fact that she had permitted herself a relationship with a man after so many centuries was an aberration, a reckless act of defiance against her fate.

And yet Eric had roused her from the despair of one who waits for a redemption that will never come. He was not afraid of a woman who shared his strength in body and will. He'd taught her to laugh again. And when she looked into Eric's face—the face of a true warrior of the Norse, broad and handsome and fearless—she could not help but love him.

"I'm headed for the shower," Eric said, catching her glance and giving her a sly look in return. He padded toward her, remarkably graceful and light on his feet, his naked chest streaked with sweat. He lifted a tendril of her hair, rolling it between his fingers. "Care to join me? I'll wash your back if you'll wash mine."

His meaning could not be clearer, and she was eager enough to join him in bed after his long absence. But she dodged aside when he bent to kiss her.

"There's something I have to take care of first," she said, smiling to take the sting out of her rejection. "I'll join you in a few minutes."

Eric let her go and winked. "I'll be waiting." He strode away, and Mist was left wondering what was wrong with her.

But of course she knew. Over the past few months, truly happy for the first time since her voluntary exile, she had begun to acknowledge just how much she had changed. Little by little she had accepted the unthinkable: she had truly become a part of this world . . . the one world that had survived Ragnarök's ice and fire. Midgard, a place without magic or gods who intervened in the affairs of men.

Of course, Midgard's very survival was a puzzle in itself. The prophecies had foretold destruction and renewal, the return of Baldr from Niflheimr, a new beginning for gods and mankind in a paradise of peace and plenty.

No such paradise had ever arisen, for Midgard had remained untouched by the chaos of war between the Aesir and Loki's children. War and famine and sorrow continued unbroken, and the Aesir were forgotten. No one, not even the sons of Odhinn himself, would come to claim the treasure she guarded. It had become obsolete. Like her.

With a sigh Mist walked out of the exercise room, past the blacksmith shop that occupied a third of the warehouse flat, and into her small kitchen. She could hear Eric singing in the shower. Geisl jumped up on the kitchen table and chirruped, demanding his rightful share of affection. Stjarna bounded up beside him, green-gold eyes far too intelligent for any ordinary cat.

Mist picked Stjarna up and stroked his dense gray fur. Breeders called them Norwegian Forest Cats now; a thousand years ago they had been sacred to the Lady.

So much lost.

"Do you think it's the same with the others?" she asked him. "Have they given up, too?"

Stjarna licked her hand sympathetically. He didn't know any more than she did, and she'd lost contact with the other *valkyrjur* decades ago. Only two other survivors of the final battle lived in San Francisco, and Vídarr and Váli had abandoned the old ways soon after she'd settled here. Mist had despised them for it then. Now, settled in a life with a man she had come to love—a life where her only "enemies" were muggers, petty thieves, and the occasional gangbanger—she finally understood.

Setting Stjarna back on the table, she gave Geisl a brief pat and walked down the short hall to the second bedroom. The rune-wards that guarded the door had never been disturbed except by Mist herself. She released them with a word, lifted the key on its chain from around her neck, and unlocked the door.

Two dozen swords, axes, daggers, and knives, each lovingly forged by her own hand, hung in oak-and-glass display cases built into the walls. Mist locked the door behind her, passed by the swords and axes, and went directly to the knife case, which held eight weapons with hand-carved grips and edges sharp enough to slice flesh like tissue. Each knife was unique, but no one of them appeared substantially different from any other except in subtle elements of design and embellishment.

The one she chose, like the others, was perfectly balanced for a hand that would never wield it in battle, a fine object that might have found a home in some collector's case among his or her other most valued possessions. But when Mist closed her fingers around the grip, it sang. Sang of a past she could scarcely remember. *An axe age, a sword age.* An age of heroism and blood and doom.

Mist knew the magics. She knew the runes and spells and songs, though her skill was only enough to guard what she held in her hand. The chant she sang now came without thought, for she had sung it a hundred times. A thousand.

The knife shuddered in her fist. Then it began to grow, the blade widening, the grip lengthening inch by inch until it was as long as her arm, long enough to touch the floor and reach above her head.

Gungnir. The Swaying One, the spear that could not miss its mark. The magic weapon Odhinn had entrusted to her in the final moments of his life, as he and the Aesir had entrusted the other treasures to her sisters.

But Gungnir was hers to guard with her life. The rune-spells that protected it from enemy hands also hid its true shape, and would continue to do so until . . .

Mist closed her eyes. There was no "until." The evil ones were no more than dust and ash. The old heroism was only a dream. Never again would she ride Gyllir on the battlefield and carry the bravest warriors to Valhöll. She was only an ordinary woman now, a forger of fine weapons, a teacher of lost arts.

It's time. Time to bury the dead and begin to forget.

Realizing that she was gripping Gungnir's shaft far too tightly for her own good, Mist relaxed her fingers, sang the spell, and watched the spear shrink to its former size. She hung it carefully back in the case, locked and warded the door, and went in search of Eric.

He was gone. A scribbled note lay on the kitchen table; he'd been called in to work and didn't know when he'd be back. *Sorry,* the note read. *See you tonight.*

Shaking off her disappointment, Mist took a solitary shower, threw on a sweater, and went out to the garage. The sky was flawlessly blue, crisp and lovely, and Mist could smell the tart, briny scent of the bay half a mile to the east. Ordinarily she would take Muni into the city, but this time she had errands to run in South San Francisco, home of the only comprehensive ironworking supplier in the entire Bay Area.

Her Volvo was ancient and often unreliable, hardly the kind of transportation she had been accustomed to in her former life. It rumbled and complained like the great hound Garmr, chained at the gates of Gnipahellir until the final days.

But Garmr was gone, like Fenrisúlfr and Loki and the great serpent Jörmangandr, the giants and dwarves who had fought the Aesir and álfar. Not even shadows remained.

Hardly aware of the drive, Mist completed her errands, her trunk and backseat groaning under the weight of the supplies. When she returned to the warehouse, Eric was still gone. She unloaded the car, arranged the supplies neatly in the shop, and set herself to completing the custom sword she had been making for one of San Francisco's more influential politicians, a man who had never fought a real battle in his entire life.

Mist paused to wipe the sweat from her forehead and stared into the glowing coals in the firepot. Even Eric, strong and skilled as he was, wore tailored suits and went to an office every day, his sphere one of endless documents, dull meetings, and deadening paperwork.

That was the world he lived in, the world she'd chosen for his sake. And hers.

Mist finished her work well after ten that night. Eric hadn't returned or left a message on the cell phone he had insisted she buy several months ago. She found herself strangely restless in spite of her hard work at the forge. She fed the cats, put on her leather jacket, and left the house.

Dogpatch was far from quiet even at this time of night; it was becoming fashionable with young professionals who frequented the growing number of clubs, restaurants, and galleries tucked between warehouses and ancient Victorian cottages. It seemed even more crowded now that Christmas was coming; colored lights festooned the old houses and shops, and someone had set a decorated tree on the roof of the recording studio across the street. Mist bypassed the busier streets, heading north and west toward Potrero Hill and the Mission District.

It was a long walk to Golden Gate Park on the opposite side of the city. Mist reached it before midnight and entered the park from Arguello Boulevard. Unlike Dogpatch, the park was deserted except for the homeless and vagrants who spent their nights wrapped in tattered blankets under bushes, huddled against the damp winter chill. There would be no Christmas for them.

Christmas. Yule, as it had been known before the coming of the White Christ. The time when the barriers between the planes of gods and men were thinnest.

Mist shivered and laughed at herself. There were no barriers, and no one to cross them. The solstice was nothing but an excuse for celebration, an end to the darkness and the coming of a new year.

She crossed Martin Luther King Jr. Drive and headed toward the Arboretum. Fog began to settle over the nearest trees, turning the park into a ghostly realm of indistinct shapes and ominous silence.

The fog. Mist stopped, lifting her head to test the air. Fog like this came in the summer, when warm Pacific wind blew over the colder waters along the coast. A sudden, bitter chill nipped at Mist's hands and face. There was nothing natural about this cold, or the icy vapor that stretched frigid fingers along the ground at her feet, slithering and hissing like the World Serpent bent on devouring everything in its path.

Disbelief shook Mist with jaws of iron. She knew the smell of the vapor and what it portended. But the *jötunar*, the frost giants, were as extinct as the great sloths or woolly mammoths that had walked the North American plains.

It wasn't possible. She must be going mad. Too many years alone. Empty years, centuries, millennia, protecting a weapon that would never be used again.

A low, screeching howl pulled Mist out of her bitter reverie. A face emerged from the vapor, rising two heads above Mist's generous height. Broad, heavy, filled with anger and fell purpose.

The cold eyes fixed on hers. The mouth, with its rows of teeth filed to points like daggers, gaped in a grin.

"*Heil*, Odhinn's girl," the *jötunn* said, his voice deep enough to shake the very ground under Mist's feet. "Or can it be that I am mistaken? Is this what the *valkyrjur* have become, mountless and dressed as thralls?"

Recovering her senses, Mist reached slowly inside her jacket for the knife she carried against her hip. It was too late now to draw the runes and burn them, and she had no song prepared that would work against a *jötunn*. She had never imagined she would need it.

"How are you called, giant?" she asked in the Old Tongue.

"I am Hrimgrimir," the *jötunn* said. "I know you, Mist, once Chooser of the Dead."

Mist shook her head, trying to dislodge the nightmare that had seized her mind and senses. Hrimgrimir was the frost giant who guarded the mouth of Niflheimr. His mistress, Hel herself, had perished at Ragnarök. Like the others, he should no longer exist.

"From whence have you come, Frost-Shrouded?" she asked. "From what dream of venom and darkness?"

Hrimgrimir laughed. "No dream, Sow's bitch." He blew out a foul, gusty breath. "A pity that you chose *her* side. You might have lived to see the new age." He reared out of the vapor, huge hands curled, his power and giant-magic swirling round about him like the sleet he wore like ice-forged armor. "You will tell me where it is before you die."

Mist felt his assault in body and soul, and her fingers slipped on the grip of her knife. She staggered back, pulled it out, and rubbed the runes engraved with such painstaking care by Odhinn himself. Like Gungnir, the knife began to stretch, to broaden, to become what it was meant to be.

"My kitten will silence your boasts," she said into the howling wind that beat against her. She lifted Kettlingr and took a step forward, body bent, legs tensed to leap. A great ice-rimed hand swung toward her like a mallet meant to crush and shatter.

She struck in turn, swinging Kettlingr upward as the hand descended. The *jötunn* howled. Hot black blood splattered over her as her rune-kissed blade sank into flesh.

Mist jumped back, ready for another attack. It never came. The vapor fell like a curtain in front of her, a writhing wall of white maggots sheathed in ice. She swung again, but her sword whistled through empty air. The vapor began to recede as quickly as it had come, crackling angrily and leaving a crystalline film on the grass.

Shaken, Mist let the battle-fever drain from muscle and nerve and bone. A cold sweat bathed her forehead and glued her shirt to her back.

This was no nightmare. A *jötunn* had returned from the dead, bringing with him an evil no child of Mist's adopted city could imagine.

Wiping her moist hand on the leg of her jeans, Mist sang Kettlingr back to its former size and sheathed the knife. The shock was nearly gone, yet the sense of unreality remained. Where had Hrimgrimir come from? No *jötunn* could walk the earth unnoticed for long. If there was no Jötunheimr, where could such a creature have found refuge from the final battle? Had she been drawn to the park tonight because she had felt his presence? Why had he tried to kill her?

Because no giant can meet a servant of the Aesir without enmity. But it was more than that. He'd known who she was. He'd been waiting for *her.*

"You will tell me where it is before you die."

Mist stared blindly at the trail of blackened grass Hrimgrimir had left in the wake of his retreat. All the assumptions she had made that morning crumbled like bones scoured by the relentless assault of time and nature. Odhinn had been right. The ancient evil had come for the Swaying One.

She fought off a wave of panic and forced herself to concentrate. Hrimgrimir had threatened her, but he'd given up and fled in the middle of the duel. And what use would a lone survivor, evil or not, have for Gungnir when there were no battles left to fight?

"You might have lived to see the new age."

Whatever he'd meant, a "new age" didn't sound like something one *jötunn* could create on his own.

Moving quickly, Mist followed the giant's trail, her boots crunching on the frozen grass. The park was still silent save for the wind in the treetops and the distant roar of a motorcycle on Lincoln Way. The fine hairs on the back of her neck stood as rigid as a newly forged blade. She had gone only a few hundred feet when the track disappeared completely. No trace of the *jötunn* remained.

And yet, as she stood still and opened her senses to the unseen, the feeling of something out of place began to grow again. Something different this time. Something that froze her blood as surely as the *jötunn's* cruel wind.

From her jacket pocket she withdrew the small piece of driftwood she always carried, though she had never thought to use it for such a purpose. She was a *valkyrja,* not a sorceress. The magic might fail, or even turn against her.

Still, she had to try. She unsheathed the knife, held the driftwood against the trunk of the nearest tree, and began to carve. The runes sizzled as she cut them into the wood: *Ūruz, Thurisaz, Ansuz.* As she completed the last, the wood twitched in her hand as if it were alive and seeking freedom.

She couldn't grant it life, only fulfillment in the flames. She sheathed the knife, withdrew a lighter from her other pocket, and set fire to the driftwood.

In three breaths it was consumed. The runes, drawn in crimson strokes, hung disembodied in the air. Then they, too, faded, and Mist felt their power seep through her skin and pierce her heart.

Without hesitation she turned onto a narrow, dusty path that wandered among a dense grove of Monterey pines. Her search brought her to a heap of discarded clothing spread over the pine needles, half hidden under a clump of thick shrubbery.

Mist cursed. The magic *had* turned against her, mocking her meager skill. She'd wasted too much time already. She was about to leave when the pile of ragged garments heaved, and a hand, lean and pale, reached out from a tattered sleeve. She gripped her knife. A low groan emerged from the stinking mound. She smelled blood, plentiful but no longer fresh.

Against her better judgment, she knelt beside the man. She expected an indigent, perhaps injured by some thug who found beating up helpless vagrants a source of amusement. But the hand, encrusted with filth as it was, appeared unmarked by the daily struggle for food and shelter. It was long-fingered and elegant, more accustomed to lifting golden goblets of mead than sifting through rubbish in a Dumpster.

She started at the thought. Mead had been the most favored beverage of gods and heroes and elves. And dwarves, and giants, and all the others who had fought for the dark at Ragnarök.

But this one was no giant or dwarf. Hesitantly she touched then pulled aside the blankets. A tall, lean form emerged, dressed in shirt and trousers too short and wide for his body. He lay on his belly, legs sprawled, cheek pressed against the damp earth.

And his face . . .

Mist had seen its like countless times in Valhöll, laughing among the Aesir and the warriors, fairer to look upon than the sun. It had always been accepted that the most beautiful of all creatures were the *ljósálfar*, the light-elves of Álfheimr, allies of the gods.

This man was not so beautiful. His face was a mask of gore and mud, one eye swollen shut and his nose broken. Yet his features could not be mistaken.

A *jötunn* had come to Midgard. Now one of the *álfar* had come as well, risen against all reason from the final death. It couldn't be coincidence.

Mist touched the *álfr's* shoulder. "Can you hear me?" she asked in the Old Tongue.

The elf stirred, his fingers digging into the soil. He made a sound that might have been a word, rough and raw. Mist had no water to give him, no spell to ease his pain. *Álfar* healed quickly; she had no choice but to let nature take its course.

"Who . . . ," he croaked, opening his one good eye. "How . . ."

"Be easy, my friend." She removed her jacket and laid it over him. "You're safe."

The eye, bright blue amid the red and brown of blood and dirt, regarded her with growing comprehension. "Safe?" he whispered. With a sudden jerk he rolled to his side, pushing her jacket away. "The *jötunn* . . ."

"There is no *jötunn* here," she said, pushing him down again. "Lie still, jarl of the *álfar*. All is well."

The sound he made might have been a laugh. He lifted himself on one arm and looked into her face. "Who . . . are you?"

Mist hesitated. She had never been afraid to use her real name among men, for there had been no one left to recognize her for what she was. Now things were different. The laws of Midgard—the natural, mundane laws that had ruled her for centuries—had been broken.

But he was of the *ljösálfar,* who had fought alongside the gods at Ragnarök. And he might have the answers she desperately needed.

"I am Mist of the *valkyrjur,*" she said.

He closed his eye and released a shuddering breath. "Then my coming . . . was not in vain." He lifted a shaking hand to rub his swollen lips. "I am Dáinn."

Dáinn. She recognized the name. It was not uncommon among both elves and dwarves. But she knew in her heart that this was no common elf.

"Bringer of the Futhark," she said slowly. "Teacher of the runes."

He raised himself higher and sat up with a wince. "Yes." There was a great weariness in his voice. "I have been gone a very long time."

Gone. The memories flooded back, images of bloody conflict and hopeless courage. The elves had fought beside the Aesir, and died beside them.

All but one. Dáinn the Wise, who had walked away when Heimdall had sounded the call to arms. Dáinn the coward. Dáinn the cursed.

Mist drew away from him as if he were Fenrir himself. "Is that why you're here?" she demanded. "Did you flee to Midgard when you ran from the great battle?"

The *álfar* had always been proud, but Dáinn made no effort to refute her accusation. He began to rise, a little of his elvish grace returning, then sank back down again like the faithless weakling he was.

"The great battle?" he said. "The final destruction of the gods?" He sighed, gazing into the darkness. "Does it seem to you that the world has ended?"

Mist couldn't pretend that she didn't understand his question, and it stung all the more because she had been thinking the same thing that very morning.

"Have you seen Baldr return from Hel?" Dáinn asked, relentless in his strange detachment. "Where are Vídarr and Váli and the sons of Thor?"

She could have told him that Vídarr and Váli were alive in this very city, one the owner of a Tenderloin bar and the other a common drunk. The sons of Odhinn were living proof that the prophecies had failed. *They* had known all along how useless it was to cling to the old ways. Mist had finally admitted they were right.

Now she knew they had been very, very wrong.

"There was an ending, yes," Dáinn said into her silence. "The Aesir and their allies were scattered, sent into limbo and robbed of their power. But there was no Ragnarök. The gods did not die. And their enemies—" He broke off, and when he spoke again it was in plain English. "Their enemies still live."

Mist felt the shock pass through her body and settle in her gut, roiling and churning like worms in a corpse. Somewhere the gods lived on, forgotten by men. Freyja, Heimdall, Tyr. Odhinn himself. The Allfather, who had passed Gungnir to her with his final breath.

"Go to Midgard," he had said. *"You will not fare alone. Each of your sisters will bear a weapon that must not fall into the hands of the evil ones. As long as you live, you will guard Gungnir. Until . . ."*

He had died then, slain by Fenrir, and with the other *valkyrjur*. Mist had left the dying to their fates. She had believed she would have little time to guard the spear, since she, too, would be obliterated in the final destruction.

The joke had been on her. Odhinn himself hadn't believed the prophecies. He'd known that the world to come would be just as cruel as the old; riven by war, greed, and suffering. He'd known that his enemies would survive.

"They have returned," Dáinn said, struggling to his feet. "The *jötunn* Hrimgrimir has come to Midgard in search of the treasures. I was sent ahead, but he—"

"Who sent you?" she demanded, gripping his arms. "Have the Aesir also returned?"

"The Aesir have no power here. Not yet. Freyja came to me in a dream. . . ."

Freyja. Freyja the beautiful, the Lady, who received half the slain warriors chosen by the *valkyrjur*. Mist remembered the other things Hrimgrimir had said before his attack.

"Sow's bitch," he had called her. Syr, the Sow, was another name for Freyja. But Mist had always been Odhinn's servant. It was for him she had fought, for him she had abandoned the honor of death in battle in favor of an immortal life of solitude.

"A dream?" she echoed, pushing her dark thoughts aside. "Why the Lady? Why should she come to *you*?"

Dáinn acknowledged her contempt with a twist of his lips. "I still have some small magic remaining to me, and the Lady has not lost all her power. She still has the *seidr*, her spell magic. It is that which keeps the gods alive." His gaze turned inward. "The Aesir can see but little from where they now reside, yet what they see is worse than any seer's foretelling."

"Tell me!"

"She charged me to find the treasures and warn their guardians against the invasion."

The invasion. The "new age." How many *jötunar* had come to Midgard? If the giants had found the other *valkyrjur*, the other treasures . . .

Panic surged in Mist's throat. "Was it Hrimgrimir who attacked you?" she asked, giving him a shake. "How did he get to Midgard?"

"There are passages, ways between the worlds that have been opened by dark *seidr*."

"What worlds? Does Jötunheimr still exist? Asgard?" She grimaced at her own stupidity. None of that was important now. "How did he find you?"

"I do not know, but he knew I was looking for you."

"And you couldn't stop him? What happened to *your* magic, *álfr*?"

For the first time a flicker of real emotion crossed Dáinn's face. "I had to let him win. My task was more important than any temporary victory. It was necessary that he believe I was no threat to him or his allies."

Mist didn't believe him. He'd let himself be beaten to a pulp and ground into the dirt like an ant on a battlefield. He was worse than useless.

But there was no time to question him further. "I have to go back," she said. "Gungnir—"

"Is it safe?"

Mist didn't bother to answer him. She jumped to her feet and began to run. She was halfway home when Dáinn caught up with her. She ignored him and kept on running.

The streets of Dogpatch were quiet now in the small hours of the morning. Dáinn was on her heels as she came to a skidding stop at her door and released the ward that guarded it from anyone but her and Eric. A dozen long strides carried her to the display room.

The case was open. Gungnir was gone.

Mist spun to the nearest wall and slammed it with her fist. Dáinn burst through the doorway, rags flapping.

"Loki's piss!" Mist swore. "Short-wit, incompetent . . ."

"It will do no good to curse yourself now," Dáinn said, unnaturally calm. "We must find him. Do you know the runes?"

"Of course I know them," she snapped.

"Then help me."

He sat cross-legged on the floor and closed his eyes. Mist sat across from him, preparing her mind and body for the *galdr*. Dáinn began to sing. His voice moved through the air in eddies and swirls like water in a stream.

A prickle of bone-deep awareness washed through Mist as Dáinn's spirit mingled with hers. It was like a violation, unseen hands reaching and plucking at her soul.

Sorrow. Such profound and terrible sorrow.

Breathing deeply, she tried to let the distraction of Dinny's presence roll away like summer's fog in autumn. It was no use. Her disdain for him was too strong. She could only hinder him now, and failure could have consequences too terrible to contemplate.

Careful not to disturb the elf, she got to her feet and walked into the kitchen. The cats were nowhere in sight, but on the table lay a folded piece of paper, not the one Eric had left before. A sense of unfocused dread stiffened Mist's fingers as she reached for the paper.

"It was not the *jötunn*," Dáinn said from the doorway.

The needle-sharp prick of ice filled Mist's lungs. She picked up the note and unfolded it. The runic script seemed to pulse on the page like entrails spilling hot from a warrior's belly.

My apologies, sweetling, it said. *I had hoped to enjoy you one last time, but it was not to be. I will cherish your gift. You may be sure I will use it well.*

The final symbol was the figure of a coiling snake. It came alive as she watched, hissing and seeming to laugh with its gaping jaws. Then it was still again, and Mist dropped the paper onto the table. It burst into flame and disintegrated into black ash.

"Eric," she whispered.

"Loki Hel's-Father," Dáinn said. "You *knew* him?"

The accusation in his voice was well deserved. She had been far worse than the short-wit and incompetent she had called herself. Eric had never loved her. He had deceived her from the moment they'd met. She hadn't been wise enough to see through the shape he had taken to seduce and set her at her ease.

Hrimgrimir had been no more than a distraction. It had always been Eric.

"I didn't know," she said numbly. "I believed . . ."

"You *believed*." His short laugh was raw with despair. He ran his finger through the ashes. "No one knew *he* had pierced the veil. We share two burdens now, shield-maiden."

Mist didn't ask what the second burden was. All she could see was Eric's laughing face when she had told him he had become nearly as good as she was.

"I'll kill him," she said.

"As Heimdall killed him?"

His mockery was all the more savage for its gentleness. She met Dáinn's gaze across the table.

"Can you find him?" she asked.

"If he hasn't left Midgard."

The questions she wanted to ask nearly choked her, but she left them unspoken. "Start looking," she said.

Dáinn dipped a finger into the ash and lifted it to his forehead. With quick, sure strokes he sketched a bind rune above and between his brows. It seemed to catch fire, and Dáinn grimaced in pain.

"A passage," he murmured.

"What do you mean?" She leaned over the table, forcing him to look at her. "*What* passage?"

"A bridge to the otherworlds." He smeared the ash with his fingers. " 'Gullin' is its name."

Golden. The Golden Gate Bridge. An echo of Bïfrost, which had once joined Midgard with the realm of the Aesir.

"Are you sure?" she asked.

"There is no certainty."

To Hel with that. It was the only lead they had, and there was no time to waste. The bridge was nearly eight miles northwest as the crow flies, longer on surface streets. Dawn was just breaking; there wouldn't be much traffic, and that meant the car would be faster than going on foot.

"Let's go," she said.

She ran into the shop, snatched up several small, dusty pieces of wood she kept on a high shelf, and dashed for the garage. Dáinn caught up with her as she reached the Volvo and threw open the door. She didn't wait to ask if the *álfr* had ever been in an automobile before, but he didn't hesitate to get in. She was already pulling out of the garage by the time he had closed his own door.

Chanting a hurried runespell to hold any overzealous cops away, Mist kept her foot on the gas all the way up Van Ness and screeched a reckless left turn onto Lombard. In minutes they were on 101 and nearing the bridge.

"Where?" she asked.

He touched his forehead, tracing the runes afresh. "Over the water," he said. "We must go on foot."

That was cursed inconvenient. There wasn't any way for a pedestrian to get onto the bridge from the San Francisco side without attracting unwelcome attention.

"We'll have to drive across," she said. "You tell me where to stop."

"If I can."

"You will." She gunned the engine and sped for the toll plaza, slowing only to pay the toll and pretend she had no intention of breaking every speed law on the books. The moment she was on the bridge she pushed on the accelerator, passing slower vehicles as if they were standing still.

"Here," Dáinn said when they were half a mile across. Mist stopped in the right lane and jumped out.

There was nothing to show that this span of the Bridge was different from any other. Dáinn vaulted over the railing that separated the pedestrian walkway from traffic. Mist followed him to the suicide barrier. Blue-gray water seethed far beneath them, choppy with a rising wind driving west from the Bay.

The faintest pressure in the air lifted the hairs on the back of Mist's neck. "I feel it," she said.

Dáinn wasn't listening. He cocked his head and closed his eyes. The air around him shimmered, and the ground under Mist's feet vibrated with barely leashed energy. The "passage" the *álfr* had spoken of was in this very place, an invisible mouth waiting for the right spell to open it again.

And there was more. She could feel Eric's presence, a shadow of his being altered and twisted into a form almost unrecognizable. She drew her knife.

"Where is he?" she asked him, struggling to control her seething emotions.

The *álfr* spread his hands in front of him as if he were reaching for something solid. "He was here, but he did not pass through. Something blocked his path."

"Then where has he gone?"

"I don't know."

"Is there anything you *do* know?"

Dáinn bent his head. "Even Loki would need a refuge. Evil always seeks evil."

Evil. What did that mean in a world of turmoil and endless conflict? The gangs? The suppliers of illicit drugs, who killed as easily as they breathed? The corrupt politicians and greedy businessmen who set policies that made thousands suffer?

Too many possibilities. They could spend weeks sorting through every dark soul in San Francisco, both high and low. But there *was* someone who might help them. Someone she'd hoped never to see again.

Maybe Vídarr already knew about the incursion. If he did, and hadn't warned her . . .

Never. Not the son of Odhinn.

"We're going to Vídarr," she said.

Dáinn stared at her. "He is here?"

"The prophecies said he and Váli would survive Ragnarök and live in the new world. That part was half right."

"Freyja said nothing about—"

Mist jumped over the barrier and returned to the Volvo. A red Jaguar streaked past, blaring its horn.

"You said the Aesir can't see everything," she said over her shoulder. *And you're as blind as they are.* She opened the passenger door. "Are you coming?"

He got in. Mist slammed the door shut, released the brake, and made a sharp U-turn. By the time they were off the bridge Dáinn was singing again.

She let him be. His magic, such as it was, was still stronger than hers. She didn't dare rely on him, but she couldn't afford to throw away even the smallest advantage, or the weakest ally.

Vídarr's club was in the Tenderloin, a scarred and graffitied doorway squashed between a seedy hotel and a pawn shop. In spite of the dubious neighborhood, Bifrost was popular with artists, musicians, and the more affluent youth from other parts of the city. Mist hadn't been inside the door for a decade, and she'd planned to keep it that way.

Plans of any kind were useless now. Mist wove through the increasing traffic, cutting through back streets and ignoring one-way signs. But her efforts to avoid the worst congestion weren't good enough. It was taking too damned long.

She pulled up to the nearest curb. "We'll have to run," she said.

Dáinn was out of the car a second after she was. She set off south, fiercely grateful for the chance to move her body again. She might not trust her own magic, but legs and arms, muscle and bone, were tools she honed to obey her will without thought or hesitation.

Tucked between the wealth of Nob Hill and the busy downtown of Civic Center, the Tenderloin was an abrupt descent both figuratively and literally. She and Dáinn ran past liquor stores, strip joints, and more than one dealer on the prowl for addicts looking to score. Panhandlers and drunks stared after them in astonishment, but they were only a blur in Mist's eyes.

Though it wasn't even eight o'clock, Mist knew that Bifrost would already be jumping. No cops would come knocking, for the simple reason that Vídarr had set runes to repel them; she could see them glowing in the air and feel their potency. Vídarr might have rejected his heritage, but he still used magic when it suited him.

Mist opened the door and walked in. Vídarr employed a doorman to keep out any "undesirables" who might slip past the wards, but she didn't recognize the big man standing just inside the door. He did a double take when Dáinn came up behind her.

"Where's Vid?" she asked the doorman.

He folded his massive arms across his chest. "Vid ain't available," he growled.

"He'll see me." She shoved past him.

"Hey, bitch!" He clamped one beefy hand over her shoulder. "You ain't—"

Mist spun around and punched him in the stomach. He let her go with a woof of astonished pain. She nodded to Dáinn, and they continued into the black, smoky pit of the bar. A dozen sets of eyes assessed them from the shadows. The radio blasted Norwegian death metal from huge speakers hung on the walls. Sullen kids with multiple piercings huddled over tables strung against the wall opposite the bar, and hipsters ignoring the city-wide smoking ban, argued over coffee and cigarettes.

They were of no interest to Mist. She didn't bother to ask the bartender where she could find Vid, but kept moving through a tightly packed crowd of inebriated slackers and entered the door behind them.

The clientele in the back room was of a far different caliber than the kids in the public area. The dozen men and women were all mature, attractive, and reeking of wealth . . . the kind who dined every night at French Laundry, had their clothes tailor-made in Paris, and lived in apartments and penthouses worth more than all the Lady's gold.

But there was something strange about them, a strangeness that stopped Mist in her tracks. They stared at her as if she had crashed an exclusive wedding wearing nothing but her sword. As if she were an enemy.

"Leave," Dáinn whispered at her back. "Leave now."

Mist barely heard him. "Who are you?" she asked, looking at each hostile face in turn.

Glances were exchanged, but no one answered. Dáinn gripped her arm. "There are too many," he said.

And suddenly she knew. "Where is he?" she demanded of the crowd, loosening her knife. "Where is your master?"

Hard eyes fixed on hers. Several of the men began moving toward her, getting taller by the second. Faces blurred, becoming coarse and ugly with hate. Fists lifted. An unmistakable chill rose in the room.

Hrimgrimir emerged from the crowd, grinning with hideous delight. "So we meet again, halfling. Or should I call you 'cousin'?"

His pointed teeth were red in the dim light. "You must be eager for death. We will be happy to oblige you."

Pulling her knife free, Mist sang the change. Dim light raced along Kettlingr's blade. Her chances of survival were slim, but she had no choice. No choice at all.

"You have more strength than you know," Dáinn said from very far away. She felt a light touch on her cheek. "Feel it, warrior. Let it come."

Some force beyond understanding burst inside her. *Hafling* cousin. She had no time to digest the revelation. Dáinn was gone, and Hrimgrimir and his kin were already upon her.

Kettlingr flew up to meet the attack. The blade skittered against a wall of ice that dissolved as soon as the sword completed its swing. Mist sang, and her *jötunn* blood, the blood she had not known she possessed, sang with her. Strength greater than that of mortal or Valkyrie throbbed in blood and blossomed in bone. Battle runes flared before her eyes. The giants retreated with cries of rage and dismay. She advanced, slashing at any flesh within reach. For a moment it seemed that she might even win.

But the new power didn't last. She felt herself falter under the weight of uncertainty. They were her *kin*. Any one of them might be . . .

She never completed the thought. Hrimgrimir roared and swung a giant fist, knocking her against the wall. Somehow she kept her grip on Kettlingr, but the blow had paralyzed her arm. She knew then that she was going to die, and *she* would not be returning.

Sliding up the wall, she grinned into the giant's face and prepared herself for the final, crushing blow. Hrimgrimir bellowed and raised his hand. The back door swung open, and a thickset blond man staggered into the room, his head swinging right and left in confusion.

"Wa's goin' on here?" he drawled, leaning heavily against the door frame. "Can' a man ge' any sleep?"

Hrimgrimir and the other *jötunar* swung to face the man. "Get out!" Hrimgrimir snarled.

"Mist?" The man took another step into the room, eyes widening. "Issat you?"

She caught her breath and worked her shoulder, feeling it come back to life again. Váli was a drunk and a slackard, but he wasn't as stupid as he looked. He had some part in all this. He *knew* what was happening, and he was trying to help her.

With a hoot of laughter, Váli stumbled his way past the *jötunar* with arms extended. "So . . . gla' to see you," he said, his full weight crashing into Mist. "Missed you."

Smothered in his bearish embrace, Mist felt the pressure of his body pushing her away from the wall. He was moving her toward the door to the bar, inch by subtle inch.

"Get out of here," he hissed, his mouth pressed to her ear.

"Where is Vídarr?" she whispered.

"You can't see him." They reached the door, and Mist heard the hinges creak. "Save yourself."

Save yourself. Vídarr wasn't in league with the evil ones. He was in trouble. Bad trouble.

Without warning, Mist shoved Váli aside and ran for the back door, swinging Kettlingr in a deadly arc. Hrimgrimir swiped at her and missed. The rest were too startled to intercept her before she got to the back door and flung it open.

Vídarr sat in a battered chair in what served as his office, his face blank as uncarved stone. His eyes barely flickered as Mist entered the room.

"Well, you have created quite a disturbance," a voice said from the shadows behind the chair. "I had hoped you would take warning and flee. After all the pleasure you've given me, I had intended to spare you."

Eric. But it wasn't Eric's voice. And the figure that emerged from the shadows was not tall and broad, but as lean and wiry as a stoat. Tight black leather covered him from neck to toe. His long, handsome face was smiling. The expression wasn't friendly.

Mist wasn't feeling particularly friendly herself. "I've come for Gungnir, Slanderer," she said.

"How charming." Loki walked past Vídarr without a glance in

his direction and stood before her, hands on hips. "You always were impulsive, my dear. That was what made you so good in bed."

Mist swung Kettlingr at his head. Loki sent the sword spinning to the floor with three short words and a wave of his hand.

"It's no use," Vídarr said, his voice thick with despair. "You can't beat him."

"Listen to him, Villkatt," Loki said. "Like you, Odhinn's son has been corrupted by his long residence in Midgard. He proved remarkably clumsy in his attempts to interfere." Loki reached for the glass of red wine that stood on the nearby desk and sniffed it critically. "In fact, we had nearly reached an arrangement to the advantage of both of us."

Mist ignored the pain in her hand and stared at Vídarr. "What arrangement?"

"To use Bifrost as headquarters for my future endeavors. Did you know there are other hidden rooms beyond this one? Very suitable for what I have in mind."

"Stealing the other treasures," she said. "But what good would it do you to keep them here? Why didn't you take Gungnir back to wherever you came from?" She took a step toward him. "Why didn't you go straight through the passage on the bridge?"

For a moment Loki's smug expression darkened. "No more questions." He relaxed and smiled again. "I'll give you one chance, sweetling. Join me, or you'll have no more use for such inconvenient curiosity."

He was probably right. She'd always known the odds of beating him were slim; he was, after all, a god, and her *jötunn* blood wouldn't be enough to defeat the Sly One. Dáinn had abandoned her, and even Vídarr had failed to stand up to him.

Still, giving up was not an option. And there was one thing she still didn't understand. Why was Loki offering her a chance to join him? Why had he felt the need to sneak around in the first place, pretending to be her human lover, if he didn't think she was a threat to him?

There was only one way to find out.

"You were always a coward," she said. "Go ahead. Strike me down."

He laughed and sneered at her bravado, and yet he hesitated. Vídarr's eyes fixed on hers, as if he were trying to tell her something important. Something that might change the game completely.

"What are you afraid of, Slanderer?" she taunted. "My sword is out of reach. You need have no fear of a fair fight."

Loki's face contorted with rage. "Pick it up," he snarled.

Mist dove for the sword before he could change his mind. In seconds she had snatched it up, secured her grip and was ready for attack.

Her enemy wasted no time. All at once Gungnir itself was in Loki's hand, and he was aiming straight at her heart. The Swaying One hummed in his grip as he let fly. Mist swung Kettlingr with all her strength, desperately singing the runes that might make the difference between life or death.

She wasn't fast enough, but no cold metal pierced her chest. Gungnir pierced the door behind her shoulder. Loki's mouth gaped in disbelief as she struck, her blade sinking into his left arm.

She knew it was little more than a distraction. He would heal almost instantly. Still, she brought Kettlingr to bear once more . . . and froze as Loki's burning hand clamped around her neck.

"You have tried my patience once too often," he said into her face, his spittle spraying her cheeks.

"And you've . . . tried mine." She wheezed a laugh. "You were never . . . as good as you thought you were. In anything."

He shook her like a child's straw doll. "Perhaps I won't kill you first," he said. "Perhaps I'll take you one last time, and show you just how good I am."

A shudder of loathing drained the strength from Mist's body. To die was one thing. To suffer such humiliation after what she and Eric had shared . . .

No. She stared into Loki's eyes. "Try it, and I'll roast your balls like chestnuts."

Loki flinched, and his grip relaxed. *He's afraid.* It made no sense, none at all, yet she could feel it, see it in his face.

But what was the key to his fear?

"Freyja is the key."

Dáinn's voice, speaking inside her head. This time she was grateful for the intrusion. She shaped an urgent question out of her thoughts, but Dáinn heard it before she was finished.

"Loki has always feared and desired the Lady," he said. *"He taunted and mocked her and called her whore because he wanted her but could not have her."*

But that had nothing to do with Mist. Loki's grip had tightened again, and Mist felt her breath stop in her throat. It was over. She had nothing left with which to fight.

"Halfling," Dainn's silent voice whispered, unraveling like thread caught in a kitten's claws. *"A jötunn was your father. Your mother . . ."*

Dáinn's presence faded, but he left in her mind a single image. An image of a face she knew, a beauty beyond compare.

Mist silenced her disbelief. She had nothing to lose. She met Loki's gaze, letting him feel every last particle of her contempt.

"Is that why you pretended to be an honorable man and lied your way into my bed?" she wheezed. "If you couldn't have the mother, you'd take the daughter?"

Loki's fingers loosened again. "She was a whore," he said, his voice not quite steady. "She lay with every *álfr* and god in Asgard, every giant and dwarf in Jötunheimr and Svartâlfheimr. You're nothing but a—"

He broke off, his face blanching under his shock of red hair. The illusion came over Mist without any effort on her part, a radiant warmth that filled her with a peace she had never known. Loki dropped her and stumbled away.

"Freyja," he croaked.

Mist raised her hand, and Kettlingr flew into it like a tame sparrow. "It is you who have the choice, Laufeyson. Come back to us."

Loki's face slackened. "I . . . I want—"

Vídarr slammed into him, and Loki staggered. The spell was broken. Loki knocked Vídarr aside with a sweep of his arm and leaped up on the desk. He crouched there, hatred in every line of his body.

"You haven't won, bitch," he said. "It isn't over. In the end you'll come begging at my feet, eager to service me like the whore you are."

And then he was gone, vanished into the shadows, the stench of his evil dispersing like a frenzy of roaches exposed to the light.

Mist closed her eyes. The warmth and joy and power were already abandoning her, leaving her an empty sack of skin and bone.

"Mist." Dáinn came up behind her, breathing hard. "Are you well?"

She turned on him, letting anger erase her despair. "Where were you, coward? You had words in plenty, but where was your magic?"

Dáinn said nothing. He simply walked away. Vídarr got to his feet, popping his shoulder back into its socket.

"Mist," he said. "You have to believe I never—"

Váli came into the room, grave and utterly sober. "There will be time for explanations later," he said. "We have more urgent concerns, including a heap of *jötunar* to deal with."

Mist didn't ask what he meant. She pulled Gungnir from the door, sang it small again, and strode past him into the other room. There literally was a heap of giants, most unconscious and the rest groaning in pain.

"*He* did it," Váli said, jerking his head toward Dáinn, who stood quietly in a corner. "I helped a little. But he kept them from interfering while you dealt with Loki."

Laughter choked Mist's reply. Had *she* dealt with Loki, or had it been Freyja all along?

My mother. Mist wasn't just half *jötunn*. She was half goddess as well. It would take some time to digest that knowledge and understand what it might mean to her. And to the battle that was coming.

She walked slowly over to Dáinn, who refused to meet her gaze. "I'm sorry," she said. "I didn't know."

"It doesn't matter," he said.

But it did. She'd thought of Dáinn as a traitor to his people and to the Aesir. And he had left her during her fight with the *jötunar*. Still, she might have to revise her opinion. So much was changing. The world was growing dark, and her sisters had to be warned. She couldn't do it alone.

"It isn't over," she said, swallowing her pride. "I need you."

He finally looked up, his mouth quirking in a weary half smile. "I have nowhere else to go."

She nodded and looked over her shoulder. Váli was busy with a bottle, and Vídarr leaned against the wall, his expression locked as tight as a virgin's legs on her wedding night.

Maybe they'd help, too. Vídarr still had some explaining to do. But now they had a little time. Maybe it was enough.

"Well," she said to the room in general, "let's get this rubbish cleaned up. It stinks in here."

BEYOND THE PALE

Nancy Holder

Who rides, so late, through night and wind?
—Johann Wolfgang von Goethe, "The Erl King"

*L*inks! *Verdammt,* left!" Lukas yelled at Meg, his voice crackling through her headset. "He's there!"

Ebony trees and jet-black bracken jagged into silhouettes as Meg galloped wildly through the snowstorm. Her hair, braided and pulled back with an elastic band, hit her back like a fist. Deluged by sleet, still she sweated under her standard-issue German police riot helmet. Unlike the others, she'd painted no insignia on it, no coat of arms, no totem. Just her last name: ZECHERLE. The miner's light attached to the front strobed icy blue on ferocious boughs of fir and pine. Wet splatted on her mask. She smelled the cold, and the mud, and her own stinking fear. Of smoky magick, there was no trace. And of their quarry, no sight.

To her left, the Black Forest raged and shook. To her right, boulders jutted toward treetops, and behind them, she knew, a waterfall cascaded. As if the icy flow had leaped the riverbanks, she was drowning in darkness and snow.

"Meg!" Lukas bellowed. "Reply!"

"Where?" she shouted into her headset. The mouthpiece was loose and she let go of the reins of her massive black stallion, Teufel, with one hand and held the mic to her mouth. "Shit, *where?*"

"You *must* see him! Twelve o'clock!"

Doggedly, she squinted through the protective mask. No night-vision goggles, no GPS, nothing. If the Great Hunt got you and dragged you across the Pale, you were worse than dead.

If they didn't get that baby back . . .

Snow. Darkness.

"Then my Sight's not working," she announced.

"*Bitte?*" Lukas cried. "Not *working?*"

Through her earphones, she could hear the others responding in disbelief. It almost made her smile; they were so serious and smug. But she was clearly in deep trouble, so she spared no time for pettiness.

"I see trees and rocks," she said. "Period, *kaput.*"

"Meg, where are you?" That was Sofie, Lukas's twin sister.

"Where the fuck are *you?*" she shouted back.

Static crackled in her ears and snow rushed at her; tree branches smacked her chest, bolted into Kevlar body armor. Teufel grunted, then sailed over a fallen log long before she put her spurs to his flanks. She understood now why they didn't use motorcycles or ATVs, which had been her first question when Lukas had explained about the magickal Haus of the Knights—Haus Ritter. He'd rolled her eyes and told her she was a typical arrogant American, and that the old ways were best because the old gods were alive and well in Germany. Well, yeah, *heil Hitler* to you, too.

"Meg, just focus," another voice advised, in the polished, aristocratic British accent of Heath, who had deposited a hundred thousand pounds into a trust fund for her brother and paid off her parents' refi, just like that, when Meg had protested that she couldn't leave the States because her parents were too wiped out to deal with anything except their favorite TV shows. "Your Sight manifested. It can't go away. It doesn't work like that."

"It *did* go away," she yelled, furious. "I'm blind out here!"

Desperately, Meg scanned the flashing landscape dead ahead, then to her left, right. The German Black Forest glared back at her, far from still. Pines and firs shuddered and bowed. Snow poured from the sky. Aside from the voices of her team crackling in her ears—the four other Gifted Border riders on her patrol—the howling wind overpowered every sound, including the steady rhythm of her own horse's hooves and the staccato pounding of her heart. In their world—of magick, and evil—she was blind, deaf, useless. It was only through sheer accident that she'd wound up on point, ahead of the others on the craggy slopes of the alpine mountain.

Or maybe it had been by design: Sofie had insisted that Meg wasn't ready to ride, that she'd slow them down. Two minutes ago, the snotty German chick had been in the lead. Now Meg didn't know where Sofie was, and her precious Sight had failed. Maybe Sofie had cast a spell of some kind to get rid of the deadweight. What had Sofie said? *We travel light, or we die.* Sofie's thick German accent had made her sound like a mad scientist in a bad movie.

"Turn left!" Lukas shouted.

Setting her jaw, squinting, Meg pressed her heel against Teufel's flank and the horse turned sharply—directly into the path of a low-lying pine bough. Meg flattened against her horse's neck, holding on tight as Teufel soared over it, landing very hard. These animals weren't bred for grace. Or long lives.

Like horse, like rider.

Icicles rattled down on her helmet and shoulders. Thank God for her body armor, uncomfortable though it was. And her kicker boots, which she'd insisted on wearing. She wasn't losing her steel toes for anything. Though truth be told, her feet were freezing.

"Meg?" That was Heath, again, eagerly welcomed into their ranks six months ago by Lukas and Sofie. Meg was the newer newbie. Not a lot of eagerness on Sofie's part when Lukas showed up with Meg, like a little boy with a stray puppy he wanted to keep. Heath was a European and he had a strong Gift. Plus he was incredibly hot, and Sofie was on her own Great Hunt to get him into bed. Meg supposed it made sense for Sofie to be a little bit German-centric, given her vocation as a Bavarian Border guard. But Meg would have thought she would be a little more human-centric, given what they were guarding the Pale from.

"Where are you?" Heath persisted.

"Unknown." She was out of her element; this was crazy. "I can't see anyone."

"I'm coming for you," Heath said.

"*Nein*. Heath, keep going." That was Sofie. "We're almost at the Pale."

How did Sofie know? What could she see?

White-hot lightning crashed, revealing a rider to Meg's left— Edouard, the fifth member of their team. The Haitian held up his gloved hand in salute. She returned it as Teufel increased his speed, slaloming around trees like a skier.

"Eddie at nine o'clock," she announced.

Sofie said something in rapid French, Eddie's language, and Eddie answered. Everyone on the team spoke at least two languages; unfortunately, Meg's second language was Spanish, and no one else spoke it. After a month in Bavaria, Meg still couldn't understand 90 percent of what Sofie said—in any language. Her accent was very heavy.

"Going ahead of you, Meg. I'm too close to the Pale," Eddie informed her, rising in his saddle jockey-style.

Like her, he was dressed in black body armor over a black cat suit, camouflage for their night ride. Their saddles were black leather, too, and each had an Uzi and a crossbow strapped behind it. She was a good shot with a submachine gun; she had that going for her. But what use was that if she could never see the target?

A curtain of snow swallowed Eddie up. To dodge another tree limb, Meg cantered left, in the direction from which Eddie had just retreated.

"*Also*, Meg, *vorsicht!*" Lukas yelled as Teufel lost his footing, and dizziness hit Meg like a fist. Vertigo fanned from the center of her forehead, smacking her temples and ripping in a zipper down the back of her neck. Jerking on the reins, she imagined the top of her head exploding and her brains shooting like a geyser toward the moon.

She knew she was skirting the Pale. The Great Hunt must have crossed over. If so, Team Ritter's mission had just failed. Humans, Gifted or not, couldn't cross the border between the realm of Faerie and humankind. Or so they'd told her. They seemed to be telling her a number of things that might not be true.

She thought of that little Mexican baby, six weeks old. Her stomach clenched as the old anger overtook her. She wasn't turning back, not this time.

Screw it, she thought.

"Giddyap," she ordered Teufel. Not the proper German command, but she couldn't remember what it was. She put her spurs to him, and he obeyed. She grabbed her mouthpiece and held it still, wanting to make sure she was heard. "Proceeding for extraction."

"Nein!" Lukas yelled.

"No, abort!" Heath's voice cracked in her ear.

Dimly she heard the four of them shouting at her as she leaned forward and kept her head down. The pommel pressed into her stomach as she gathered up Teufel's mane in her fists.

For one strange moment she saw herself back home three months ago, out in the desert with the temperature topping 110. Before she'd known there was a Great Hunt or a Pale. Before she'd met Lukas. Red hair in a bun, khaki fatigues, mirrored sunglasses, Beretta in her hand and another in Jack Dillger's. Opening the door to the stolen U-Haul and seeing what the *coyote* had left—seven desperate Mexican nationals attempting to cross illegally: six dead, one alive; and that one nearly dead and begging for water, and begging more desperately not to be sent back across the border.

"Lo intentaré de nuevo." I will try it again. He said it through cracked, bleeding lips, and then he burst into heaving sobs, crammed as he was among corpses.

Holding the baby in her arms, Meg had started to cry, too. She never broke down in front of anyone; she was a tough bitch, but that day her mirrored sunglasses could do only so much. That damn desert day of the dead she had cracked apart, right down the middle.

Shortly after that, Lukas had contacted her. And now she was here at a very different border.

The howling wind shimmered into silvery wind-chime voices:

> *Oh, come and go with us,*
> *Death never visits us*
> *Oh, come and go with us . . .*

"Pull back. Don't cross. You will die. Repeat: do not cross," Lukas said.

Her tears:

The baby had worn a tiny gold chain and a religious medal around his chubby neck. He was curled in the limp arms of his dead teenage mother, and for one hopeful moment, Meg had thought he was still alive. She had gathered him up, feather light; his little head fell back and his last breath came out, a death rattle in a dried husk. Still she had hoped, prayed, whispered to him just please, *por favor, hijo,* to whimper, to take a breath. Part of her mind had registered that he was dead; another part spun fantasies, bargains that would pull him back to earth and make his lungs inflate. She was here; she would save him. It would be all right.

It would never be all right again.

Jack didn't tell anyone that she'd cried and gotten sloppy drunk and yanked at the waistband of his jeans, Okay, what about just once; they had a strong partnership and they'd be fine afterward. Or that she'd wound up drinking even more, sitting on his couch and watching the remake of *Night of the Living Dead* and sobbing, "Why? Why?" And Jack, bless him, fully clothed, bless him, had said, "I *know.* I thought George Romero got it right the first time."

She asked for a week of leave and spent it driving through the desert, looking for more stalled vehicles. She'd ridden Mesa, her dappled mare, along dusty trails bordered with deer weed, white sage, and manzanita that she couldn't reach with a vehicle. Sweating in the heat, thinking of the baby, armed with a rifle.

Glad Jack hadn't asked for a new partner. Yet. Watching the ghostly forms in night vision, in the surveillance center. Men, women, children, pushing through holes in the fences; wading the swell of a stream; white blurs like phantoms. Was she looking at the *coyote* who had left the baby to die?

In a phone call, her cousin Deb, who lived in Fargo, North Dakota, had told her that every winter, she and her friends routinely got in their cars and trolled for stranded drivers, whose car engines had frozen, whose hoods were buried in snow.

"So it's in our blood," Deb had concluded.

In her blood.

After the baby died, Meg doubled her visits to Matt in the care facility.

Matt, her big brother. Matt and Meg. Once a West Pointer, an athlete, a practical joker. Growing up, she'd hated it when he hit on her friends. Then at twenty, he'd been struck by lightning; his heart had stopped; his frontal lobe had been fried. She'd been eighteen. How could that happen? He'd been caught in a downpour at a party; he wasn't alone. There were twenty-seven other people there.

She researched the histories of people who had been struck by lightning. A man named Roy Cleveland Sullivan had been struck seven times, and had some "deficits," but he lived to tell the tale. Then he committed suicide at the age of seventy-one.

Matt couldn't even ask for more applesauce.

Their parents checked out emotionally when they checked Matty into the facility. Meg slipped the orderlies extra money so he would never sit in dirty diapers. So they wouldn't drug him. So if he ever did remember her, he would be able to tell her that they had treated him well.

Her parents protested only mildly when she dropped her plans to get a teaching credential and instead became a Border Patrol agent. None of her friends understood. So she dumped them. Of course, she didn't understand it, either.

The Mexican baby, Matt, and the child in the glowing white snowstorm. Meg wasn't losing this one, too.

"Giddyap, Teufel," she told her horse, who responded as if he spoke her language.

Haus Ritter—the House of the Knights—had been after the Erl King for a thousand years. Their lineage was long and illustrious. They had snatched back hundreds—maybe thousands—of babies, right out of the arms of the Erl King's goblin minions. There were stories, paintings, songs about Ritter heroes who had died in glorious service to the cause. But no one had ever crossed the border between Faerie and forest and returned to tell the tale.

"*Meg!*" Lukas bellowed at her. His voice echoed off the rocks. The snow-battered moon blazed. Too close; too close; someone fired off a warning round; maybe they figured she had lost her mind, which is what supposedly happened to humans when they crossed the Pale. Which was about to happen to the kidnapped child, if it wasn't already dead.

"Meg, stop!" Eddie cried. "Look, *look*!"

"*Zurück!*" Lukas bellowed.

Then, through the din, something *clicked* in the bony ridges above and below her eyes, sounding like the cocking of a rifle. It was the same sound and sensation that Lukas had magickally caused in San Diego, to manifest her Second Sight. Now, as then, shimmers of luminous colors spiraled and pinwheeled all around her. The smoky odor of magick permeated her mask; and her heart skipped multiple beats. Her Second Sight was back, and the Great Hunt roared up in front of her, fifty yards away.

Holy shit.

It was blurred at first, as if she were looking through the surveillance cameras back in San Diego. White and glowing, horses and riders.

Then forty yards away, the cantering parade snapped into sharp relief. Cut out in black by the brilliant lights, dozens of spiky goblins in medieval armor rode black chargers, capering and gibbering as they galloped, a thundering horde. There were at least a dozen of them sitting so high in their saddles that she figured the smallest to be at least six feet tall. Orange flames flared from the horses' nostrils; sparks flew from their hooves. Hellhounds of ash and smoke bayed at their heels, disintegrating, re-forming—

Thirty yards.

Twenty.

At the lead rode the majestic Erl King himself, Master of the Great Hunt, exactly as Lukas had described him. Dressed in ebony chain mail and a solid black chest plate, the demon lord of the forest towered over the goblins. His black helmet was smooth, with no helm—no eyeholes—topped with curved antlers that flared with smoky flames; fastened at the shoulders, his cloak furled behind like the wake of an obsidian river. In his right chain-mail gauntlet, he held the reins of his enormous warhorse. His left clasped a squirming bundle against his chest—the baby.

He must be freezing.

The child had been snatched from his crib, where he slept bundled in pajamas. His name was Garriet, and he was nine weeks old. While they were suiting up and Lukas was detailing the mission, Meg had asked for a picture. Sofie had snorted.

"He'll be the baby in the Erl King's arms," Heath had deadpanned. "But if by chance there's two, grab them both, Meggie."

The Erl King had stolen many thousands of children through the centuries. His goblins put changelings in their emptied cribs—often passing for human children, but evil creatures to the core. Adolf Hitler had been a changeling. Jack the Ripper. Charles Manson. There were other places where he could cross the Pale; it was the job of Haus Ritter to guard it here.

What will he do to Garriet if we don't get him back?

No one could tell her. Their primary mission was to isolate the Erl King and kill or wound him, approach, and snatch back the child. It seemed an impossible task. Lukas and Sofie had done it once before, when they were nineteen. They were twenty-seven now, and this was the first verified theft since.

"I see them," Meg whispered into her microphone. "My Sight has returned."

"*Bon, c'est bon,* Meg," Eddie said, his voice taut with excitement.

Then light flared around the Great Hunt, saturating the surroundings with a hazy green glow. Lightning crackled. Sparks flew. Thunder roared down the mountain. The ground shook beneath her, and Teufel whinnied.

A great wailing rose around her.

"*Scheiße.* They're across," Lukas announced. "Abort."

A goblin rose in his stirrups, turned, and waved at her. His face was a mass of scars and hollows, as if someone had taken a Halloween mask and melted it.

She'd been taunted before. You didn't last in the Border Patrol if you gave in to your impulses. But adrenaline was pumping through her system so hard and fast she was quivering. There was no way this was over.

"I can get them," she insisted.

"They're beyond the Pale, love," Heath reminded her.

"It's over," Sofie chimed in. "Retreat, Meg."

Shaking her head, Meg pressed her thighs in a viselike grip against Teufel's flanks, reached behind, and started to grab her Uzi. She rethought. On this side of the Pale, standard-issue ammo could kill her targets. But if shot from this side to the Pale, the chambered rounds were ineffective. The crossbow bolts, coated with magicks, would work. She didn't know why. She didn't care at the moment. Problem was, she had yet to master the crossbow. In target practice, she shot wide.

She had to get closer if she was going to save that baby.

"I'm going," she said, urging Teufel forward. He tossed his head and broke into a run.

Then she heard singing, in silvery tones, angelic and sweet:

> *Oh, come and go with us . . .*
> *Where death never visits us . . .*

"Eddie!" Lukas shouted. "Stop her!"

Oh, come and go with us . . .

The song washed over her, drawing out her anger like poison from a snakebite. Buried anger over her helplessness—

Where death never visits us . . .
"*Eddie!*" Lukas bellowed.
"*Mwen regret sa,*" Eddie said.

Something slammed into her side like a huge, spiked fist; it tore through the layers of her protective armor and sliced into her skin. Fireball heat tore through her body; then she went cold, and began to slide from her horse.

Oh, come—

"No," she gritted, "crap."

Losing consciousness, she slumped sideways. Into snow, she prayed; if she hit the rocks, or if she fell under Teufel . . .

Through the glowworm-like radiance, the image of the Great Hunt stretched and glimmered. She held out a gloved hand, as if she could scoop the riders up in her fist. Vibrations buffeted her ears; then banshee wails shot up around her. Death. Death was riding with the Hunt. The baby . . .

The wailing.

Just wolves, she thought, tears forming, grabbing the pommel and canting farther right. *No, no, I was so close. So close again . . .*

"Don't go," she ordered the Erl King. "Don't, you bastard."

The King of the Elves turned his head in her direction. Although Teufel was still racing forward, she froze from head to steel-toed boot. Behind his black mask, he looked at her. Saw her. She felt it as if he had laid a hand on her shoulder, or her cheek . . . icy cold, but gentle. Chills skittered up and down, ghost fingers on the xylophone of her spine.

She had never been more afraid, nor felt more alive, than in that moment.

"I know you," she whispered.

He inclined his horned head slowly, in her direction. The chills got worse; but so did an incredible euphoria, as if she were the most powerful being who had ever lived.

He held her gaze, in his black mask and flaming antlers. Then he nestled the child beneath his chin.

And then she was gone.

In the hospital:

She'd heard her brother's voice from behind the bandages, issuing from the hospital bed, after the lightning strike: *"Meh meh meh."*

"He's trying to say my name," she'd told his neurologist.

"I'm so sorry, but it's just a reflex. He doesn't even know who you are," the doctor had replied.

Their parents were drinking coffee in the waiting room. They couldn't seem to make it down the hallway to see him. The nurses had all traded looks and the social worker had been called. Something about her parents' denial. Something about he was their son, for God's sake. They should at least *see* him.

In the desert:

When she had held that lifeless Mexican baby and tried to will it into living, she forgave her parents for being too afraid to face Matt. Maybe that was where the tears had sprung from, and the messy way she'd hit on Jack. He'd told her he'd been tempted until she started talking about her brother.

"You got issues, hon," he'd told her.

We travel light, or we die.

————

When she awakened, she was lying on the floor of Haus Ritter's dark blue van, and her armor was off. She was bare to the waist with a heavy blanket covering her, and she felt loopy, drugged, and supremely pissed off. Bathed in snowfall moonlight, Lukas knelt beside her, his hands resting one on top of the other, beneath the blanket, molded against her left side. His eyes were closed, his dark eyebrows furrowed as he whispered under his breath. Warmth spread from his skin to hers; he was performing a healing spell.

She studied his face. Lying jerk. The first time she'd met him, in San Diego, she had allowed herself to be mesmerized by his movie-star looks. Craggy jaw, oceanic blue eyes fringed with heavy lashes, deep hollows in his cheeks tinged with perpetual dark brown beard stubble.

She and Jack had just spoken to a class of students at UC San Diego about the rights of undocumented workers. How "illegal immigration" boiled down to sneaking across the Mexican border to El Norte—the North, the U.S.—paradise, fairyland—to get raped, robbed, murdered, to *die*—and she had stared at all those idealistic, liberal kids who stared at her as if she were the Great Satan, hearing *nothing* of what she was saying—the agents, killed in the line of duty—and decided to tell them the story of the dead baby in the desert. Not to help them understand, but to punish them.

"So how again do you define illegal immigration as a victimless crime?" she concluded in a flat voice brimming with venom.

It was too much; she'd been too brutal. Jack had intervened by passing out a stack of the public affairs officer's business cards. Then he'd driven straight to the Elephant Bar. To unwind, he said. Trouble was, his divorce would be final in nine days; and after a few Dos Equis and tequila shots, they both started crossing over into that fairyland of their own, which involved intimacies they shouldn't take and confessions that were mostly lies, but kind lies, designed to comfort and tempt each other.

But any love that was made there would definitely die. Meg had realized they were crossing the line sooner than Jack did. She'd excused herself to go to the bathroom and whipped out her cell phone, about to call herself a cab, when Lukas had appeared at the other end of the dimly lit hall, like a desperado calling her out at high noon.

"You're awake," Lukas murmured now, lifting his hands from her chest and pulling the blanket up to her chin. Tenderly, gently.

"Did we—?"

"Nein." Blue eyes in a face puffy with cold and despair. "No."

She clenched her fists to keep from exploding. "The whole thing was bullshit," she said. "I couldn't see. And you made Eddie *shoot* me."

"To stop you from killing yourself," he replied. "Crossing the Pale is like stepping on a livewire. I told you that."

> *Oh, come and go—*

"How did I end up on point? I couldn't *see*!"

"Something affected your Sight," he agreed.

"Maybe the Erl King did it," Eddie said, looking over his shoulder at them. Mid-twenties, he was very sculpted, with a hooked nose and deep hollows in his cheeks. Her distant relative, carrying magickal DNA or "auric vibrations," as Lukas referred to them. So they'd been told.

"How?" Meg asked.

"Who can say?" Sofie said.

Lukas glanced toward his sister, his expression hooded. "Well, it's never happened before."

"And her parents didn't manifest any Gifts," Sofie added.

"I was *not* adopted." She scowled at the back of Sofie's head as Lukas handed her a large gray sweater. She pulled it on over her head. They'd been over this. If magick could have saved Matty, *someone* in the family would have used it.

"Sometimes it's dormant," Lukas reminded them both. "It's not exactly genetic. Auric vibrations are like magick bloodlines."

"Then maybe magick forces we don't yet understand have affected her Ritter vibrations," Sofie interjected. "We need to find out if we can count on Meg's Gift."

God, did she *blind me?* Meg wondered. Maybe Sophie liked being the queen bee of the patrol unit. There was definitely no love lost between the two of them, but would she actually sabotage someone on a life-and-death mission?

"We'll do a thorough investigation," Lukas assured her.

There was a lull. Everyone looked tired and glum. They'd been on a high before the mission. Eddie and Heath had known about their special powers, but they hadn't realized there was a worldwide confederation of magickal groups—hundreds of thousands of people—who were "different." Gifted, in their parlance.

The van trundled over ancient cobblestones. Snow piled on skyscrapers of glass and steel, and on Victorian heaps whose roofs were skewered with chimneys and satellite dishes. It smacked at an angle against "perpendicular" whitewash-and-wood beams of Renaissance architecture, most of it decidedly "faux," and all of it reminding Meg of Legoland back in California.

Heath, who looked to be around thirty-five, sat facing her on the floor, wrapped in a dark blue blanket, looking cold, tired, and frustrated. His face was ruddy from the cold and his crazy blond Rasta braids were soaked with either sweat or snow or a combination. Sofie was driving, and Eddie was riding shotgun, tipping his head back against the seat.

"How's Teufel?" Meg asked.

Lukas grimaced. "Feeling guilty. You need to have a chat with him and let him know he didn't do anything wrong."

He probably means that literally, she thought. What would have happened to Teufel if she had crossed the Pale? In the heat of the moment, she hadn't given it a moment's thought. Her San Diego mount, Mesa, was a great quarter horse, and Meg felt affection for her, but she belonged to the Border Patrol and as such, was ridden by other agents. Meg had worked hard not to develop too close an attachment to her.

Here, things were different. Each rider was assigned his or her own horse, and no one else rode it. It was expected that some sort of magickal bonding would take place. Meg had been riding Teufel since she arrived, and if that was happening, she didn't have the Gift to know it.

Moving stiffly, she elbowed herself to a sitting position, giving her head a quick shake when Lukas moved to help her. At the same time, Heath reached over to the left and showed Meg a thermos.

"Tea?" he offered.

When she didn't move, Lukas took it and unscrewed the black matte plastic cap. He poured steaming brown tea into the cap and held it out to her. She wasn't going to drink any of it, but she opened her mouth and the scalding, astringent liquid dribbled onto her tongue.

"It wasn't a good time for any of us," Heath said to her. "But at least we know it's real. The Hunt." His voice reeked with awe.

"Yeah, swell," she retorted, to hide her freak-out. This was all a little too real for her comfort. "*You* didn't get shot."

Eddie turned around, looked down at Meg, and grimaced.

"I'm sorry," he said. "It was just a little . . ." He waggled his fingers. He had a special little Gift in addition to Second Sight—he could hurl blasts of debilitating energy from his hands. Sort of like hitting someone with just a little bit of lightning.

"I'm okay," she told him, remembering her euphoria, wondering if that was why she was crashing so hard now. Nothing else would have stopped her. She'd been seized by madness, designed to lure her across the Pale, so she would die.

"We weren't fast enough. We'll get better," Heath put in.

I *was fast enough*, Meg thought.

The van fell into another silence. Heath said, "We debriefed while you were out." He smiled faintly. "Lukas told Eddie it was quite common to wet your pants the first few times."

"*Guete ou*. Lucky for you," Eddie shot back, but Heath didn't even acknowledge his salvo.

It was very different back home, even after deaths and murders and some moron's intestines exploding because they were filled with bags of heroin. Her *compadres* at the Border Patrol pulled crazy practical jokes on each other, drank together. That was why Jack had been so shaky when she had broken down crying over the baby.

Six months' leave of absence. That left all kinds of doors open. Jack would probably be in the middle of his first rebound.

"We're home," Lukas announced, almost as if he could read her mind, and she needed reminding that Germany was home now.

The crowning jewel of Ritterberg was the castle, Schloss Ritter, only half of which stood intact. Wars and time had pulled it down. Meg didn't understand why they didn't repair it—they could use magick, couldn't they? It was like a distressed version of Disneyland, fairy-tale chic: circular turrets, crenellated walls; it was truly spectacular. The vast refurbished rooms, updated kitchens, and bathrooms were the official home to the 357 members of Haus Ritter, one of the hundreds of houses that composed the world of the Gifted— people who could use magick.

What kind of magick? she'd demanded, throwing back more tequila and eating the nachos Lukas had ordered for her. Magick to read minds; to read memories off objects; to become invisible; to travel through time; to conjure and wound and kill. Magick to hurl fireballs and bursts of energy; magick to protect. Different Gifted possessed different Gifts. In Meg's veins ran the blood of Haus Ritter—the German House of the Knights, sworn to guard the Bavarian section of Germany from all the supernatural elements that roamed within. She was a Border guard, maintaining a line watch of the Pale as it traced its route through the Black Forest, where the Erl King rode with the Great Hunt. There were four such units, and hers had been created a year ago, when Lukas and Sofie had found Eddie.

It was a world Meg had never dreamed existed until Lukas came up to her in the hallway of the Elephant Bar. It probably helped his case that he was very handsome and that she was drunk, and he got her drunker. He confessed later that he'd also used a bit of charm on her, plopping herbs in her drink that would make her listen. Drugging her, in other words.

It had taken her longer to believe him than he'd thought it would—nearly a month—during which he awakened her Second Sight and showed her the specters of their shared history: the ghosts of fallen knights whose last name was Zecherle, like hers; and Ritter, which was his.

In the Middle Ages, *Ritter* simply meant "knight" in German—any nobleman with a coat of arms who protected his lands and his folk. But *Haus* Ritter was another matter—a secretive, dedicated family of Gifted warriors, who were unaware that the world over, there were other magick-using families dedicated to other causes—in some cases good but in many, many others, evil.

That changed with World War II, and the Nazis' fascination with the occult. Just as the Houses began to contact each other, fear of discovery by the Ungifted sent them underground. As Germans, Haus Ritter suffered terrible losses—conscripted into armies; shipped to the death camps; fleeing Europe. The Erl King was busy in those days, riding boldly across the Pale and stealing Bavarian children—Aryan, Jewish, Gypsy, Mediterranean, and African children—while the Nazis were blamed; and the weakened Ritters seemed powerless to stop him.

Then World War II ended. Resuming the title of Guardian of the House—*Wächter*—Andreas Ritter, Lukas and Sofie's grandfather, began the slow process of finding the scattered family members. Their father, Marcus, had been killed in a car crash in 1990—Lukas and Sofie didn't believe it had been an accident—and the leadership of the Border patrol had fallen to the twins. Through rites and rituals, they continued the search for more personnel.

On the damn desert day that Meg had let down her guard and cried, Lukas had found her. Then he boarded a plane to San Diego to meet her.

To woo her to Germany, he had shown her proof of her magickal Gift—the Gift of Second Sight. Sitting in his room at the Hotel del

Coronado, giving her a cracked, weathered leather glove, he lit candles and told her to close her eyes while he whispered strange words. After about thirty minutes, she saw visions of Ritter midnight rides, and a redheaded man who could have been her own twin, gazing at her from centuries ago and nodding encouragement. Despite herself, she was drawn in, pulled hard; she knew him, deep in her soul; blood sang to blood.

But when she'd snapped out of the trance she'd turned down Lukas's invitation, insisting he had drugged her again, and pointing out that she had a life in San Diego, and her own border to protect.

"You have more boundaries than that," Lukas had drawled. "More walls."

She took offense, even though he was right.

Lukas had suggested she come with him to Germany just to see. To visit. Then to train, just a bit. Take six months to be fair. And now, tonight, to ride with them for the first time.

What an epic fail.

She stared up at the Ritter coat of arms, barely visible in the storm: a shield bisected into fields of blue and white, superimposed by a tree trunk sawed nearly down to the roots. The Erl King's name had been mistranslated; to some, he was known as the Alder King, alder being a kind of wood. But he was King of the Other Side—the elves and goblins, the baby thieves.

Sofie downshifted and the van climbed the hill on which the castle was perched. Moving gingerly, Meg pulled her cell phone out of a Velcro pocket in her pants. The face remained black. Crap, had it fried?

"It's only two a.m.," Lukas informed her. They had gone on duty at ten p.m., and gotten the call about the child abduction at midnight. It seemed like much longer to her.

The van stopped and Lukas pulled back the door. He unfolded himself and reached out a hand to Meg. It was warm. The wound at her side was warm, too.

She moved from the door and crowded beneath an umbrella that

Eddie snapped open. Lukas looked at the two of them as if they were exotic creatures, then turned and joined Sofie at the back of the van. Heath followed. Breath rising like steam, they began unpacking the weaponry, passing out the crossbows and Uzis. The horses would be seen to and trailered back to the castle barn by stable hands.

"You don't have to carry your gear," Lukas said, but Meg gave him a look and slung the strap to the Uzi over her head, then her crossbow quiver, still loaded with bolts, and the crossbow itself. There were several metal containers of ammo; she hoisted one up, grunting under her breath at the pull in her side, and headed for the castle. Two bundled Ritter security guards stood at attention before the large ornate wooden door, which had once borne a carving of knights in pursuit of the Erl King. It was worn nearly away, and everyone used a smaller door cut into the old one.

The five filed inside, Lukas and Sofie leading. Meg was in the middle, then Heath, and finally Eddie. The entrance to the castle glowed with firelight and golden magick; it was warm if not cozy, as the cavernous ceiling stretched up into the front turret.

Wächter Andreas Ritter, the Guardian of the Haus, strode toward them as staff approached and took their weapons and ammo. Tall, gangly, with a shock of white hair and gray eyes behind wire-rimmed glasses, he was dressed in a black turtleneck sweater, black wool trousers, and boots. With his salt-and-pepper beard, he looked like an intellectual—some kind of college professor. It was hard to believe that he was over 165 years old. It was said that his great-grandfather had tried to parley a truce with the Erl King. No one could tell Meg if that was true.

The lithe older man spoke to the group in German, and everyone was galvanized by his attention. He was their resident sorcerer and guru. Sofie and Lukas spoke earnestly, and attention turned to Meg.

"You really tried it?" Andreas asked her in English. "To cross the Pale?"

She nodded, and he shook his head. "I'd like to talk to you about that. Could you come to my office in a little while? Shall we say at nine?"

"Okay," she replied.

Then Andreas turned to Sofie and spoke in rapid German: *"This is your team, yours and your brother's. Can you not control your people?"*

Meg's voice tingled with shock. She understood every word.

"Not her," Sofie replied, and Lukas shook his head.

"She's new. She's trying."

"She's dangerous," Sofie put in.

"Did you get the changeling?" Lukas asked Andreas, changing the subject.

"The extraction team hasn't reported in yet."

Damn. Suddenly German was no longer a language barrier.

"Hey," Meg began; then a wave of weariness crashed over her. She was too tired to go into it now. Too heartsick.

And not trusting enough.

"Yes?" Andreas prompted.

"I'll see you at nine," she said.

He dismissed them. The Border patrol units were elite squads with their own luxurious rooms and bathrooms. Located in a turret, hers was a large half circle, the stone floor covered with dark blue mohair carpets emblazoned with the Ritter crest, matching hangings warming the imposing heavily carved canopy bed. Medieval-looking gilt antiques—scooped chairs with leather slings, a table inlaid with a mosaic of a saint—and a real coat of armor finished off the decorations. It was so unlike her messy but pleasant condo. Her cell phone was working; she set the alarm for eight thirty. Shakily, she stripped out of her kicker boots, cat suit, and the sweater.

Naked, she shuffled into the bath and showered, luxuriating in the hot, hot water. In her mind, she replayed the mission; saw herself objectively, as if at a distance. Saw the Erl King. *He bowed his head to me. He knew me. And I knew him.*

There was no way she was going to rest if she lay down. Her busy brain was too fully engaged. So she dressed in jeans, cowboy boots, and a white turtleneck sweater. She braided her wet hair and left her room. Her boots clacked as she walked down a stone corridor illuminated with overhanging mosaic lanterns powered by fluorescent bulbs.

I saw a demon king, she thought. *And real goblins. They took a baby. And I couldn't do shit. And now I can understand German and I'm hung up about who likes me and who trusts me and what the hell is wrong with me?*

I nearly crossed into another dimension.

Her legs buckled and she held herself up against the wall. Her breath came in quick gasps; she was shaking, hard; then she slipped to the floor and pushed her back against the stone, bringing her knees to her chest and burying her head.

This is crazy, so crazy, she thought. She could remember having this same conversation with Lukas, back in California: *Fifty years ago, people who saw your Border Patrol surveillance system would have thought it was magick. What's to say that we aren't simply using some other kind of technology?*

All his rationalizations. All hers.

Maybe the Erl King was a man in a costume. The goblins, too. It's an urban legend and these guys buy into it or perpetuate it, and I'm on a reality show. Or it's some elaborate practical joke Jack cooked up. Speakers in the trees, special lighting.

Except . . . I speak German. And I was going to cross over. I couldn't stop myself.

She rested her head on her knees.

Struck-by-lightning stories: August Hellman of Arkansas was struck twice and lived to tell the tale. No permanent injuries. No brain damage. Each time he was hit, he smelled ozone and felt "a terrible sense of foreboding" seconds before.

That monster took a baby. Why? What do they do to them?

No one could tell her. No one knew.

Someone was coming; she got to her feet and wiped her face, averting her head. Living in the castle was like living in a big office building, with people coming and going at all hours, busy, busy, busy. Guarding the Pale was only one of the duties of Haus Ritter. Apparently there were vampires called *Blutsauger.* And gnomes. A lot of guarding.

Hysterical laughter welled up inside her. She thought about calling Jack. *Guess what. I'm living in an* Underworld *movie.*

She didn't recognize the man ambling toward her, apparently texting, head down, fingers flying. He wore jeans and a dark brown sweatshirt with the Ritter crest silk-screened in black.

"*Abend,*" he said casually. *Evening.*

"*Guten abend,*" she replied.

I should tell someone about all this. I shouldn't wait until nine.

She continued on down the corridor of stone, knowing that Andreas's office was on the fifth story of the castle and that she had to make two lefts before she reached the birdcage elevator, a Victorian contraption that scared her to death—

She heard a low, deep moan, and stopped walking. It was almost sub-audible, as if it were originating from underneath her. She looked around. There was nothing.

She walked on.

The moan came again.

Cocking her head, she turned down a passageway lined with oil paintings of Ritter knights, maybe Renaissance. At a T-intersection, she shrugged and forked right, turning around, wondering if she'd imagined it. It could be the water pressure in the pipes. A movie.

Except . . . she felt compelled to find it.

More woo woo, she thought.

Another moan.

Slowing, she spotted two wooden doors flush with the wall, very plain, with brass doorknobs. She tried the first one. It was locked. But the second swung open, into a dimly lit stairwell.

An ornate brass stair railing curved both up and down, and a faint light glowed from below.

Cocking her head again, she started down the stone stairs, worn and uneven but clean. She didn't know why she didn't summon someone to investigate. Why she didn't sound the alarm. It seemed the right thing to do.

She reached the landing.

Another moan.

Another floor down.

She kept going.

And going.

Then the stairs stopped. On the wall was a faded sign that read EINTRITT VERBOTEN. *No entry.* It was so dark she had trouble reading it. But no trouble at all translating it, apparently.

Passing the sign, she looped around and started down the next flight of the staircase. About halfway down, a terrible stench wafted beneath the scent of her shampoo and body splash. She knew that smell—people crowded in too tightly; sick and neglected people.

She coughed into her fist. The sound echoed. There was a rustling as if in response, and a gasp. And another moan.

She descended one more flight. The smell grew worse, sickening her; making her remember the baby in the desert, and the baby on horseback.

At the bottom of the next landing, a strip of luminous tape had been attached to the stone floor. It gave off white light, like the Pale.

I should get the hell out of here, she thought. *I'm not supposed to be here.*

Then the moan became strange sounds, like wind chimes:

"❋ ❋."

Twinkling silvery.

"❋ ❋."

And she knew they meant "home."

"Hello?" she whispered, staring at the tape. EINTRITT VERBOTEN.

"❋ ❋."

Home.

"Do you need assistance?" she asked in a louder voice.

Silence. And . . . weeping, and then a kind of gasping, like strangling. And another voice, higher-pitched:

"** **."

Help.

Meg sucked in her breath and made a semijump over the tape, bracing herself for a shock, or pain, but nothing happened. Her boots echoed. Rustling, scrabbling sounds came from the space in front of her, which was filled with vague, shadowy box shapes. As she walked forward, her eyes began to adjust.

She was standing at one end of a double row of cubes or boxes. They stretched far into the darkness, into some vast section of the castle she couldn't picture; an open space this wide, with no supporting beams or columns for the weight of the building above it, shouldn't be possible. *Magick*, she realized, and walked to the closest box, about three feet from the line of luminous tape.

The front was barred; she couldn't tell if there was an additional barrier—Plexiglas, regular glass—but something sat inside, on the floor, with long shins perpendicular to the floor, and feet that appeared to be pulled from gray clay. Long, nubby fingers were wrapped around the shins, and a bald head rested on the knees. Meg stared at it, transfixed.

What the hell?

With a hiss, it whipped its head up and glared at her, its features deep and plain, very human, its eyes filled with hatred so deep that she took an involuntary step backward.

It was a holding cell. And the thing inside it was imprisoned.

It glared, and then it slowly shut its eyes. It remained that way, head raised, eyes closed, as Meg stared at it.

Jesus, she thought.

The moan sounded again. She moved past the box—the *cage*— and was about to pass another one when she froze. There was a naked child inside, a towhead, with big blue eyes and a quivering lower lip. It was a little girl, and when she saw Meg, she shrieked and threw herself backward, much as Meg had done at the first cage.

"Hey, it's okay. I won't hurt you," Meg said.

The moan again:

"** **."

She raised a hand to the terrified toddler—*I'll be back*—and hurried on, past more cages with more children in them. Most of them were fair-haired and blue-eyed, very German. An imprisoned mini Aryan nation. A few of the prisoners were like the first one, almost claylike, but most were like the little towhead.

Then she came to a cage inhabited by what appeared to be a child half carved from wood, but unfinished—arms that ended in stumps, one leg, the torso an approximation of a chest. No sex organs. No eyes.

"** **."

It was the thing that was moaning.

She looked around, pretending to be suspicious that this was all a joke, but the sick thudding of her heart belied her actions. She was believing this.

More moans joined the first. *Home. Help.*

Their eyes were huge and sorrowful. They were lonely, and homesick, and miserable.

She understood: they were the changeling children, from beyond the Pale. They were the babies who had been put in the beds of the human children taken by the Erl King. The fruits of the Ritter extraction teams.

She thought of the Mexican baby; and Matt; and the child who had been taken tonight. Garriet. What was going on? What was this about? Why was it that these . . . children could survive on this side of the Pale, but she couldn't cross it?

She wandered among the cages and cells, seeing more misery and despair, and deep hatred. Her cell phone alarm went off: eight thirty. Sliding it off, she hurried back up the stairs, fully intending to confront Andreas.

As she headed for the birdcage elevator, she saw him striding toward the castle entrance, bundled up in a black overcoat and a white fur hat. She hurried after him; he turned his head, took note of her, and said in English, "Emergency. We'll have to postpone the meeting."

"What's going on?" she asked, not expecting him to tell her.

He frowned, shrugged. "It's the damnedest thing. Garriet's mother refused to give our extraction team the changeling. It's a mess. She's hysterical."

"Let me come with you," Meg said, striding along beside him.

He raised his brows. "You're a Border guard. This is not anything to do with you."

"I want to go."

"You should rest. It was a hard night."

"Bitte," she said in German, and he smiled at her quizzically.

"You Americans are so pushy."

"Assertive," she corrected him.

He pursed his lips and made an eye sweep of her appearance. "There's an extra coat in the car. Come on, then."

It was nearly four, and still black out. The Erl King rode only at night. They rolled in a Mercedes through the snowy streets, followed by another navy blue van. Their driver was the texter Meg had passed in the hall.

A single pedestrian fighting against the snow took the time to wave. That there were goblins and ghosties had been accepted by the locals; and that the Ritters were the ones to go to for help was appreciated. Meg was boggled. Why had she never read about any of this? Wasn't this groundbreaking, earthshaking?

Andreas was in cell phone communication with the leader of the extraction team. Since she could understand German now, she listened carefully. The house was isolated, deep in the forest. The woman was alone with the changeling. She had a gun.

"No, it's not imperative that the *Dämonkind* survive," he said. "But the woman . . . that would cause an incident. *Ja . . .*"

After a while, he flicked off the phone and sighed, looking out the window. She studied his profile.

"Are you going to put the baby in that dungeon downstairs?" she asked him.

He turned his head and looked at her.

"Where you keep all the others?" she added.

He frowned. "How do you know about that? That's classified."

Classified. Did Sofie and Lukas know about it?

"You know, where I come from, we just ship them back across the border," she said.

He raised a brow. She could feel energy moving off him in waves; a thrill of fear centered in her back. Eddie had knocked her out with the flick of his hand. What could this guy do?

"Back where you come from, they aren't evil."

"No. They're just desperate." She shifted; the wound in her side was hurting a little. "What's going on? Why does this happen?"

The snow fell as the Mercedes plowed through the storm. Unless the Erl King had gotten Garriet indoors, he'd probably frozen to death by now.

"In the earlier times, when a deformed child was born, the people would say it was a changeling," Andreas began. "A slow mind, a missing limb . . . they would say this child was not a human child. Then they would take it into the forest, and leave it."

"Charming."

"Their hope was that the faeries would take it back."

She pursed her lips. "So what are you saying, that the Erl King takes the deformed kids from us and leaves, what? Demons in their place?" She thought a moment.

"*Nein*. We don't know why he does it. But he never took the cast-offs. And he leaves . . . what he leaves."

She took a deep breath. "About what he leaves. They want to go ho—"

The Mercedes pulled to the right, and the engine went off. She looked past Andreas, to see a small white A-frame chalet sitting in the billows of snow, surrounded on three sides by fir trees. Smoke came out of a chimney set in the shingled roof, and empty flower boxes fronted a window beside the wood door, and another one above the door, where there must have been an extra little room.

The building was surrounded by what appeared to be a SWAT team in full body armor and helmets, crouched, holding crossbows. They all had Uzis slung across their chests. The soldier closest to the car looked over his shoulder at them, and made a fist.

Andreas murmured under his breath. She knew he was speaking Latin, and that he was conjuring a spell that would protect them. Energy washed over her in strong, surging waves, making her feel tall and light on her feet, and *powerful*—but it was a weak sensation compared to what she had felt at the Pale.

The soldier approached and brought Andreas up to speed: the woman was inside with the changeling; she was hysterical, armed, and defiant.

Andreas turned to Meg. She knew he was going to tell her to stay in the car.

"I'm going in with you," she said in English, although she knew how to say it in German. And in Latin.

What am I doing? What am I, period?

The *Wächter*—the Guardian—parted his lips as if to deny her request; before he could speak, she *pushed*, somehow. Her intentions— her thoughts—carried power. She didn't know exactly what that meant, but she did know she could make him say yes.

Then he blinked, and he told the soldier to form a bodyguard around the two of them. Andreas kept glancing at her, as if he knew something was up, but he didn't know what. The disorienting, manic high she had first felt at the Pale thrummed through her as they were fitted with vests and Andreas was given a radio. Then he knocked on the door and spoke kindly to the woman, launching into hostage-crisis speak. He was good at it. He was charming her magickally; maybe she knew it and maybe she didn't. The odor of the wood smoke from the chimney changed, and magick permeated the air.

Then they were in. The house was simply furnished, and a box of disposable diapers sat next to the door. The woman was around Meg's age—twenty-eight, give or take—and she was holding the silent, unmoving baby against her body, as the Erl King had held little Garriet. Holy shit, she had a Glock in her hand, the weight of which must be wearing her down. It wouldn't be long before she surrendered.

Her name was Brigitte, and her eyes were bloodshot. Her face was swollen with crying. She ticked her glance from Andreas to Meg and leaned her head against the baby's head. The baby looked like any normal little baby, with a wisp of strawberry hair and those mirror-like gray eyes of newborns. Younger than Garriet, then? She could smell the smoky magickal scent of him, like ozone before lightning.

"He doesn't want to go with you," the woman said to Andreas. In German, of course.

Andreas began to reply, but Meg spoke first.

"Ich weiss." I know.

Andreas looked at Meg sharply. She ignored him, focusing all her attention on the woman. Brigitte. Before Meg knew what was happening, her mind filled with the image of the baby in the desert, and of Matty . . . and of the Erl King, nodding at her.

Had it been so hideous in Mexico that the mother had had to cross? So terrifying in Matty's hospital room that their mom couldn't cross?

What lay beyond the Pale?

I crossed the tape in the dungeon, she thought. *I don't think I was supposed to be able to do that.*

Meg heard Andreas's thoughts, echoing in her head: *This poor woman is crazy with grief. She's trying to substitute the little monster for her little boy. Crazy, crazy.*

And then Meg thought about the possible desperation of the Erl King. Was he a cunning monster, salting the world with genocidal dictators and serial killers? Or a *coyote,* finding places for the children of the desperate?

Or something else altogether?

In the house:

It all happened so fast.

Meg reached out her hand to Brigitte. Andreas watched, hand on his radio. She knew dozens of weapons were cocked and ready.

Brigitte held her breath.

Meg nodded her head, once.

Brigitte exhaled and gave Meg the Glock.

"Gut," Andreas said, grunting his approval as he held out his hand to Meg for the weapon. He said into the radio, *"Achtung, hier spricht—"*

Then Meg raised it and aimed it point-blank at his face. "Tell them to back away," she ordered him. *"Now."*

But he didn't. First he tried to reason with her, and then he started to warn the SWAT team. So she knocked him out with the Glock, hard across his temple.

"Was?" Brigitte whispered, thunderstruck.

"Come with me. Now," Meg ordered her.

Oh, come and go with us . . .

Silently, she and Brigitte went out the front door, holding the baby. Brigitte began sobbing. The snow was pouring down. The soldiers couldn't really see what was happening. The first one to approach her asked her if Andreas was coming out.

"Ja," she told him, sounding unnaturally calm. "He's securing the interior. Get us to the Mercedes. The woman stays with us."

The soldier complied. They were halfway to the car when Andreas's voice crackled over the radio: "Stop them!"

Meg burst into action, clocking the soldier on her right with the Glock, grabbing his Uzi, aiming it at the solider on Brigitte's left. He backed away, yelling. She swept a circle, shooting *blam blam blam;* the Uzi was her weapon. She covered Brigitte as the woman sprinted to the vehicle.

Meg heard Andreas's thoughts: *Gone mad when she hit the Pale;*
she's under his control; what's happening; will we have to kill her?

Now the soldiers were opening fire, but *something* surged around
her, protecting the three of them as she charged to the driver's side,
yanked open the door, and dragged him out. Jerking him toward
herself, she kneed him; as he crumpled, she aimed her elbow at his
Adam's apple. He fell backward far enough for her to leap in, slam
the door, and peel out.

What would they do? Pursue? Kill an innocent civilian and a
Ritter—one of their own? She didn't know how to drive in snow; she
kept swerving. She flew along the road, with no thought but to save
the baby from the dungeon. Death in a U-Haul, in a cell beneath a
castle. Brigitte was screaming. The baby was silent.

Oh, come and go with us . . .

Down a lane, up into the forest. Horns were blaring; sirens. Gunfire erupted.

"What are you doing? What's happening?" Brigitte shrieked.

She felt another surge, like a mania, and kept driving, sliding all
over the icy road.

Where death never touches us.

Vertigo washed over her, and she reeled. Lights pinwheeled across
the windshield. Part of her wondered just how this had happened;
the other part of her believed it was all connected, inevitable. Even
down to Matty.

Suddenly she was thrown forward, hard, then backward. The car
stopped moving. They'd hit something. Light flared around her; she
couldn't see out.

"Are you all right? Is the baby all right?" she shouted in German,
but Brigitte was still screaming.

Meg fumbled for the Glock. The rear window shattered. She

couldn't hear anything as she flattened herself against the seat and searched for the gun. Her surroundings slid into white light, white noise. Despite the danger and the stakes—or maybe because of them—excitement tripled her heart rate.

There. She wrapped her hand around the weapon, then cracked the door and rolled out. A bullet zinged past her cheek. She dove into the snow, making herself harder to hit as she tried to take aim in the darkness. Pine boughs bobbed overhead; she'd slammed the car into a tree.

Light shimmered and whirled. Light shot up to the sky, in geysers, and silver songs exploded all round her. Her heartbeat went off the charts; her euphoria skyrocketed. She had to fight to stop shaking the Glock, double-fisting it, panting.

Where death never touches us.

She took aim, took pause, and tried to think about what she was really doing.

Saving him.

She fired off a round. How many did she have left?

Nearly blind—again—she was able to see that something had dropped in the snow. A soldier. She had hit a man. And he had been aiming his crossbow at her, not his Uzi. As if she were magick.

On her elbows, she scrabbled forward, reaching for the weapon.

The lights dampened; the silvery songs faded. She turned around and saw the glowing green light behind her, and the Great Hunt roared into focus. The goblins, the horses, the dogs . . . and the Erl King. His black mask gazed at her; his antlers burned at the tips. He was holding a swaddled baby in one arm, against his chest. Did the baby move? Meg couldn't tell.

Oh, come and go with us.

Brigitte was still in the car, shrieking and crazed. Meg didn't know if she could see the Great Hunt.

"No bullets can touch me," Meg decreed, in German, and Latin. English, and Spanish. "Nothing can touch me."

Meg reached into the car and yanked the changeling out of Brigitte's hands. He was so light. He smelled like smoke.

The car fell deeper into the snow as bullets shot out the tires. She raced back across the Pale, assaulted on all sides by the colors, the singing—a kaleidoscope. Behind her, Brigitte ran yelling; a soldier came up beside her and threw himself protectively over her.

Flailing, Meg staggered forward, holding out the baby. She lifted the crossbow, to show the Erl King that she had it. No bolts, she realized belatedly, but she wasn't about to let him know.

"Trade!" she yelled.

The goblins put spurs to their horses, heading toward her; the hellish dogs snarled and snapped. The Erl King held up his hand. The human baby in his arms squirmed.

Armor clanked.

Horses chuffed.

The *ratatatat* of the firefight died away.

In the silence, vibrant, multihued light formed a wall behind the Great Hunt. Then it undulated and wove together, descending, resting on Meg's shoulders like a cloak of many colors. It was warm, almost too hot, and it wrapped around her like body armor.

The Erl King walked his charger forward and lowered his hand toward her. He leaned down in his saddle, extending his arm.

Oh, come and go with us.

He looked at her hard through his blank black mask. And she understood—not all of it—but she knew that there were lines he, too, could not cross.

Lines that she *could* cross.

At the moment, precisely why, or how, or what that meant, didn't matter. So she took his hand, and he hoisted her up behind himself in the saddle, magickally, so that the baby in her arms was never disturbed. Then somehow, she was holding both babies, feather light, and as they squirmed, they opened their eyes and looked at her. The changeling baby trilled, and the human baby cooed.

As she settled in behind the Erl King, the colors and lights were nothing compared to his radiance, and the heat of his body as she gripped the horse's flanks with her thighs and held the babies for dear life.

> *Oh, come and go with us.*
> *Where death never touches us.*

For dear life.

"Giddyap," she said, and the Erl King's horse shot into a full gallop. Then it broke into a run, hooves sparking against the snowy ground. The hellhounds belled and bayed, spewing flames. The goblins capered and gibbered; and they laughed.

Maybe someday she could save Matty, too.

The Great Hunt soared through the night, far beyond the Pale.

ABOUT THE AUTHORS

L. A. BANKS (aka Leslie Esdaile Banks) is a native of Philadelphia and a graduate of the University of Pennsylvania Wharton undergraduate program, and holds a masters in fine arts from Temple University's School of Film and Media Arts. After a ten-year career as a corporate marketing executive for several Fortune 100 high-tech firms, Banks changed careers in 1991 to pursue a private consulting career—which ultimately led to fiction and film writing. Now, with over twenty-eight novels plus twelve anthology contributions in an extraordinary breadth of genres, and many awards to her credit, Banks writes full-time and resides in Philadelphia. Look for her Vampire Huntress Legends series and a full listing of her published works at: www.vampire-huntress.com or www.LeslieEsdaileBanks .com.

JENNA BLACK graduated from Duke University with a degree in physical anthropology and French. Once upon a time, she dreamed she would be the next Jane Goodall, camping in the bush and making fascinating discoveries about primate behavior. Then during her senior year at Duke, she did some actual research in the field, and her fascinating discovery was this: primates spend most of their time doing such exciting things as eating and sleeping. Concluding that this discovery was her life's work in the field of primatology, she then moved on to such varied pastimes as grooming dogs and writing technical documentation. She is now a full-time writer of fantasy, romance, and young adult fiction.

KAREN CHANCE grew up in Orlando, Florida, the home of make-believe, which probably explains a lot. She has since resided in several cities around the world, mostly goofing off, but occasionally writing novels in her Cassandra Palmer and Midnight Daughter series. Her short fiction has appeared in several anthologies, including *Inked*, *On the Prowl*, and *Wolfsbane and Mistletoe*. She is currently back in Florida, where she plans to continue writing while dodging hurricanes.

ROXANNE CONRAD has published more than thirty novels, including (as Rachel Caine) the *New York Times* and *USA Today* bestselling Morganville Vampires series, as well as the popular Weather Warden and Outcast Season series. She is also a contributor to several bestselling anthologies. She lives in Fort Worth, Texas, with her husband, fantasy artist R. Cat Conrad.

"Wimpy" Gothic novel heroines sent **CAROLE NELSON DOUGLAS** on a sixty-novel mission of creating strong women protagonists in genres from science fiction and fantasy to historical and contemporary-set mystery and romance. "The first woman" in several journalism areas while reporting for the *St. Paul Pioneer Press,* she became the first author to use a woman from the Sherlock Holmes stories as a protagonist, with the *New York Times* Notable Book of the Year *Good Night, Mr. Holmes*. Whether her woman characters have paranormal powers like Delilah Street, or run on brains and nerve like Irene Adler, they all enjoy being girls and showing the boys how it's done. *Publishers Weekly* starred reviews for *Dancing with Werewolves* and *Brimstone Kiss* launched the Delilah Street noir urban fantasy series, which is set in an apocalyptic Las Vegas vastly different from the contemporary Vegas of Douglas's long-running Midnight Louie feline PI cozy-noir series.

P. N. ELROD writes and edits, and is best known for *The Vampire Files,* where Bobbi Smythe hangs out with her undead boyfriend, vampire PI Jack Fleming. Elrod is a hopeless chocolate addict and cheerfully refuses all efforts at intervention. More about her toothy titles may be found at www.vampwriter.com.

NANCY HOLDER is the *New York Times* bestselling author of the Wicked series (with coauthor Debbie Viguie). *Crusade: Damned,* the second book in their new series, Crusade, will be out in August 2011. The first book of their new series, *Unleashed: The Wolf Springs Chronicles,* will debut in January of 2012. She is also the author of the young adult horror series, Possessions. *The Screaming Season,* third in the series, hit the shelves in March 2011. She lives in San Diego with her daughter, Belle, and their corgis, Panda and Tater, and two very hairy cats named David and Kittnen Snow Vampire.

Trained as an artist with a BFA in illustration from the California College of Arts and Crafts, **SUSAN KRINARD** became a writer in 1992 when a friend read a short story she'd written and suggested she try writing a romance novel. A longtime fan of science fiction and fantasy, Susan began reading romance—and realized what she wanted to do was combine the two genres. *Prince of Wolves,* her first romance novel and one of the earliest to feature a werewolf hero, was the result. Within a year Susan had sold the manuscript to Bantam as part of a three-book contract, and the novel went on to make several bestseller lists. Since then, she's written and published over fourteen paranormal and fantasy novels, and written stories for a number of anthologies, both fantasy and romance. Both the anthology *Out of This World* (which included Susan's "Kinsman") and the novel *Lord of the Beasts* appeared on the *New York Times* bestseller list. Susan makes her home in New Mexico, the "Land of Enchantment," with her husband, Serge; their dogs Freya, Nahla, and Cagney; and their cat, Jefferson. In addition to writing, Susan's interests include music of almost every kind, old movies, reading, nature, baking, and collecting unique handmade jewelry and decorative crafts.

New York Times and *USA Today* bestselling author **CHEYENNE McCRAY** has a passion for writing suspense and urban fantasy novels. Among many other awards, Chey has won the prestigious RT Book Reviews

Reviewers' Choice Award twice and has had her books nominated four times. A University of Arizona alumnus, Cheyenne McCray has been writing ever since she can remember, back to her kindergarten days, when she penned her first poem. She began to pursue publication seriously after starting her first young adult novel in January 2000. For two years Cheyenne wrote primarily young adult paranormal fiction under a pseudonym. While she loved writing young adult fiction, she found herself wanting to explore adult relationships and started writing paranormal romance and romantic suspense, also branching out to suspense/thrillers and urban fantasy. She has written eleven novels and two novellas for St. Martin's Press. In 2009 her thrilling new Lexi Steele suspense novels debuted with *The First Sin*. Then *Demons Not Included* kicked off her exciting urban fantasy Night Tracker series. Both series debuted to acclaim by readers and reviewers, and landed on multiple bestseller lists. Be sure to go to http://cheyennemccray.com to sign up for her private book announcement list and to get free, exclusive Cheyenne McCray goodies. Please feel free to e-mail her at chey@cheyennemccray.com. She would love to hear from you.

LILITH SAINTCROW is the author of the Dante Valentine, Jill Kismet, and Strange Angels series. She currently resides in Vancouver, Washington, with her children, cats, and assorted other strays.

JEANNE C. STEIN is the bestselling author of the urban fantasy series the Anna Strong Vampire Chronicles. Last April, her character, Anna Strong, received an RT Book Reviewers Choice Award for Best Urban Fantasy Protagonist. The sixth in the Anna Strong series, *Chosen,* will be released in August.

ELIZABETH A. VAUGHAN is the author of The Chronicles of the Warlands series, *Dagger-Star,* and *Destiny's Star.* She still believes that the only good movies are the ones with gratuitous swords or lasers. Not to mention dragons. At the present, she is owned by two incredibly spoiled cats and lives in the Northwest Territory, on the outskirts of the Black Swamp, along Mad Anthony's Trail on the banks of the Maumee River.

RACHEL VINCENT is the author of the urban fantasy series Shifters and the young adult Soul Screamers books. Rachel has a BA in English and an overactive imagination, and consistently finds the latter to be more practical. She shares her workspace with two black cats (Kaci and Nyx) and her number one fan. Rachel is older than she looks— seriously—and younger than she feels, but remains convinced that for every day she spends writing, one more day will be added to her lifespan.

ABOUT THE EDITORS

RACHEL CAINE is the internationally bestselling author of thirty novels, including the *New York Times* and *USA Today* bestselling Morganville Vampires young adult series: *Glass Houses, The Dead Girls' Dance, Midnight Alley, Feast of Fools, Lord of Misrule, Carpe Corpus,* and *Fade Out,* with five more to follow through 2011. She also writes the bestselling Weather Warden series: *Ill Wind, Heat Stroke, Chill Factor, Windfall, Firestorm, Thin Air, Gale Force,* and *Cape Storm.* She recently launched a third series, Outcast Season (*Undone, Unknown, Unseen, Unbroken*). She has also published an original novel for the television show *Stargate SG-1* (*Sacrifice Moon*) under the pseudonym of Julie Fortune in 2005. She has had short fiction in several bestselling anthologies, including *My Big Fat Supernatural Wedding, My Big Fat Supernatural Honeymoon, Strange Brew,* and *Many Bloody Returns.* She and her husband, award-winning artist R. Cat Conrad, live in Fort Worth.

Artist, writer, editor, and traveler, **KERRIE HUGHES** would also like to be a paranormal investigator and a size 2 but it ain't gonna happen, so she has dedicated her life to just being a Chick who can Kick Butt without having to be violent. (But she would love to go Cynthia Rothrock on some bad guys and win.) Kerrie has been editing anthologies since 2005, and in addition to *Chicks Kick Butt* has worked on the following volumes:

Love and Rockets, 2010
A Girl's Guide to Guns and Monsters, 2010
Zombie Raccoons and Killer Bunnies, 2009
Gamer Fantastic, July 2009
Dimension Next Door, 2008
Fellowship Fantastic, 2008
Children of Magic, 2006
Maiden Matron Crone, 2005